ANDY MATTHEWS & READER THOMAS

# GUSTAV & HENRI

**VOL. 1**

Or as I like to call it ...
## SPACE TIME CAKE!

## HOW TO USE THIS BOOK:
PAGES TURN RIGHT TO LEFT. DO NOT OPERATE THIS
BOOK UNDERWATER. ALL WORDS IN THIS BOOK ARE
100% RECYCLABLE AND CAN BE USED AGAIN AND AGAIN.

RED COMET PRESS
BROOKLYN

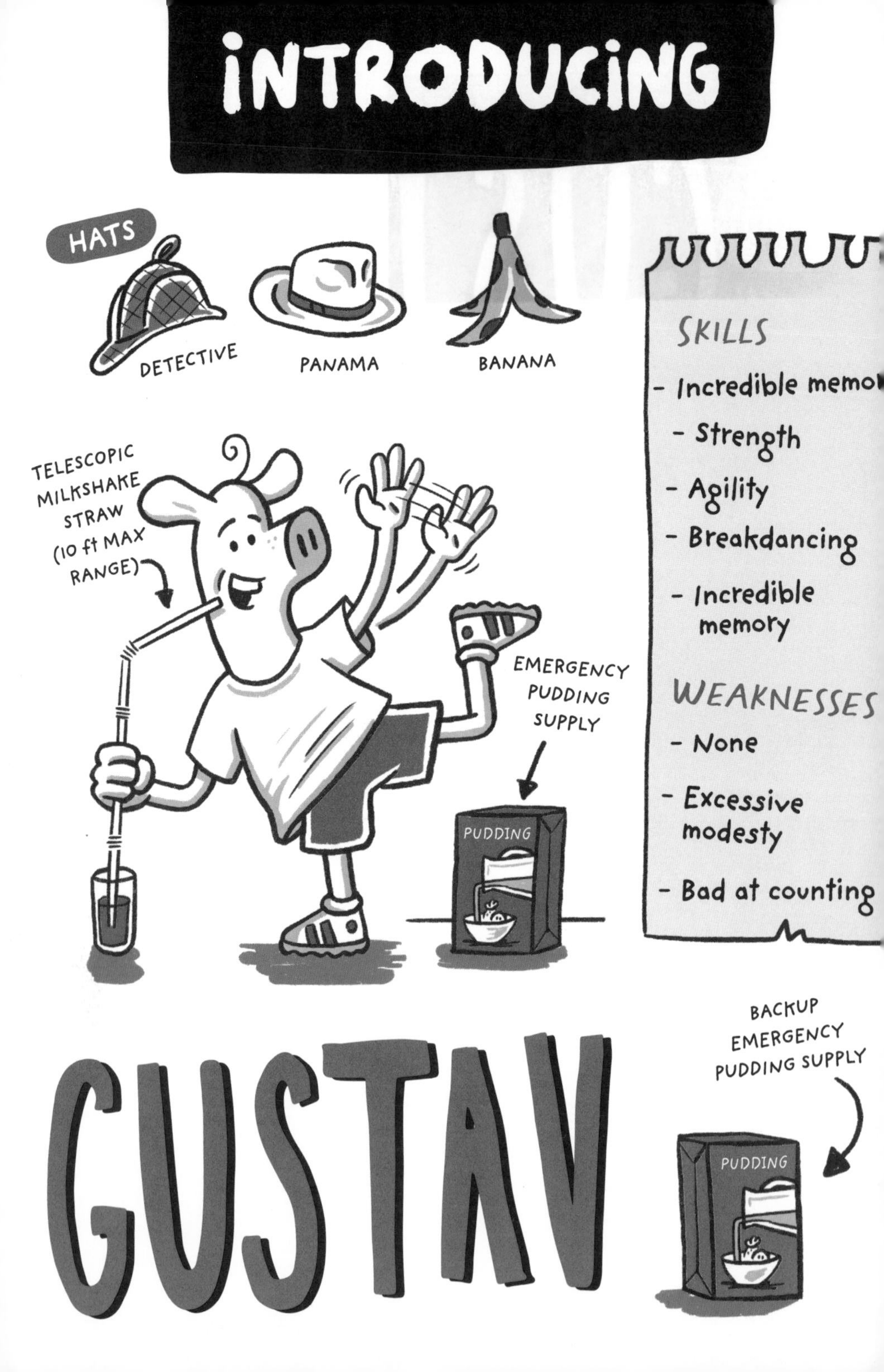
INTRODUCING
HATS
DETECTIVE
PANAMA
BANANA
SKILLS
- Incredible memo
- Strength
- Agility
- Breakdancing
- Incredible memory
WEAKNESSES
- None
- Excessive modesty
- Bad at counting
TELESCOPIC MILKSHAKE STRAW (10 ft MAX RANGE)
EMERGENCY PUDDING SUPPLY
PUDDING
GUSTAV
BACKUP EMERGENCY PUDDING SUPPLY
PUDDING

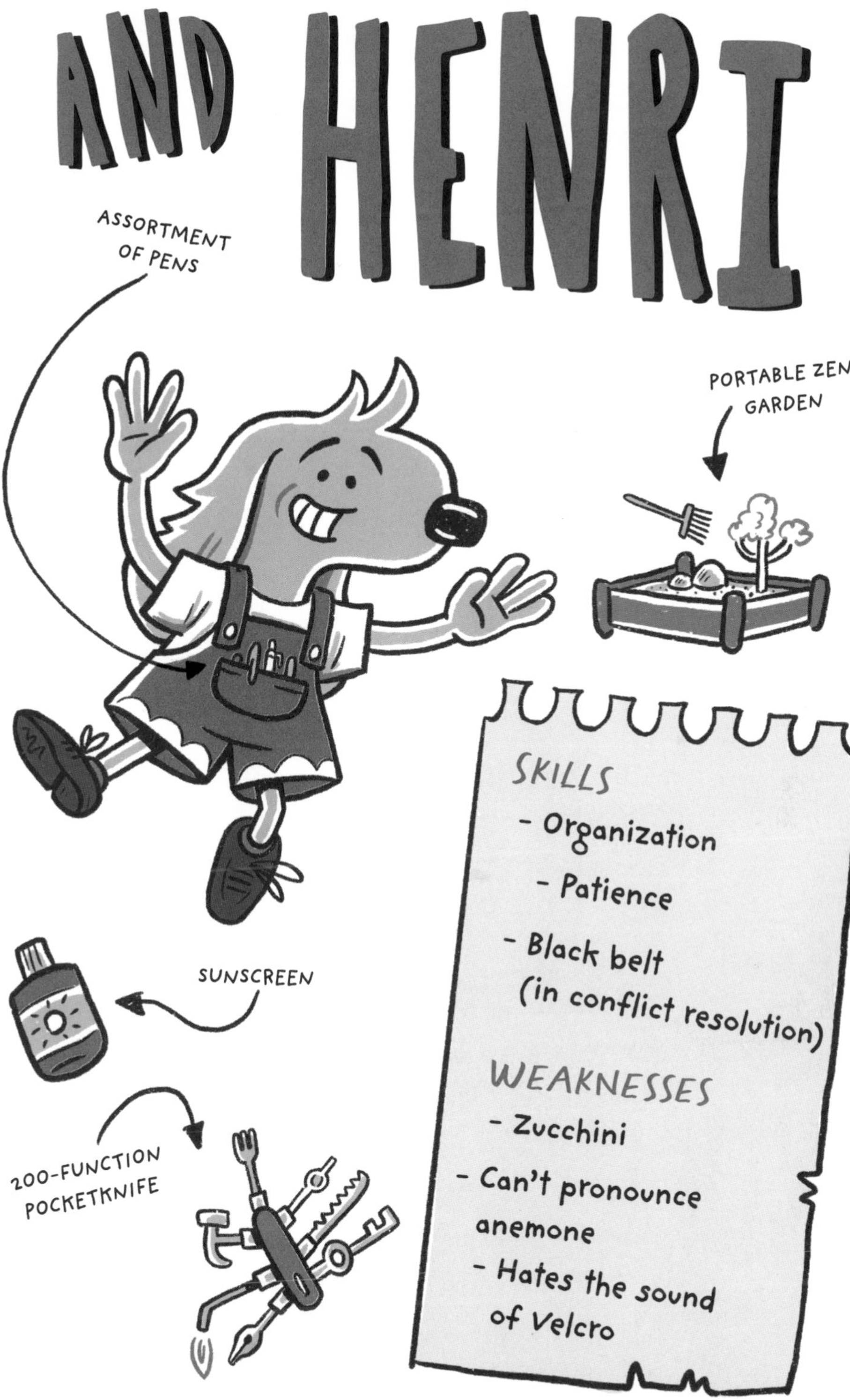
AND HENRI
ASSORTMENT OF PENS
PORTABLE ZEN GARDEN
SUNSCREEN
200-FUNCTION POCKETKNIFE
SKILLS
- Organization
- Patience
- Black belt (in conflict resolution)
WEAKNESSES
- Zucchini
- Can't pronounce anemone
- Hates the sound of Velcro

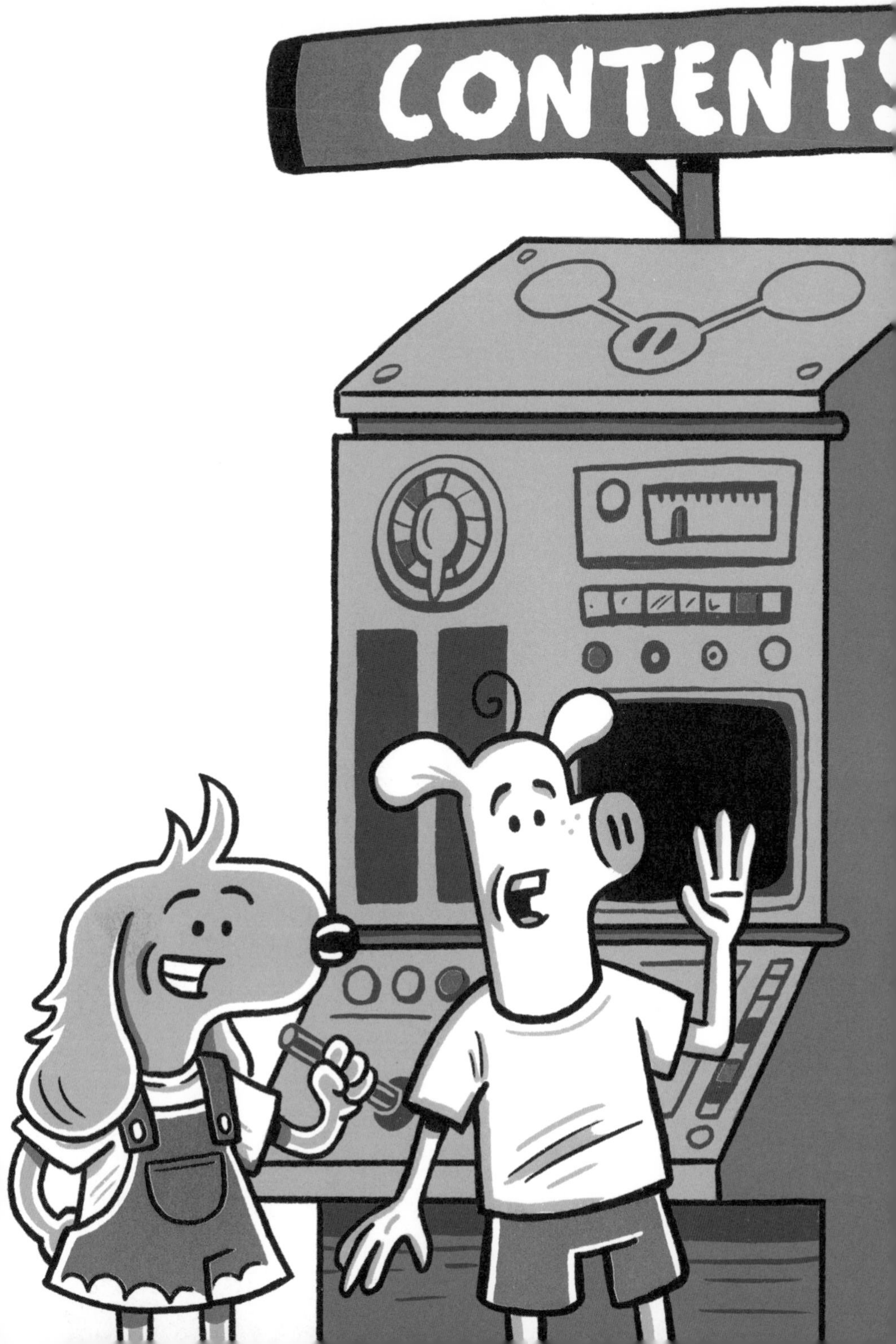
CONTENTS

**O-MATIC**

GUSTAV,
# SPACE PIG

`3`

`41`

GUSTAV,
# TIME PIG

DETECTIVE GUSTAV
AND THE **GREAT**
PIG DAY **MYSTERY**

`83`

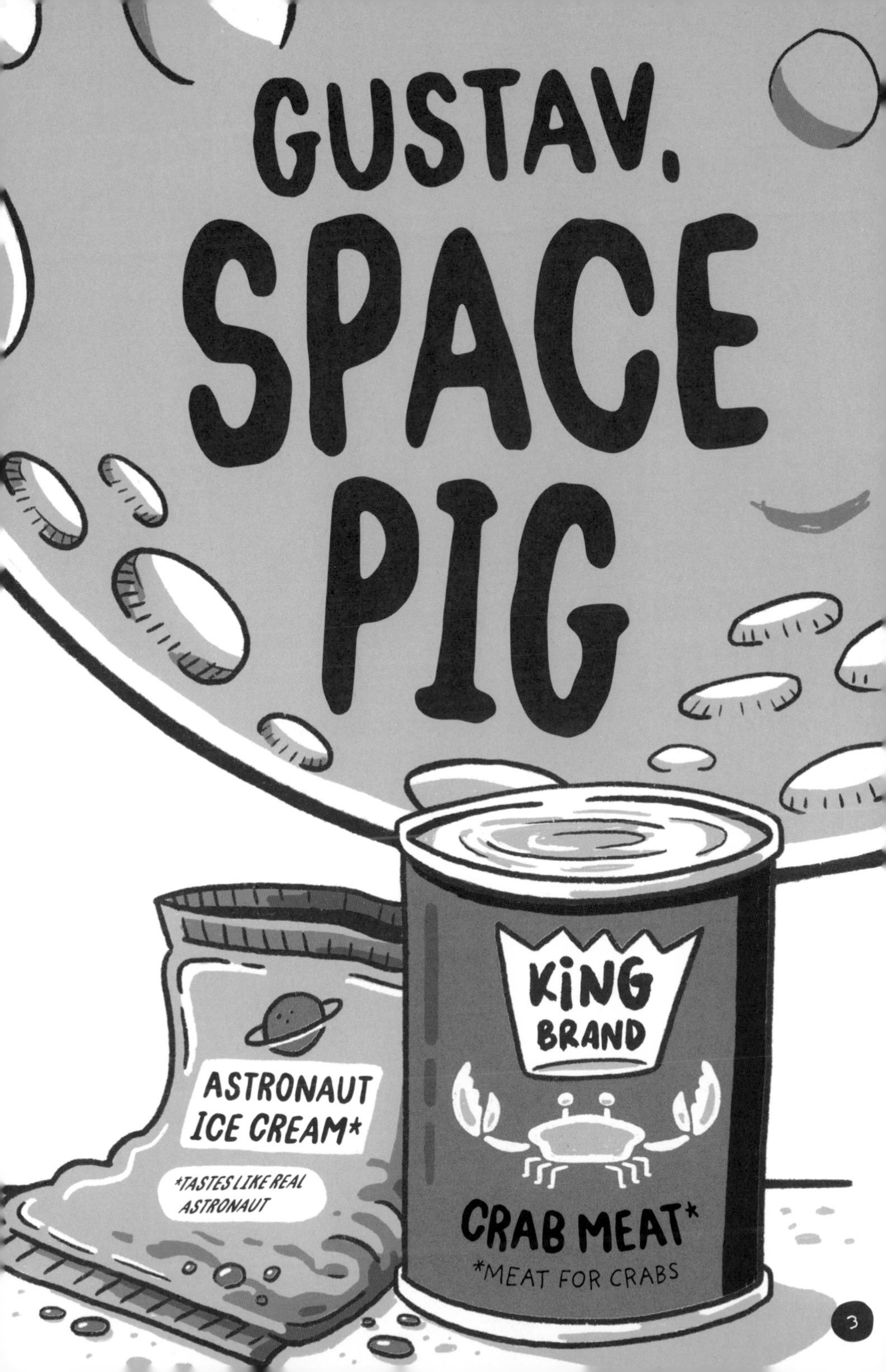
GUSTAV,
SPACE
PIG
ASTRONAUT
ICE CREAM*
*TASTES LIKE REAL
ASTRONAUT
KiNG
BRAND
CRAB MEAT*
*MEAT FOR CRABS

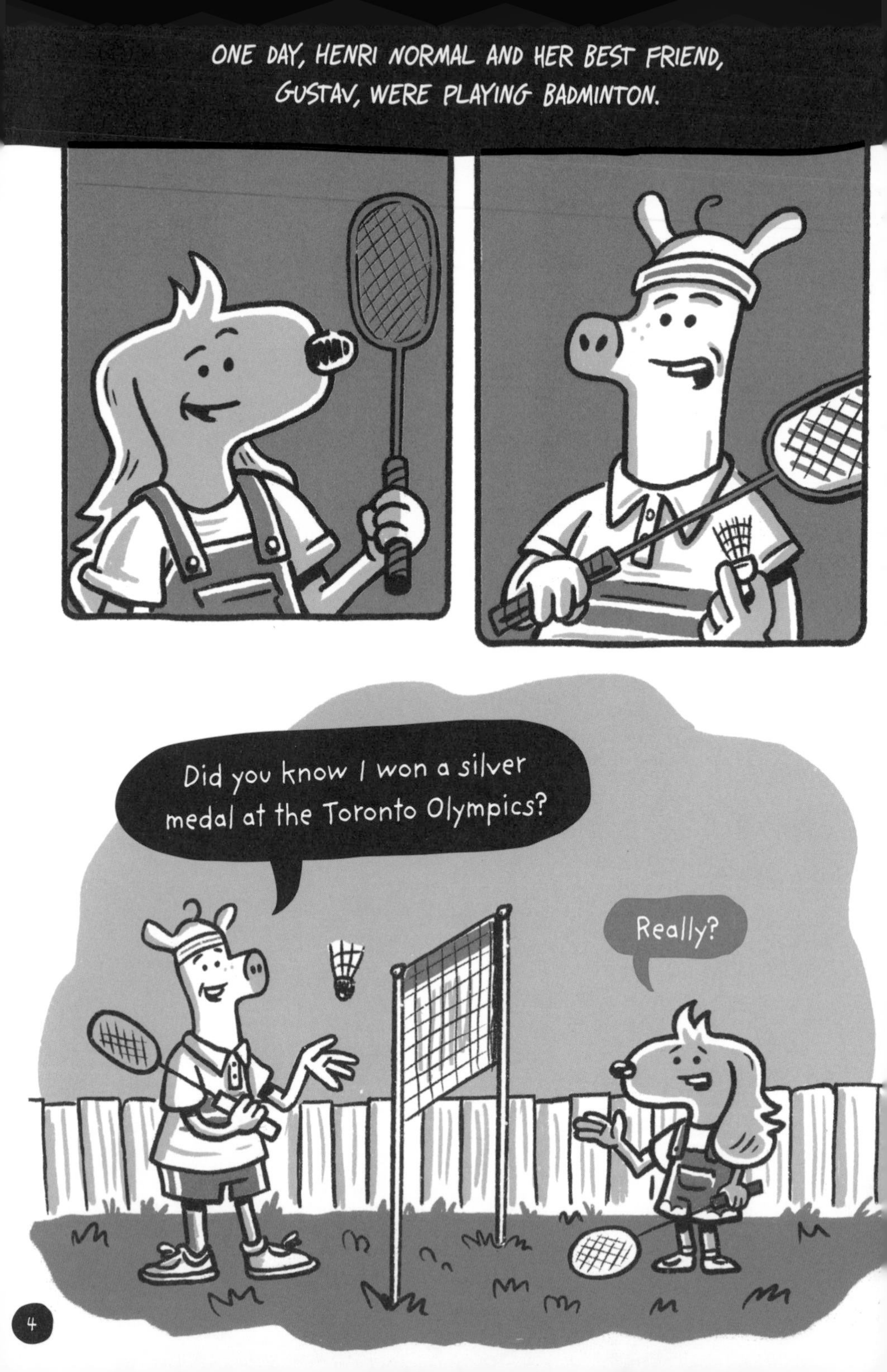
ONE DAY, HENRI NORMAL AND HER BEST FRIEND, GUSTAV, WERE PLAYING BADMINTON.
Did you know I won a silver medal at the Toronto Olympics?
Really?

It was while Gustav was demonstrating the slam shot that got him into the finals, that the shuttlecock went missing.

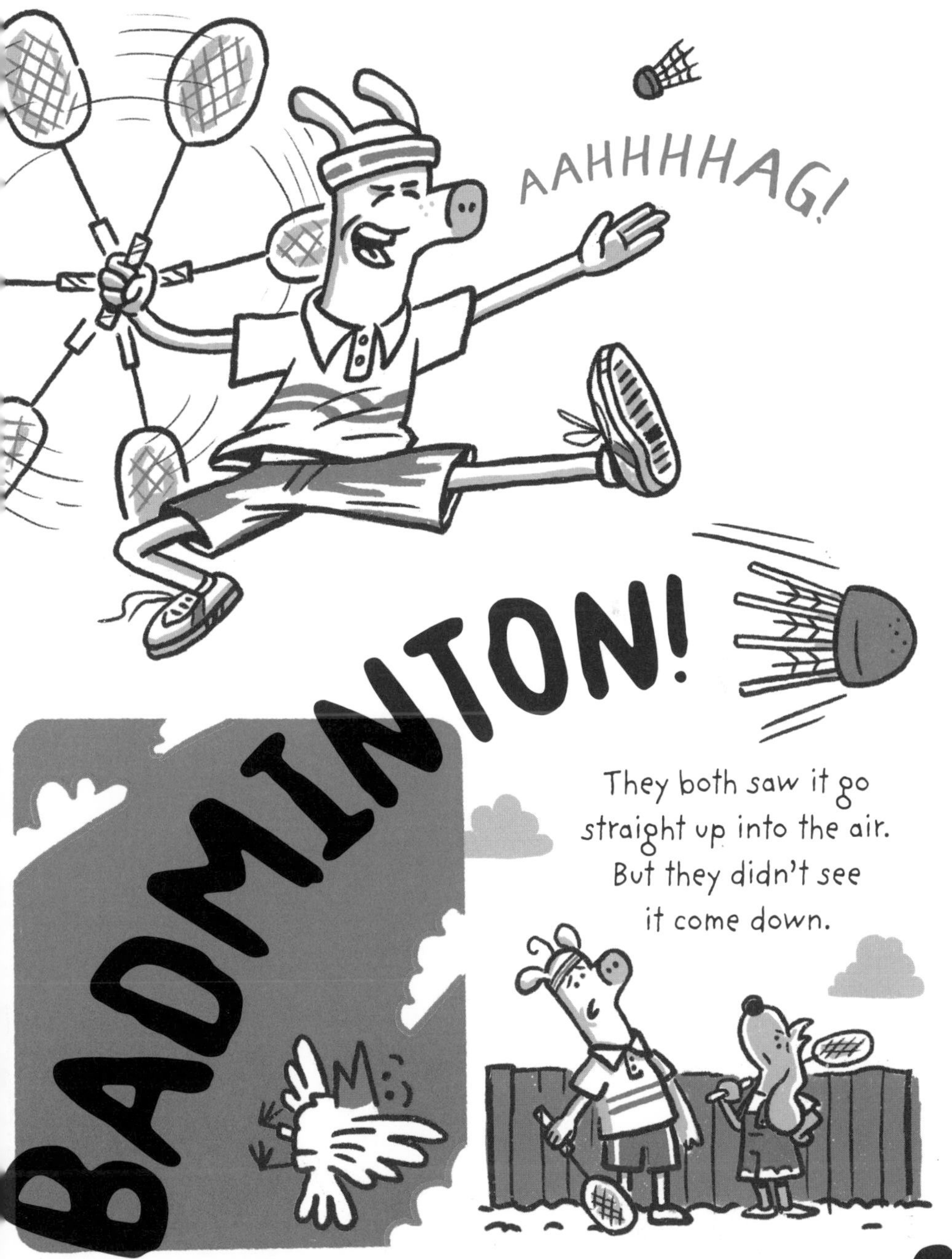
AAHHHHAG!
BADMINTON!

They both saw it go straight up into the air. But they didn't see it come down.

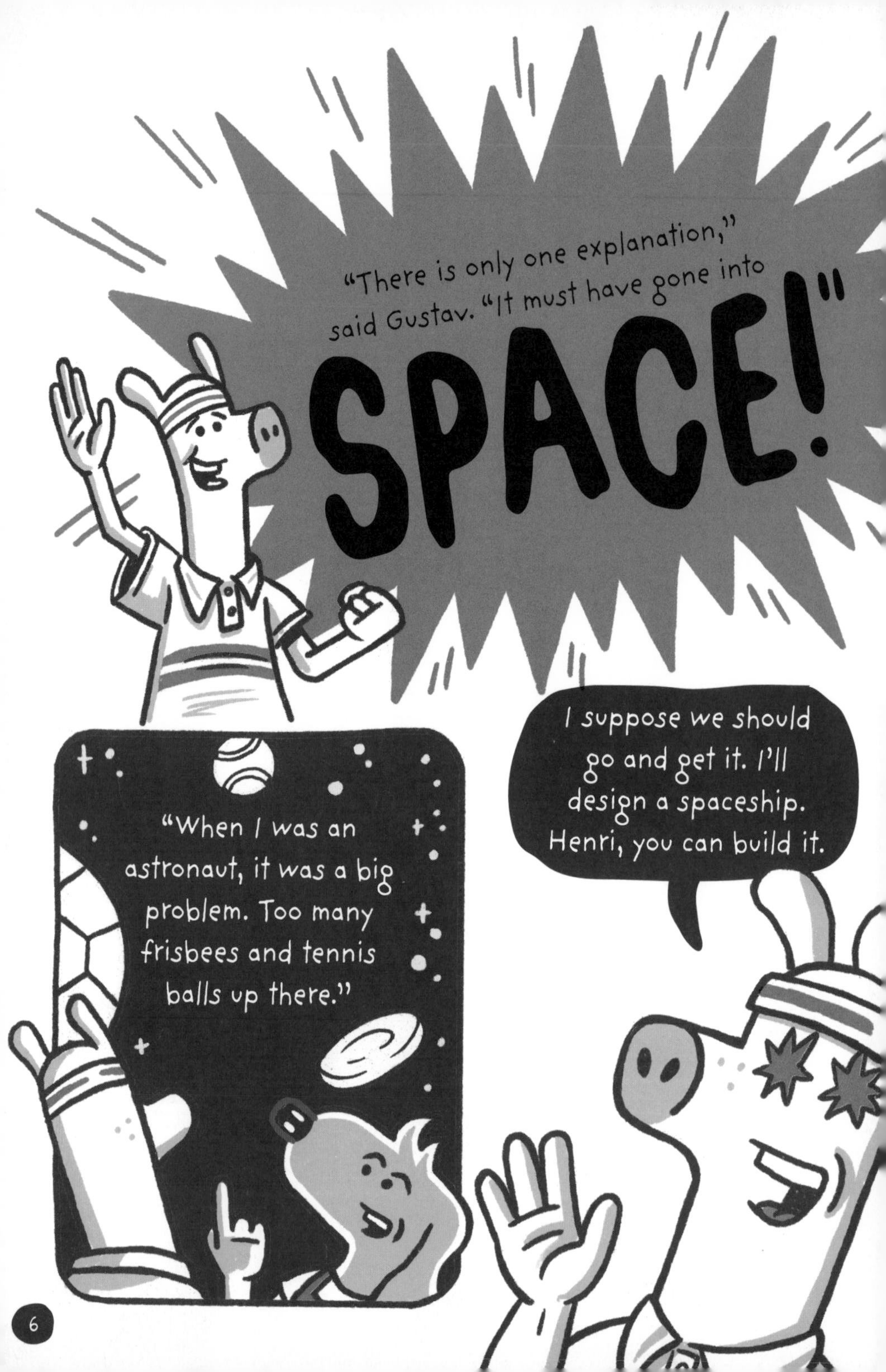
"There is only one explanation," said Gustav. "It must have gone into
SPACE!"
"When I was an astronaut, it was a big problem. Too many frisbees and tennis balls up there."
I suppose we should go and get it. I'll design a spaceship. Henri, you can build it.

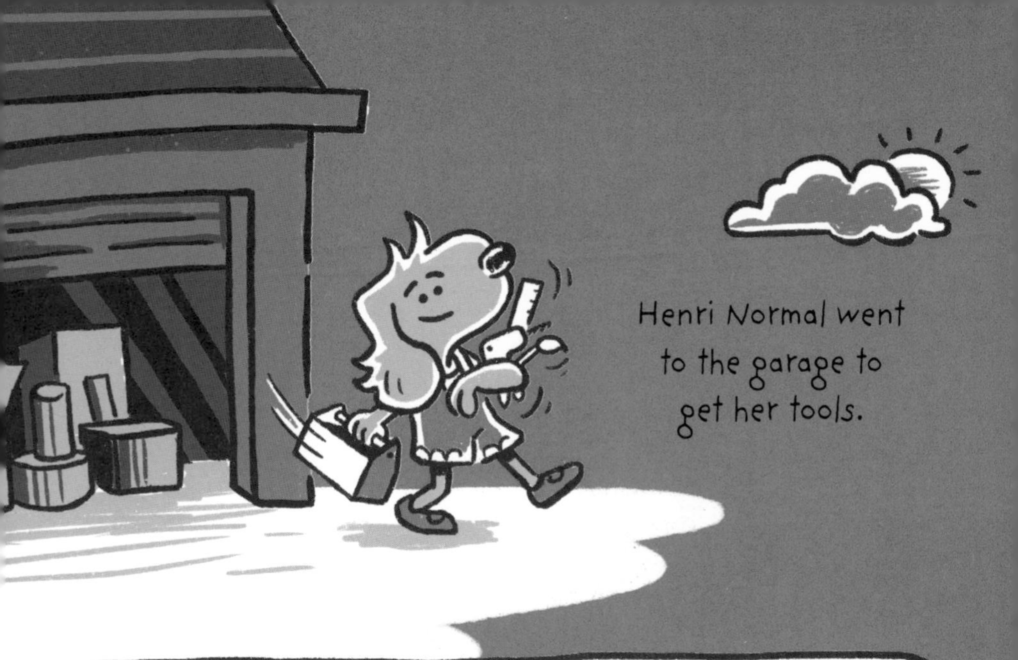
Henri Normal went
to the garage to
get her tools.

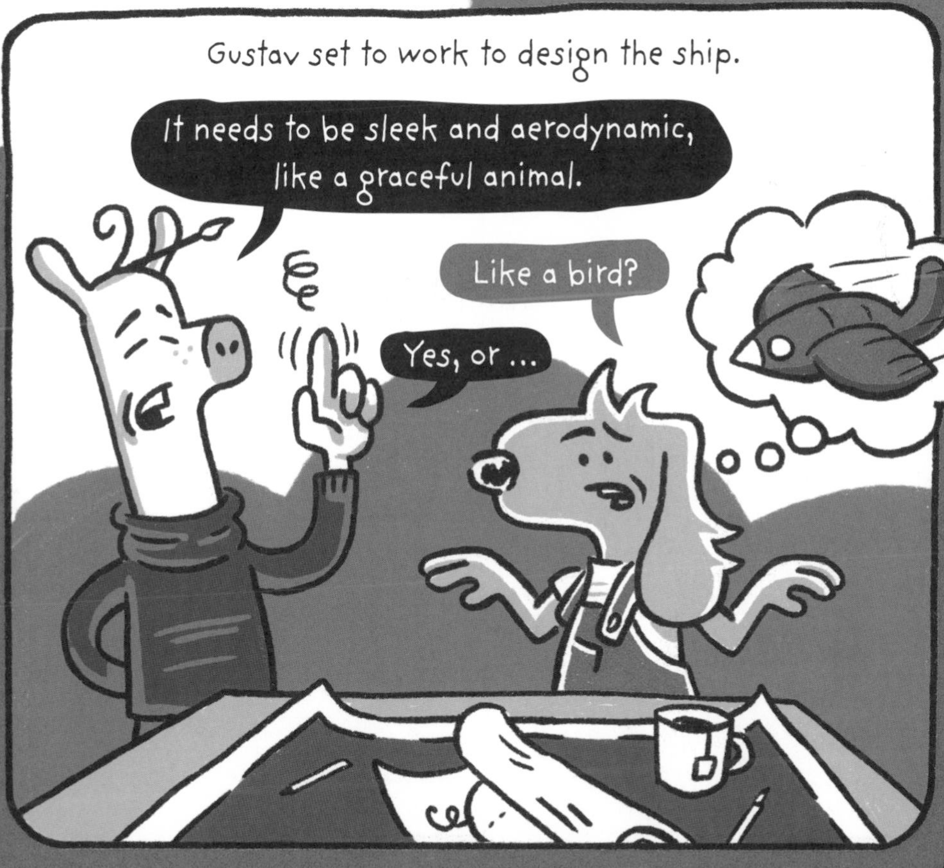
Gustav set to work to design the ship.
It needs to be sleek and aerodynamic, like a graceful animal.
Like a bird?
Yes, or ...

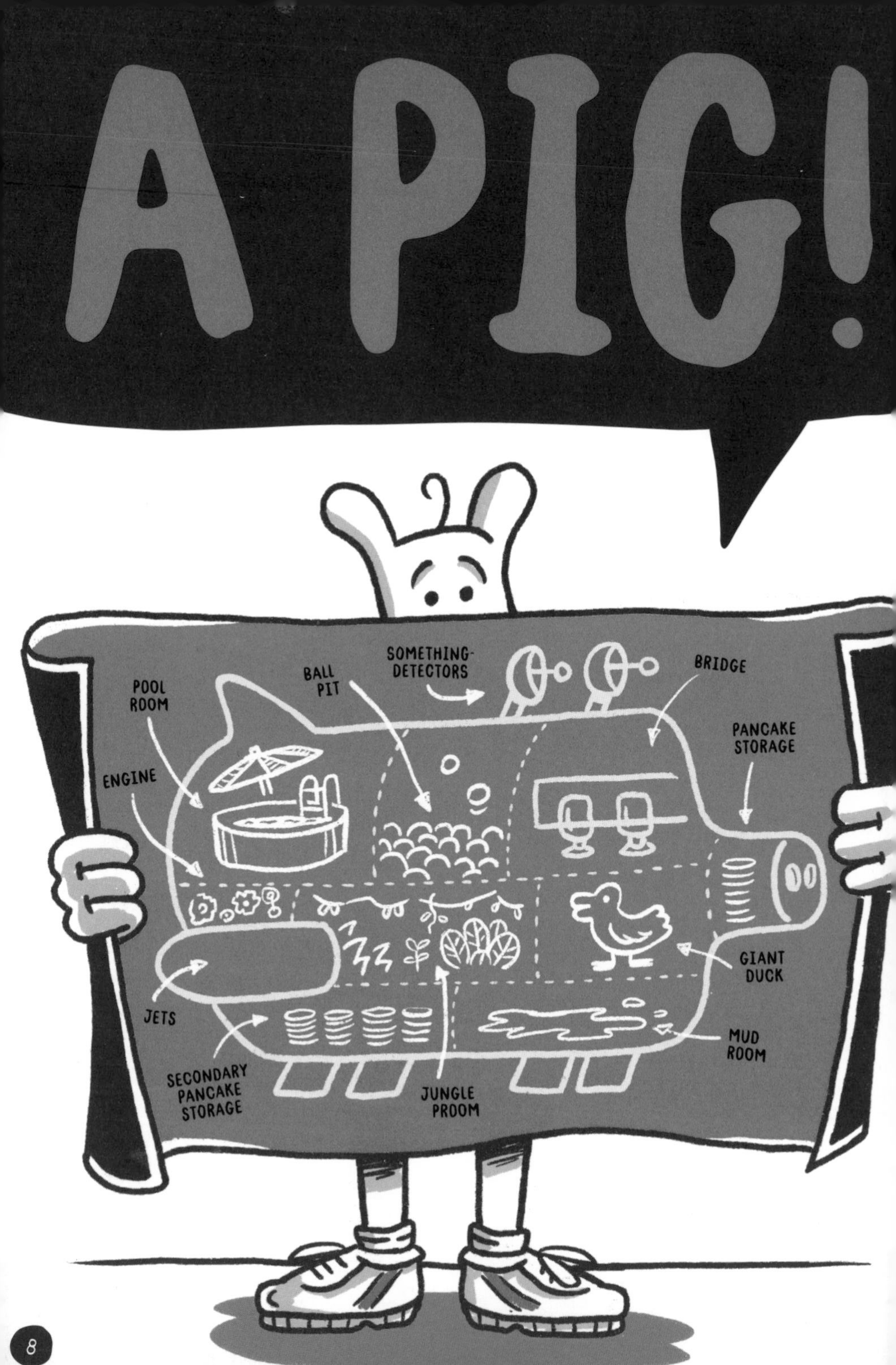

A PIG!
POOL ROOM
ENGINE
BALL PIT
SOMETHING-DETECTORS
BRIDGE
PANCAKE STORAGE
GIANT DUCK
JETS
SECONDARY PANCAKE STORAGE
JUNGLE PROOM
MUD ROOM

Henri Normal worked all night. She tried not to make too much noise, but—

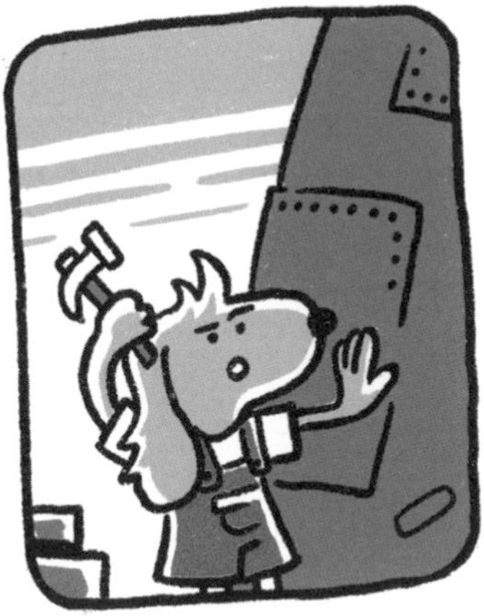

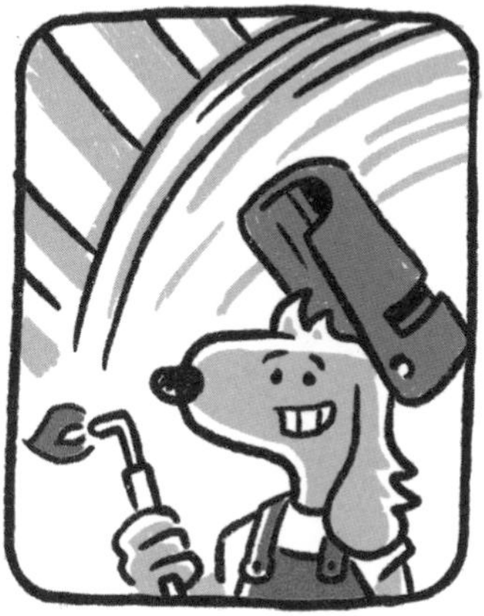

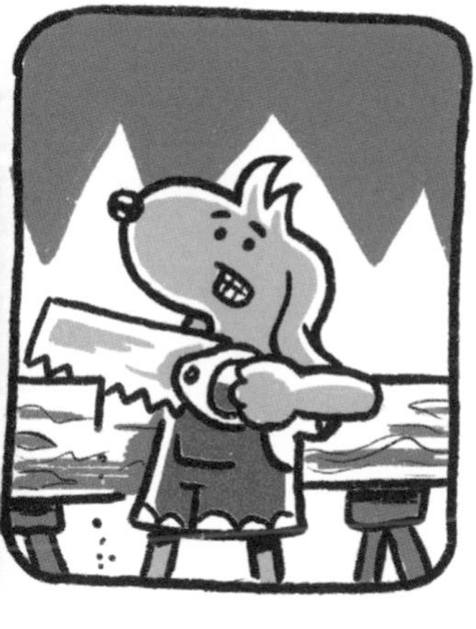

as anyone who has tried it will know—it is almost impossible to build a spaceship quietly.

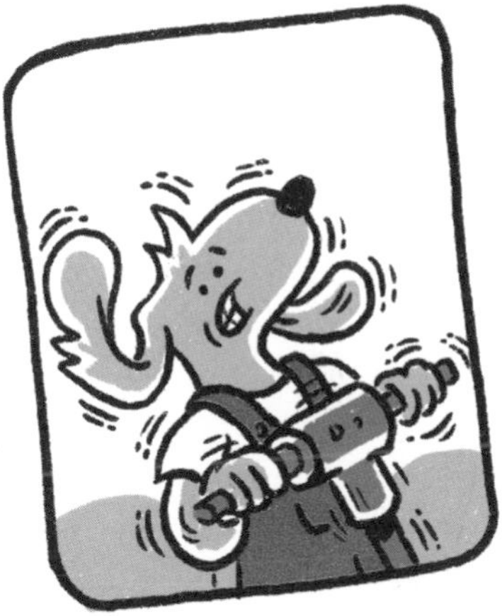

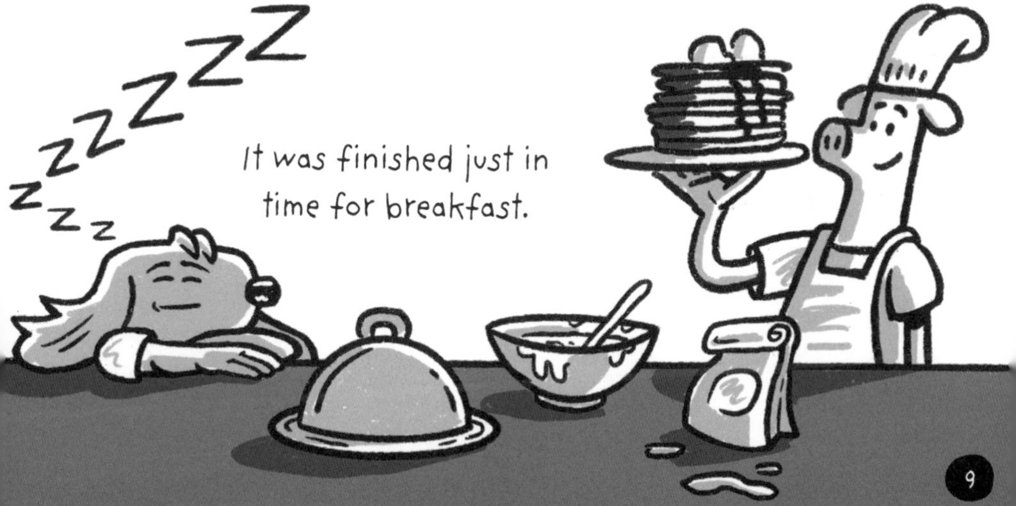
ZZZZZZZZZZZ

It was finished just in time for breakfast.

"Excellent," said Gustav, after finishing his 15th pancake.
"Now to prepare for lunch."

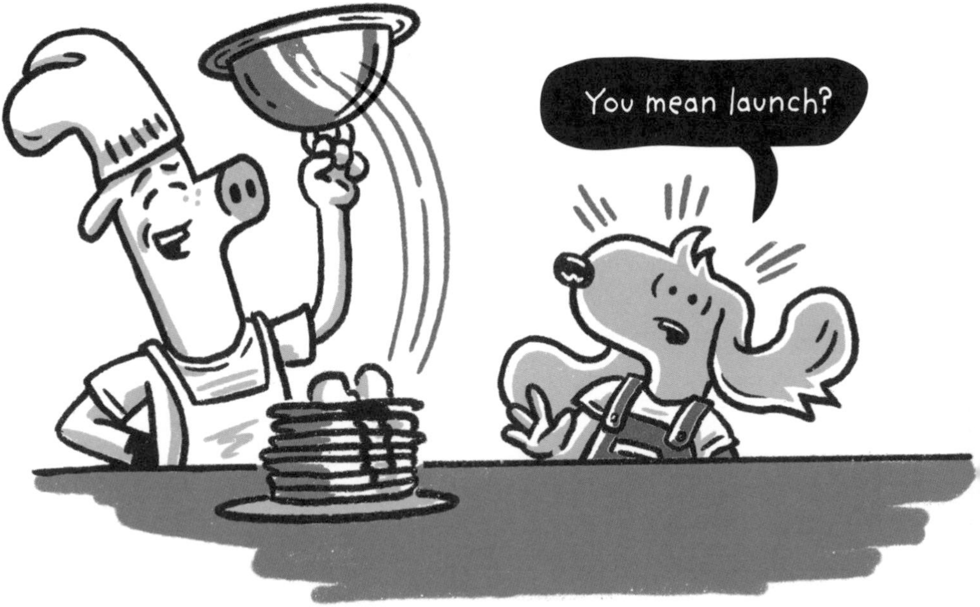
You mean launch?

"Yes," said Gustav, as they climbed into their spacesuits.
"We launch right after lunch."

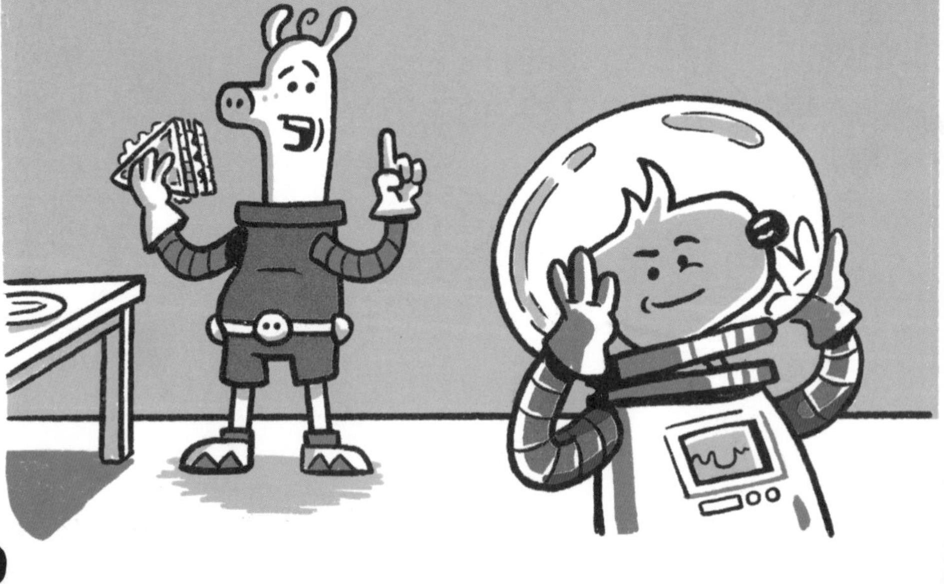

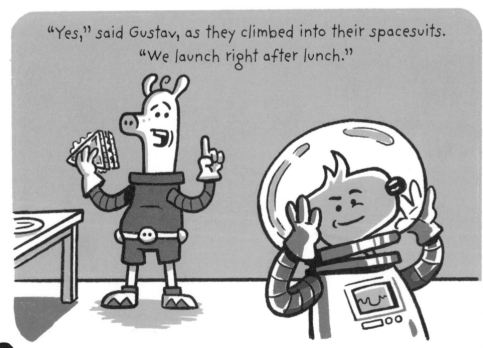

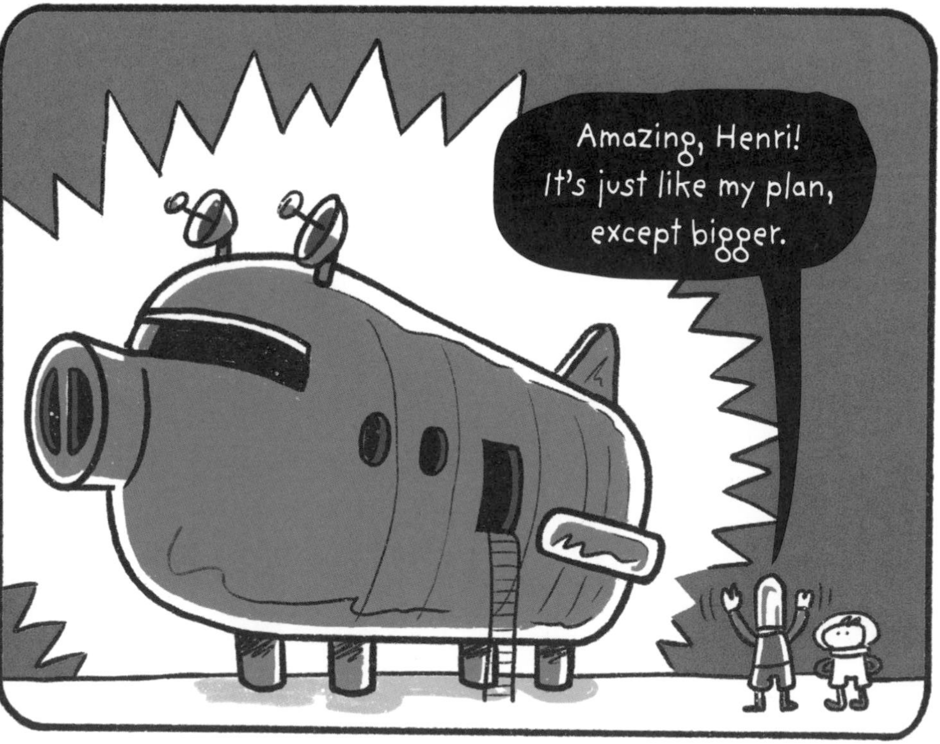
Amazing, Henri! It's just like my plan, except bigger.

They climbed aboard.

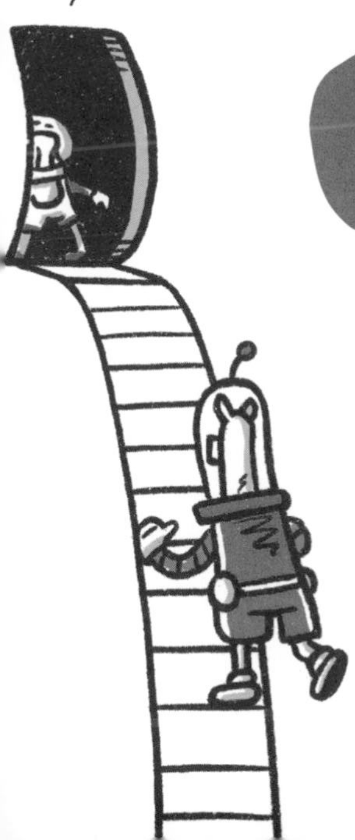

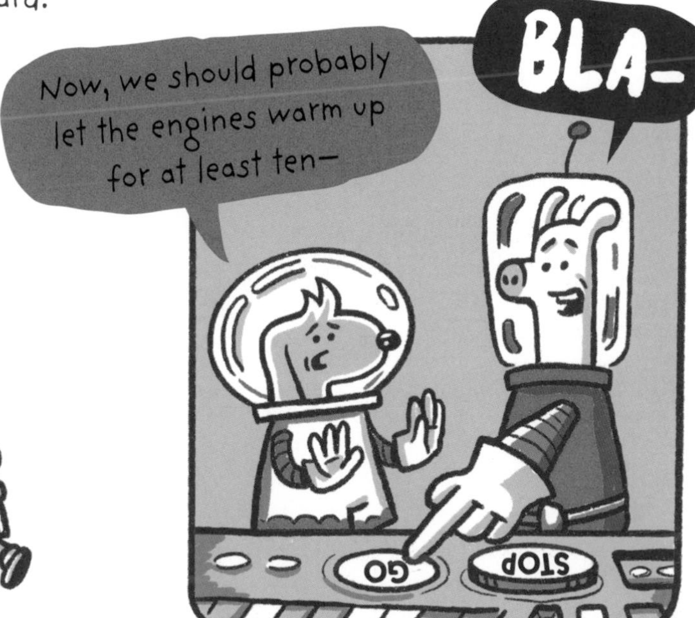
Now, we should probably let the engines warm up for at least ten—
BLA-
GO
STOP

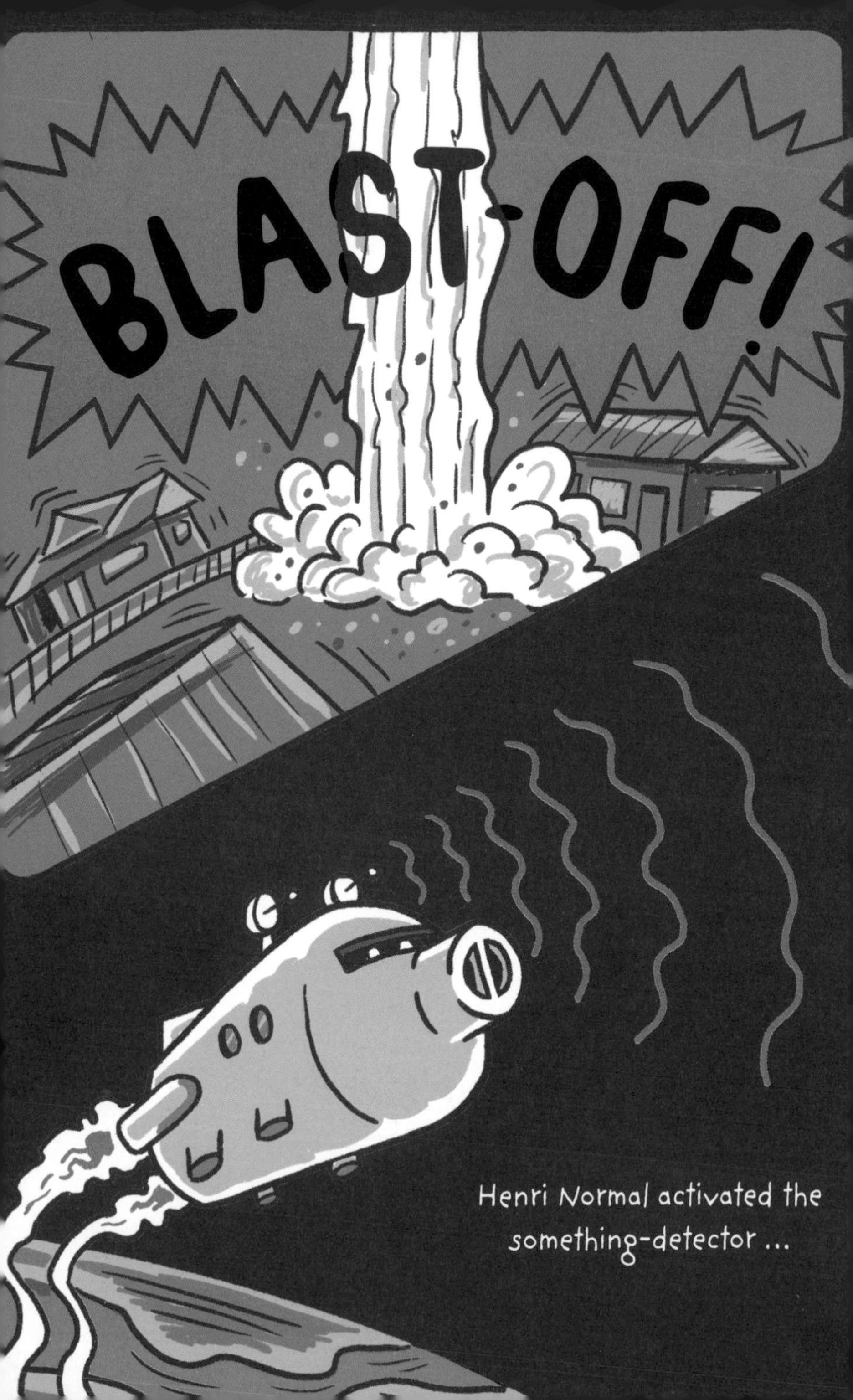
BLAST-OFF!
Henri Normal activated the something-detector ...

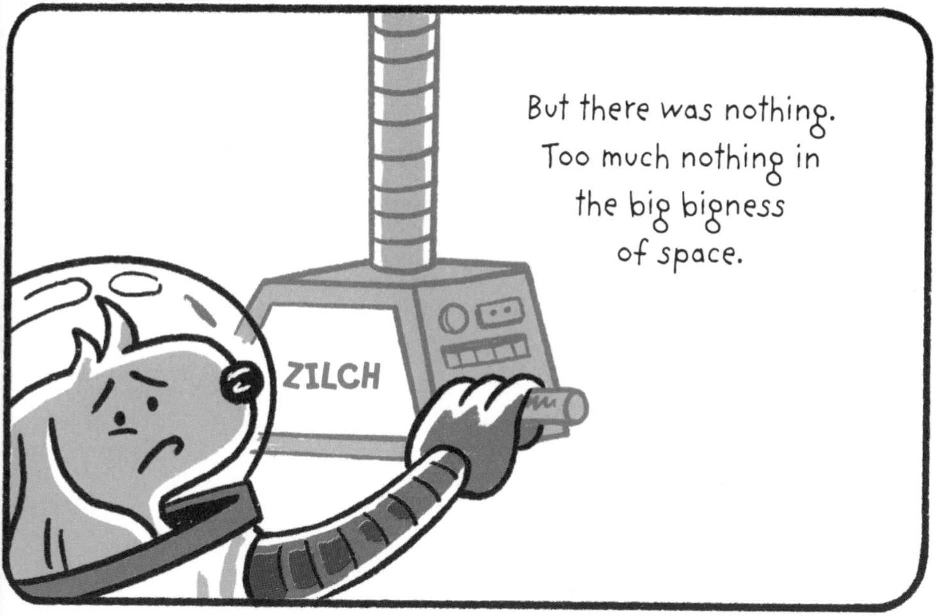
But there was nothing. Too much nothing in the big bigness of space.
ZILCH

Finally, they turned the detector toward the Moon.

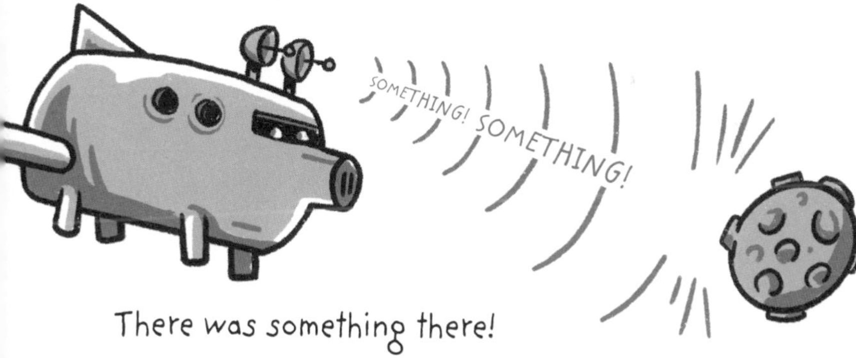
SOMETHING! SOMETHING!

There was something there!

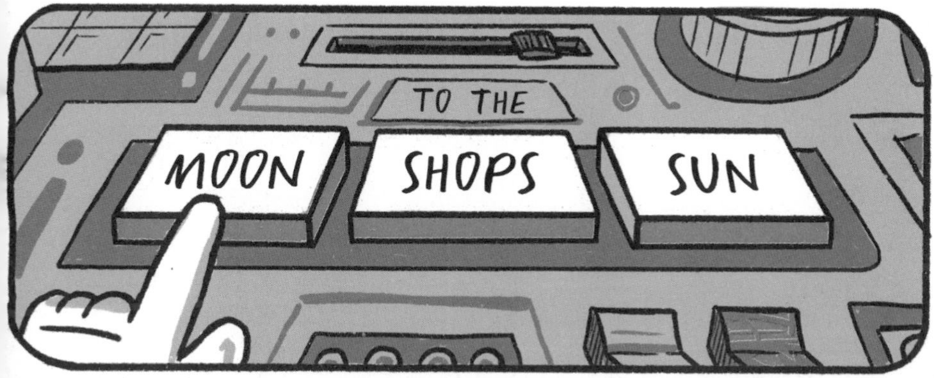
TO THE
MOON
SHOPS
SUN

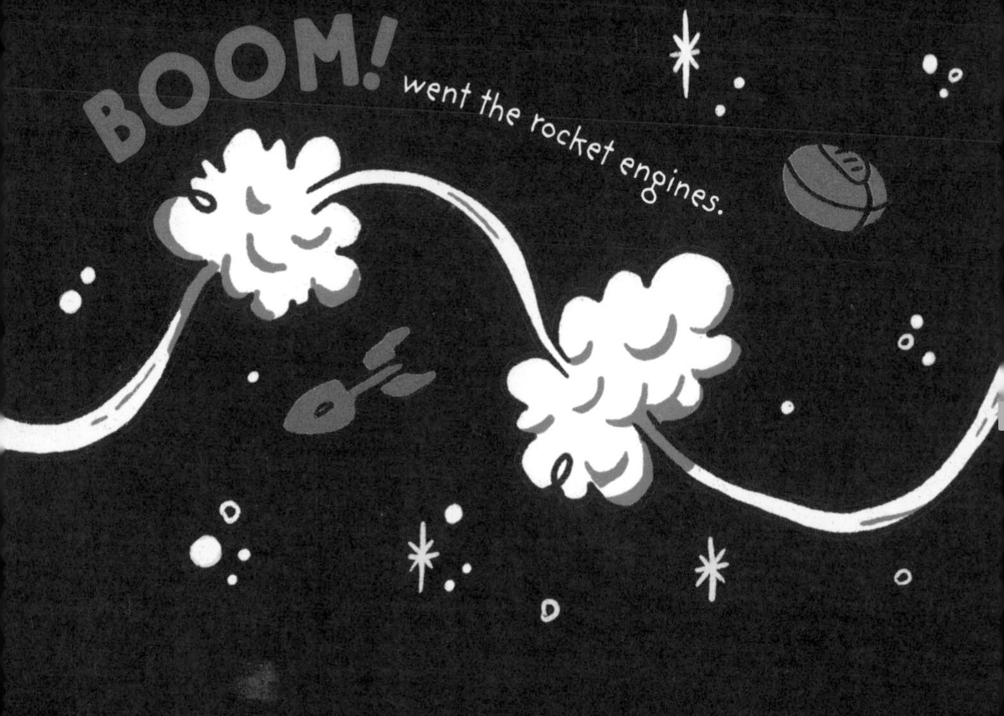
BOOM!
went the rocket engines.

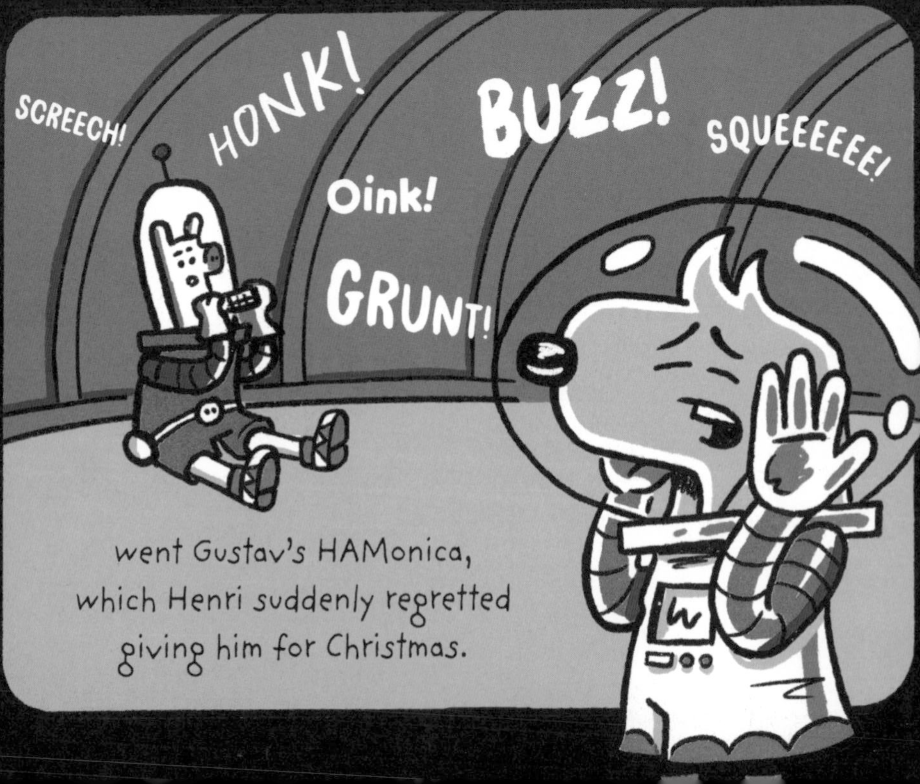
SCREECH!
HONK!
Oink!
GRUNT!
BUZZ!
SQUEEEEEEE!
went Gustav's HAMonica,
which Henri suddenly regretted
giving him for Christmas.

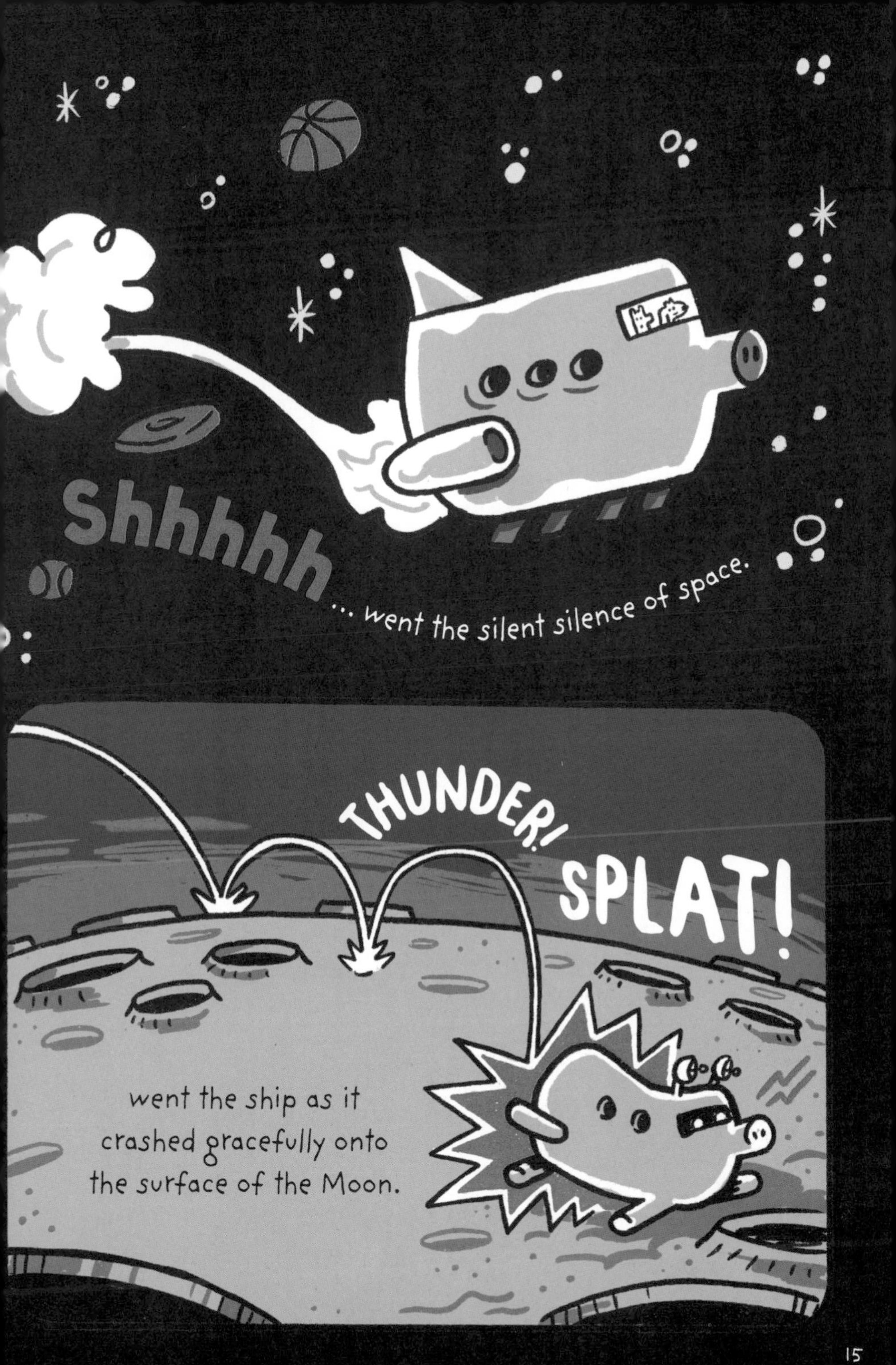
Shhhhh
... went the silent silence of space.
THUNDER!
SPLAT!
went the ship as it crashed gracefully onto the surface of the Moon.

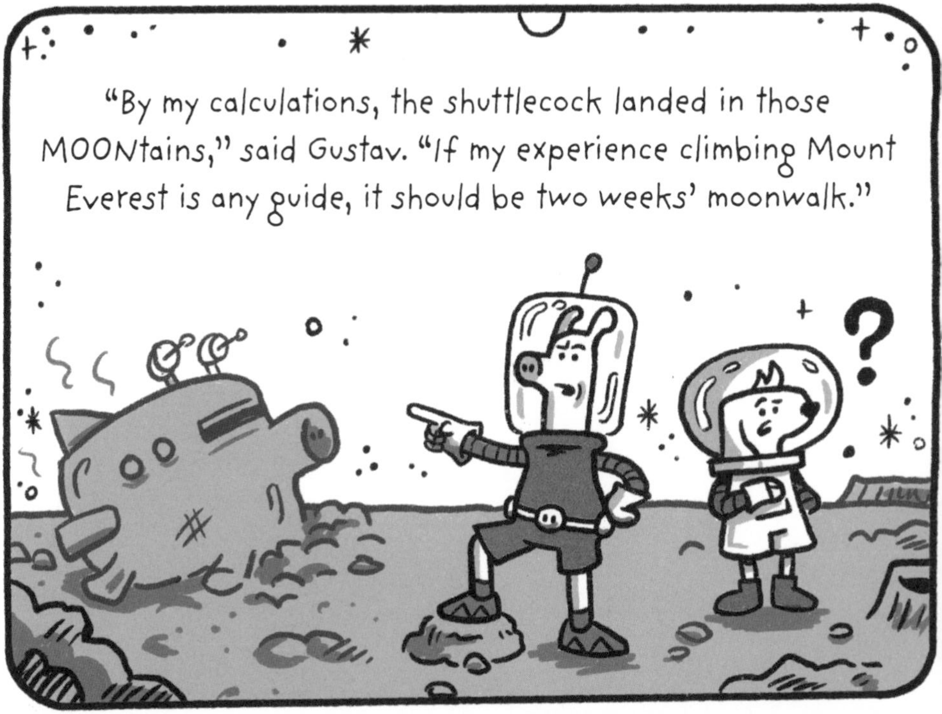
"By my calculations, the shuttlecock landed in those MOONtains," said Gustav. "If my experience climbing Mount Everest is any guide, it should be two weeks' moonwalk."

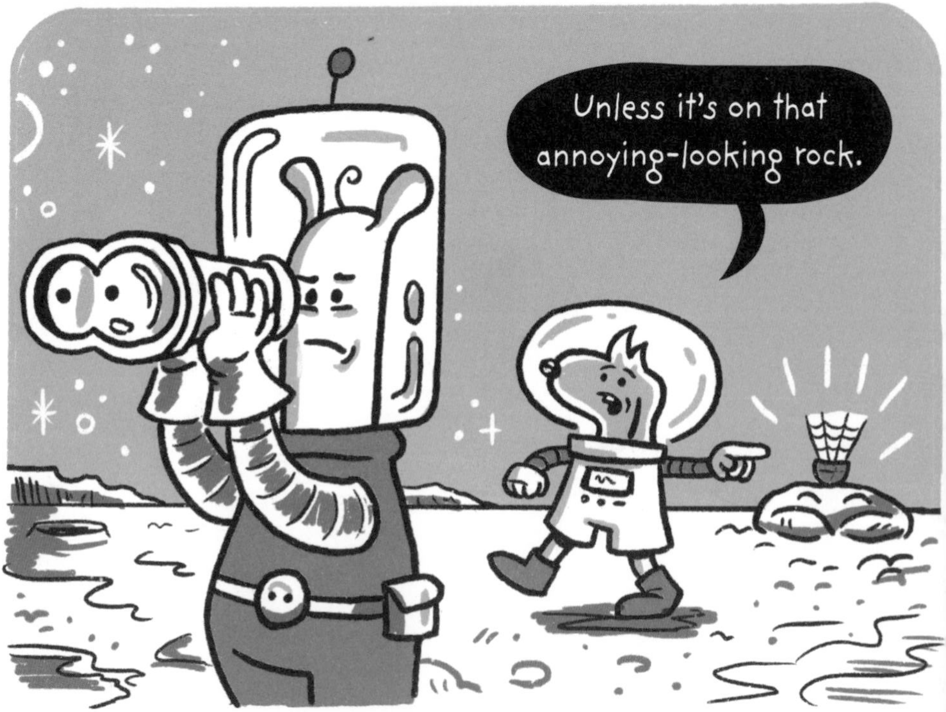
Unless it's on that annoying-looking rock.

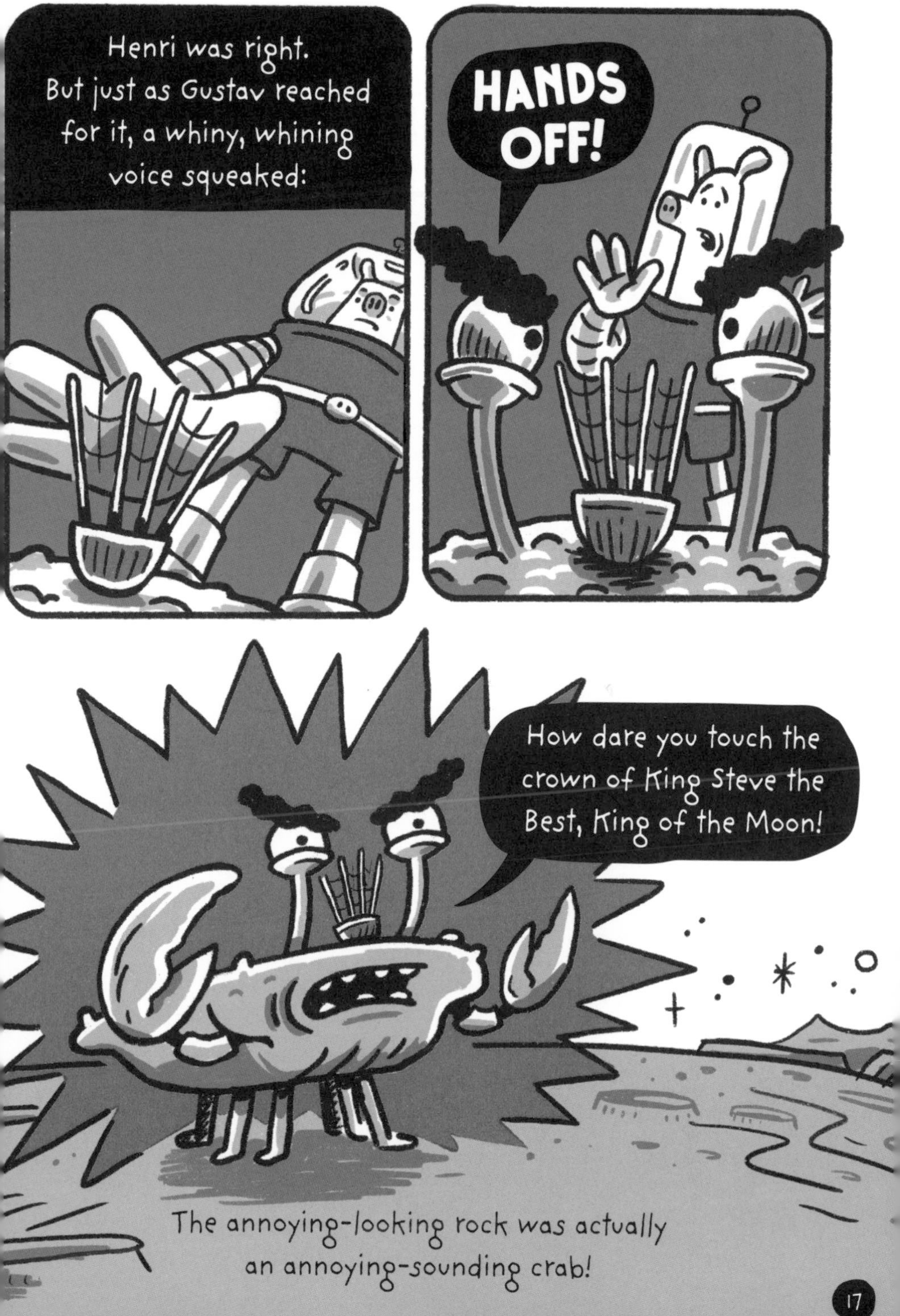

Henri was right. But just as Gustav reached for it, a whiny, whining voice squeaked:
HANDS OFF!
How dare you touch the crown of King Steve the Best, King of the Moon!
The annoying-looking rock was actually an annoying-sounding crab!

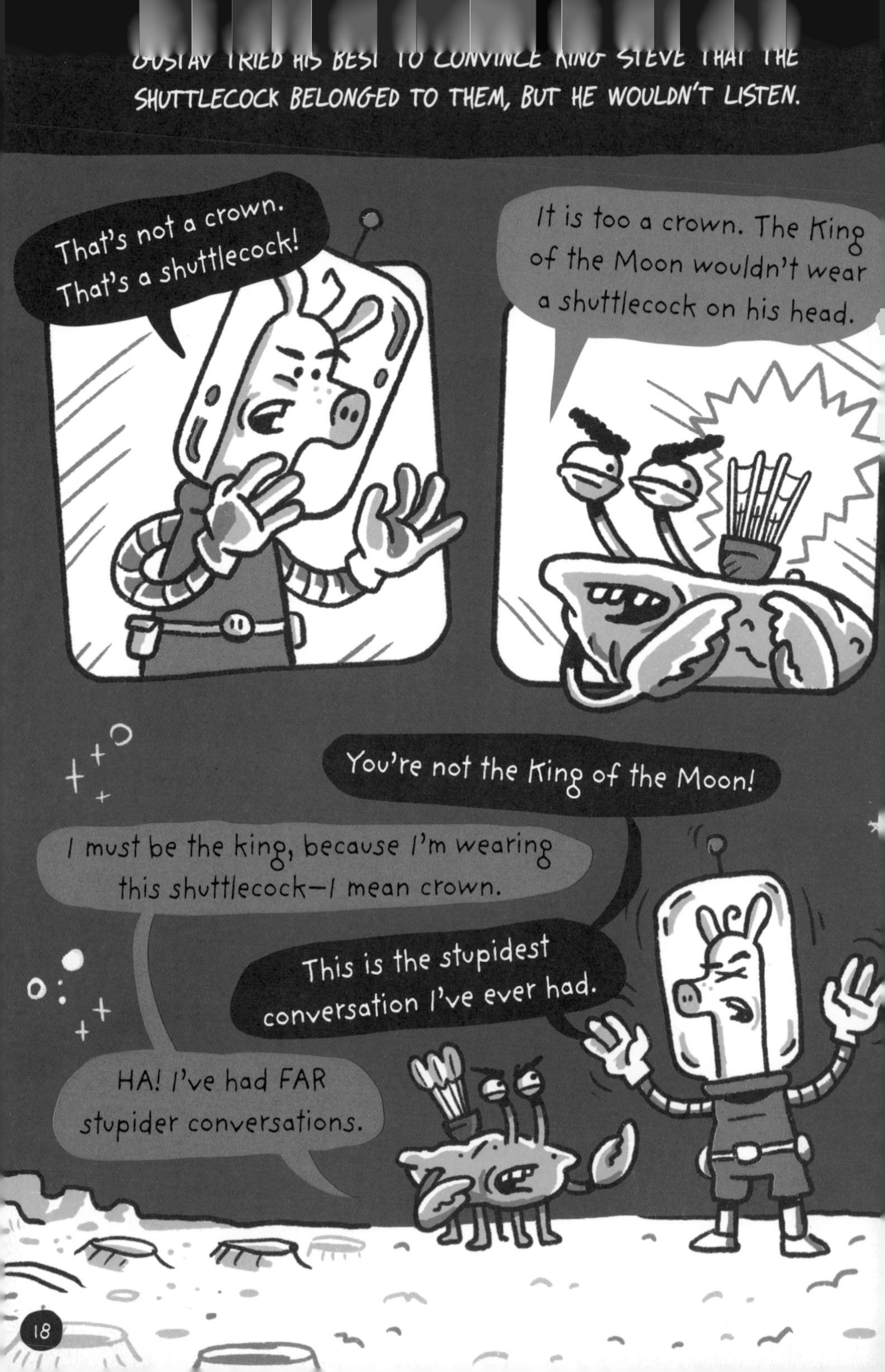
GUSTAV TRIED HIS BEST TO CONVINCE KING STEVE THAT THE SHUTTLECOCK BELONGED TO THEM, BUT HE WOULDN'T LISTEN.
That's not a crown. That's a shuttlecock!
It is too a crown. The King of the Moon wouldn't wear a shuttlecock on his head.
You're not the King of the Moon!
I must be the king, because I'm wearing this shuttlecock—I mean crown.
This is the stupidest conversation I've ever had.
HA! I've had FAR stupider conversations.

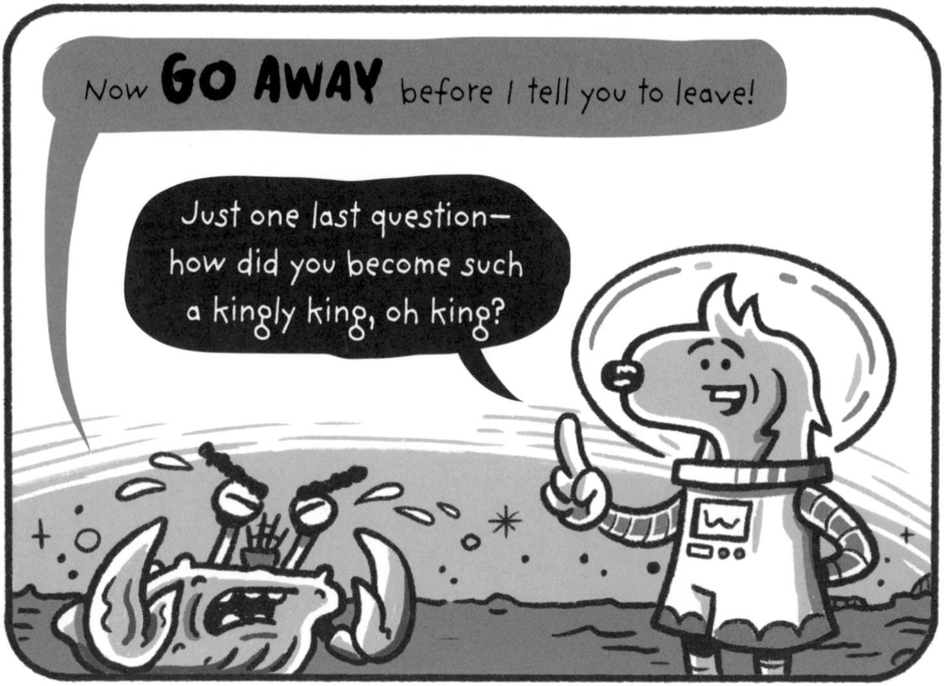
Now GO AWAY before I tell you to leave!
Just one last question—how did you become such a kingly king, oh king?

King Steve was flattered. "I had to complete two—no, five ... no, FOUR impossible challenges," he said.

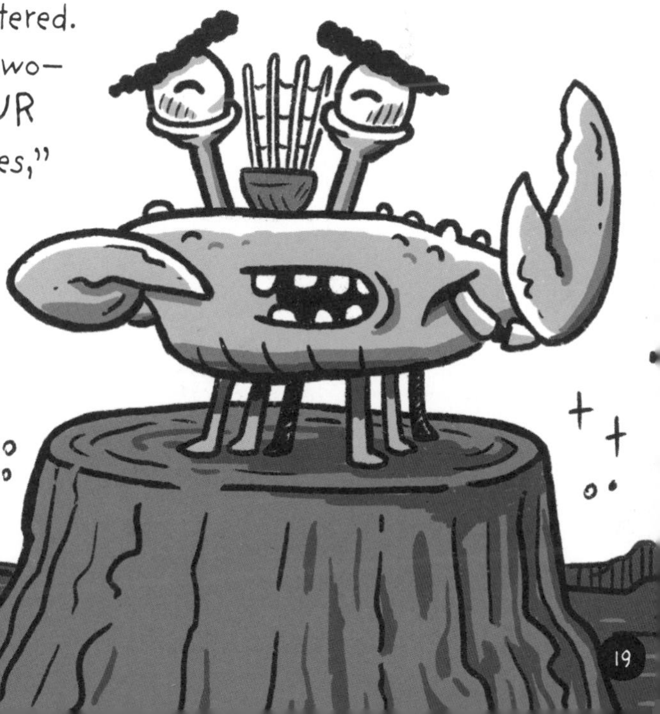

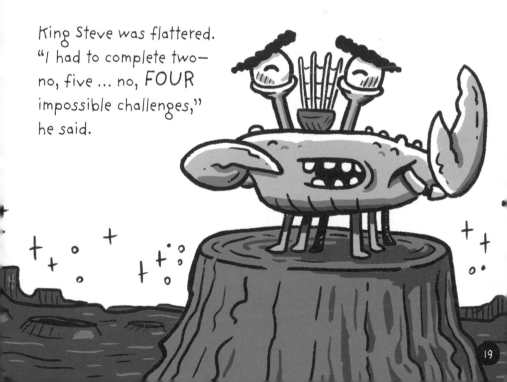

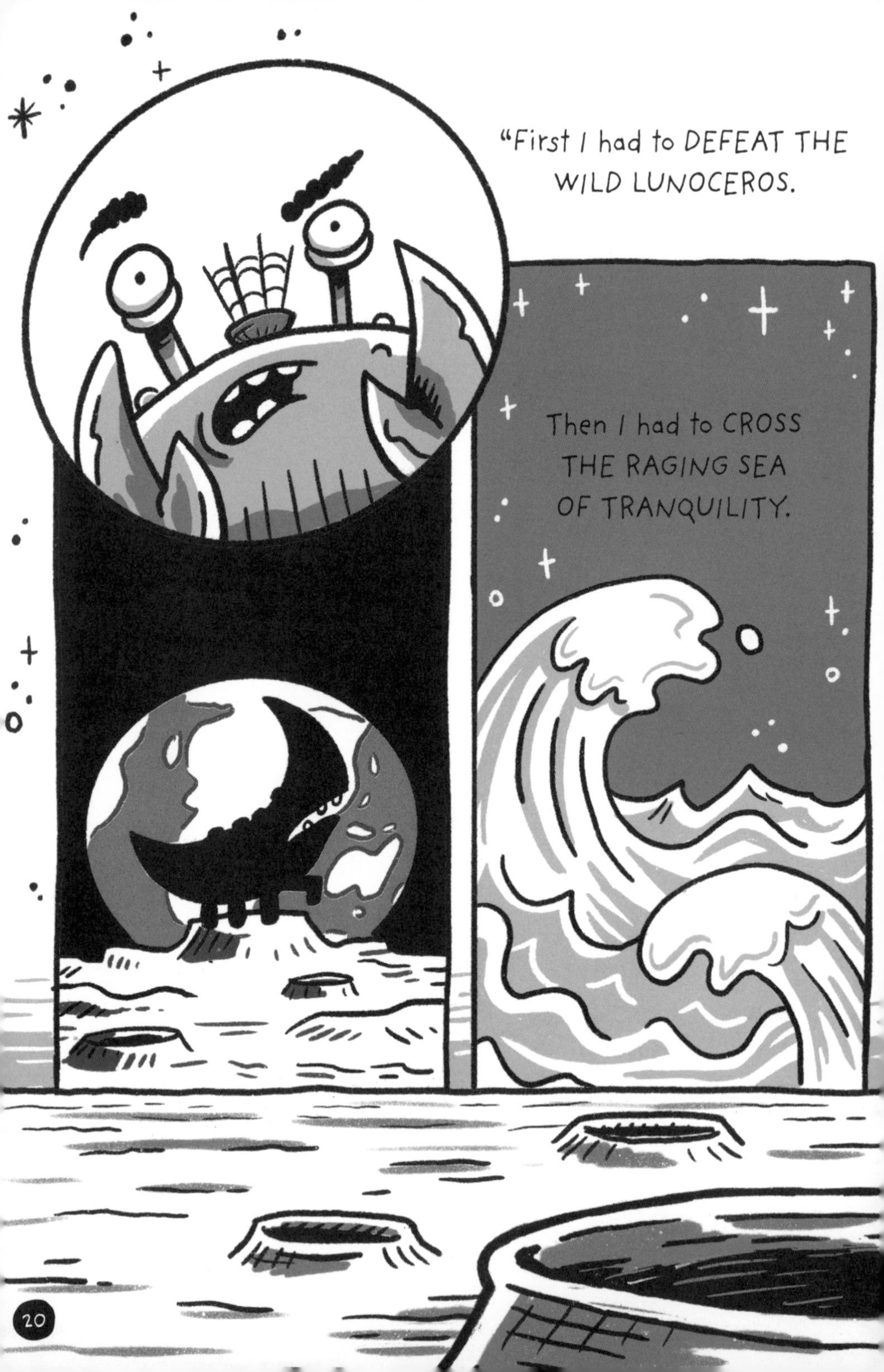
"First I had to DEFEAT THE WILD LUNOCEROS.
Then I had to CROSS THE RAGING SEA OF TRANQUILITY.

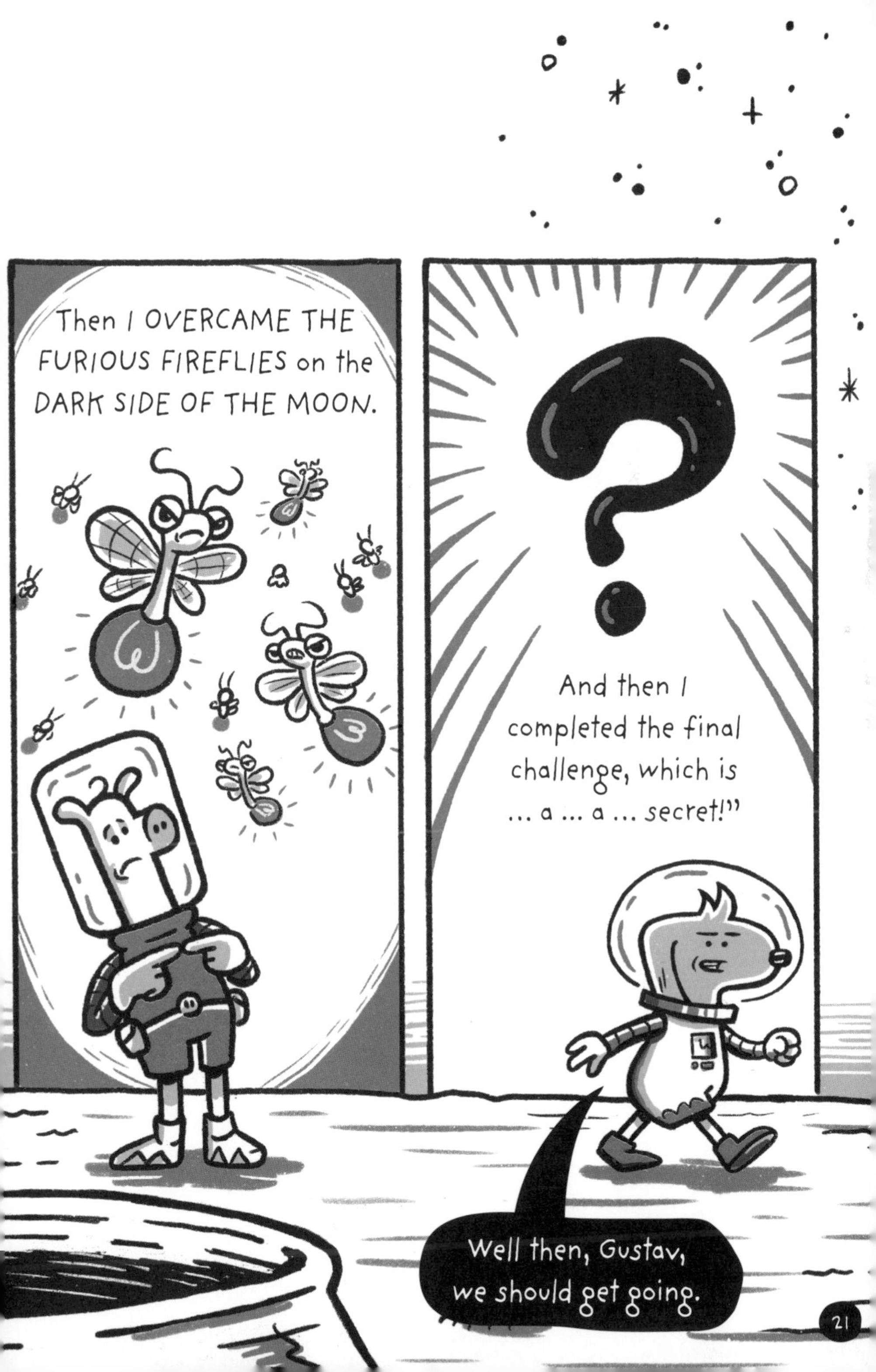
Then I OVERCAME THE FURIOUS FIREFLIES on the DARK SIDE OF THE MOON.
And then I completed the final challenge, which is ... a ... a ... secret!"
Well then, Gustav, we should get going.

"Scuttling off home, are you?" sneered King Steve.

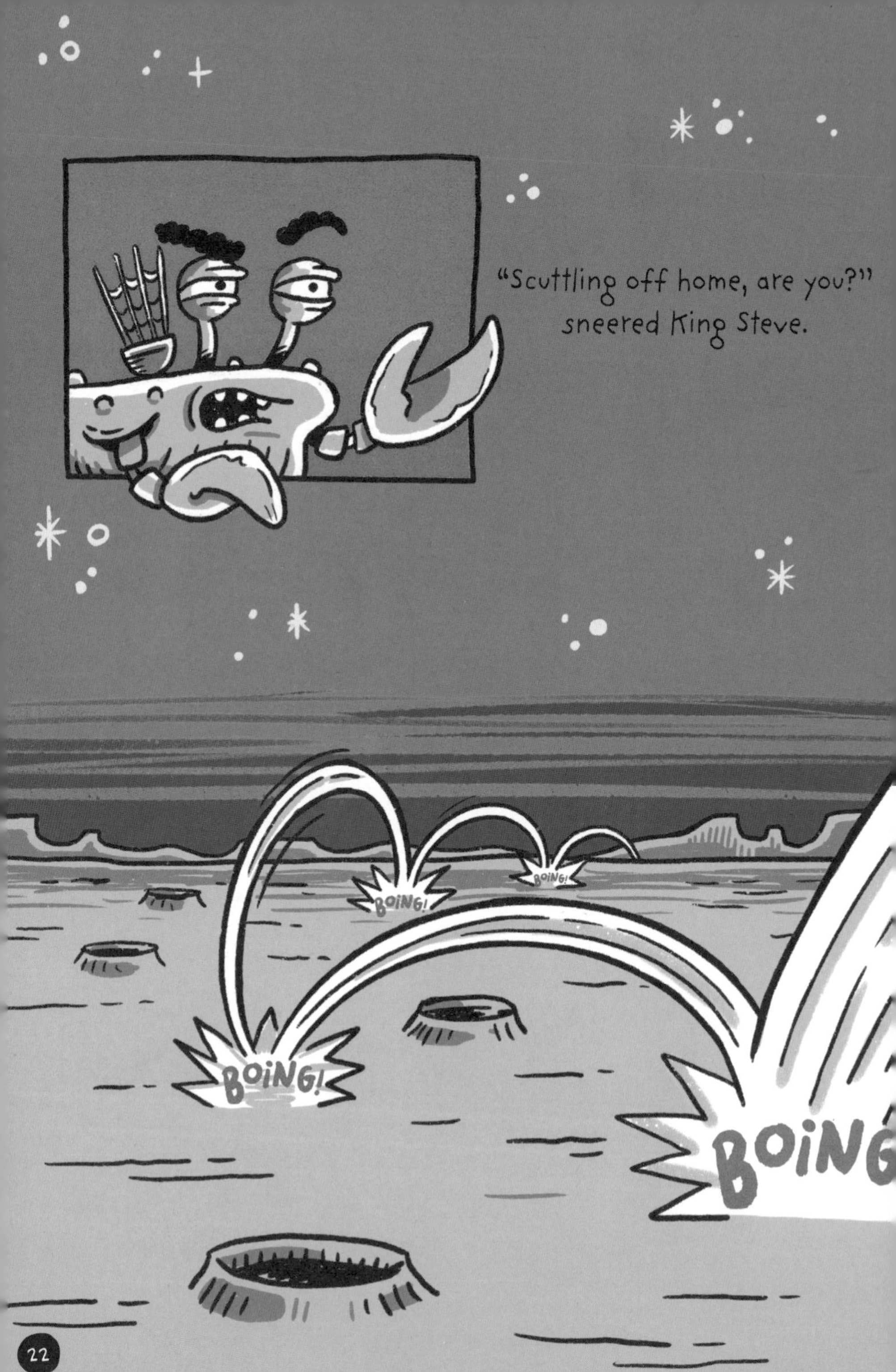
BOING!
BOING!
BOING!
BOING

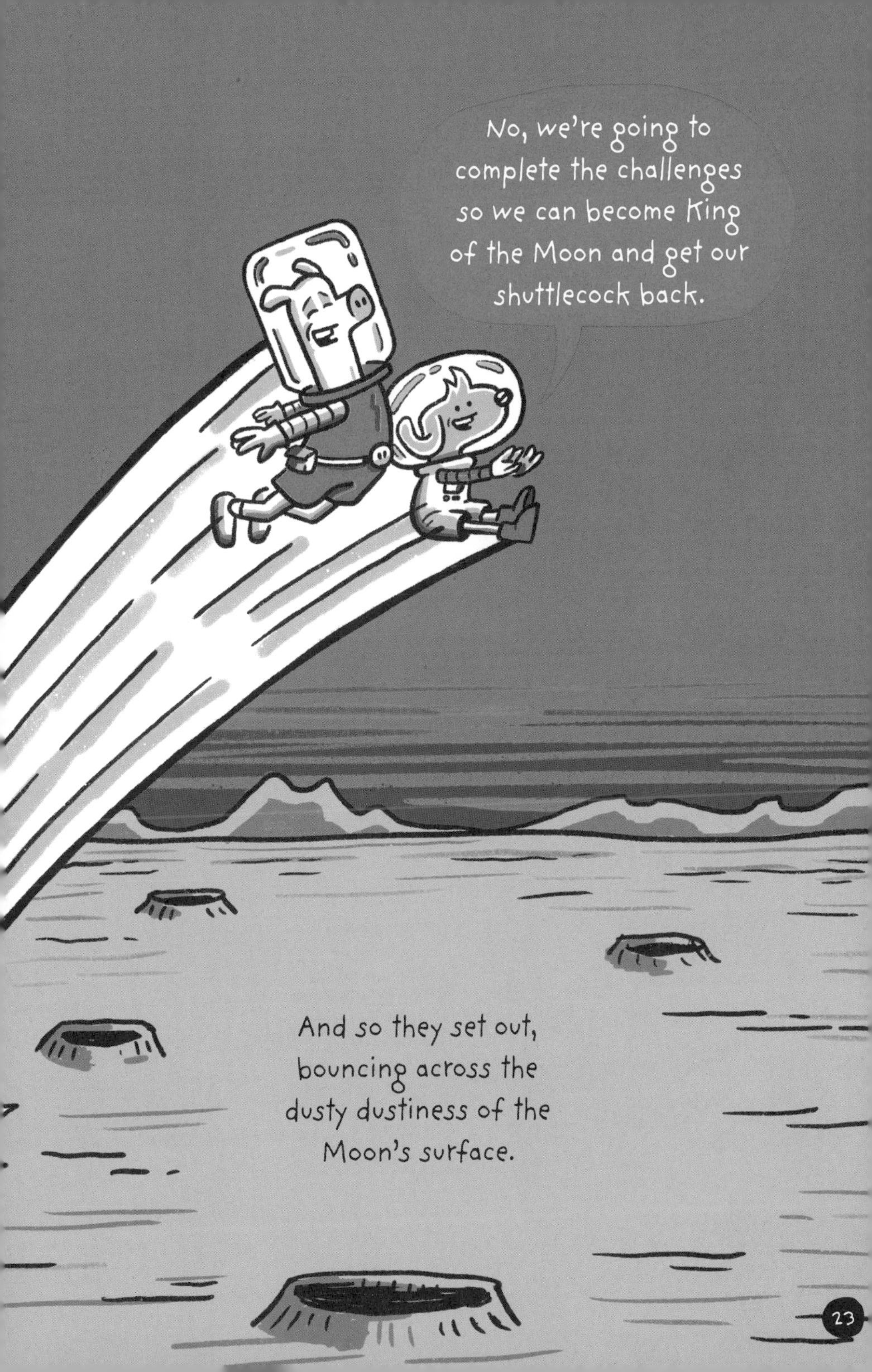
No, we're going to complete the challenges so we can become King of the Moon and get our shuttlecock back.
And so they set out, bouncing across the dusty dustiness of the Moon's surface.

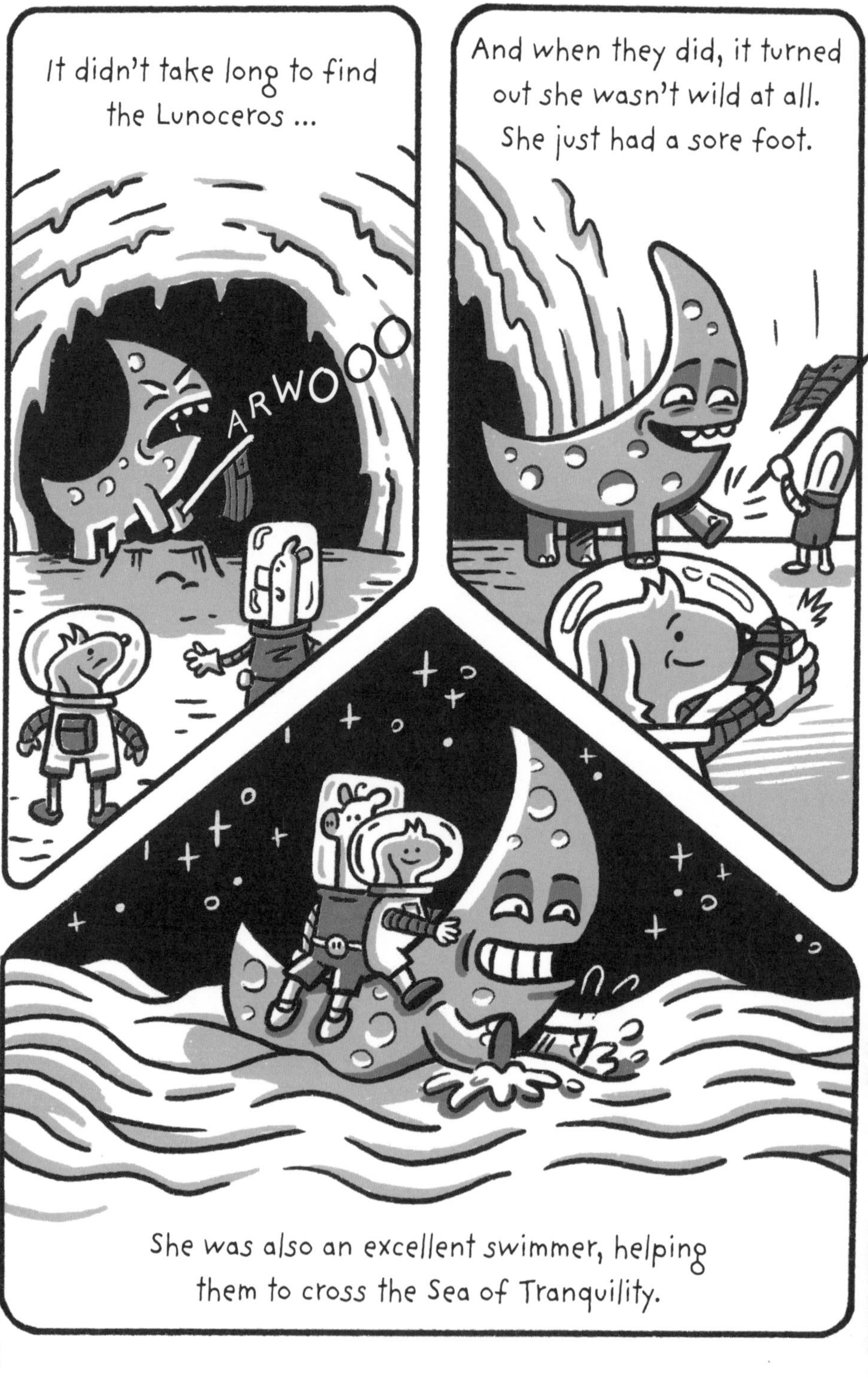
It didn't take long to find the Lunoceros ...
ARWOOOO
And when they did, it turned out she wasn't wild at all. She just had a sore foot.
She was also an excellent swimmer, helping them to cross the Sea of Tranquility.

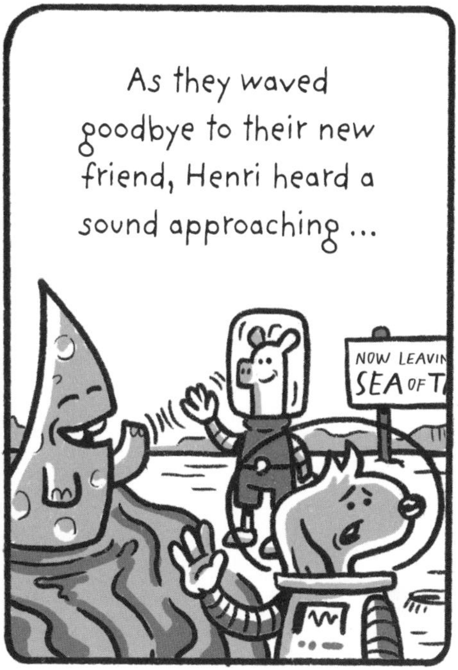
As they waved goodbye to their new friend, Henri heard a sound approaching ...
NOW LEAVIN
SEA OF T

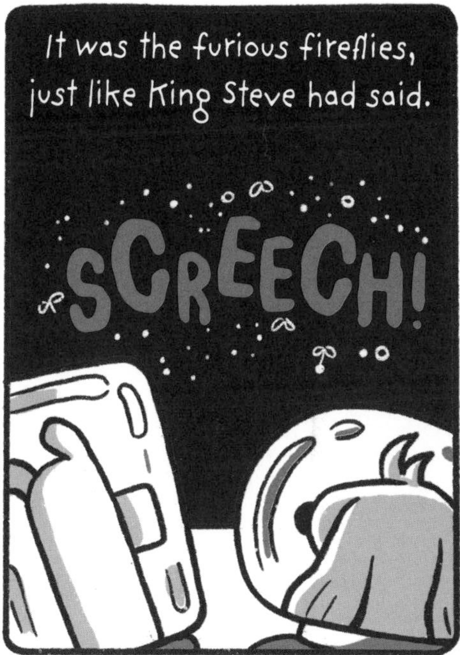
It was the furious fireflies, just like King Steve had said.
SCREECH!

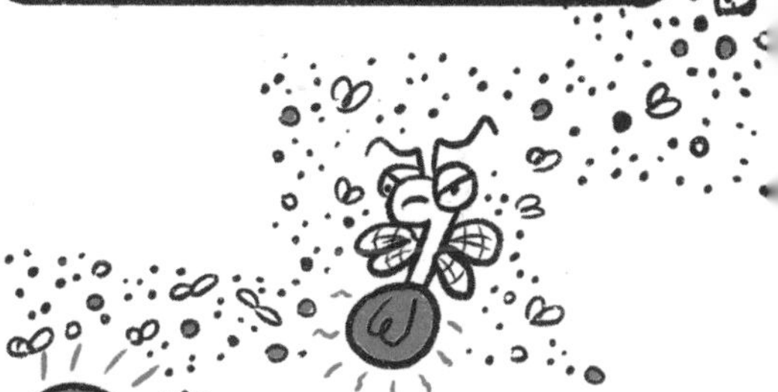

"Such horrible screeching," said Gustav. But that gave Henri an idea.

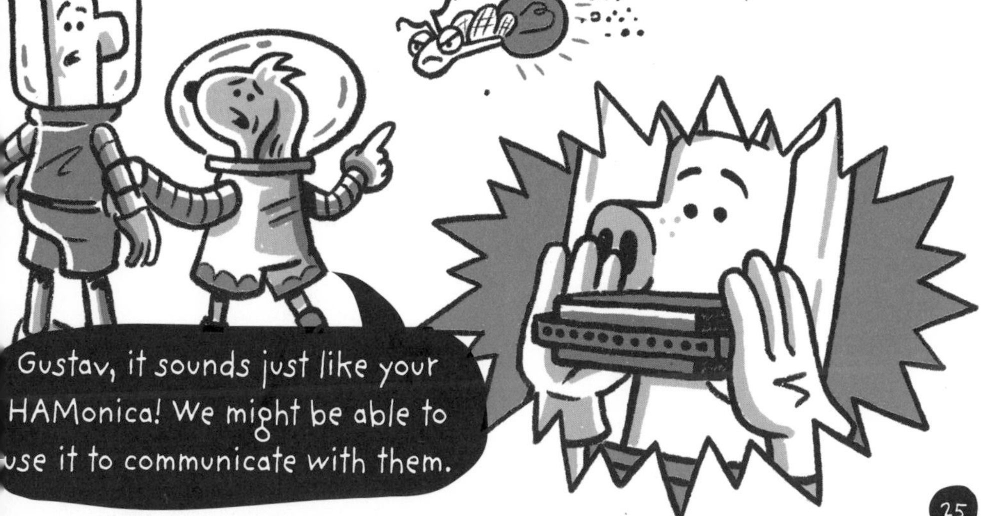
Gustav, it sounds just like your HAMonica! We might be able to use it to communicate with them.

Henri was right—the fireflies were enchanted by the instrument's heavenly grunts and squeals.

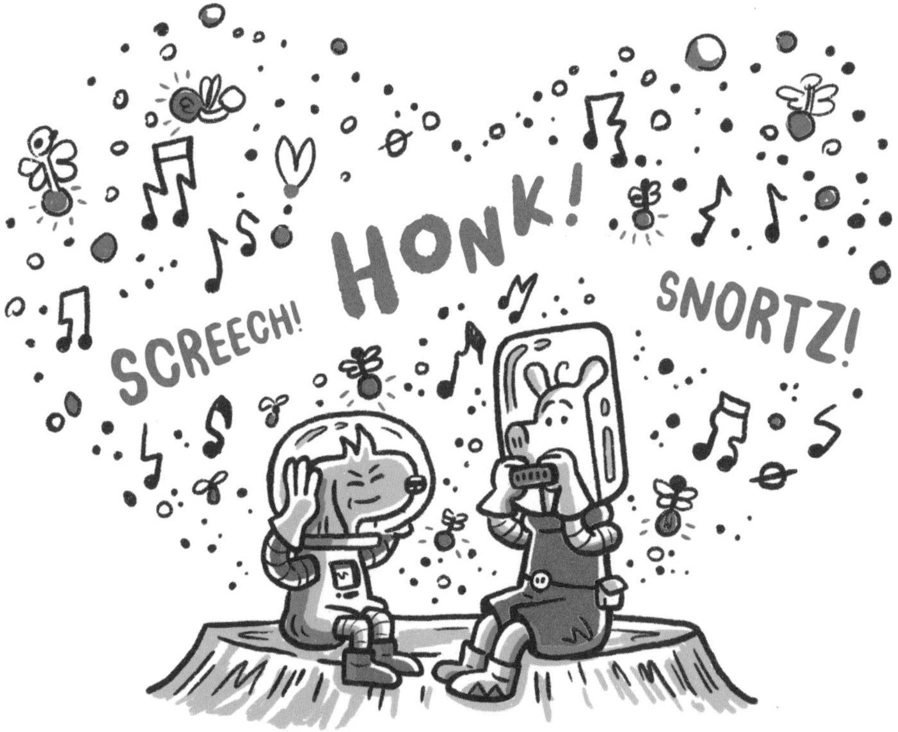
SCREECH!
HONK!
SNORTZ!

They calmed right down, and even helped to warm and guide Gustav and Henri Normal across the dark side of the Moon.

(Which was even colder than a fridge inside another fridge.)

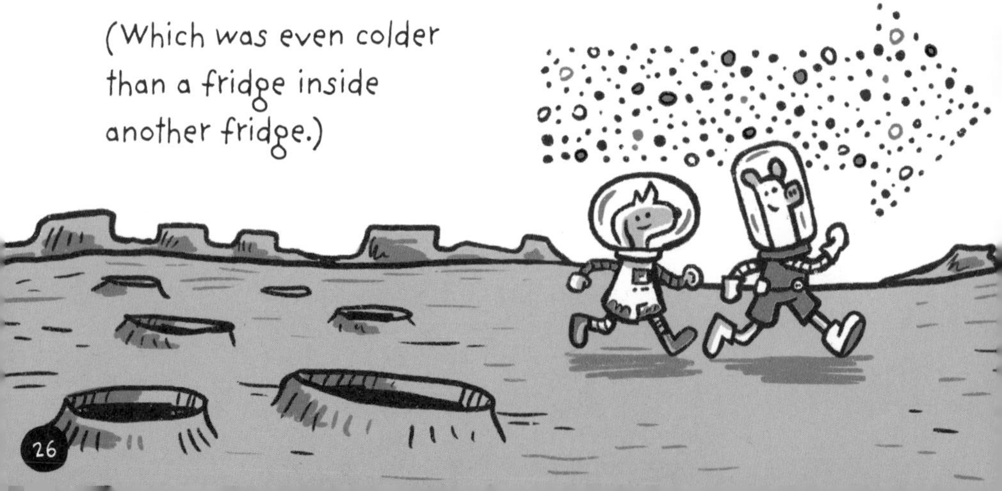

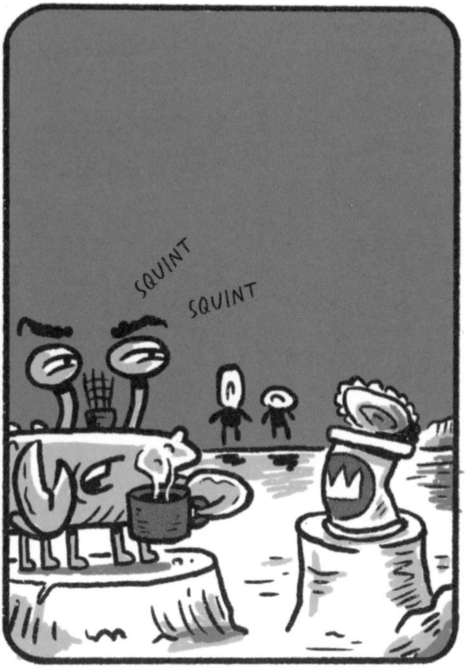
SQUINT
SQUINT
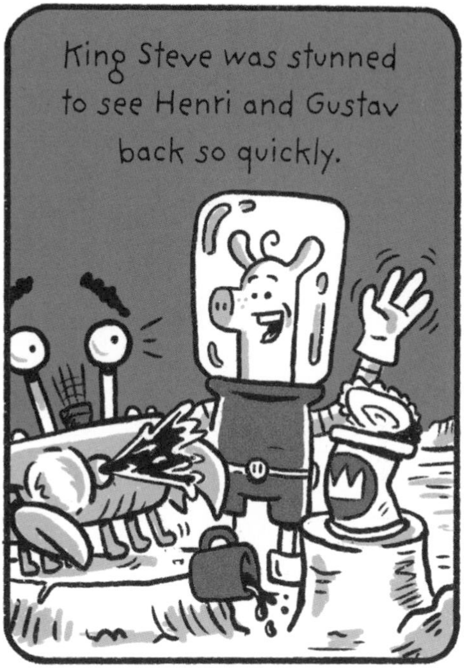
King Steve was stunned to see Henri and Gustav back so quickly.

But they still had one challenge left.
The secret challenge!

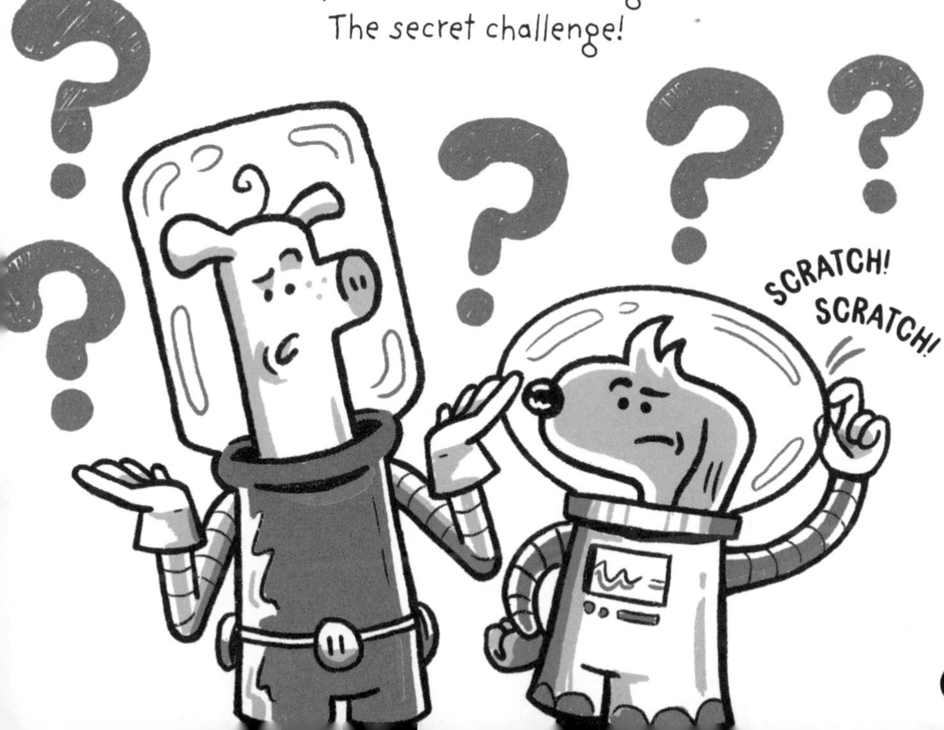
SCRATCH!
SCRATCH!

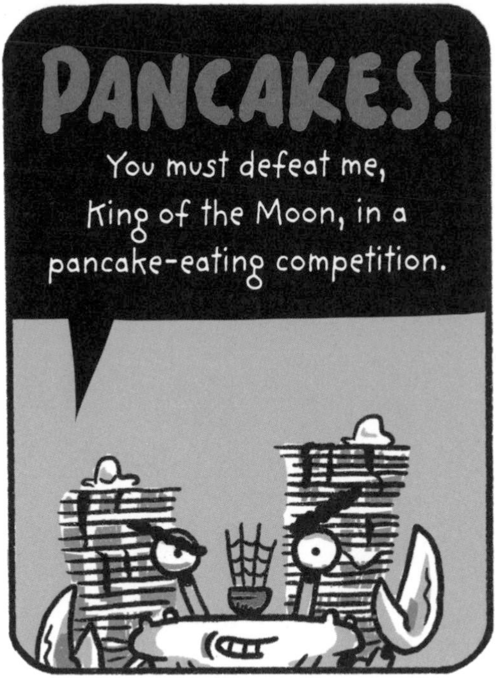
PANCAKES!
You must defeat me, King of the Moon, in a pancake-eating competition.

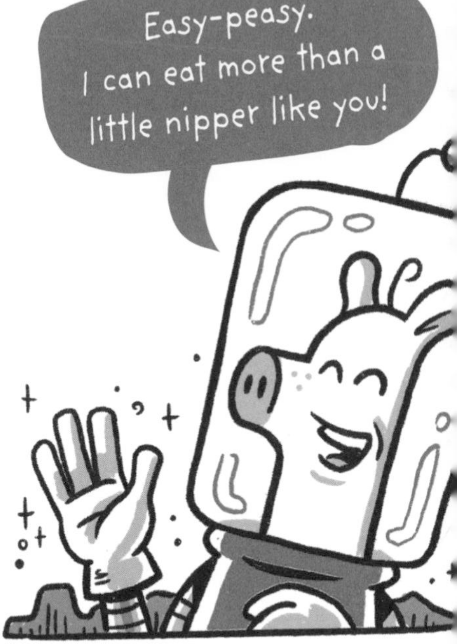
Easy-peasy. I can eat more than a little nipper like you!

But then King Steve shook himself and revealed that he wasn't a crab—he was a **BLOBSTER**.

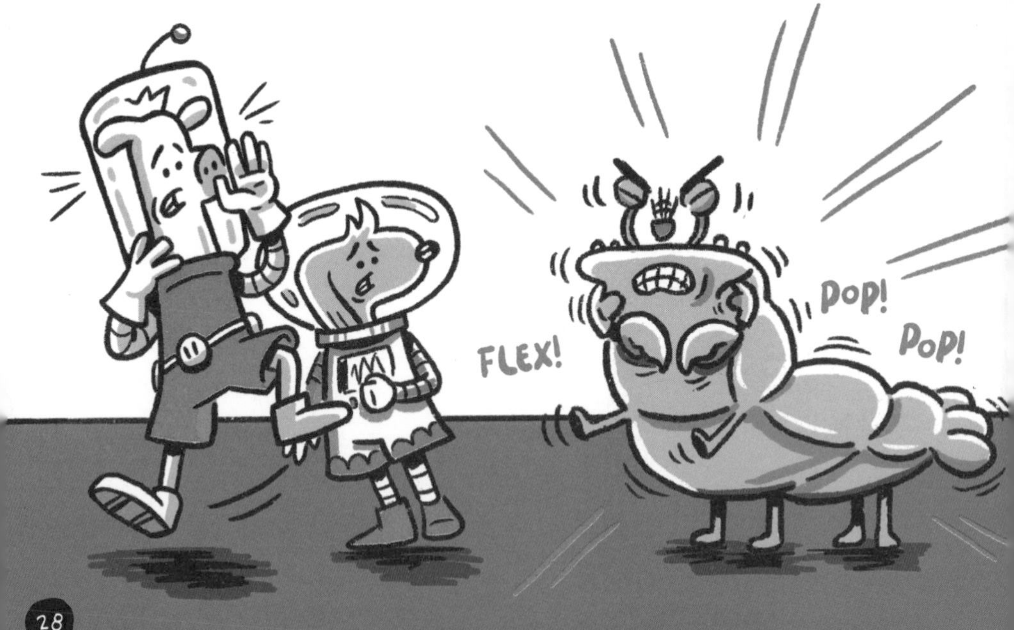
FLEX!
POP!
POP!

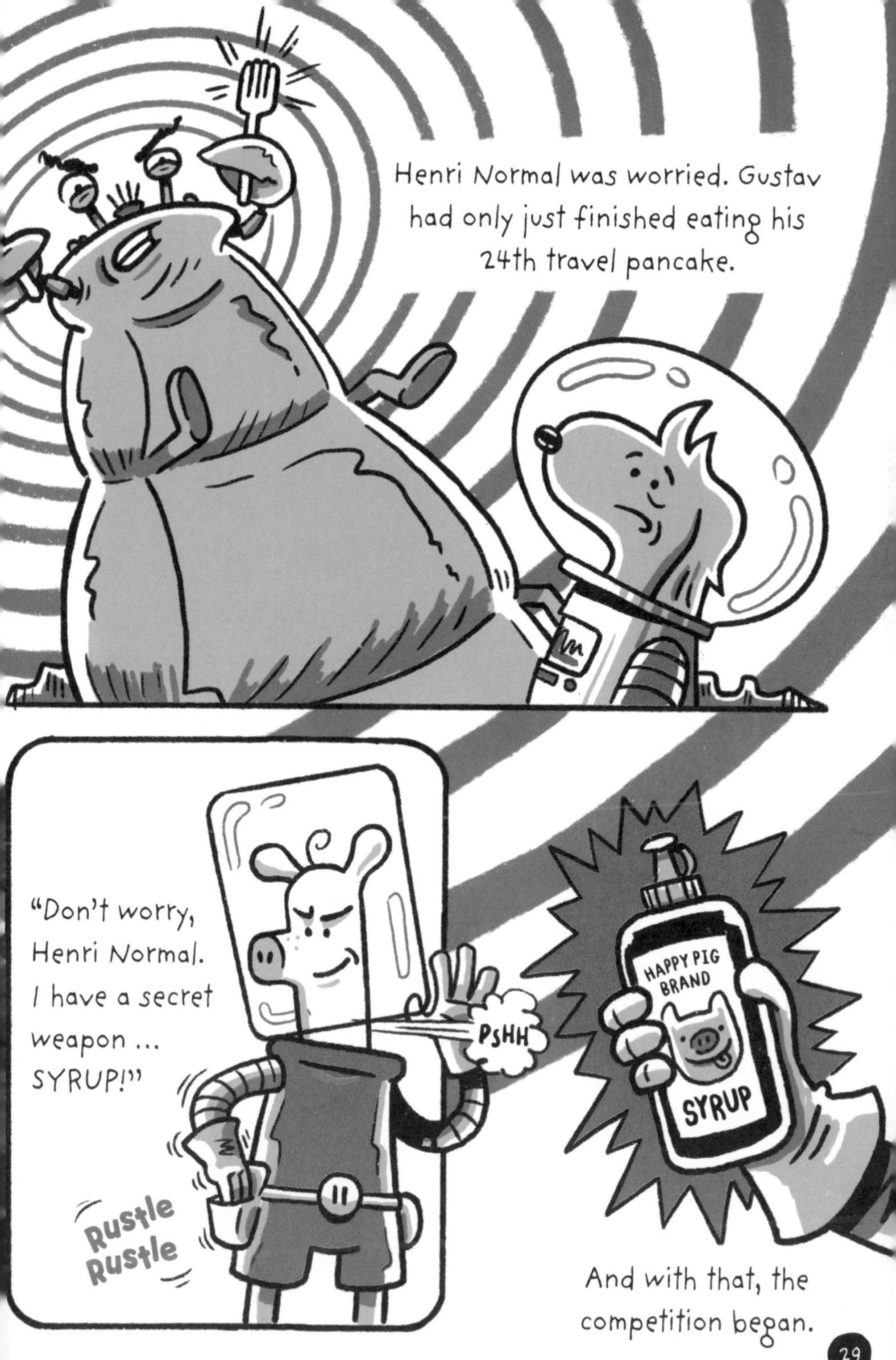
Henri Normal was worried. Gustav had only just finished eating his 24th travel pancake.
"Don't worry, Henri Normal. I have a secret weapon ... SYRUP!"
Rustle Rustle
PSHH
HAPPY PIG BRAND
SYRUP
And with that, the competition began.

They ate and gobbled

and chewed

and munched

and burped

and chomped

and swallowed

and bit

and nibbled

and gulped

until finally ...

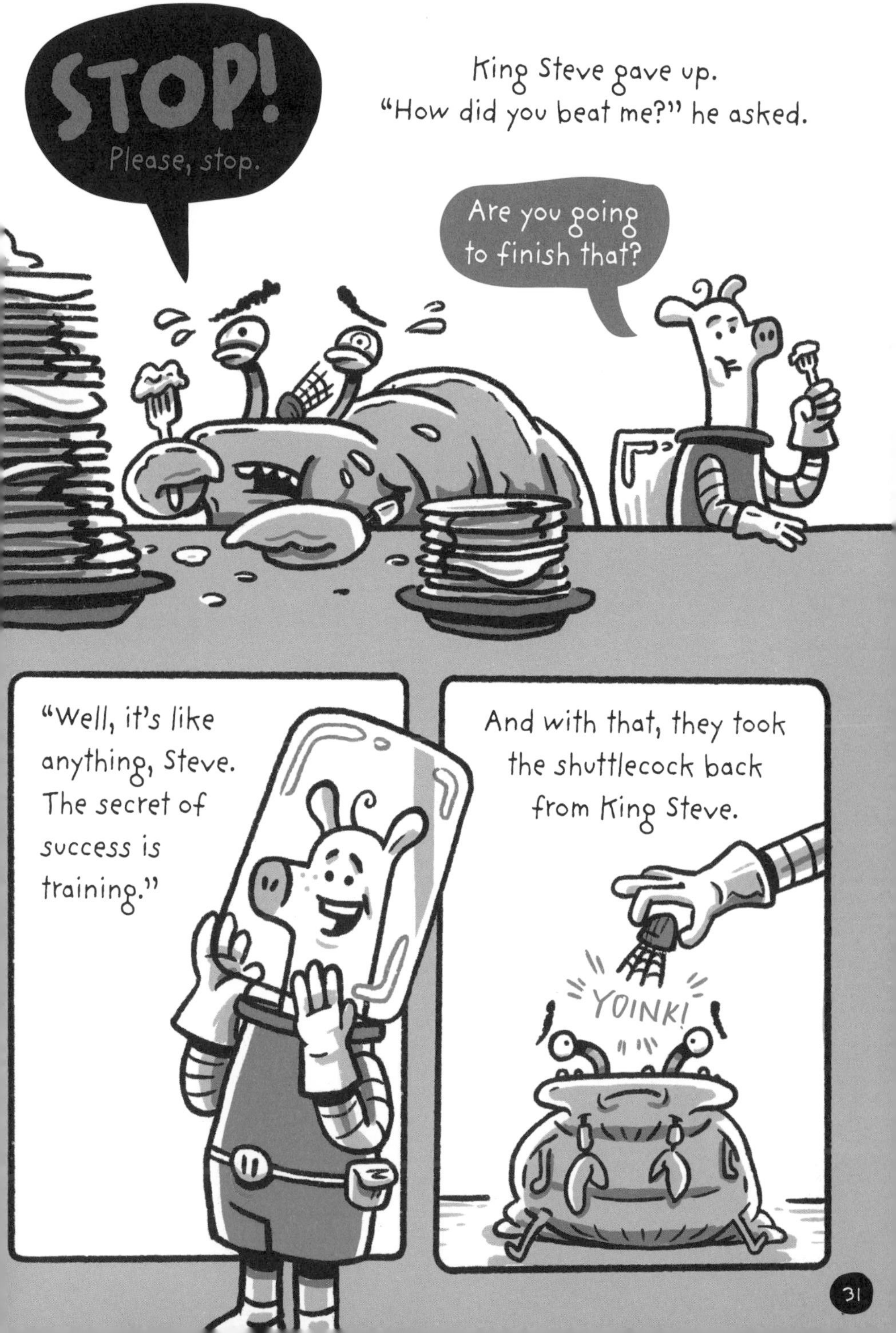
STOP!
Please, stop.
King Steve gave up.
"How did you beat me?" he asked.
Are you going to finish that?
"Well, it's like anything, Steve. The secret of success is training."
And with that, they took the shuttlecock back from King Steve.
YOINK!

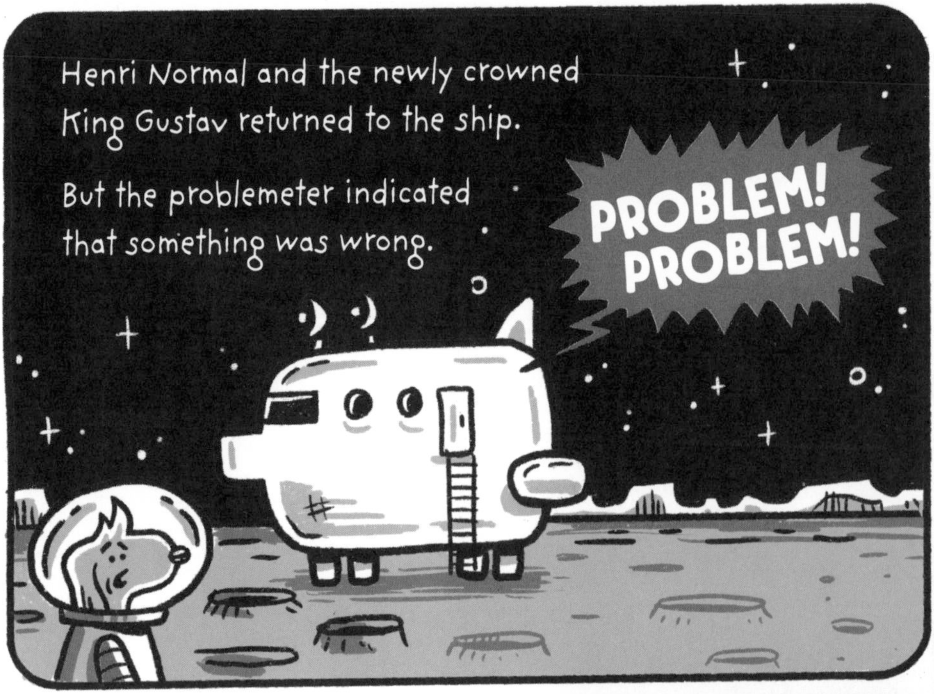
Henri Normal and the newly crowned King Gustav returned to the ship.
But the problemeter indicated that something was wrong.
PROBLEM! PROBLEM!

The ship was too heavy to escape the Moon's gravity. Also, Gustav's seat belt wouldn't do up anymore.

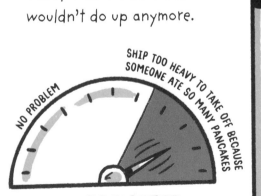

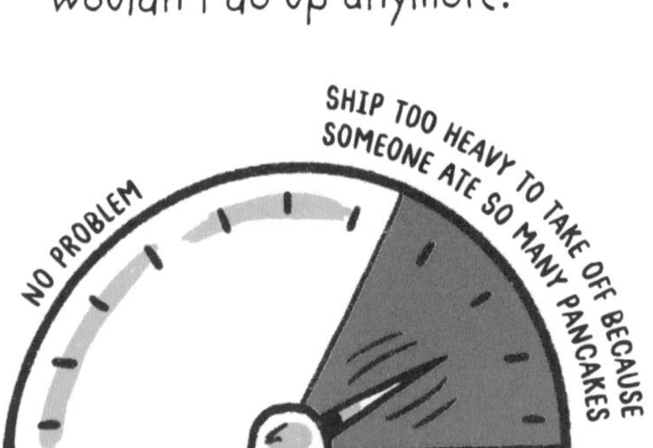
NO PROBLEM
SHIP TOO HEAVY TO TAKE OFF BECAUSE SOMEONE ATE SO MANY PANCAKES

**PROBLEMETER**

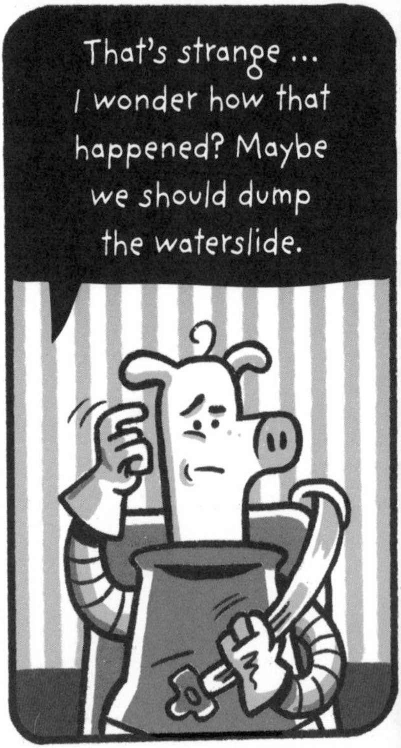
That's strange ... I wonder how that happened? Maybe we should dump the waterslide.

But even without the waterslide and the Ping-Pong table—
and the television and the bedside lamp and the mixmaster
and the backup Ping-Pong table and the emergency television
and everything else they could throw out—the rocket was
still just a teensy tiny bit too heavy to take off.

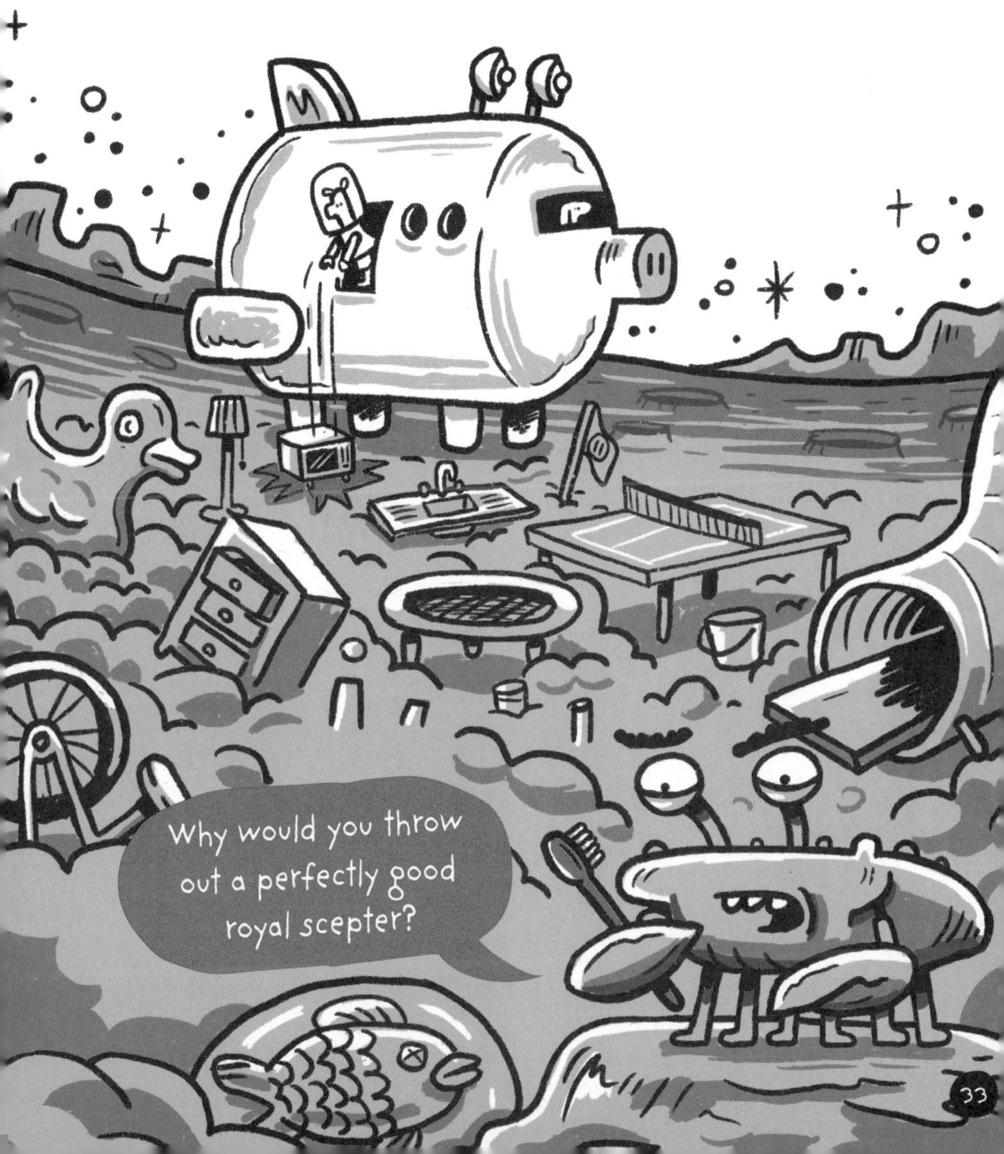
Why would you throw out a perfectly good royal scepter?

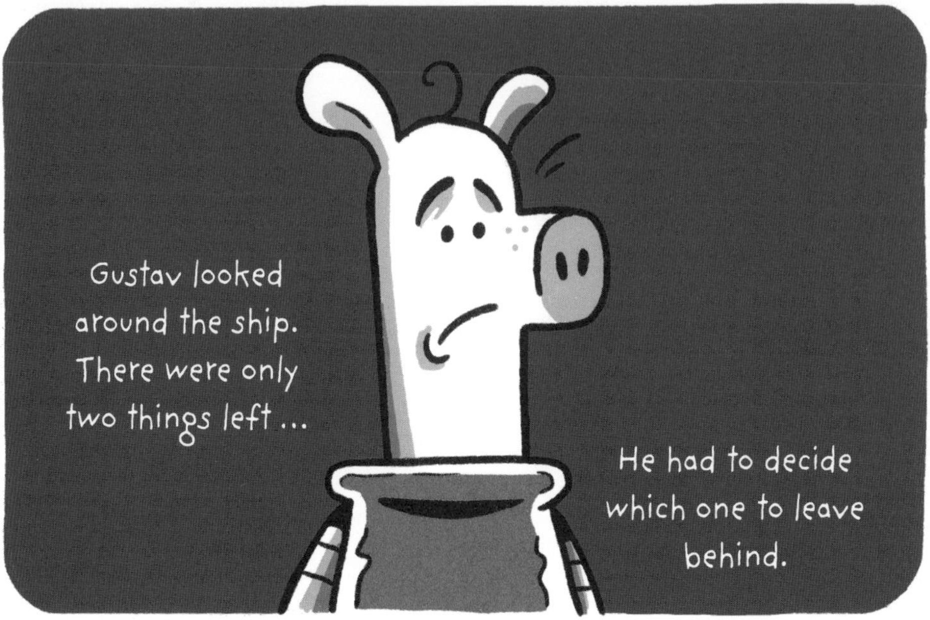
Gustav looked around the ship. There were only two things left ...
He had to decide which one to leave behind.

It was not an easy decision.

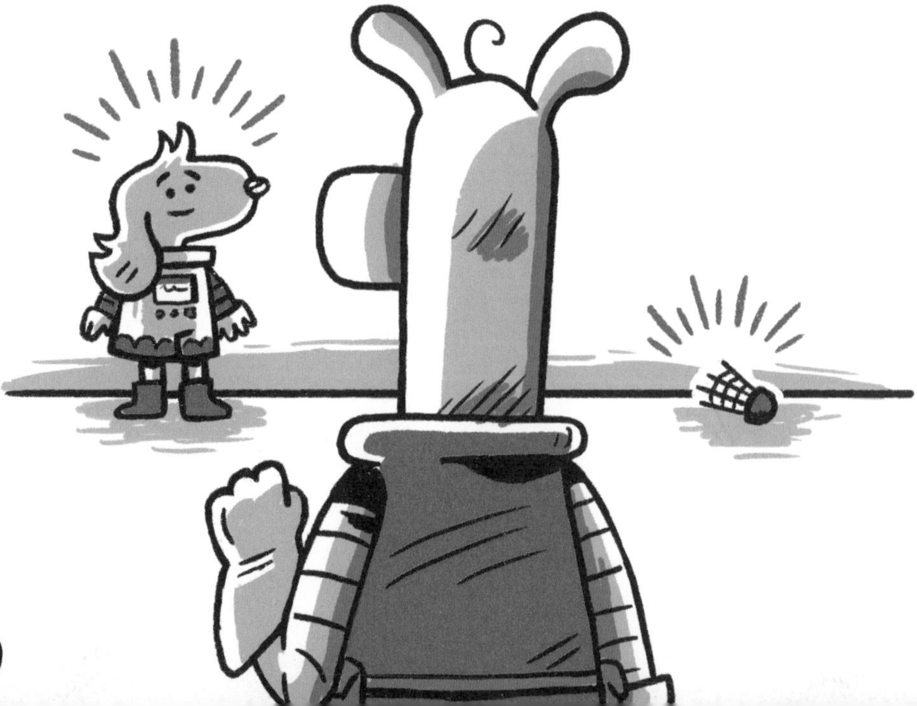

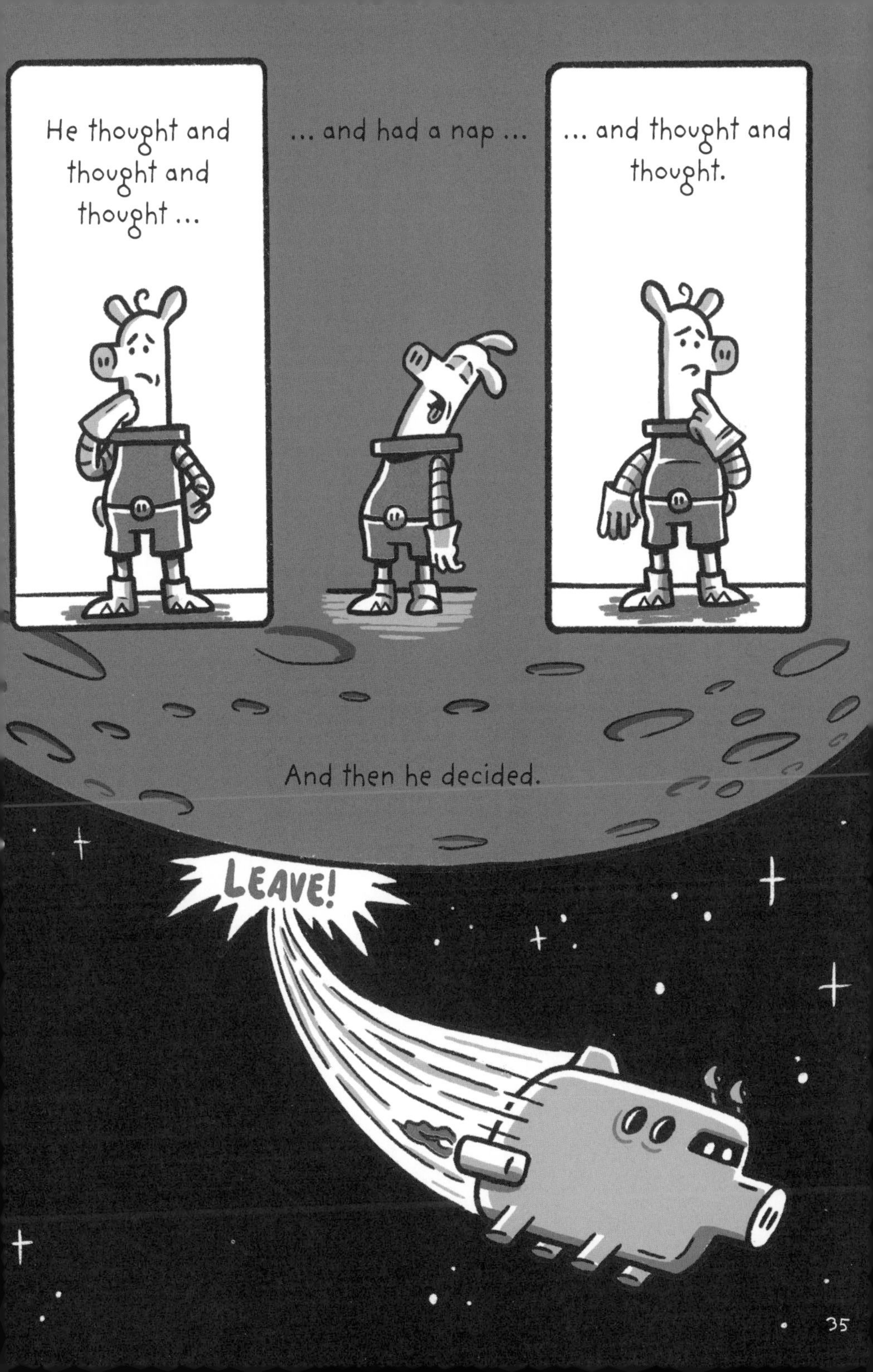
He thought and thought and thought ...
... and had a nap ...
... and thought and thought.
And then he decided.
LEAVE!

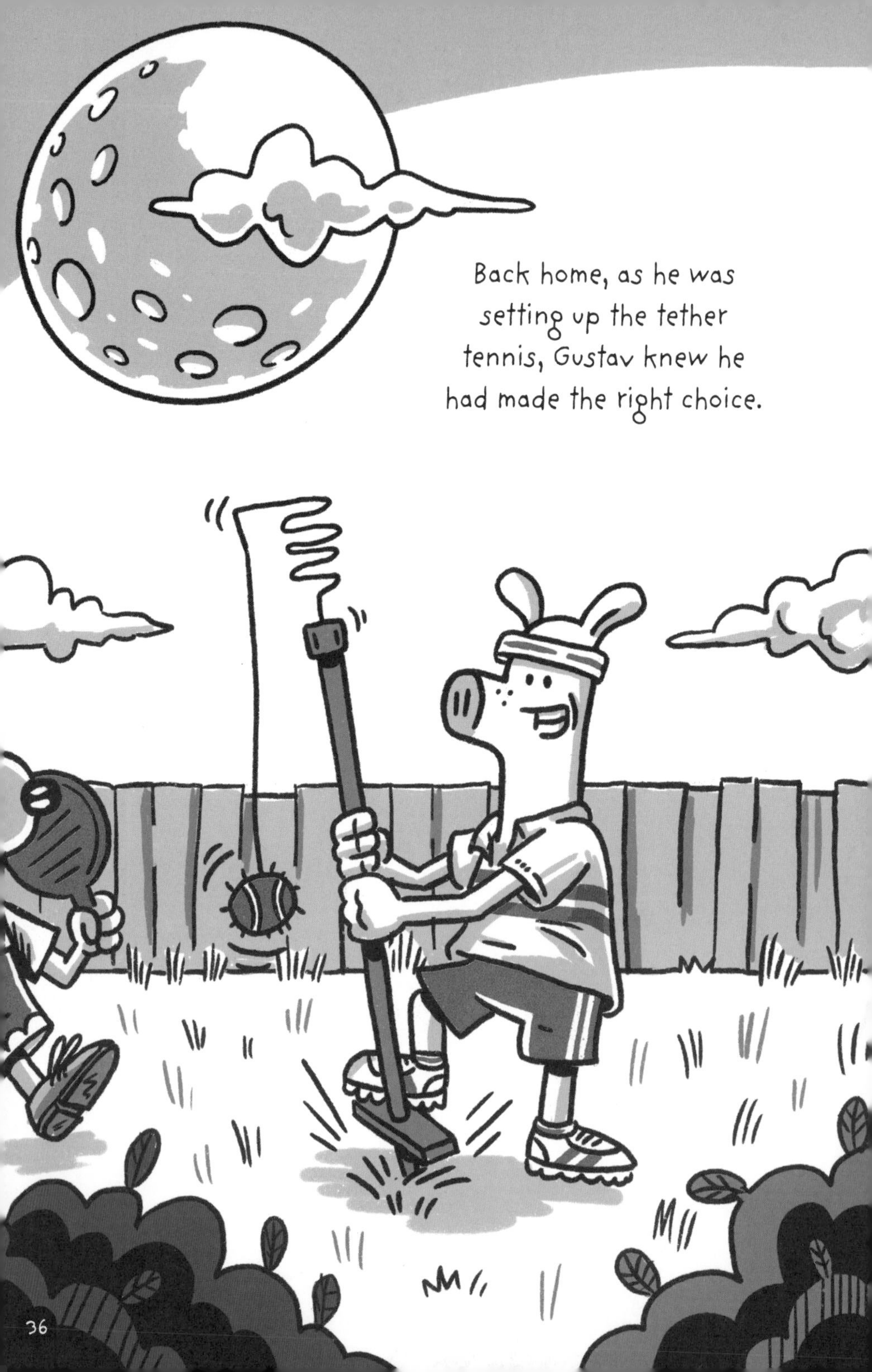
Back home, as he was setting up the tether tennis, Gustav knew he had made the right choice.

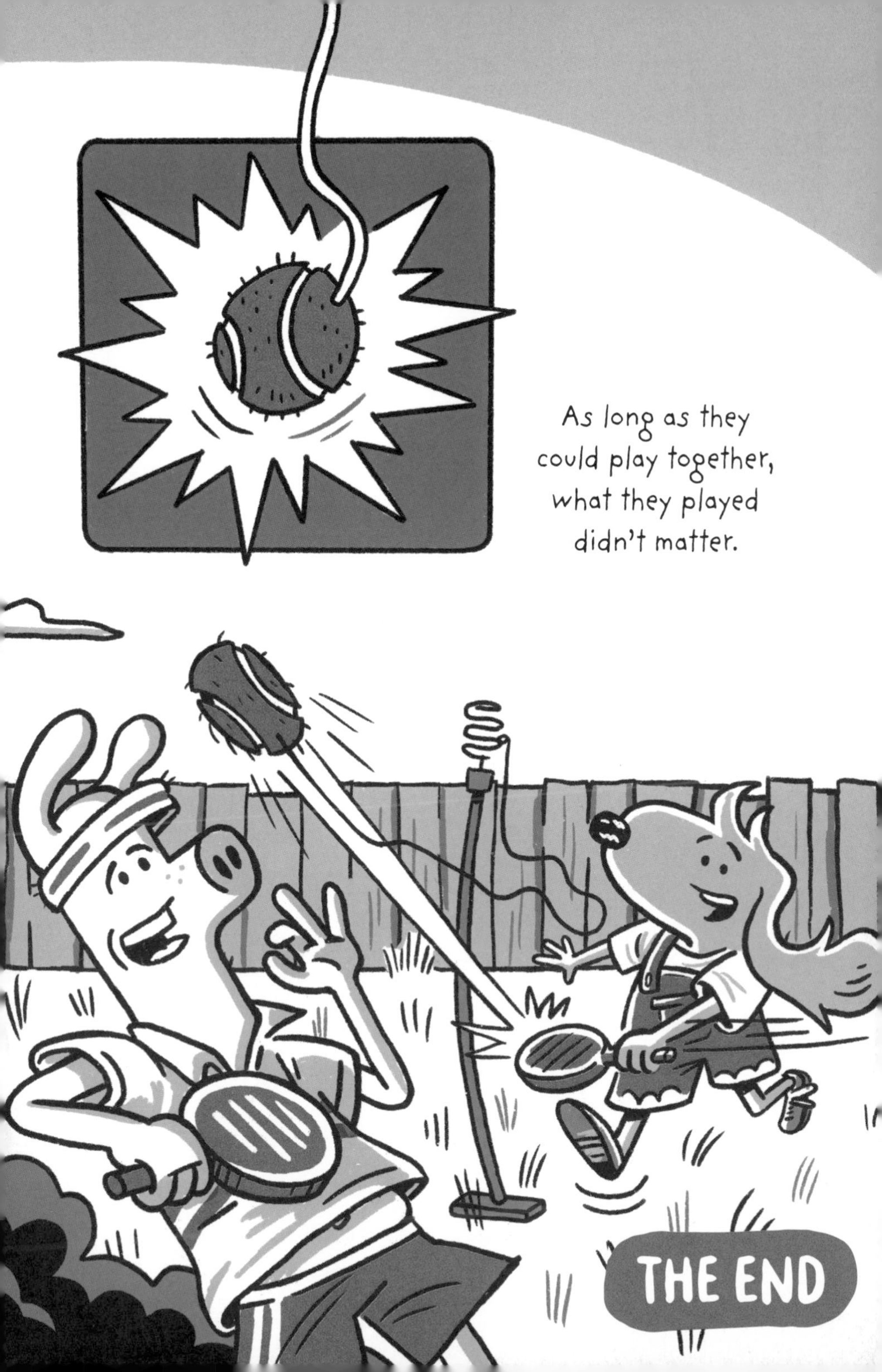
As long as they could play together, what they played didn't matter.
THE END

# ACTIVITY SHEET

## FUN ACTIVITIES FOR A LONG ~~CAR~~ SPACE TRIP

BARNEY THE BEAVER NEEDS TO GET BACK TO HIS DAM. HELP BARNEY FIND HIS WAY THROUGH THE HEDGE MAZE.

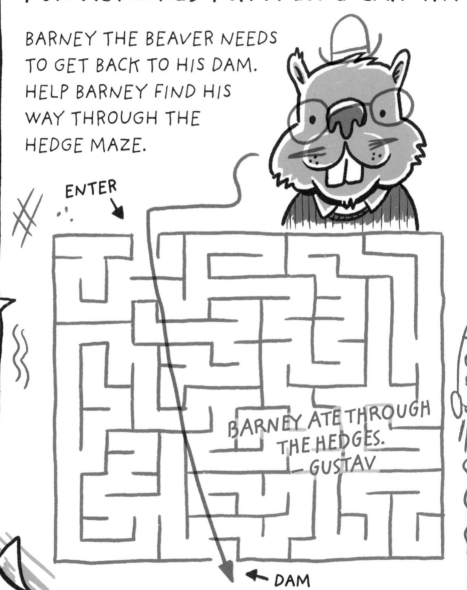

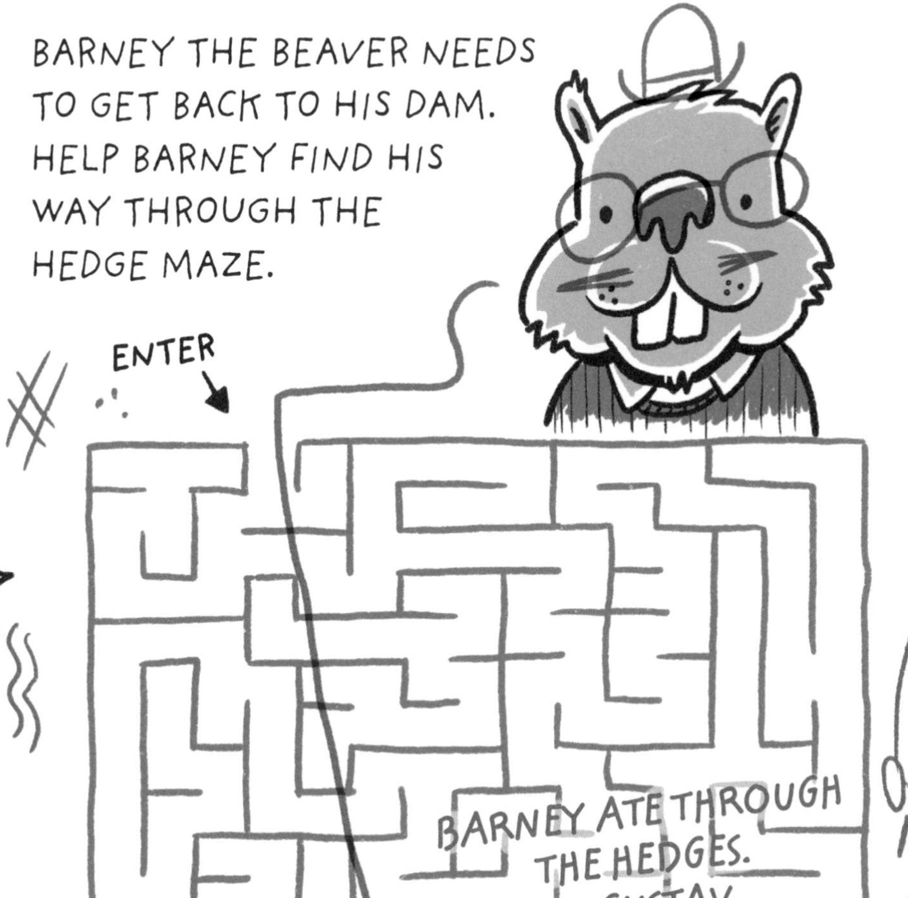
ENTER
BARNEY ATE THROUGH THE HEDGES.
— GUSTAV
DAM

# WORD SEARCH!

DRAW A LINE THROUGH THE BIRD WORDS!

| | | | | | | | | | |
|---|---|---|---|---|---|---|---|---|---|
| B | V | O | W | L | X | U | B | R | T |
| M | Z | T | X | C | T | C | G | A | E |
| U | G | T | B | A | S | F | I | Y | T |
| W | G | N | I | W | E | L | N | Q | G |
| M | E | C | U | Z | N | V | G | P | B |
| J | U | Z | U | G | T | N | W | E | L |
| O | V | Q | O | D | P | U | A | R | C |
| J | Y | O | D | Y | Q | K | A | A | G |
| P | Q | L | F | J | Y | X | M | A | H |
| A | A | I | Q | Y | P | R | X | V | T |

~~BEAK~~

~~NEST~~

~~TAIL~~

~~EGG~~

~~WING~~

EASY!
— G

# RIDDLE TIME

1. WHAT HAS ONE EYE BUT CANNOT SEE?

A SLEEPING CYCLOPS!

WHAT HAS TWO HANDS BUT CANNOT CLAP?

ANOTHER SLEEPING CYCLOPS!

. WHAT HAS LEGS BUT DOESN'T WALK?

A THIRD SLEEPING CYCLOPS OBVIOUSLY!

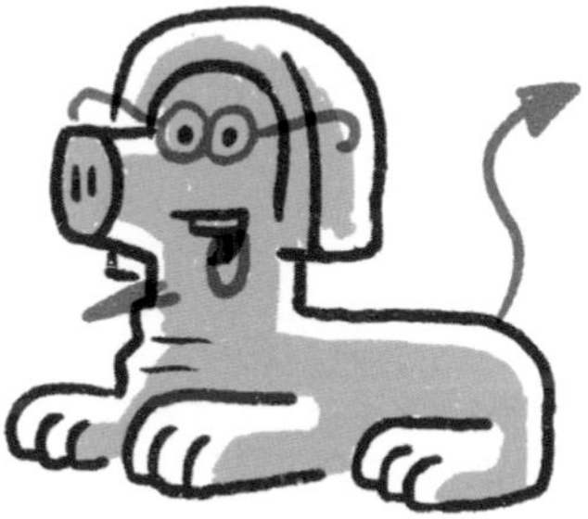

ANSWERS: 1. NEEDLE 2. CLOCK 3. TABLE

# GUSTAV, TIME PIG

**L'UNREAL AGEING CREME**

FOR THE FREQUENT TIME-TRAVELER

FIGHT THE SEVEN SIGNS OF YOUTH!

**INTERESTING BRIDGES**

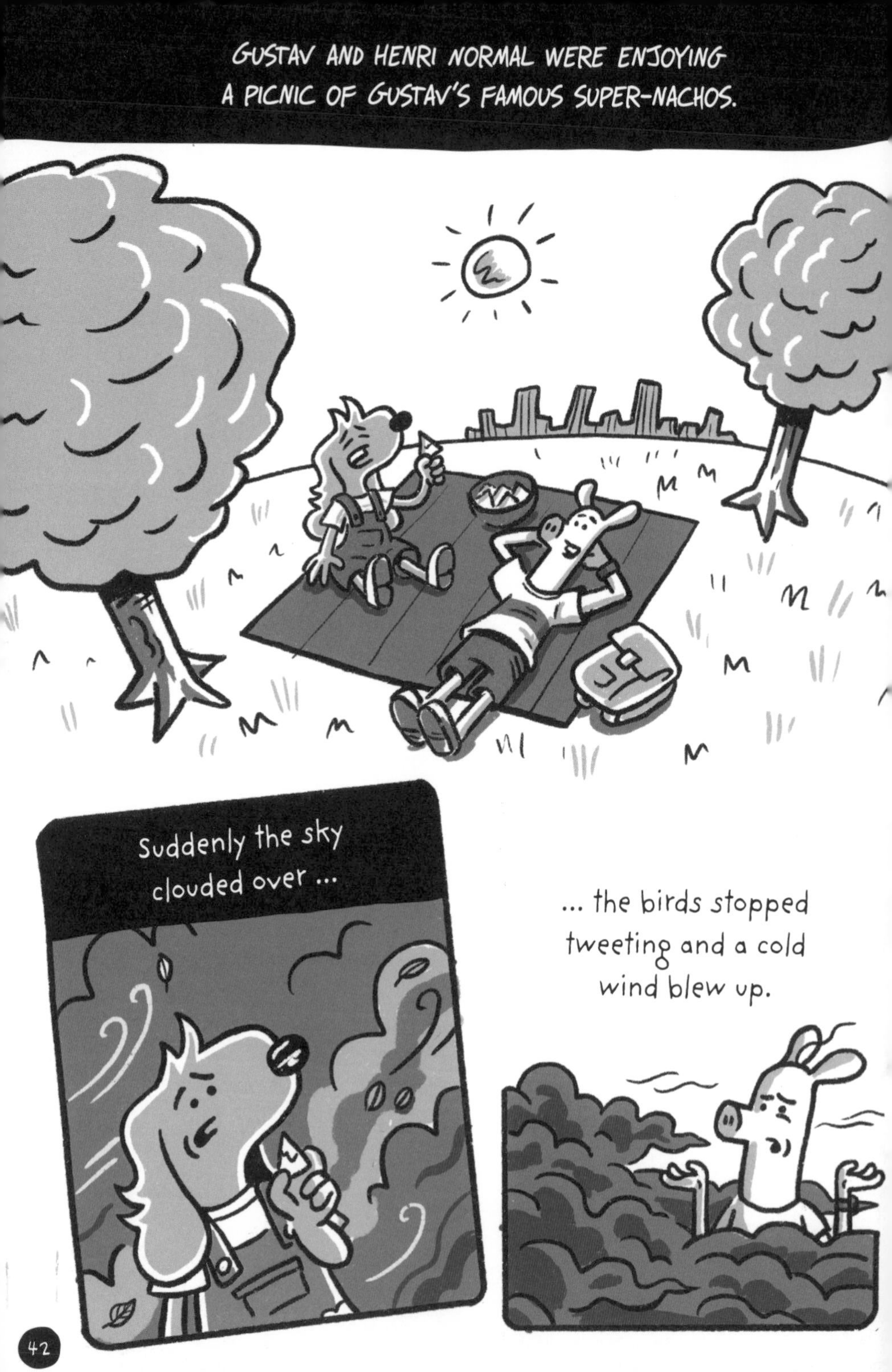
GUSTAV AND HENRI NORMAL WERE ENJOYING A PICNIC OF GUSTAV'S FAMOUS SUPER-NACHOS.
Suddenly the sky clouded over ...
... the birds stopped tweeting and a cold wind blew up.

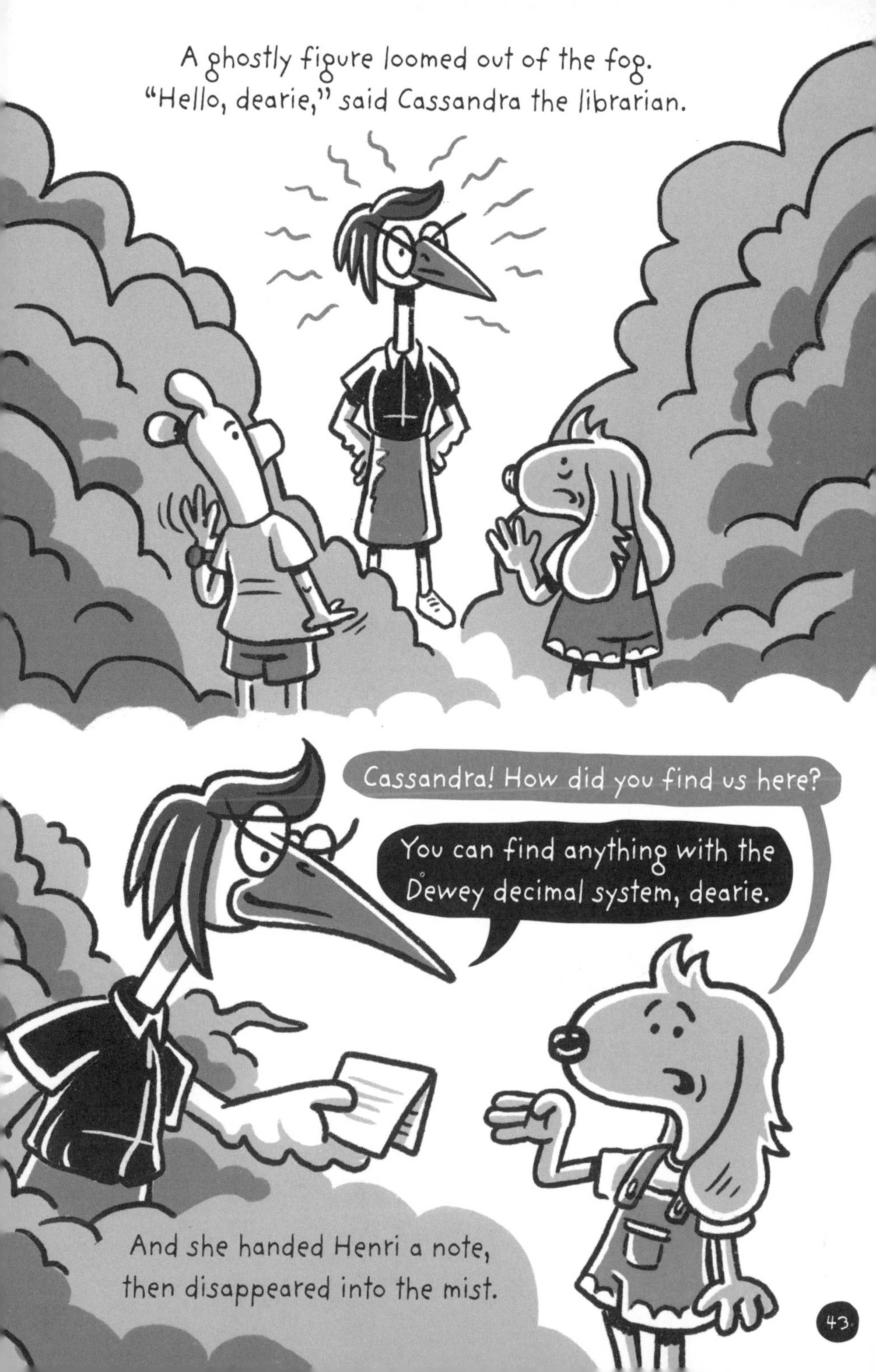
A ghostly figure loomed out of the fog.
"Hello, dearie," said Cassandra the librarian.
Cassandra! How did you find us here?
You can find anything with the Dewey decimal system, dearie.
And she handed Henri a note, then disappeared into the mist.

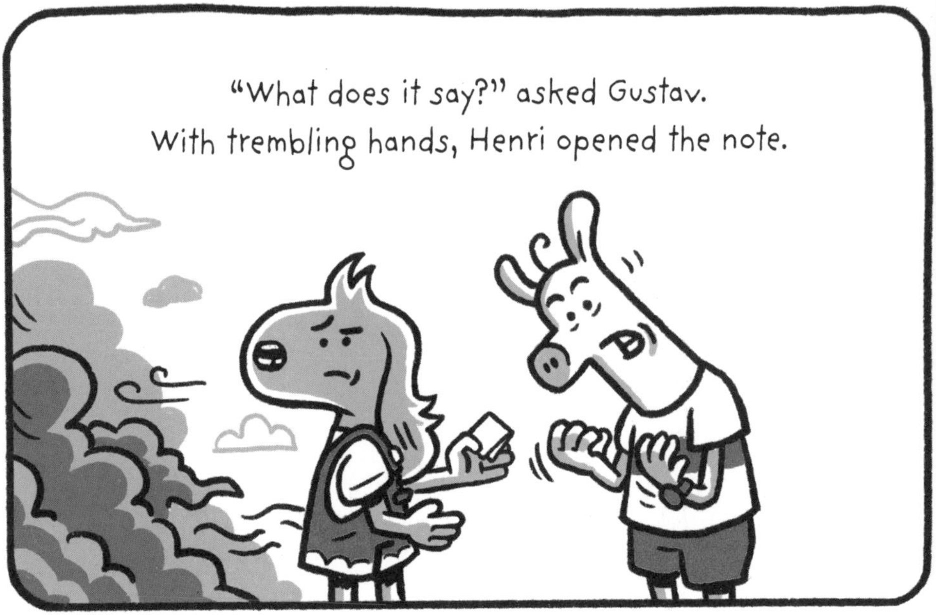
"What does it say?" asked Gustav.
With trembling hands, Henri opened the note.

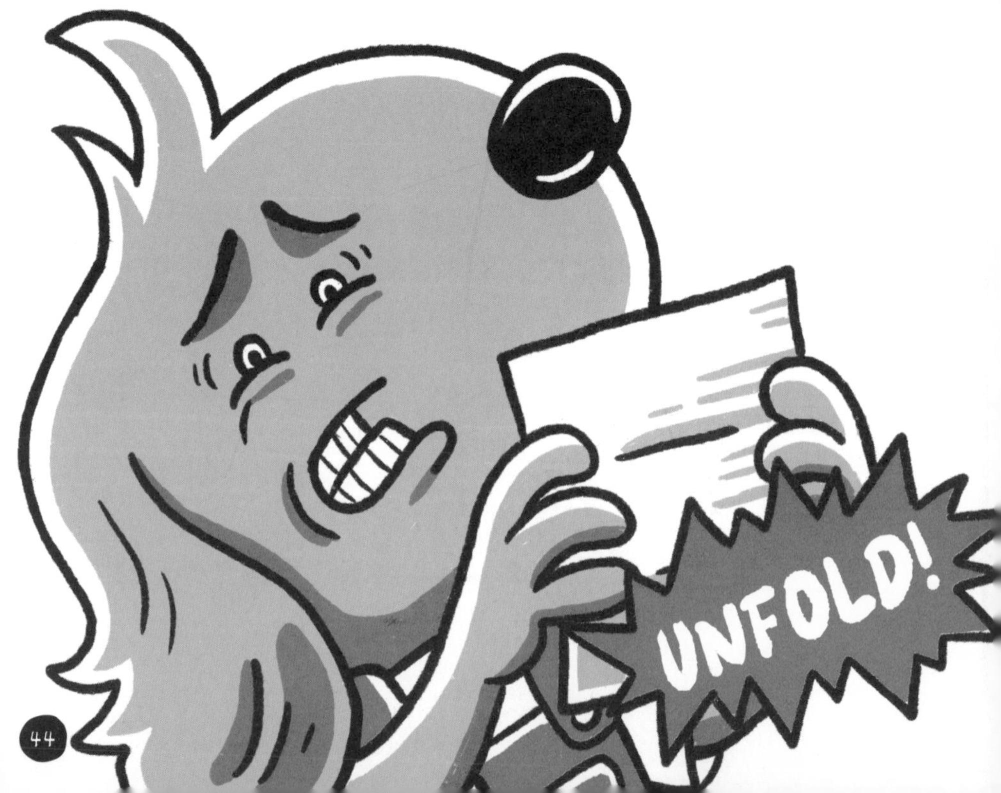
UNFOLD!

BART COBALD MEMORIAL LIBRARY
Due to failure to return the book
"Interesting Bridges" by Samuel Bug, your library card has been permanently
double-canceled.
Regards, Cassandra the librarian

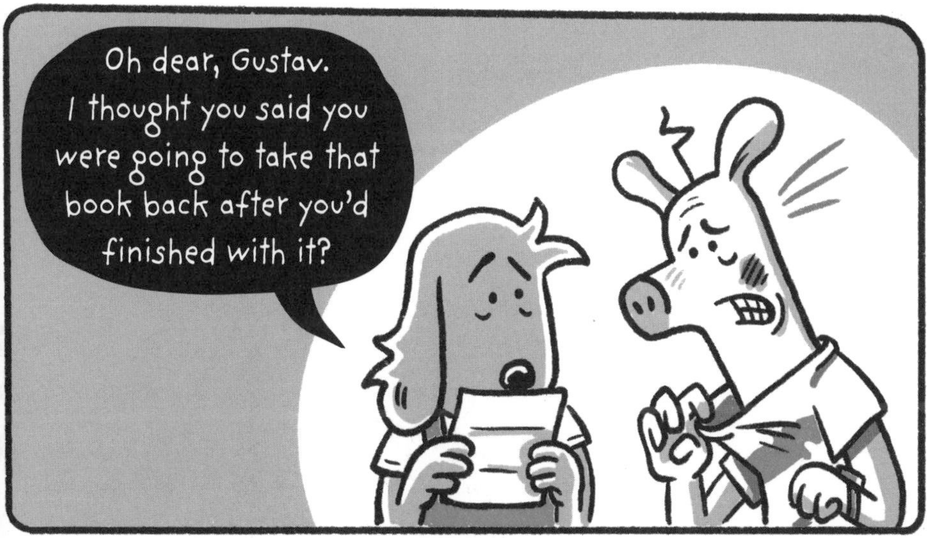
Oh dear, Gustav. I thought you said you were going to take that book back after you'd finished with it?

"I feel terrible, Henri," sighed Gustav.

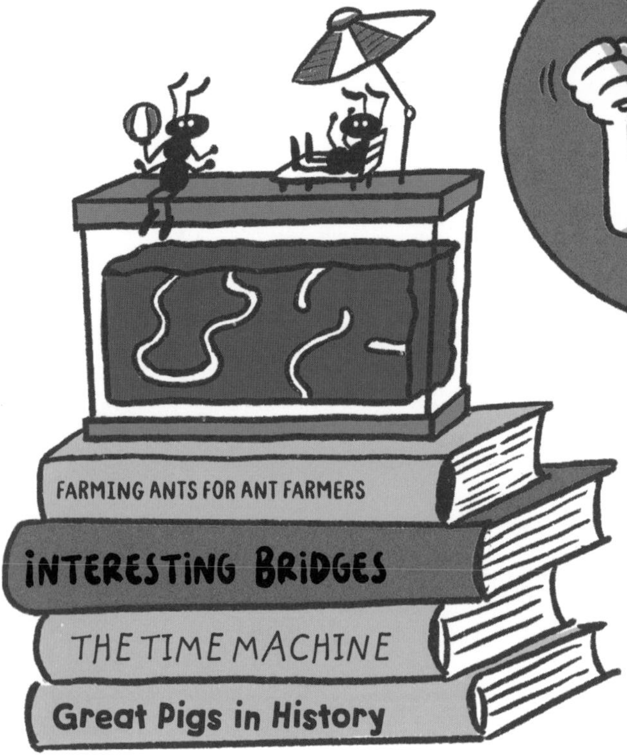
FARMING ANTS FOR ANT FARMERS
INTERESTING BRIDGES
THE TIME MACHINE
Great Pigs in History

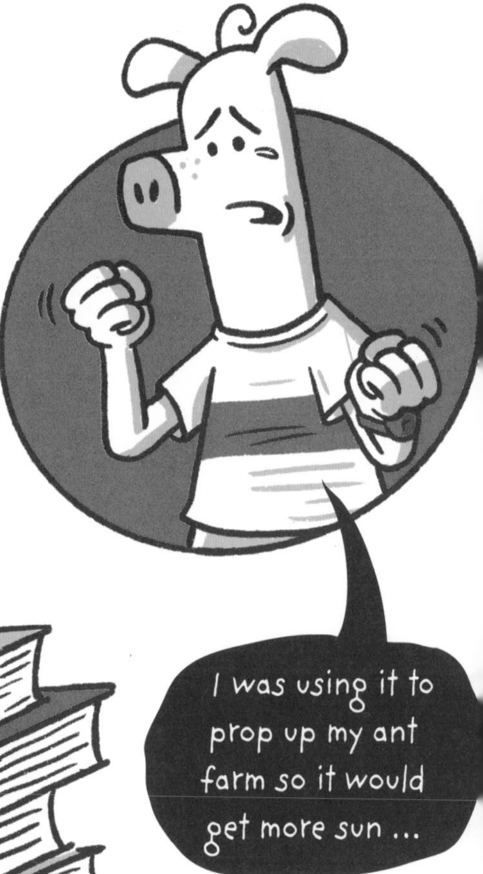
I was using it to prop up my ant farm so it would get more sun ...

"Well, there's nothing we can do now," said Henri sadly.

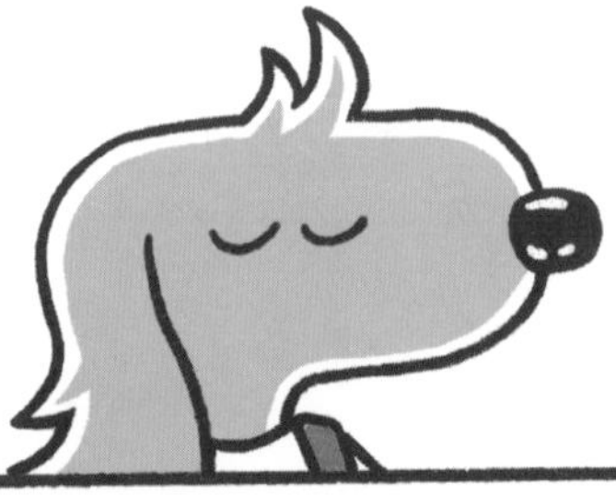

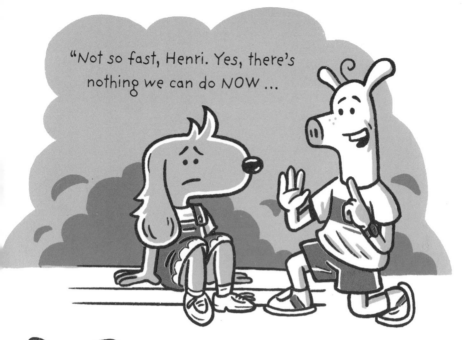

"Not so fast, Henri. Yes, there's nothing we can do NOW ...

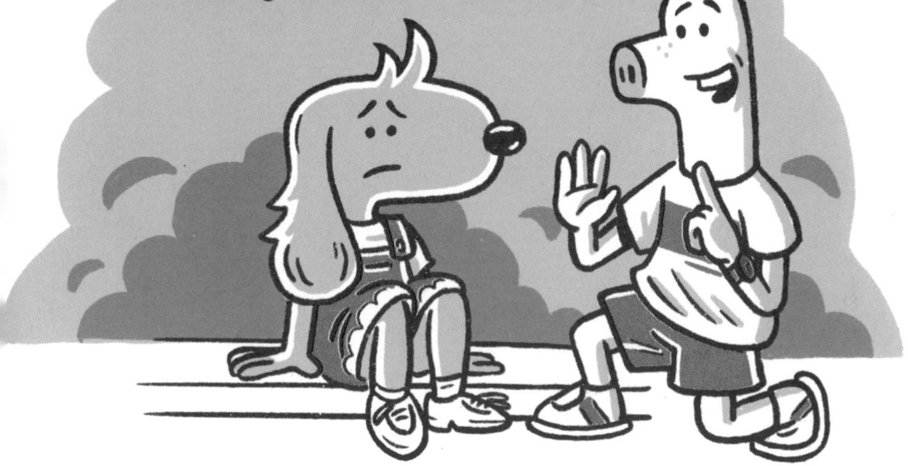

... but what if we were to

# GO BACK IN TIME?"

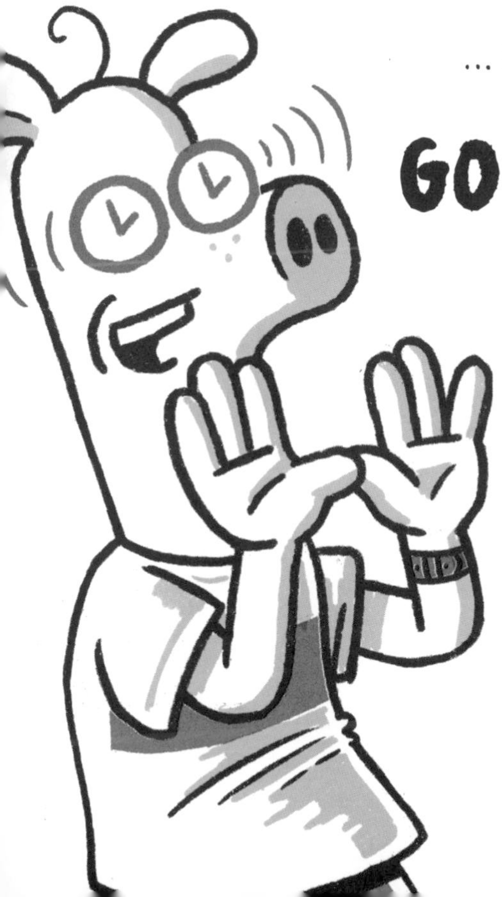

Henri shook her head.

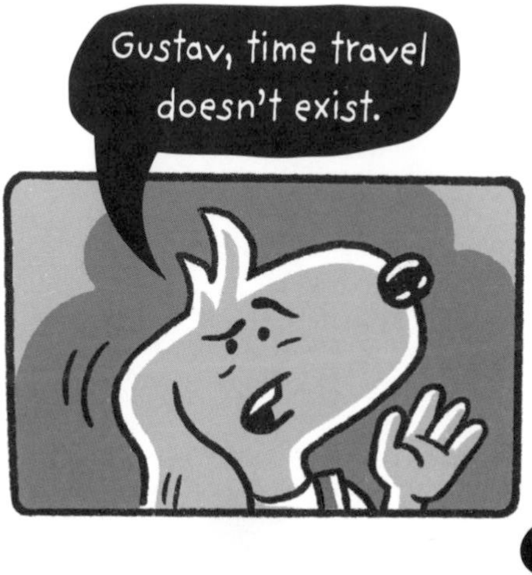
Gustav, time travel doesn't exist.

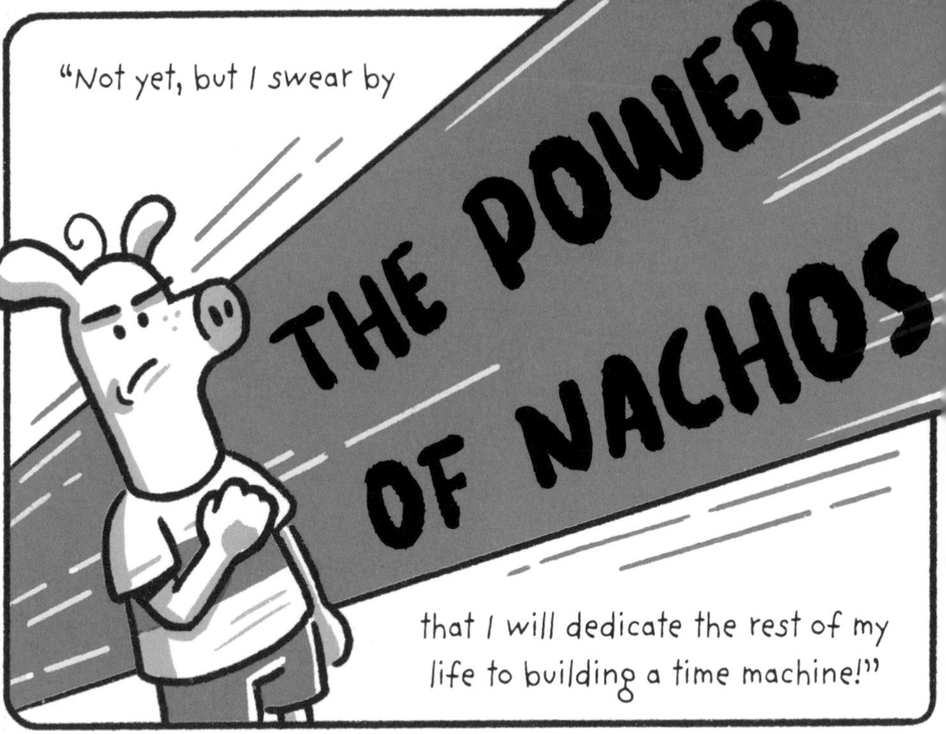
"Not yet, but I swear by
THE POWER OF NACHOS
that I will dedicate the rest of my life to building a time machine!"

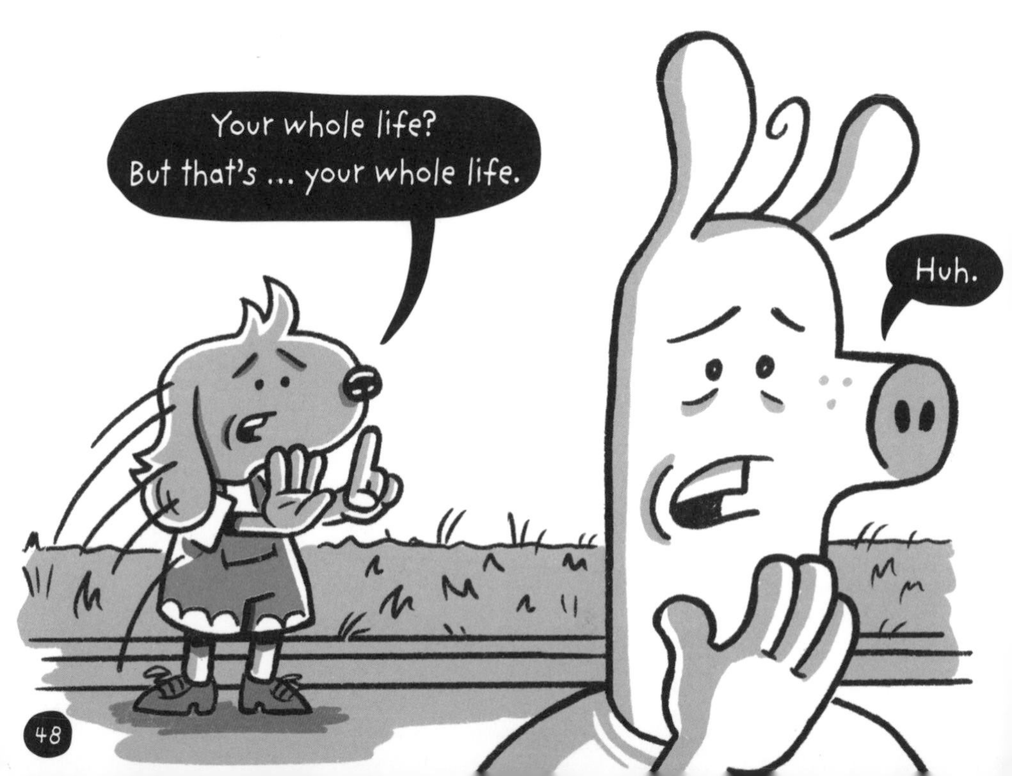
Your whole life?
But that's ... your whole life.
Huh.

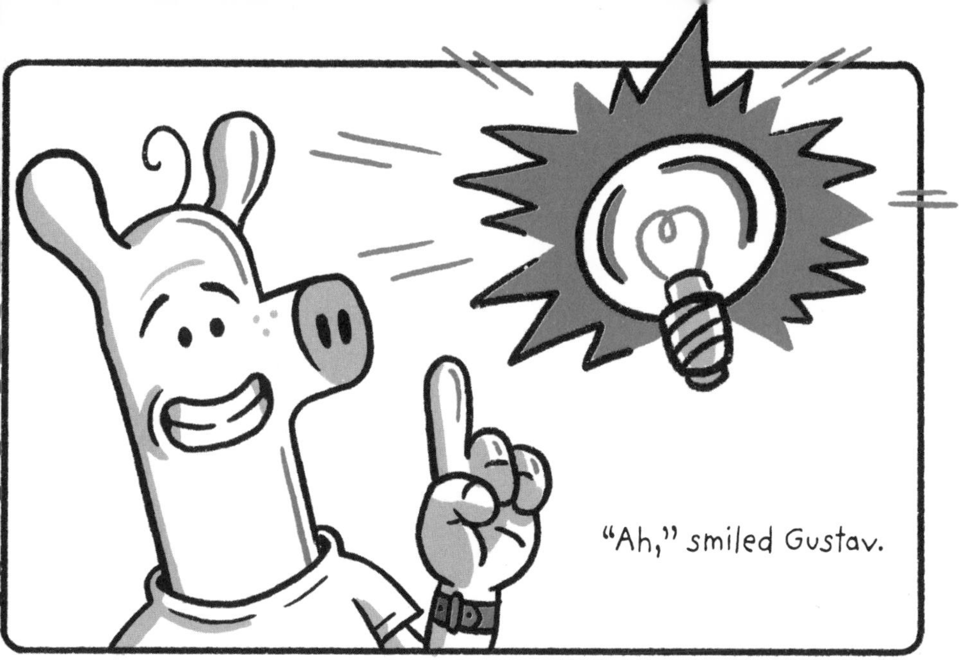
"Ah," smiled Gustav.

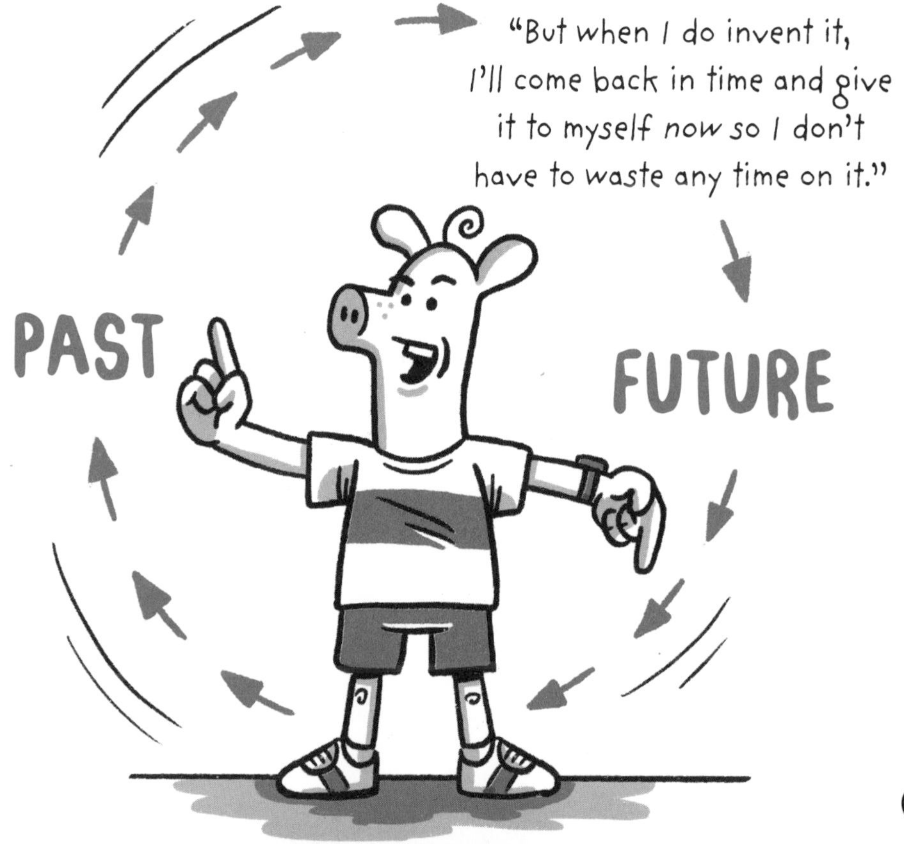
"But when I do invent it, I'll come back in time and give it to myself *now* so I don't have to waste any time on it."
PAST
FUTURE

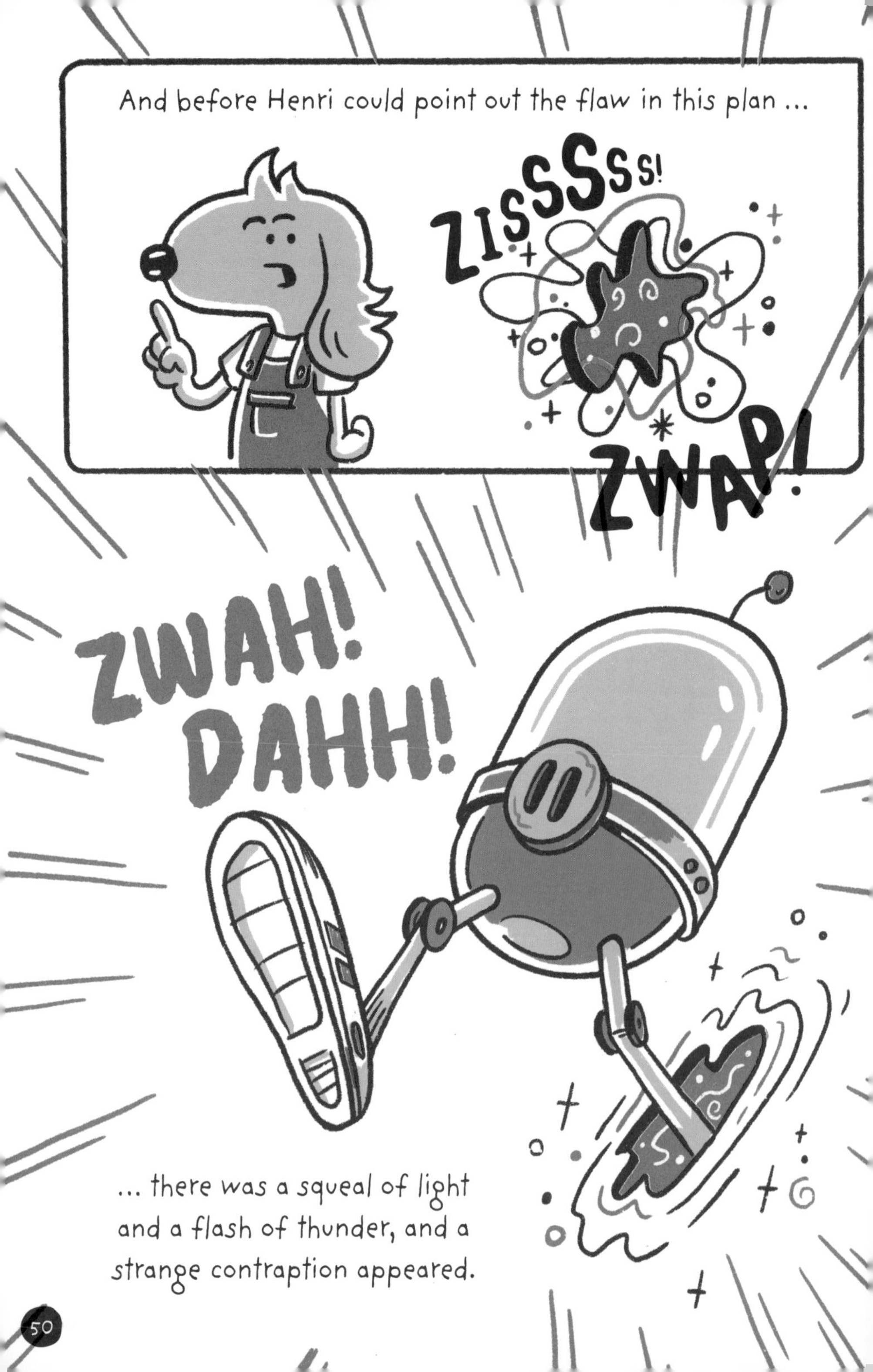
And before Henri could point out the flaw in this plan ...
ZISSSSSS!
ZWAP!
ZWAH! DAHH!
... there was a squeal of light and a flash of thunder, and a strange contraption appeared.

From the smoke emerged a pig with a long beard and an eye patch.

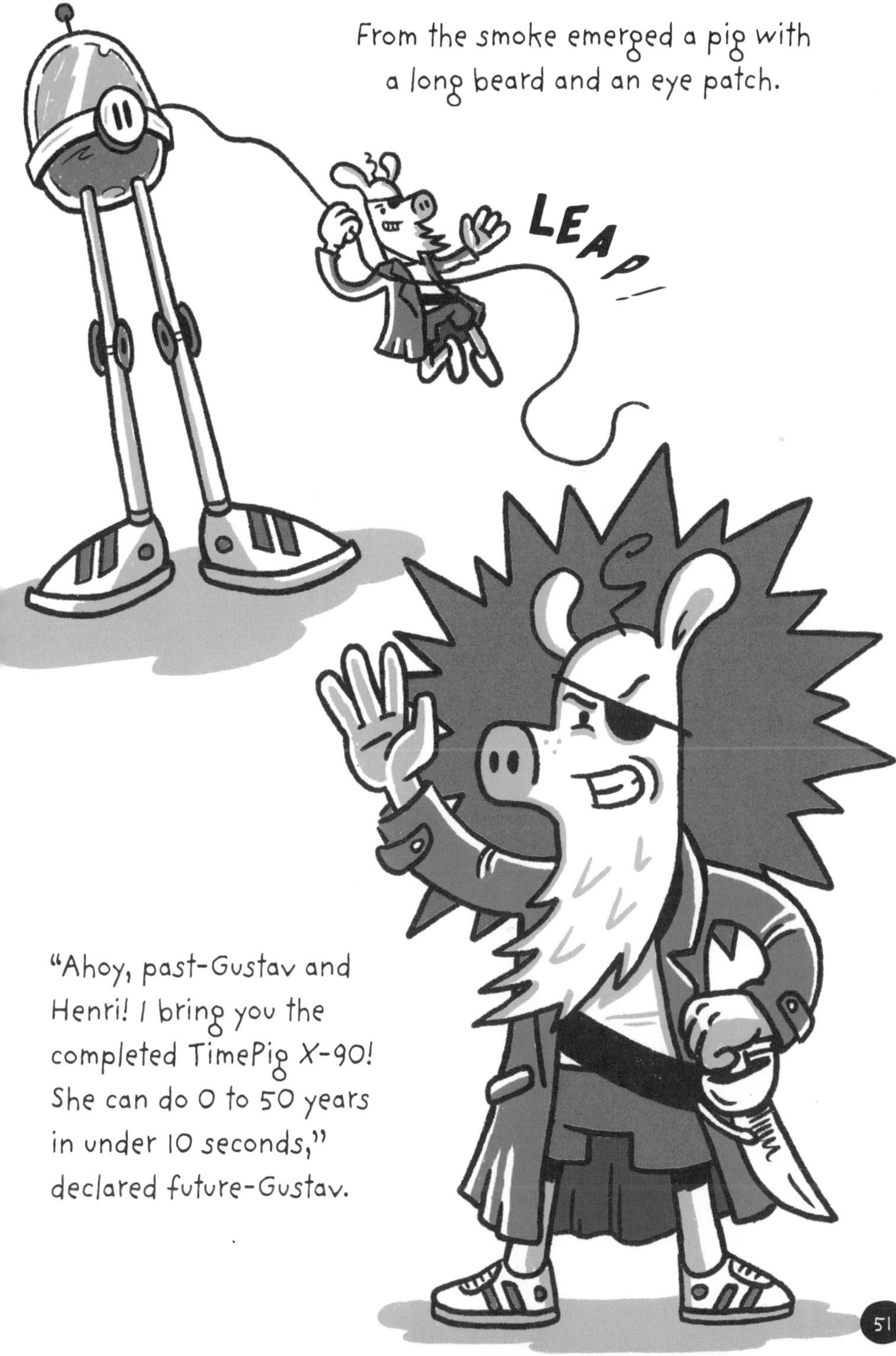
LEAP!

"Ahoy, past-Gustav and Henri! I bring you the completed TimePig X-90! She can do 0 to 50 years in under 10 seconds," declared future-Gustav.

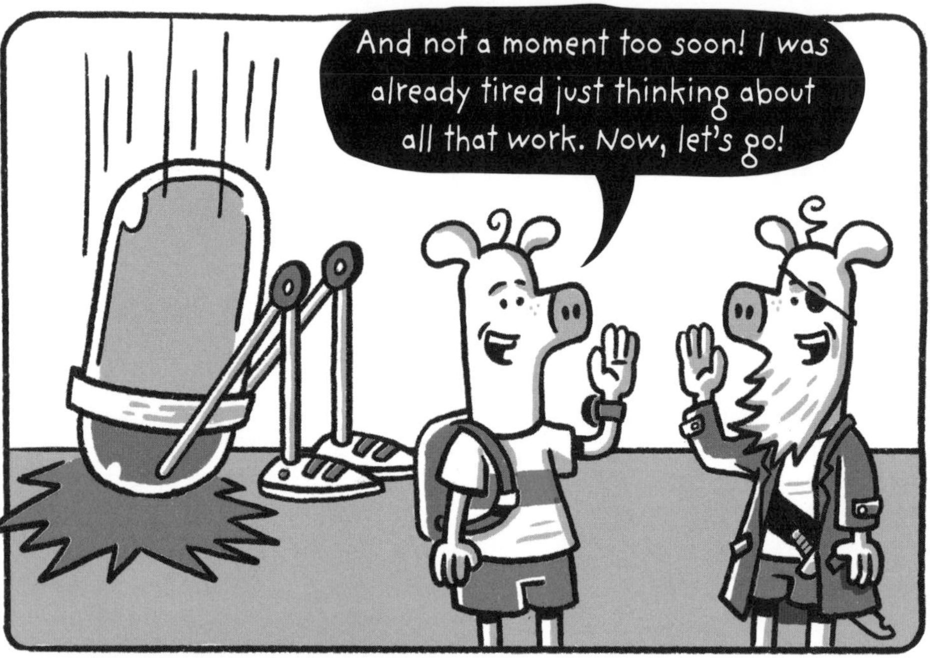
And not a moment too soon! I was already tired just thinking about all that work. Now, let's go!

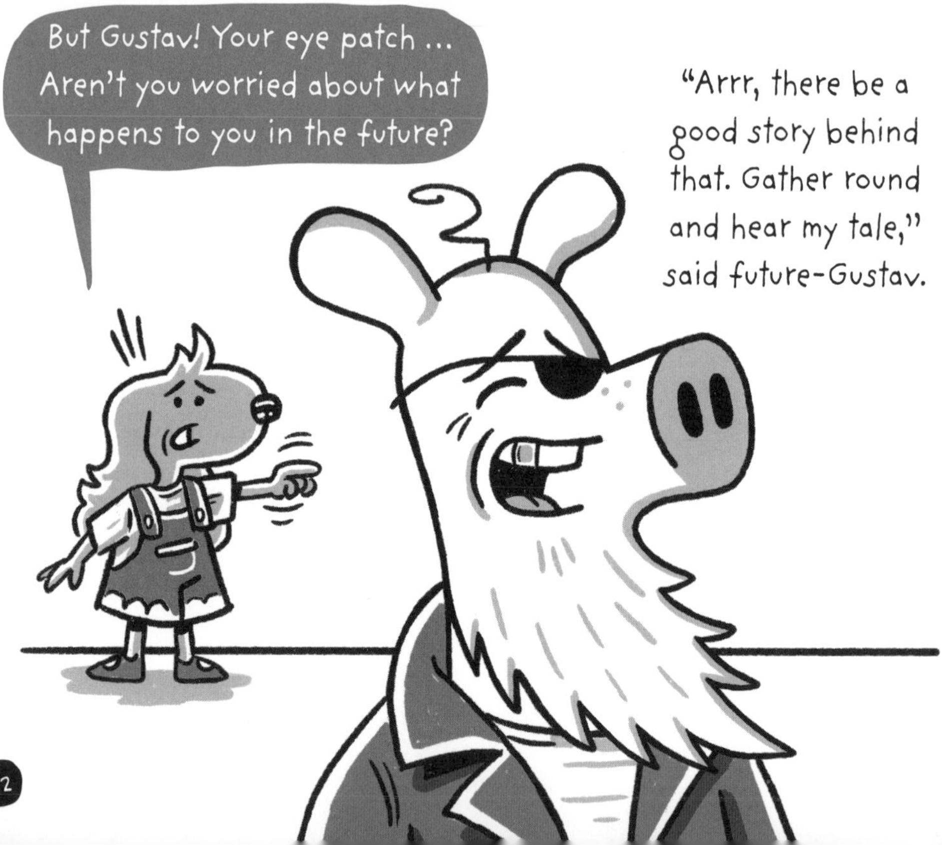
But Gustav! Your eye patch … Aren't you worried about what happens to you in the future?

"Arrr, there be a good story behind that. Gather round and hear my tale," said future-Gustav.

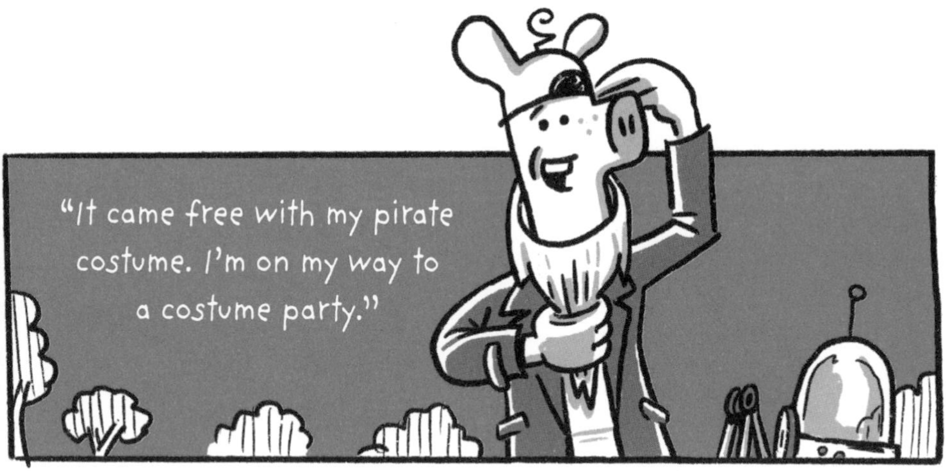
"It came free with my pirate costume. I'm on my way to a costume party."

"Come on, Henri," said Gustav. "I just have to run home and get the book, then ...

**WE HAVE AN INJUSTICE TO FIX!"**

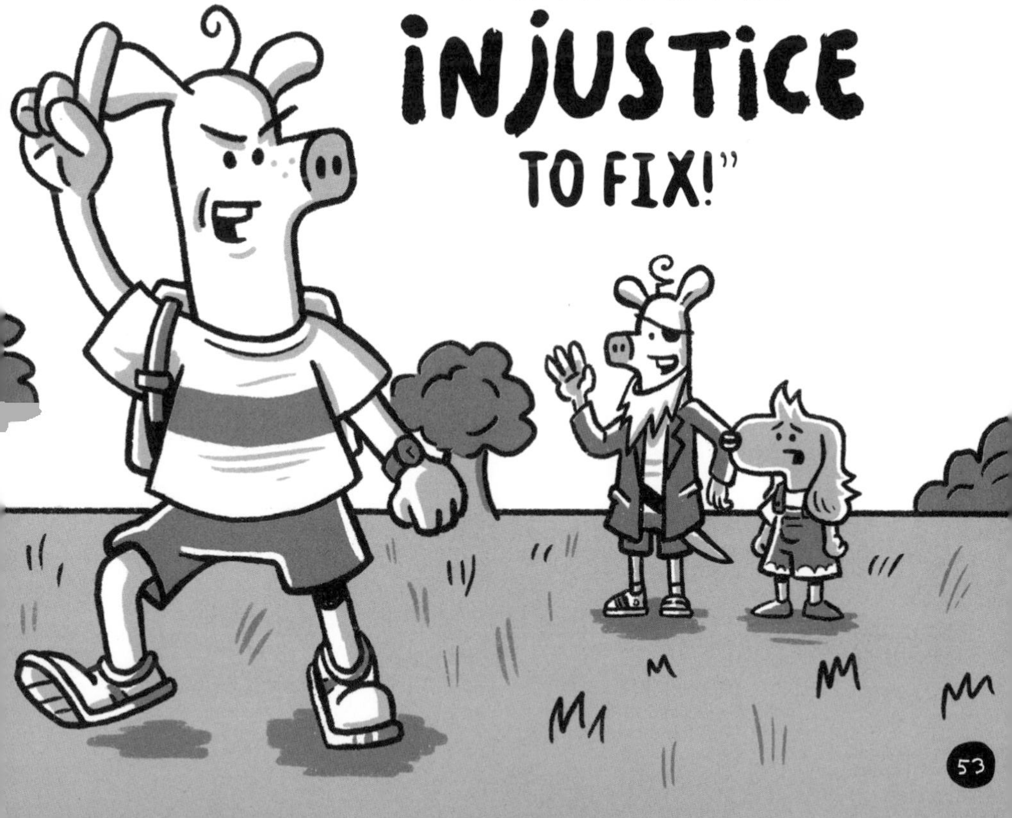

And before Henri could protest, Gustav ran home and came back with the book.

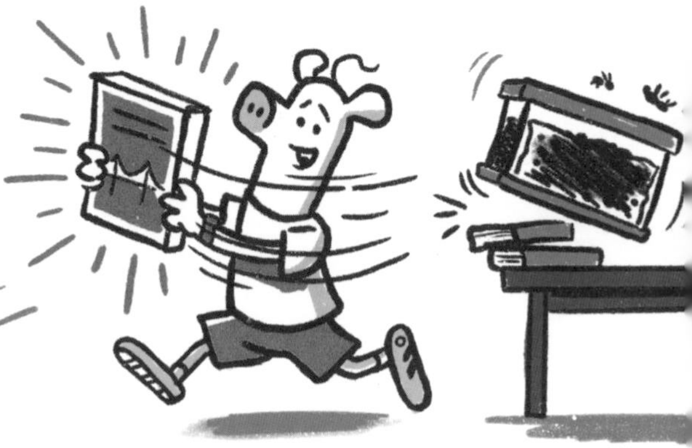

And the last of the super-nachos, which he crammed into his backpack ...

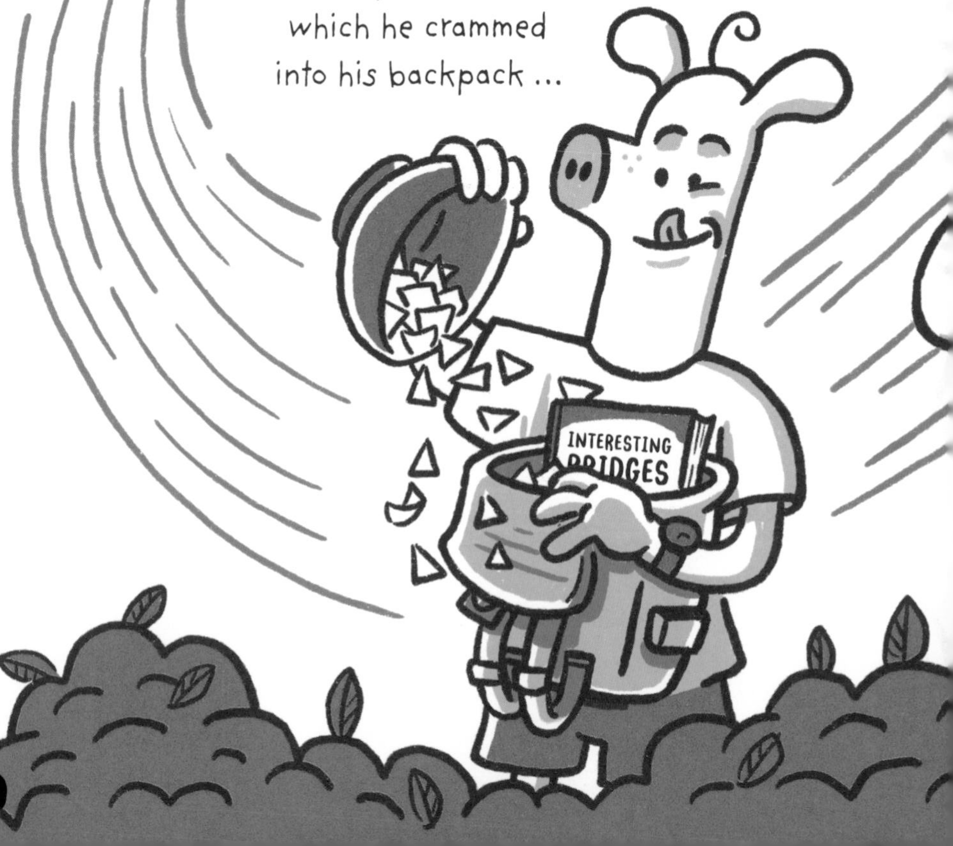
INTERESTING BRIDGES

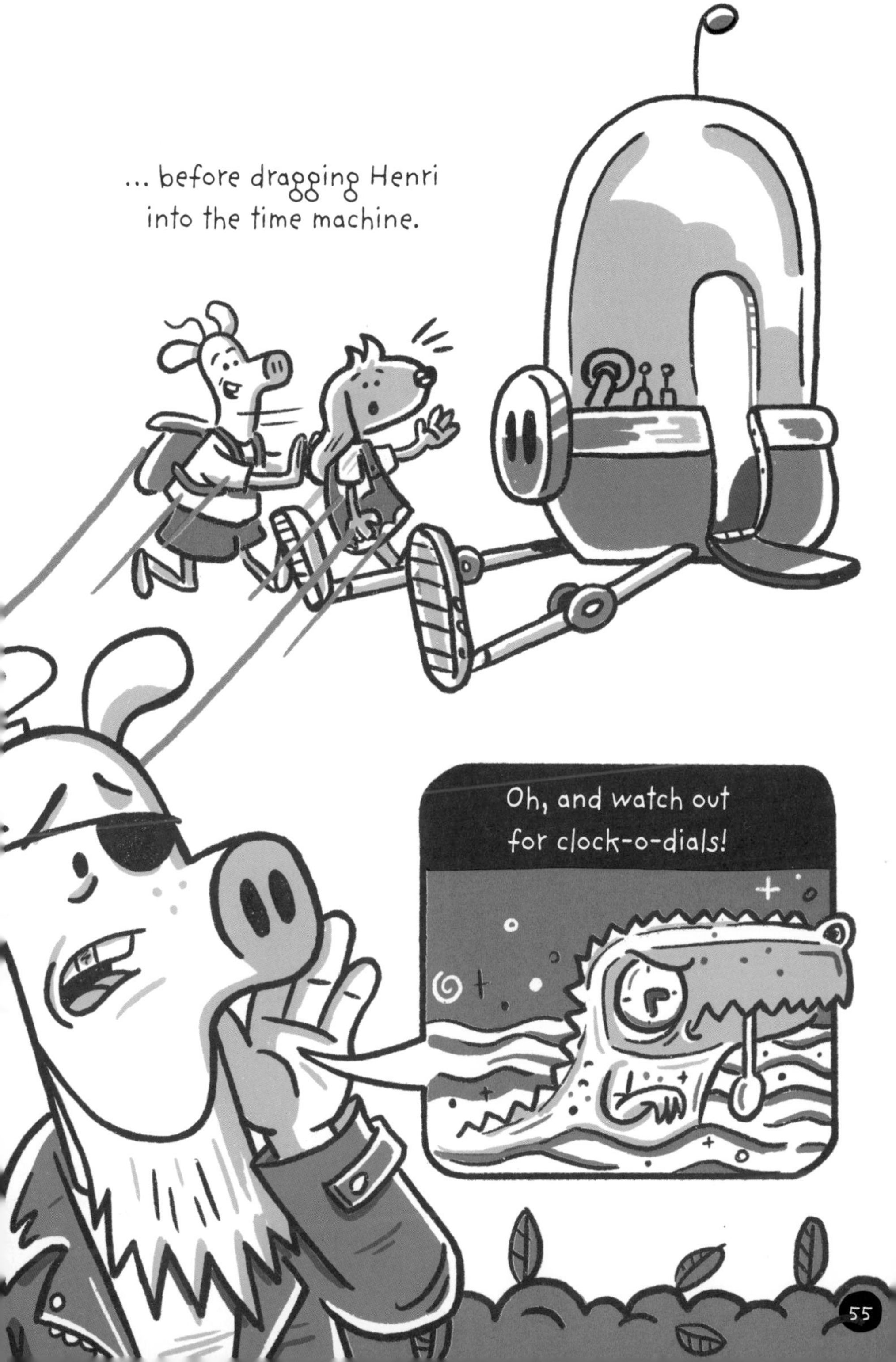
... before dragging Henri into the time machine.
Oh, and watch out for clock-o-dials!

"What was that?" asked Henri, but there was no time for an answer as Gustav shouted,

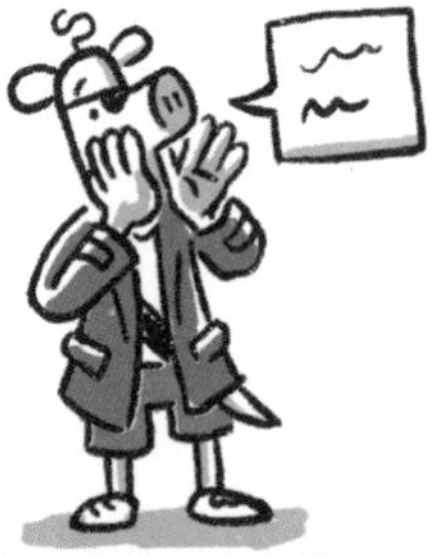

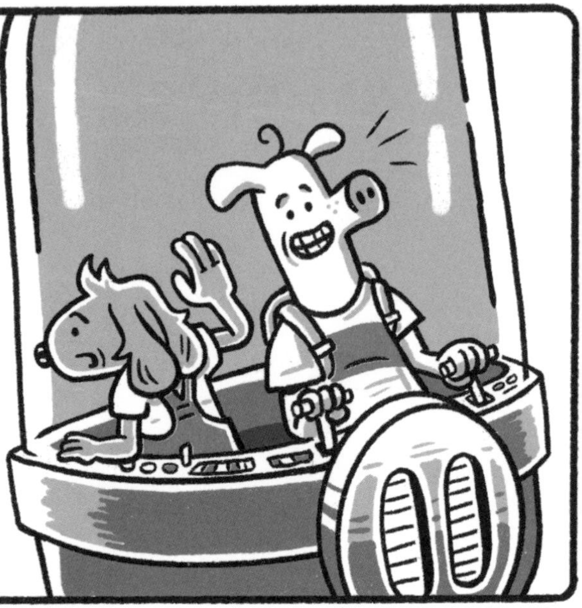

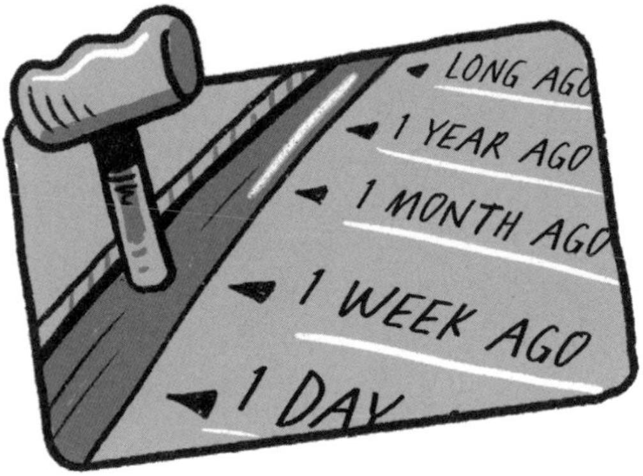
LONG AGO
1 YEAR AGO
1 MONTH AGO
1 WEEK AGO
1 DAY

"To the past!" and slammed "one week ago" on the whenever-lever™.

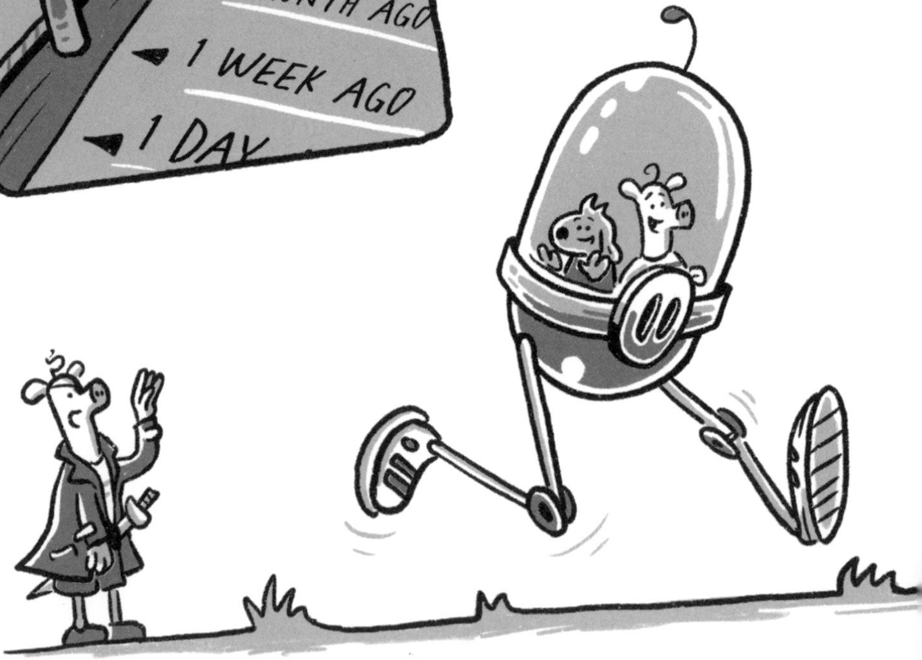

A glowing portal opened in front of them ...

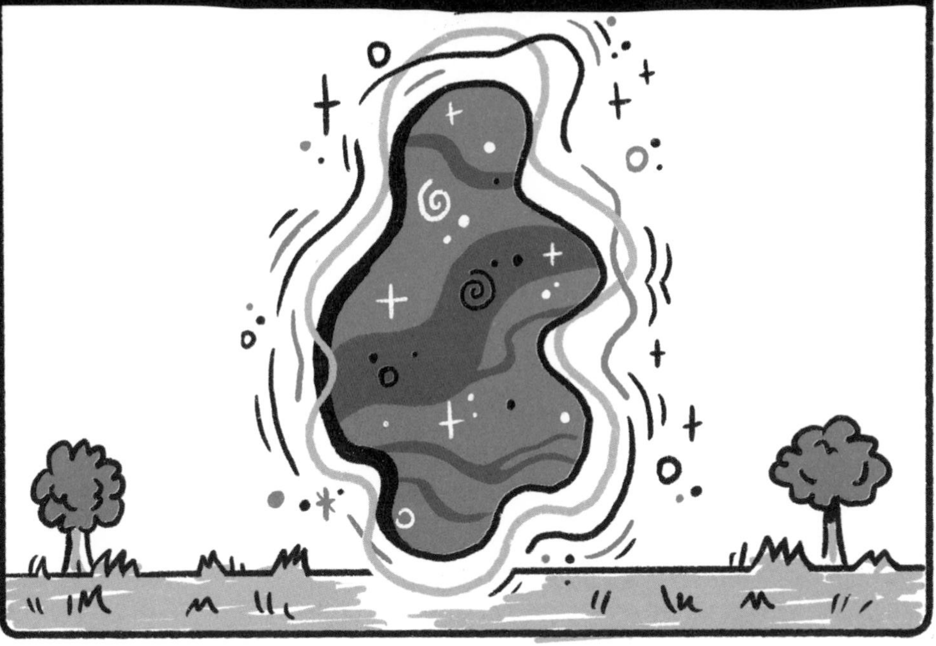

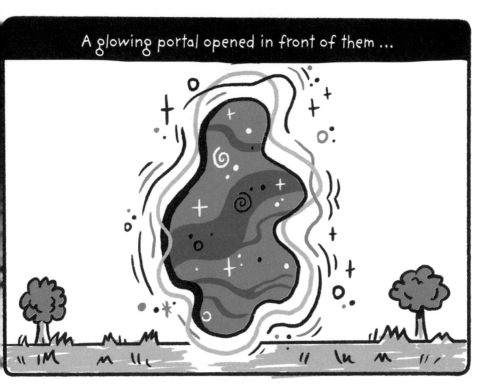

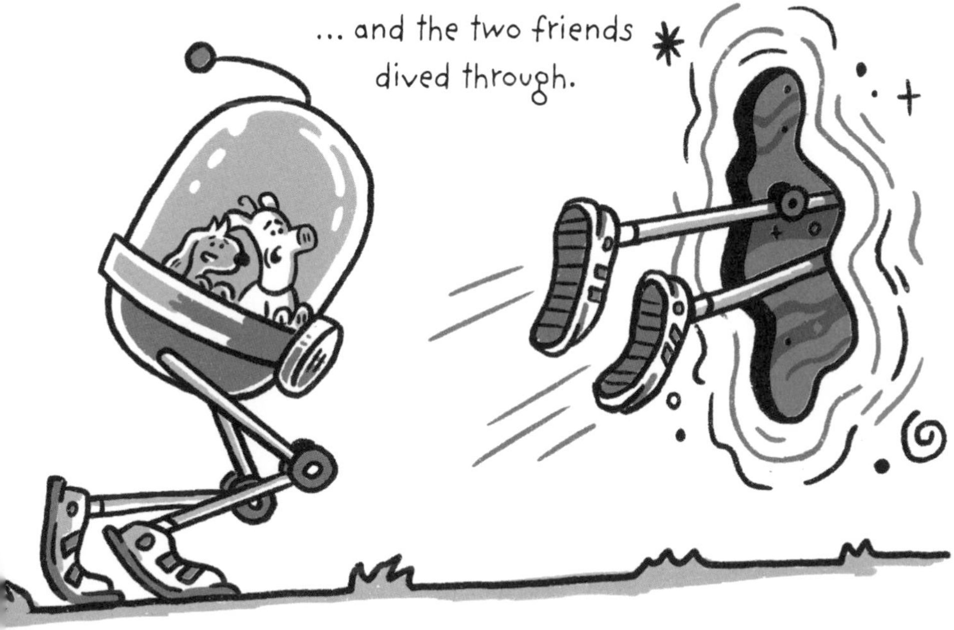
... and the two friends dived through.

With a squeal and a flash, the TimePig disappeared.

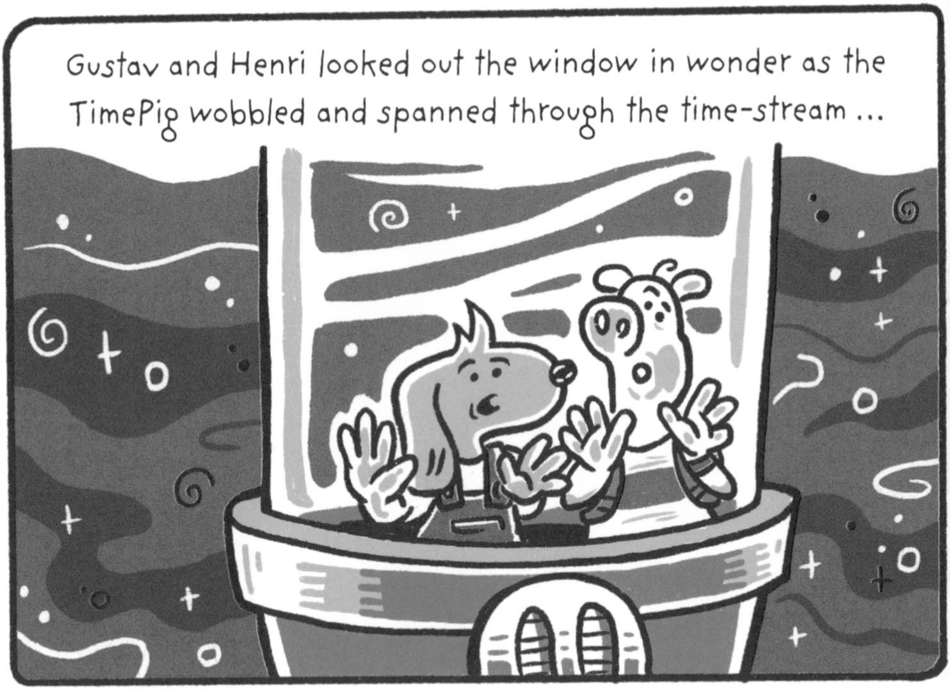
Gustav and Henri looked out the window in wonder as the TimePig wobbled and spanned through the time-stream ...

... and then reappeared with a thud outside the library.

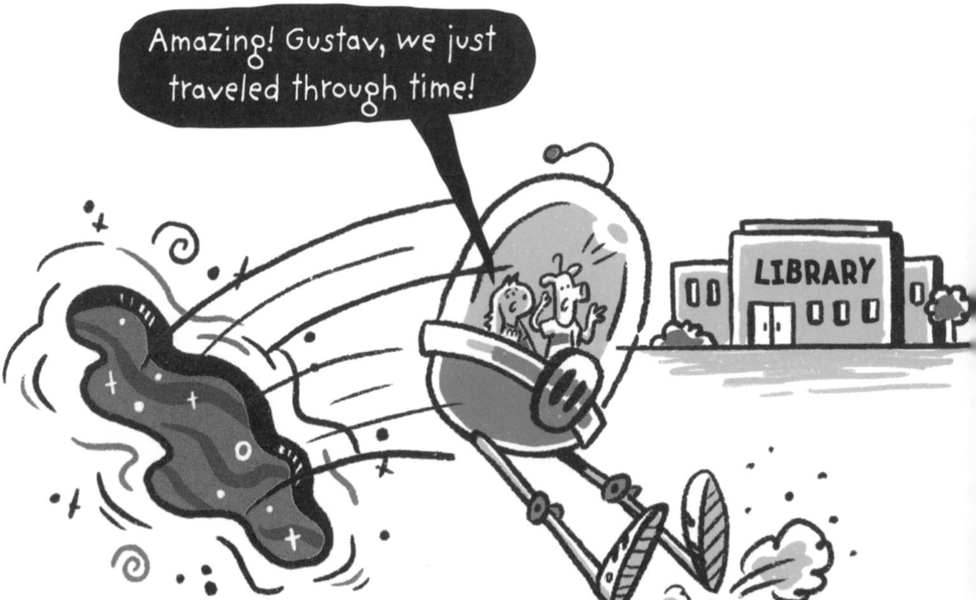
Amazing! Gustav, we just traveled through time!
LIBRARY

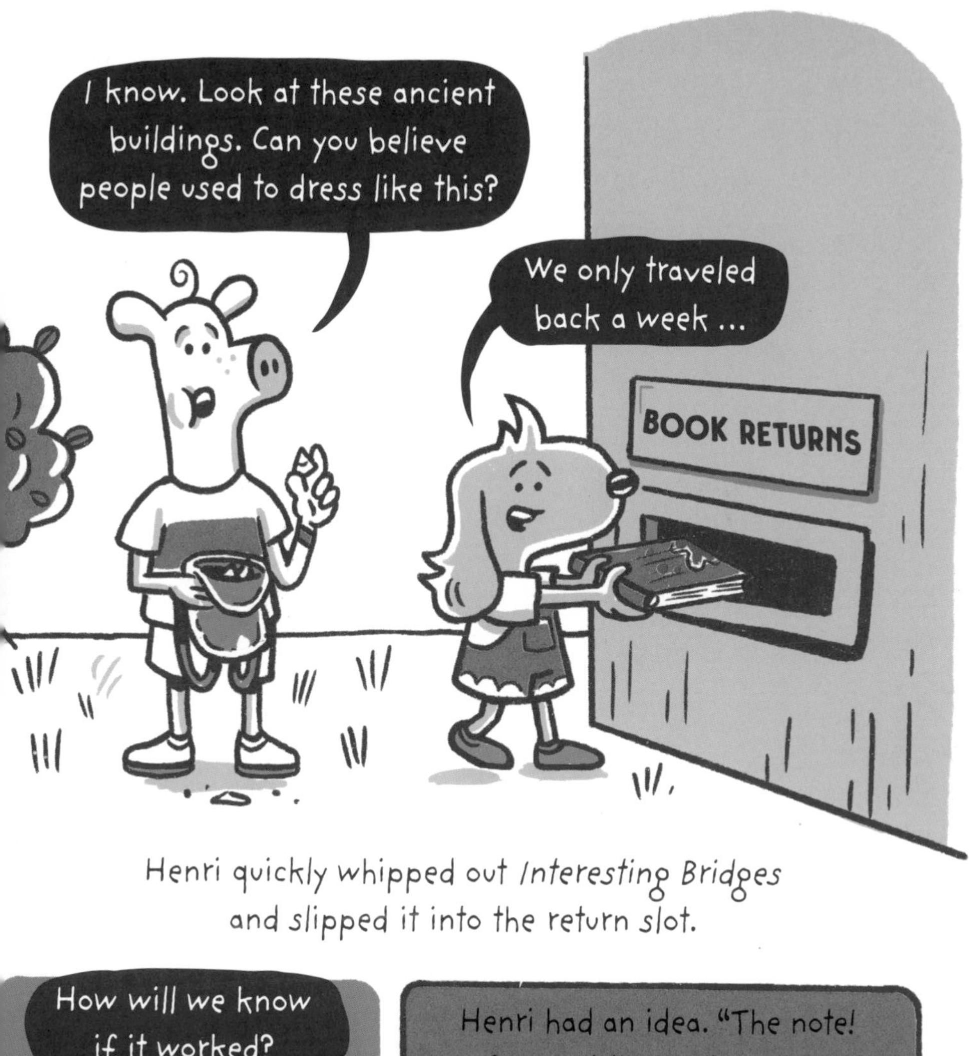
I know. Look at these ancient buildings. Can you believe people used to dress like this?
We only traveled back a week ...
BOOK RETURNS

Henri quickly whipped out *Interesting Bridges* and slipped it into the return slot.

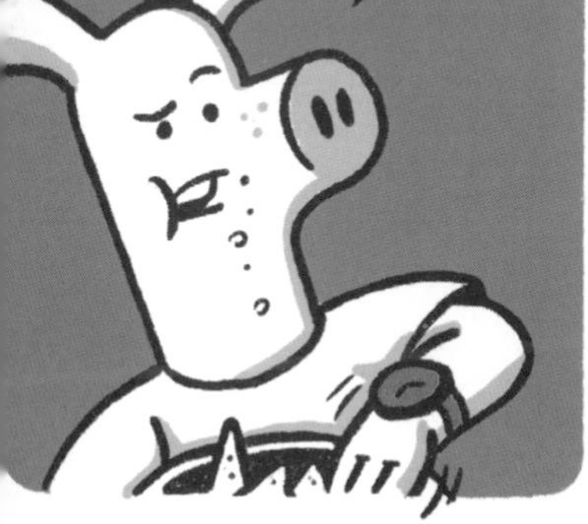
How will we know if it worked?

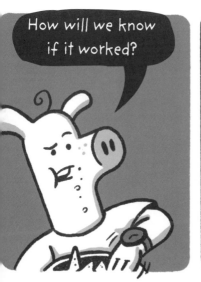

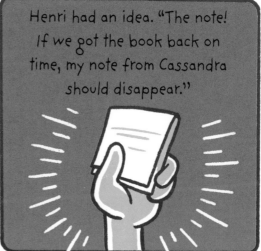

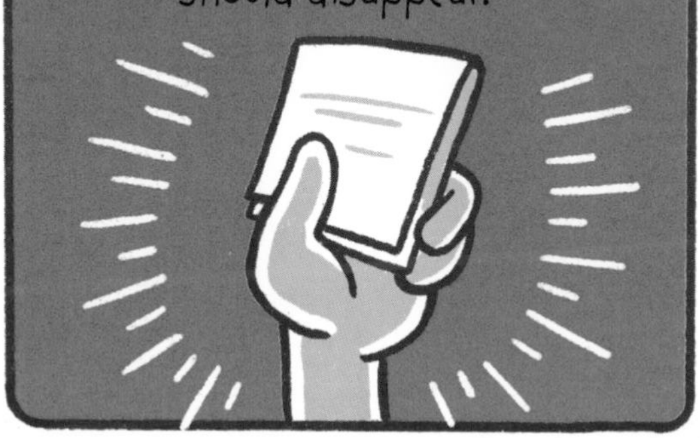
Henri had an idea. "The note! If we got the book back on time, my note from Cassandra should disappear."

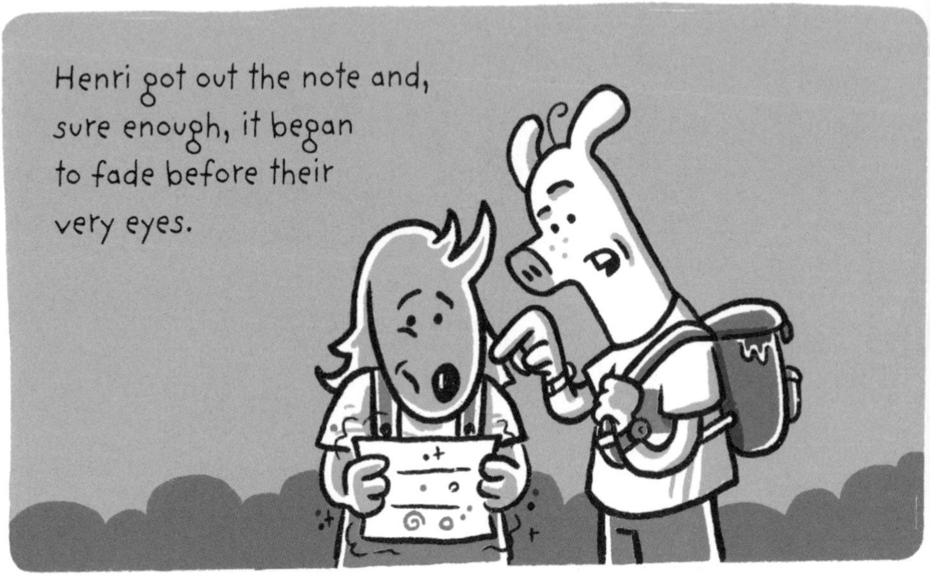
Henri got out the note and, sure enough, it began to fade before their very eyes.

But instead of disappearing, the words just changed.

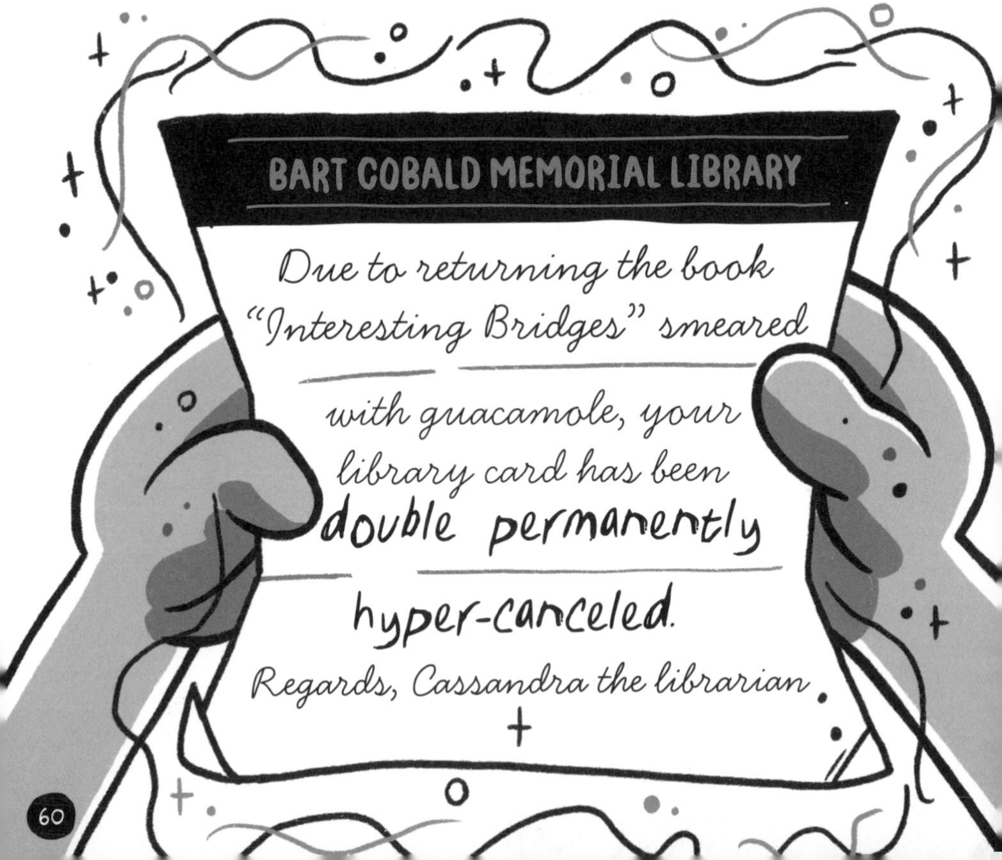
BART COBALD MEMORIAL LIBRARY
Due to returning the book "Interesting Bridges" smeared with guacamole, your library card has been double permanently hyper-canceled.
Regards, Cassandra the librarian

Gustav slapped his forehead.

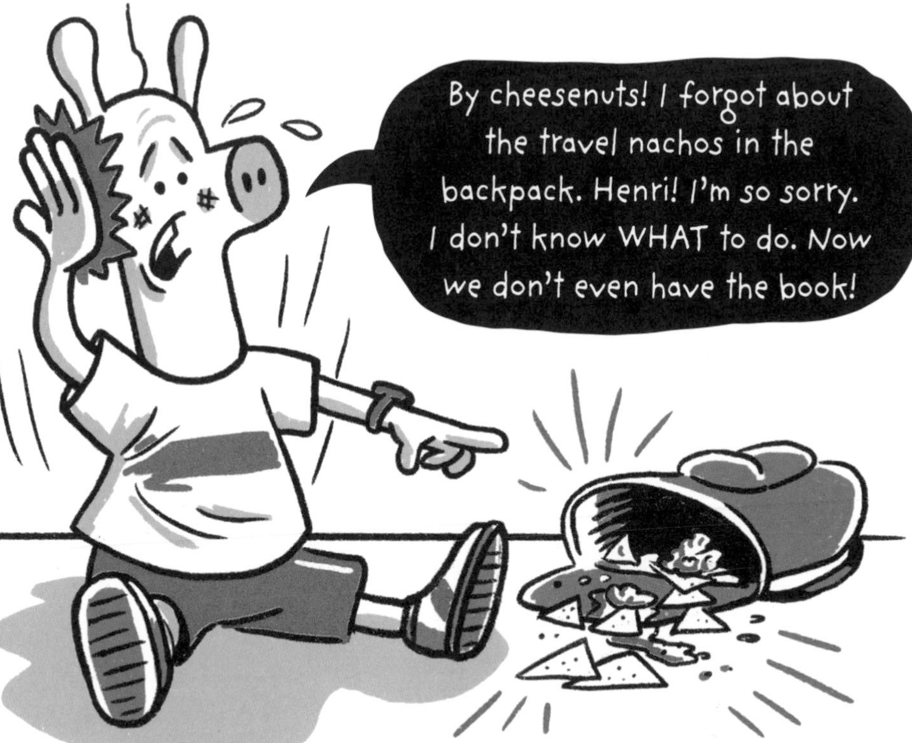
By cheesenuts! I forgot about the travel nachos in the backpack. Henri! I'm so sorry. I don't know WHAT to do. Now we don't even have the book!

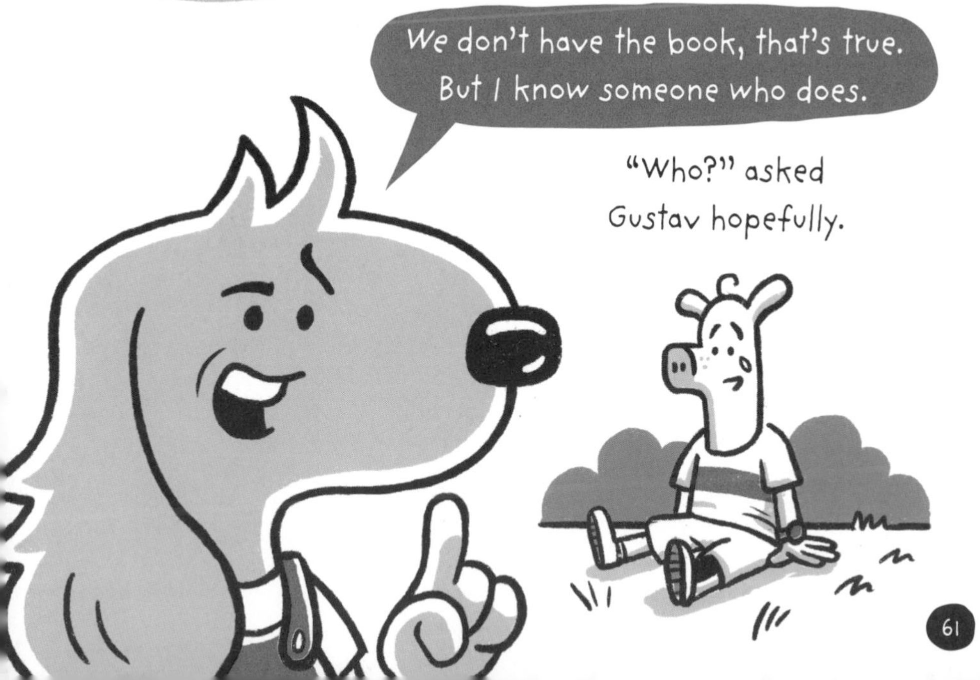
We don't have the book, that's true. But I know someone who does.

"Who?" asked Gustav hopefully.

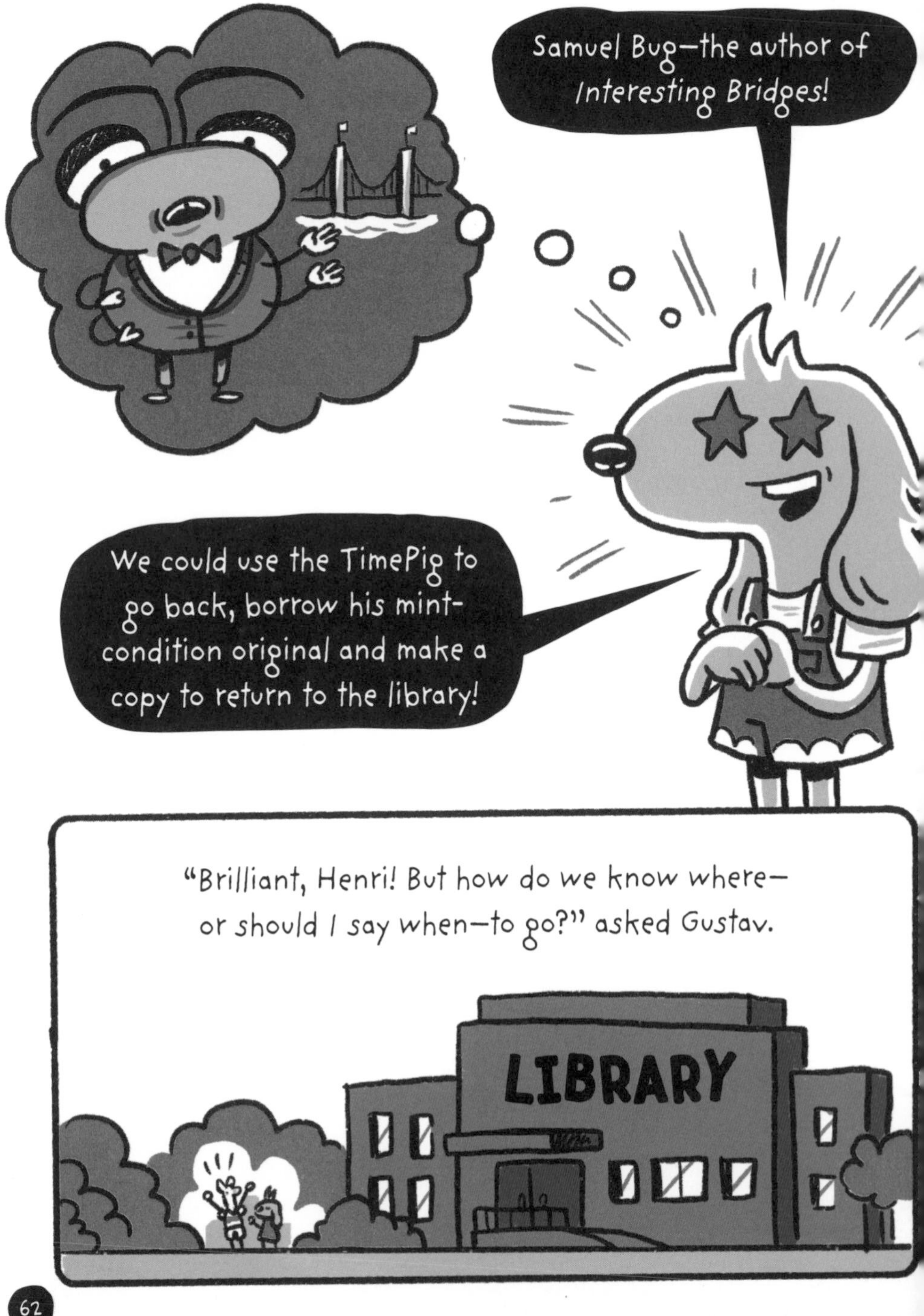
Samuel Bug—the author of *Interesting Bridges*!
We could use the TimePig to go back, borrow his mint-condition original and make a copy to return to the library!
"Brilliant, Henri! But how do we know where—or should I say when—to go?" asked Gustav.
LIBRARY

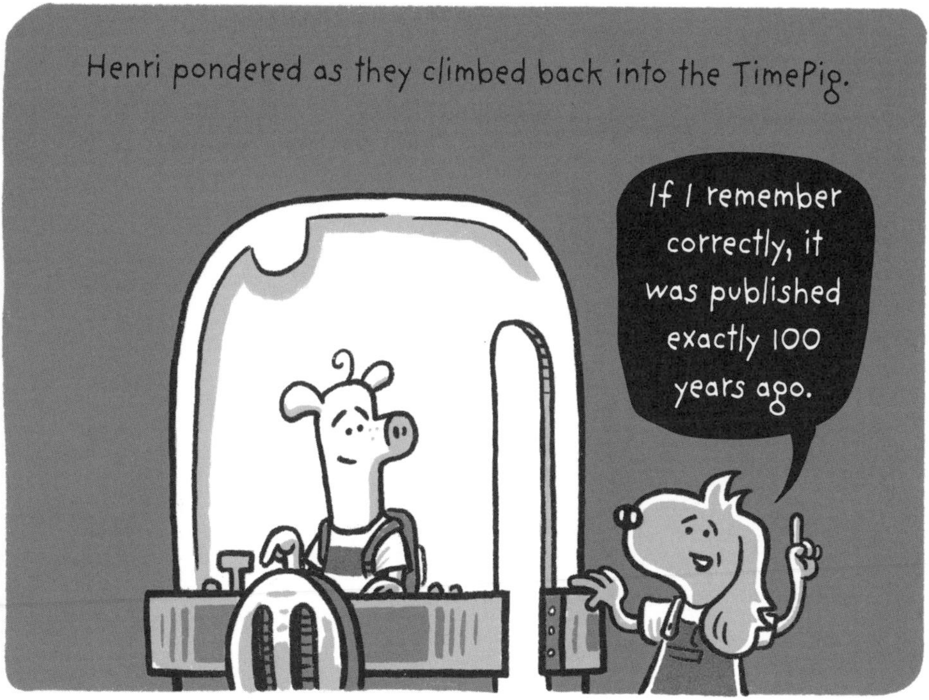
Henri pondered as they climbed back into the TimePig.
If I remember correctly, it was published exactly 100 years ago.

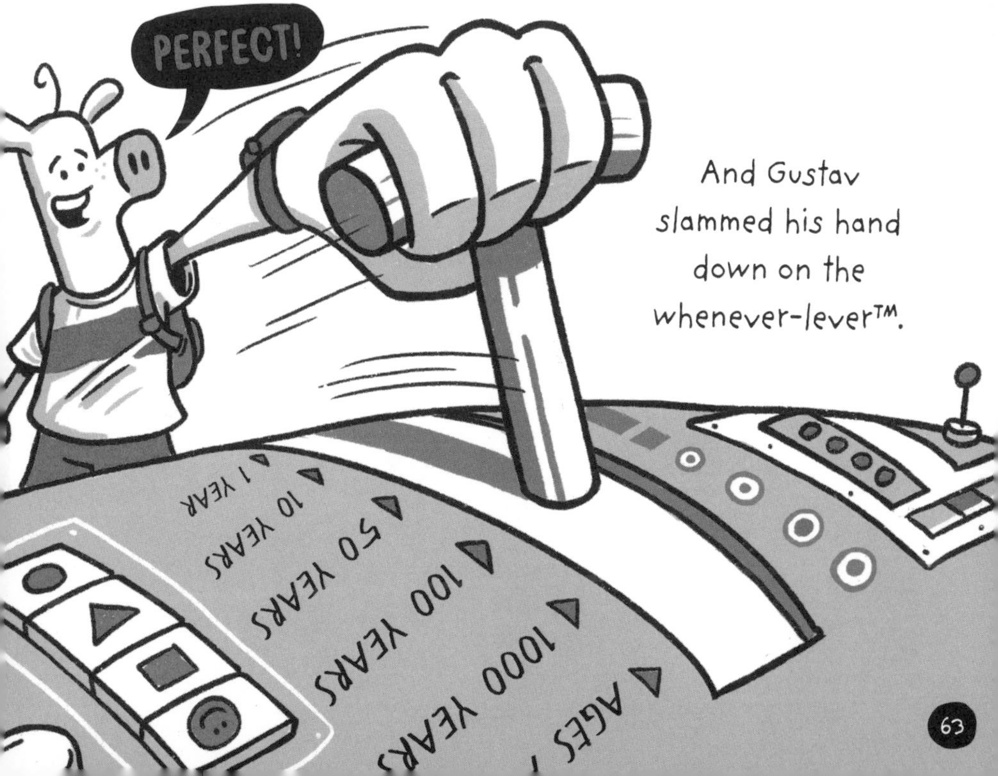
PERFECT!
And Gustav slammed his hand down on the whenever-lever™.
1 YEAR
10 YEARS
50 YEARS
100 YEARS
1000 YEARS
AGES

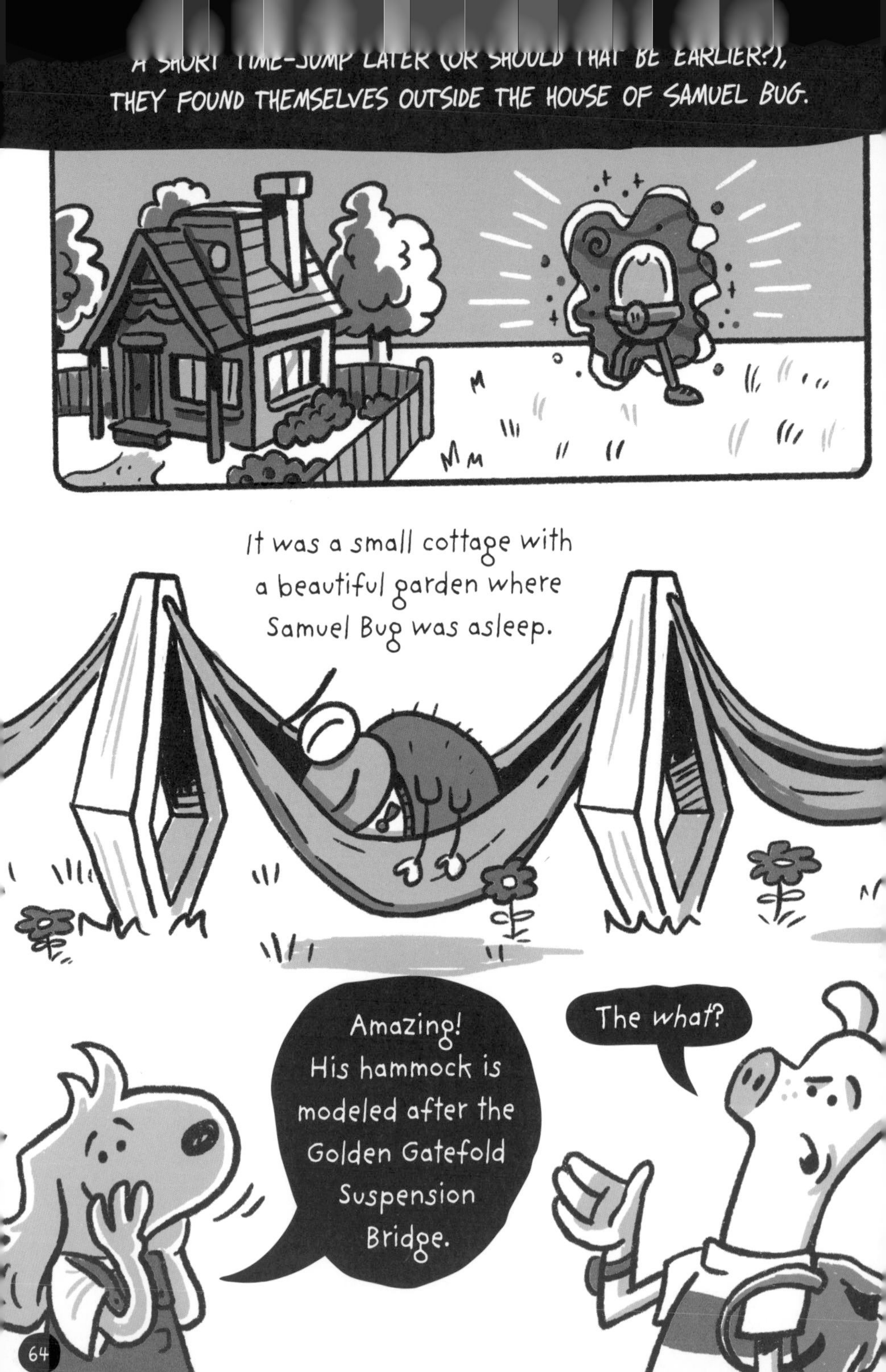
A SHORT TIME-JUMP LATER (OR SHOULD THAT BE EARLIER?),
THEY FOUND THEMSELVES OUTSIDE THE HOUSE OF SAMUEL BUG.
It was a small cottage with a beautiful garden where Samuel Bug was asleep.
Amazing! His hammock is modeled after the Golden Gatefold Suspension Bridge.
The what?

"The most interesting bridge in the world! The book has an eighteen-page reinforced fold-out diagram."

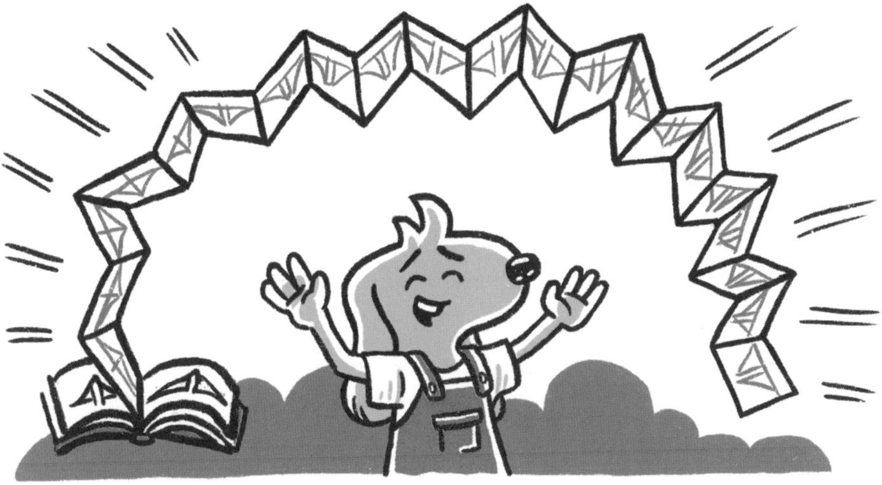

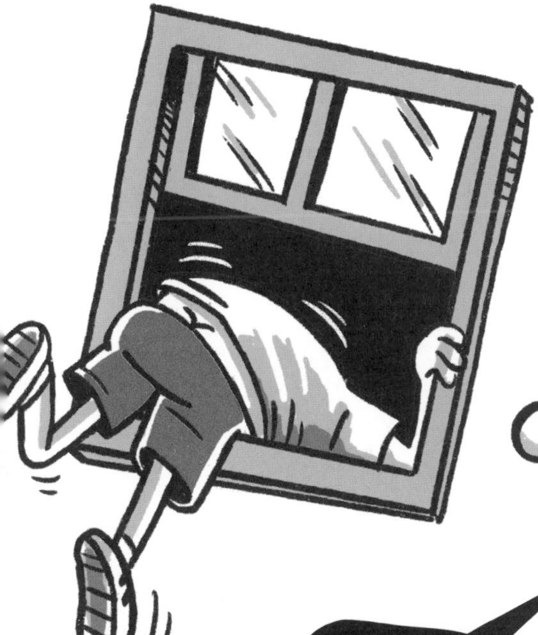

"And speaking of the book," said Gustav, reaching through an open window.

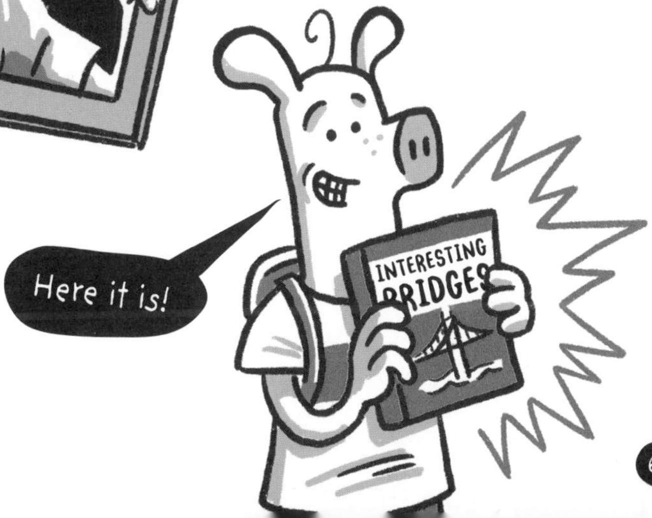
Here it is!
INTERESTING BRIDGES

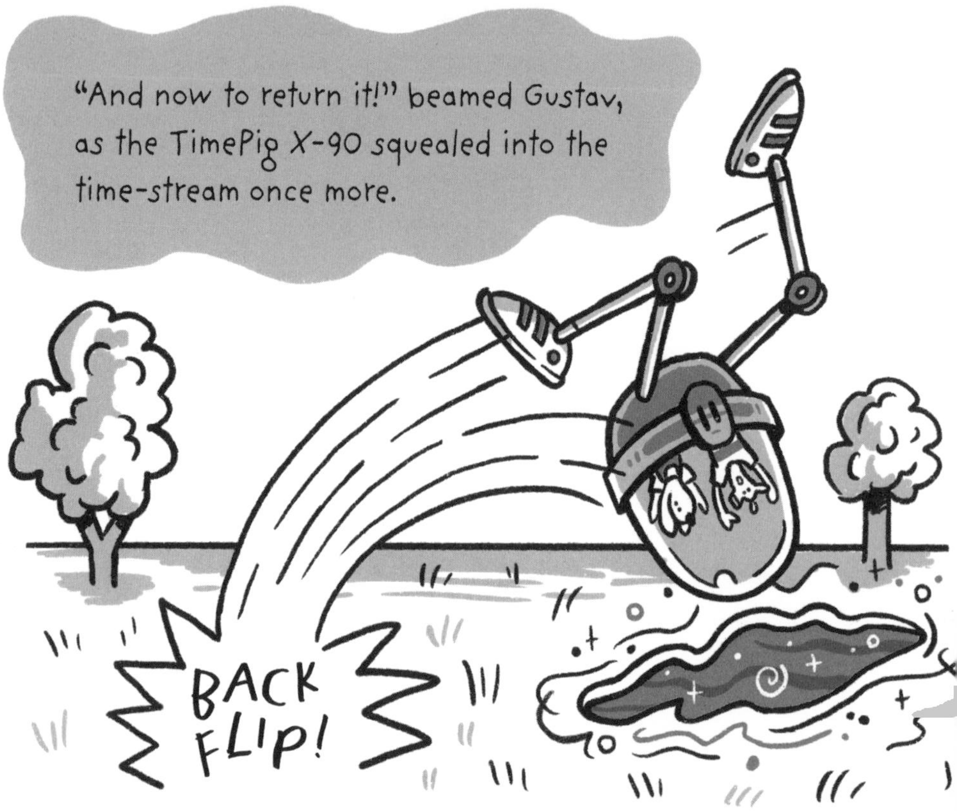
"And now to return it!" beamed Gustav, as the TimePig X-90 squealed into the time-stream once more.
BACK FLIP!

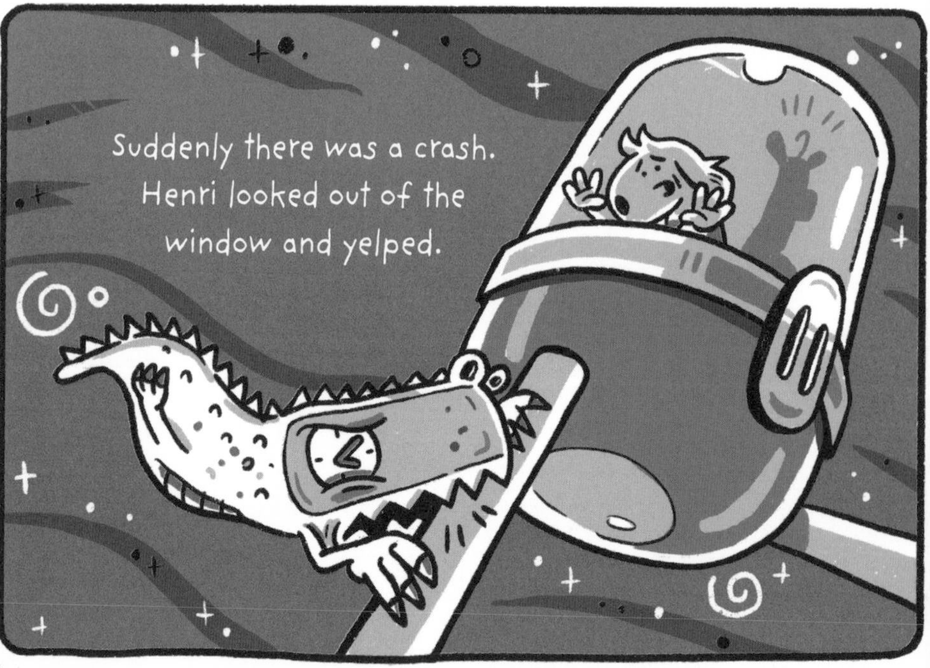
Suddenly there was a crash. Henri looked out of the window and yelped.

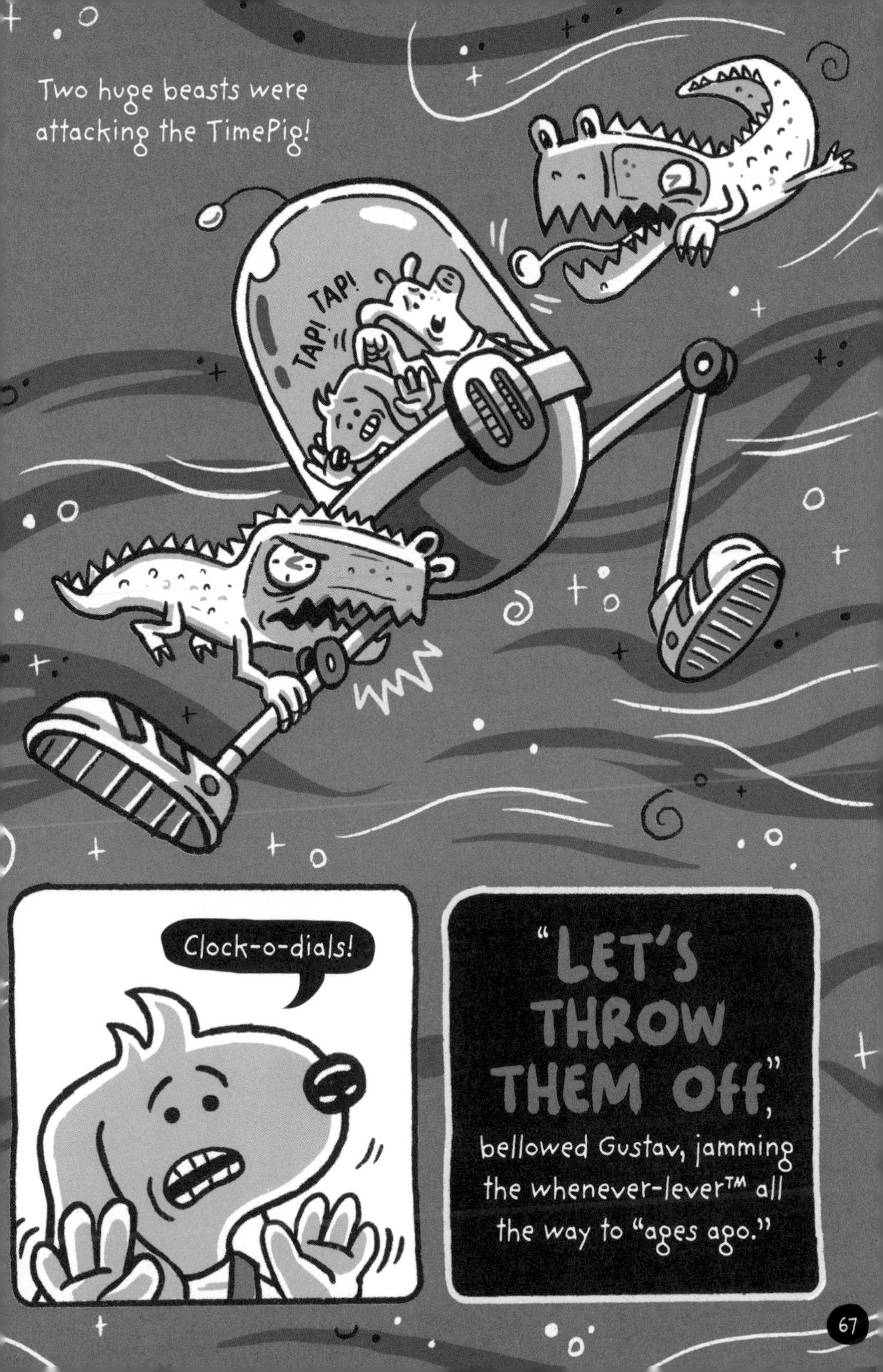
Two huge beasts were attacking the TimePig!
TAP! TAP!
Clock-o-dials!
"LET'S THROW THEM Off," bellowed Gustav, jamming the whenever-lever™ all the way to "ages ago."

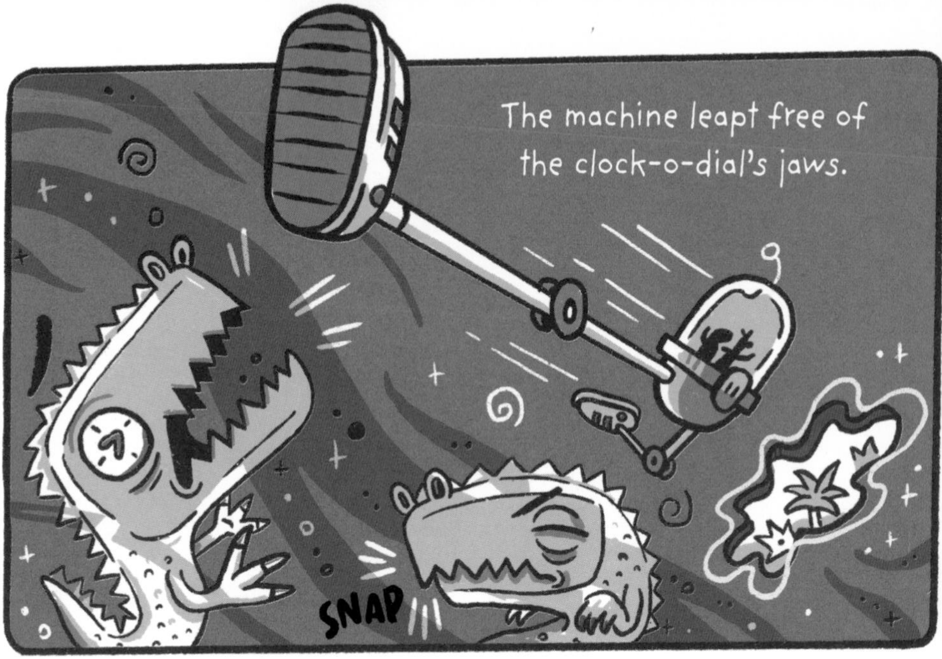
The machine leapt free of the clock-o-dial's jaws.
SNAP

The TimePig tumbled through a glowing portal, sending Henri and Gustav crashing into a strange forest.

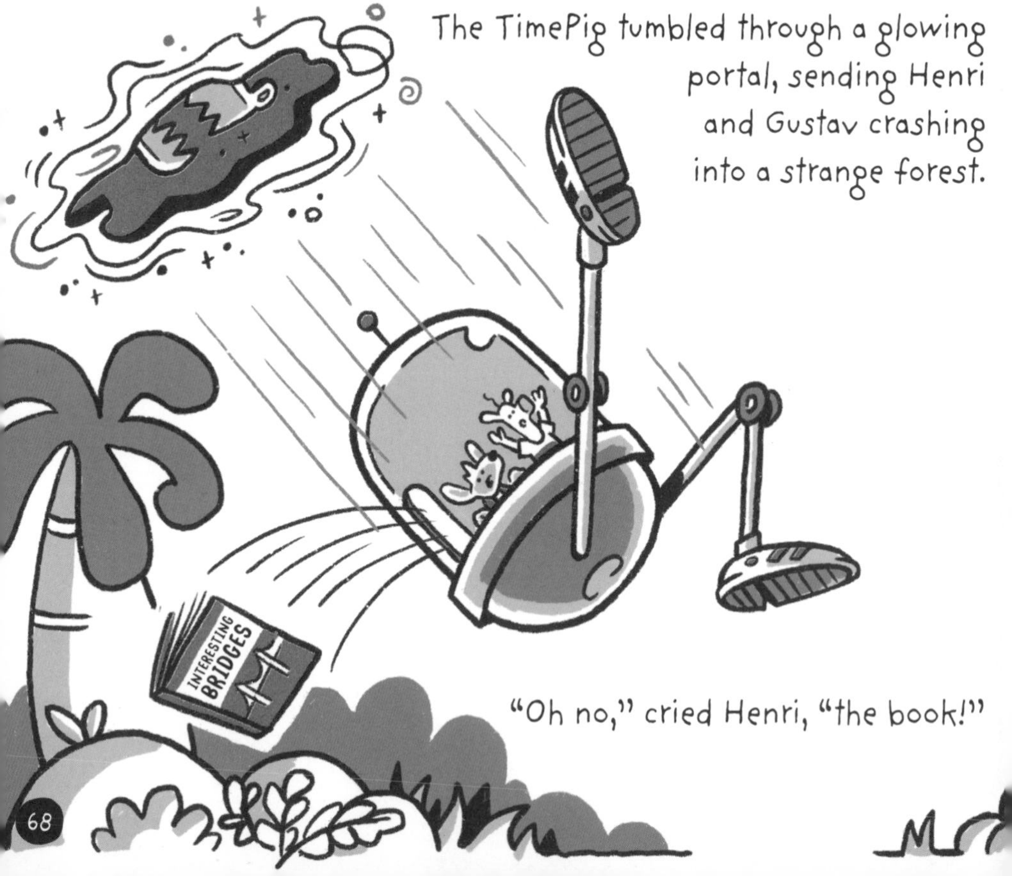
INTERESTING BRIDGES

"Oh no," cried Henri, "the book!"

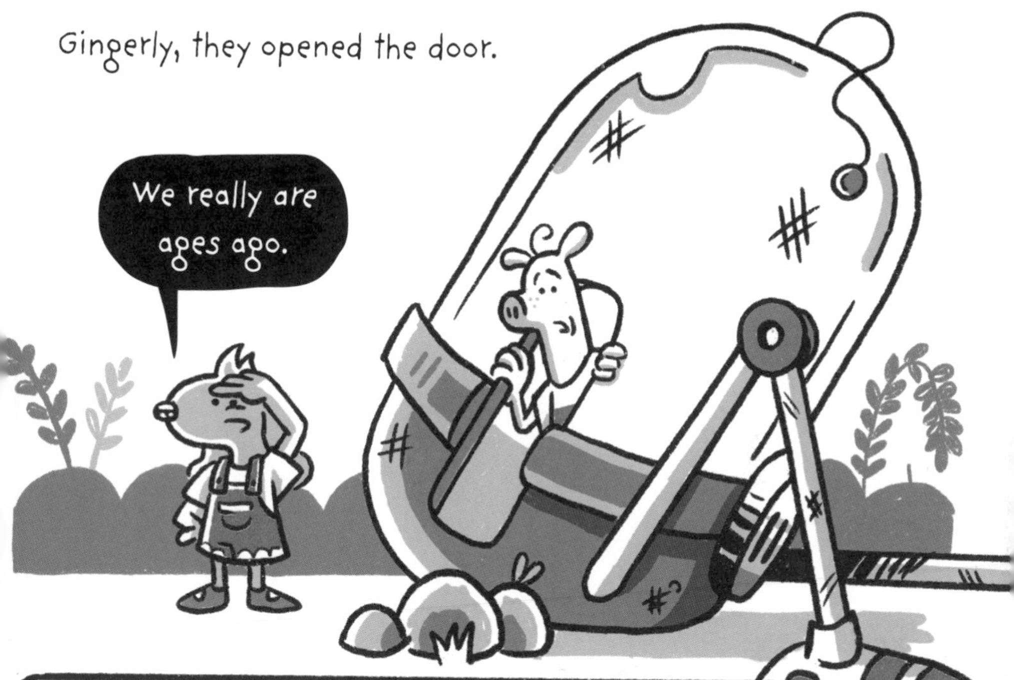
Gingerly, they opened the door.
We really are ages ago.

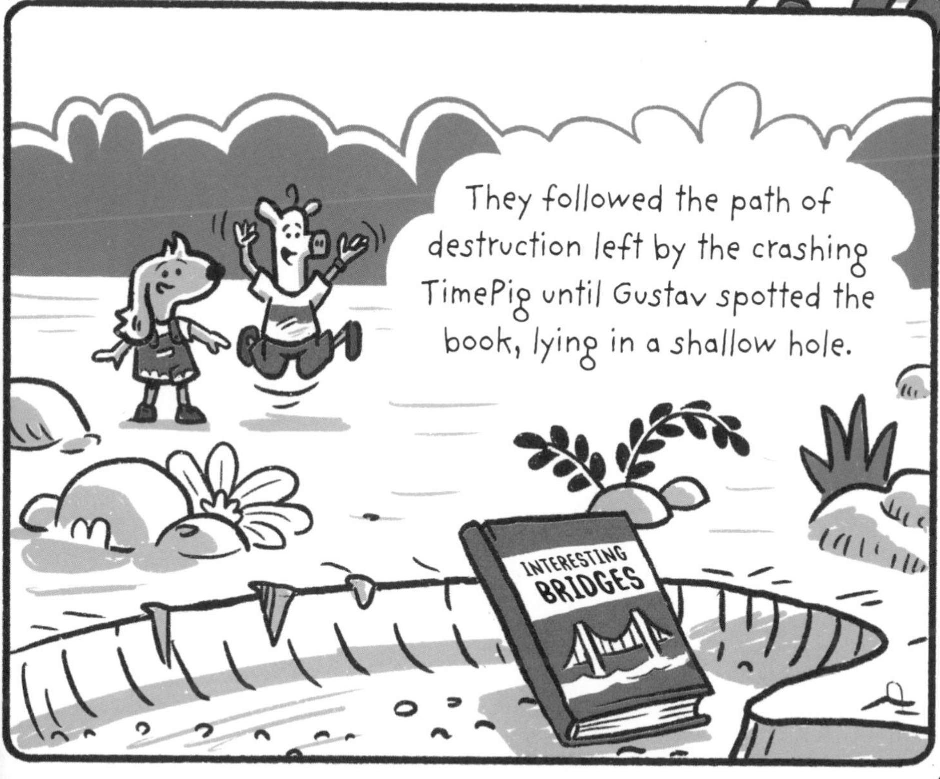
They followed the path of destruction left by the crashing TimePig until Gustav spotted the book, lying in a shallow hole.
INTERESTING BRIDGES

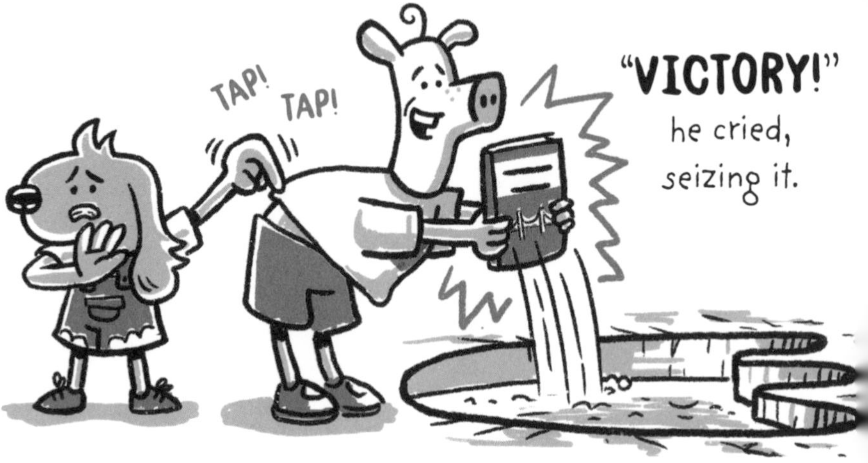
TAP!
TAP!

**"VICTORY!"** he cried, seizing it.

"Um, Gustav," said Henri quietly, "does that hole look ... a bit foot-shaped, do you think?"

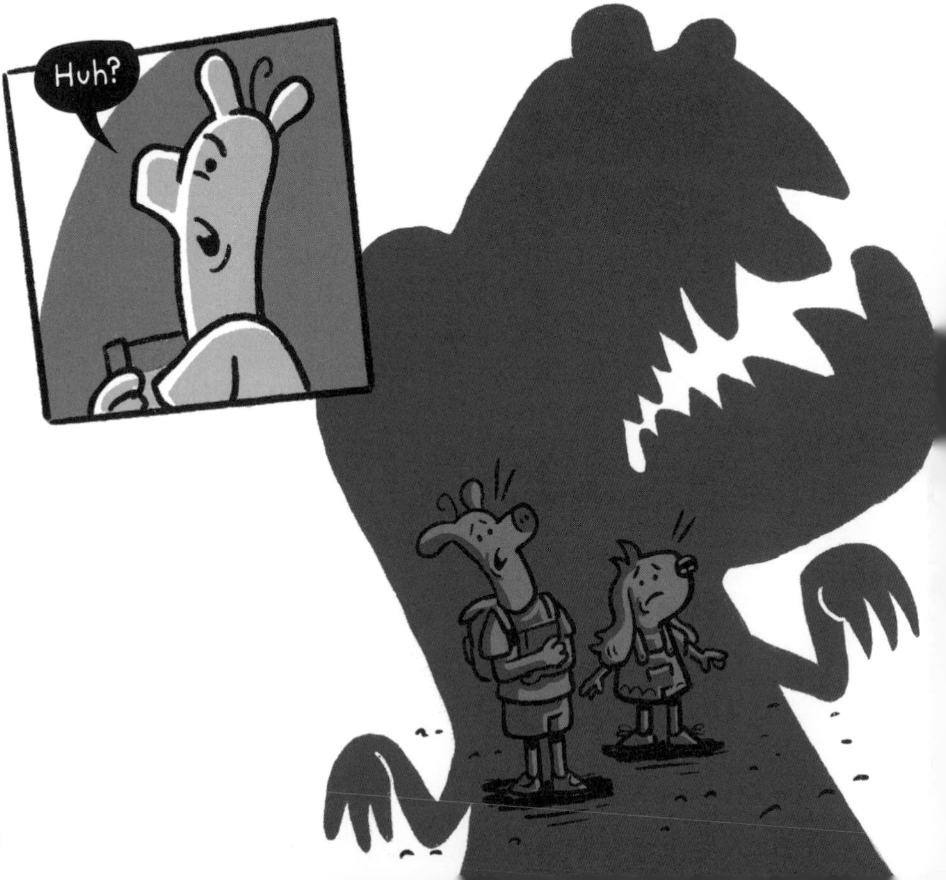
Huh?

"Can you believe we used to dress like that?" grunted Gustav as they ran through the jungle, the T-rex thumping and roaring behind them.

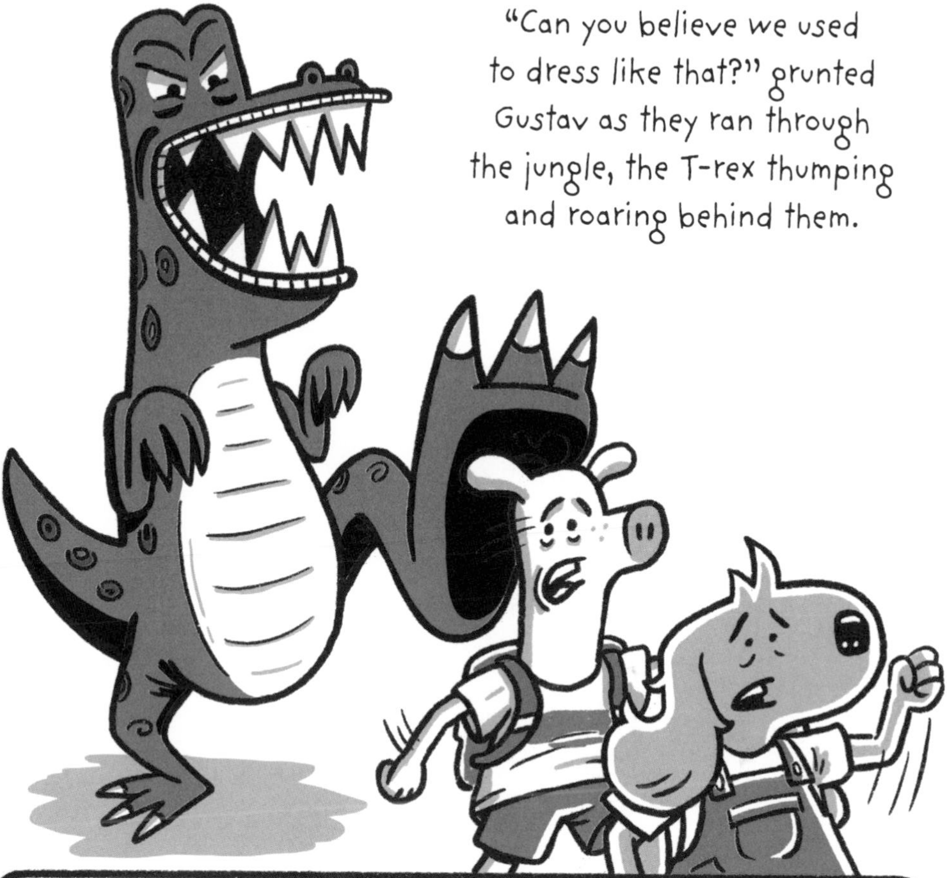

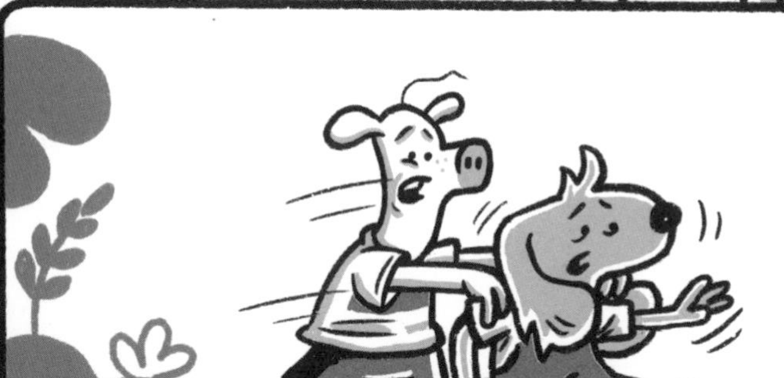

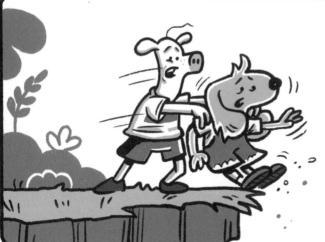

**SUDDENLY** they came to a juddering stop on the edge of a deep ravine.

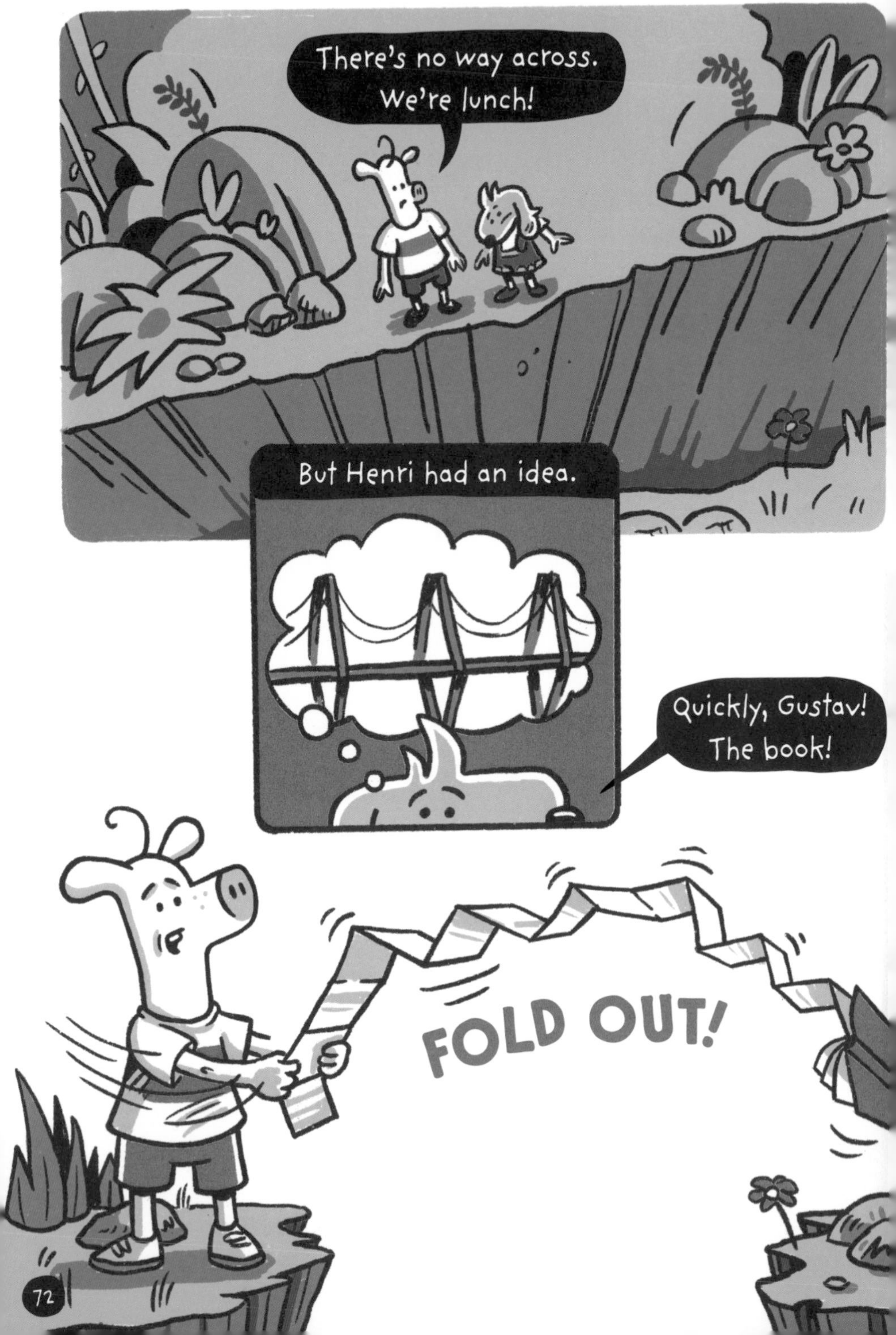
There's no way across. We're lunch!
But Henri had an idea.
Quickly, Gustav! The book!
FOLD OUT!

And together they scuttled across the eighteen-page reinforced fold-out diagram of the Golden Gatefold Suspension Bridge,

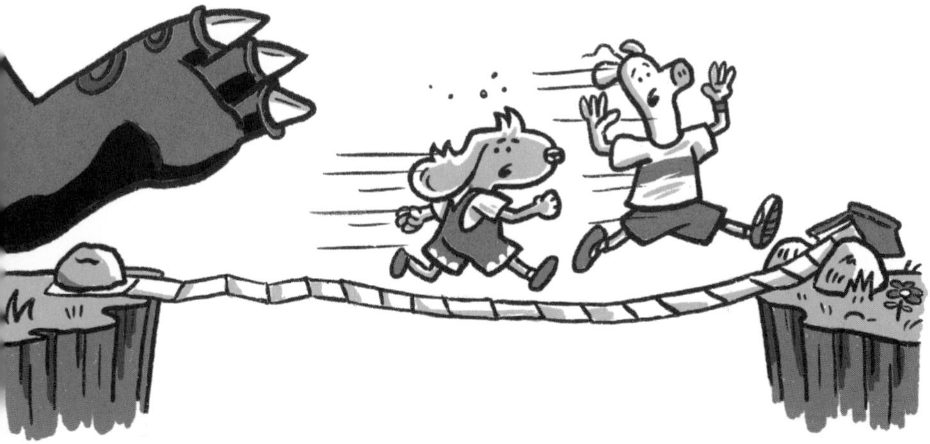

only just making it to safety before the T-rex sent the bridge—and the book—crashing into the river below.

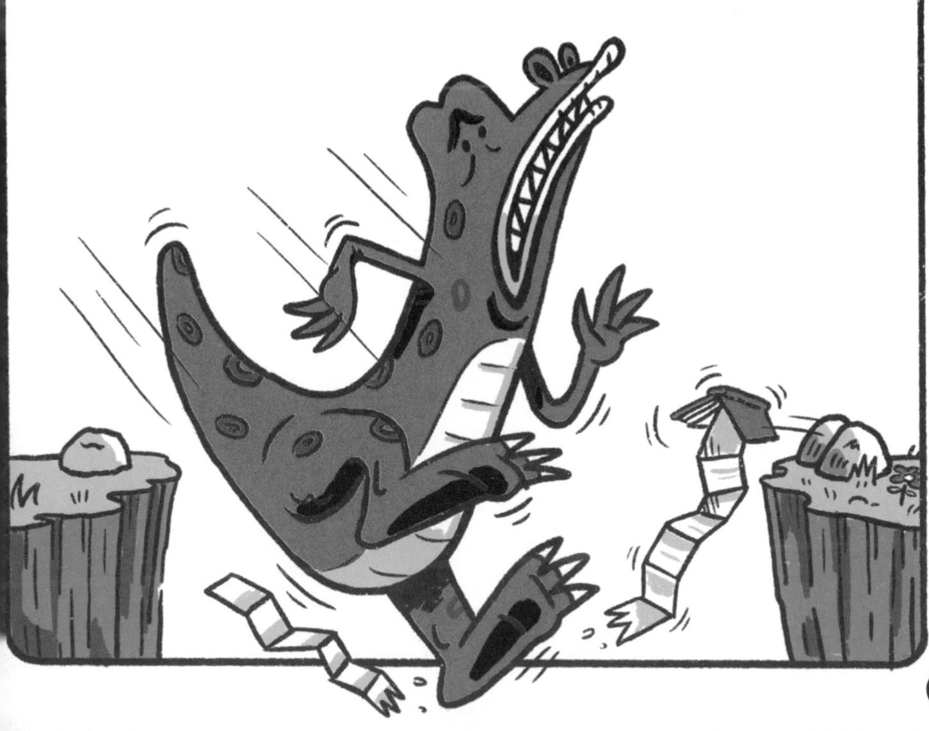

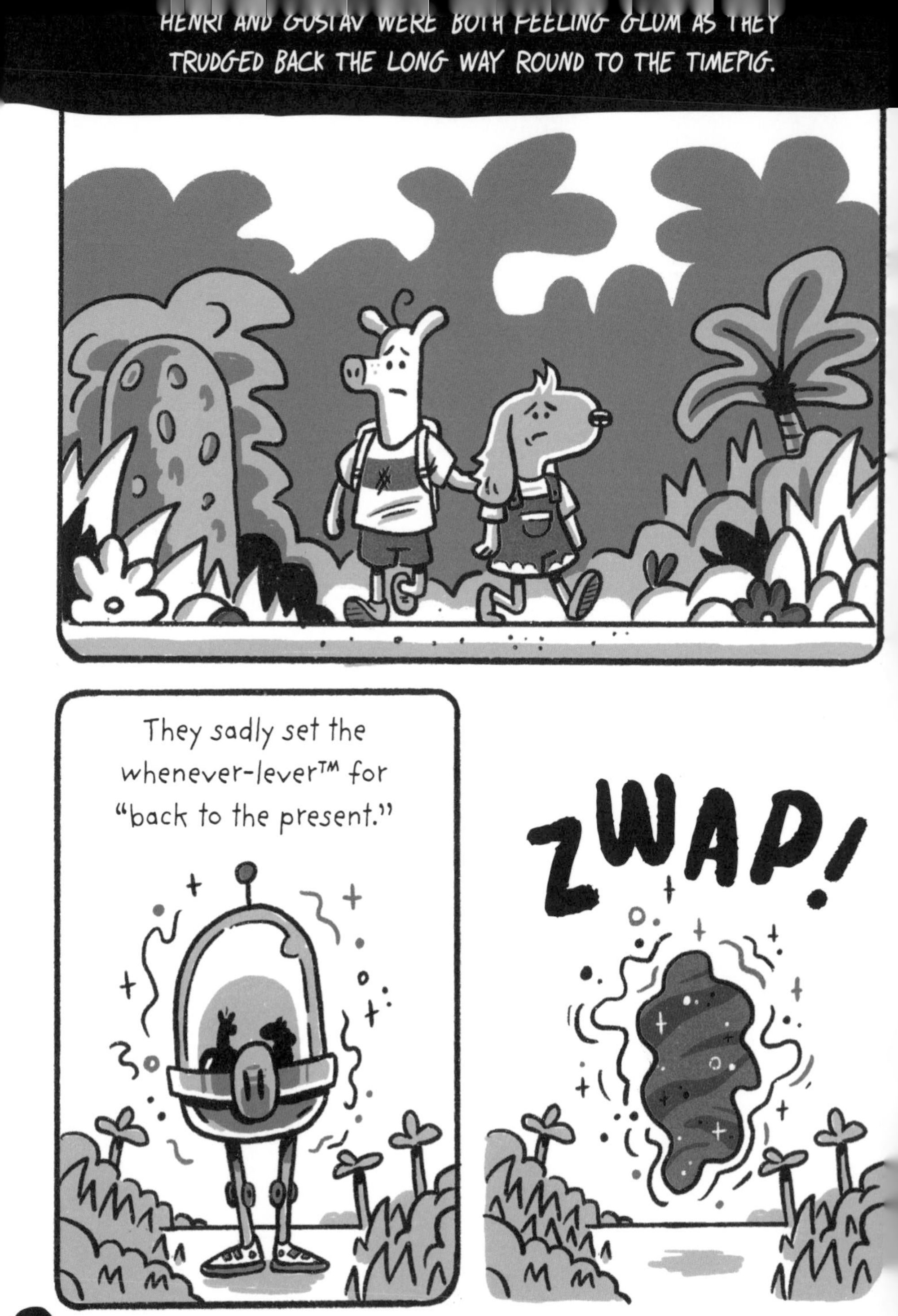
HENRI AND GUSTAV WERE BOTH FEELING GLUM AS THEY TRUDGED BACK THE LONG WAY ROUND TO THE TIMEPIG.
They sadly set the whenever-lever™ for "back to the present."
ZWAP!

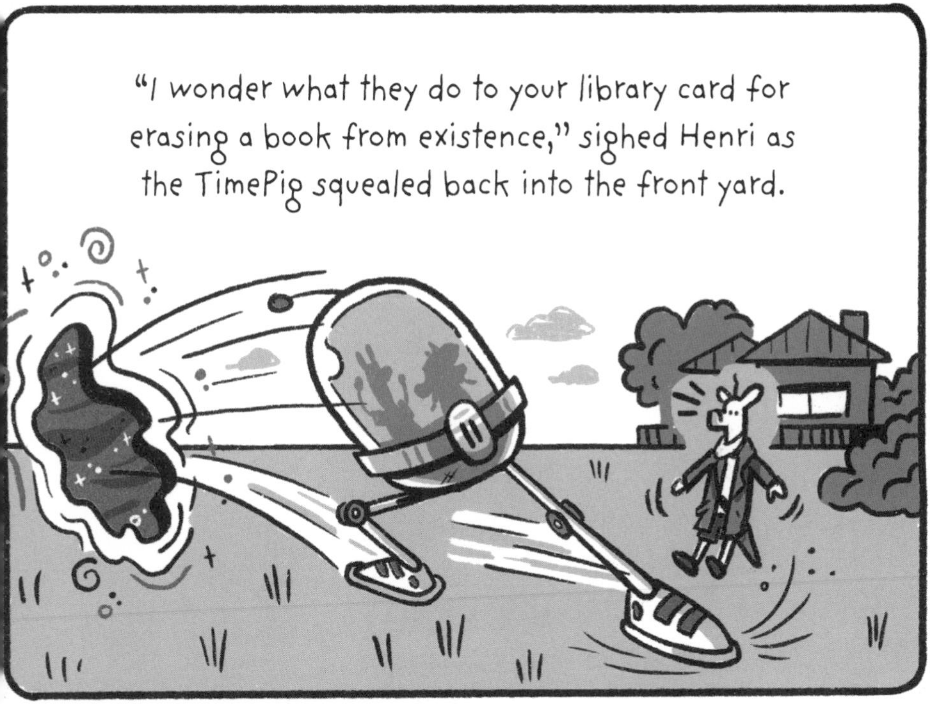
"I wonder what they do to your library card for erasing a book from existence," sighed Henri as the TimePig squealed back into the front yard.

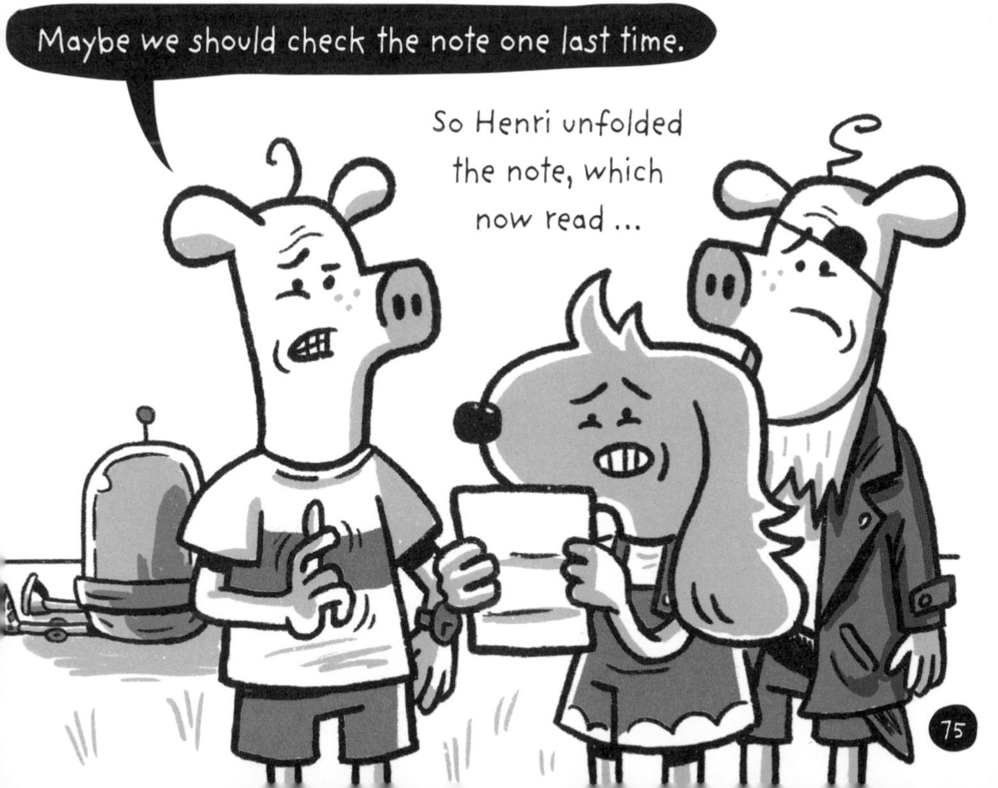
Maybe we should check the note one last time.
So Henri unfolded the note, which now read ...

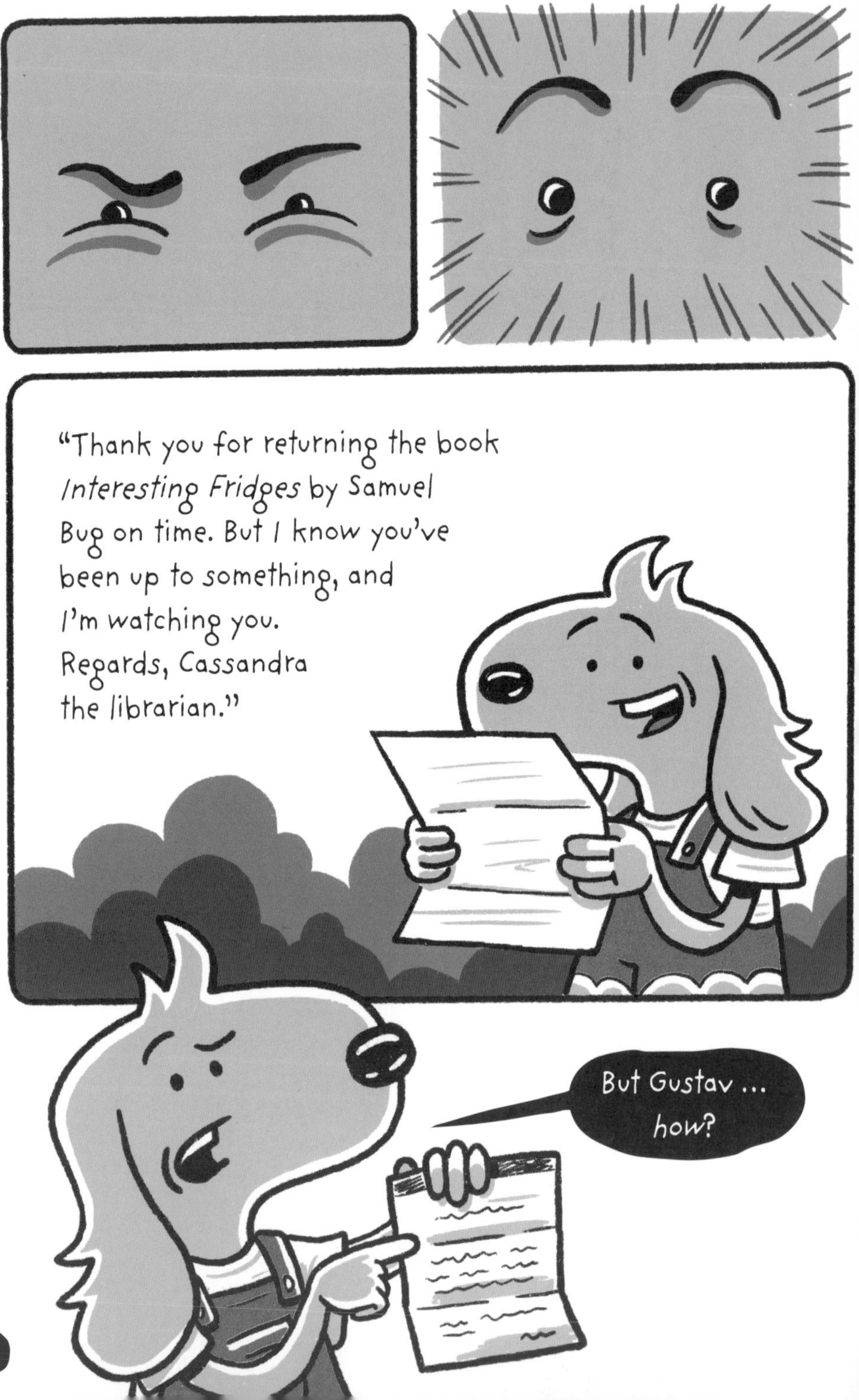
"Thank you for returning the book *Interesting Fridges* by Samuel Bug on time. But I know you've been up to something, and I'm watching you. Regards, Cassandra the librarian."
But Gustav ... *how?*

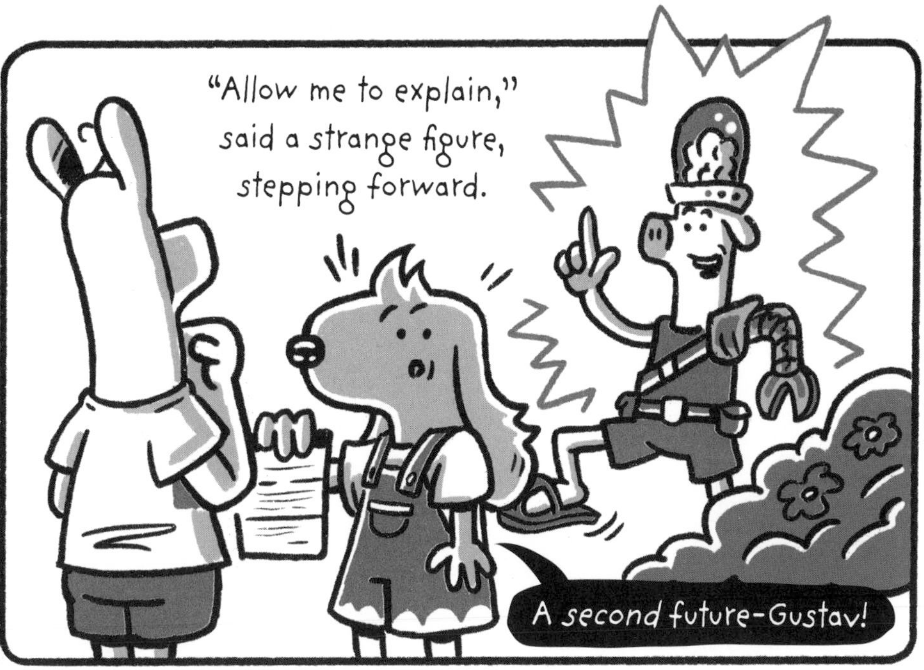
"Allow me to explain," said a strange figure, stepping forward.
A second future-Gustav!

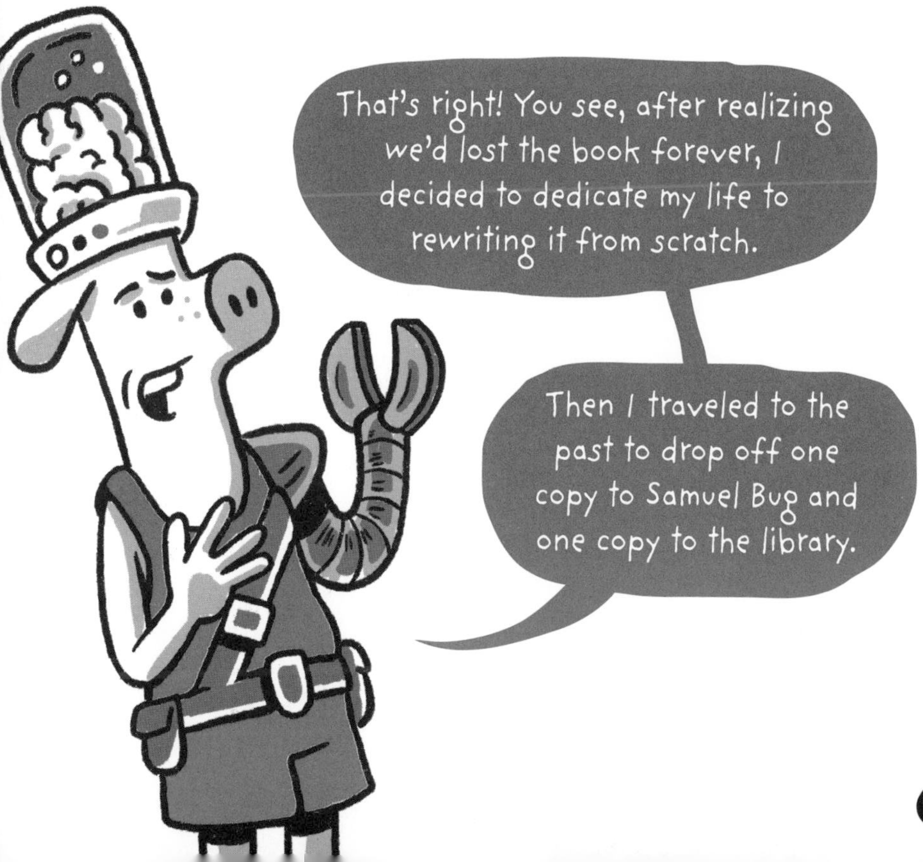
That's right! You see, after realizing we'd lost the book forever, I decided to dedicate my life to rewriting it from scratch.
Then I traveled to the past to drop off one copy to Samuel Bug and one copy to the library.

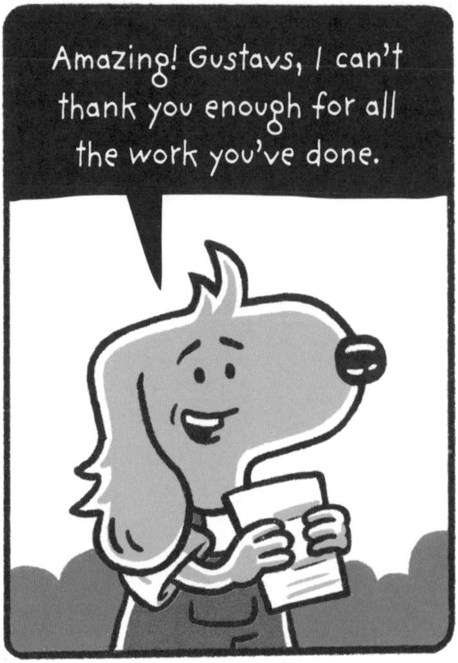
Amazing! Gustavs, I can't thank you enough for all the work you've done.

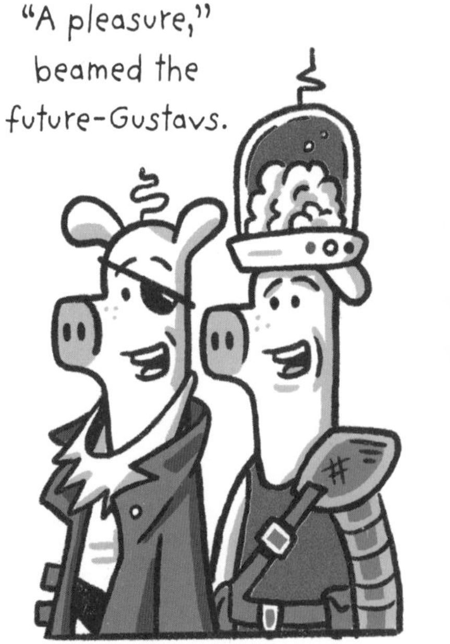
"A pleasure," beamed the future-Gustavs.

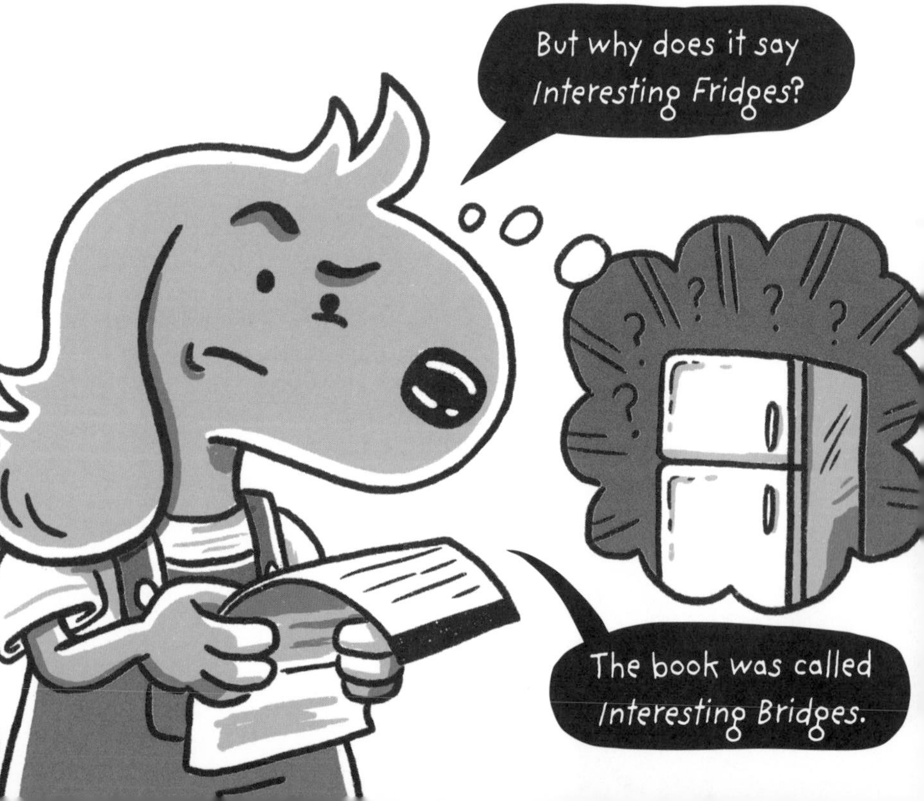
But why does it say *Interesting Fridges?*
The book was called *Interesting Bridges.*

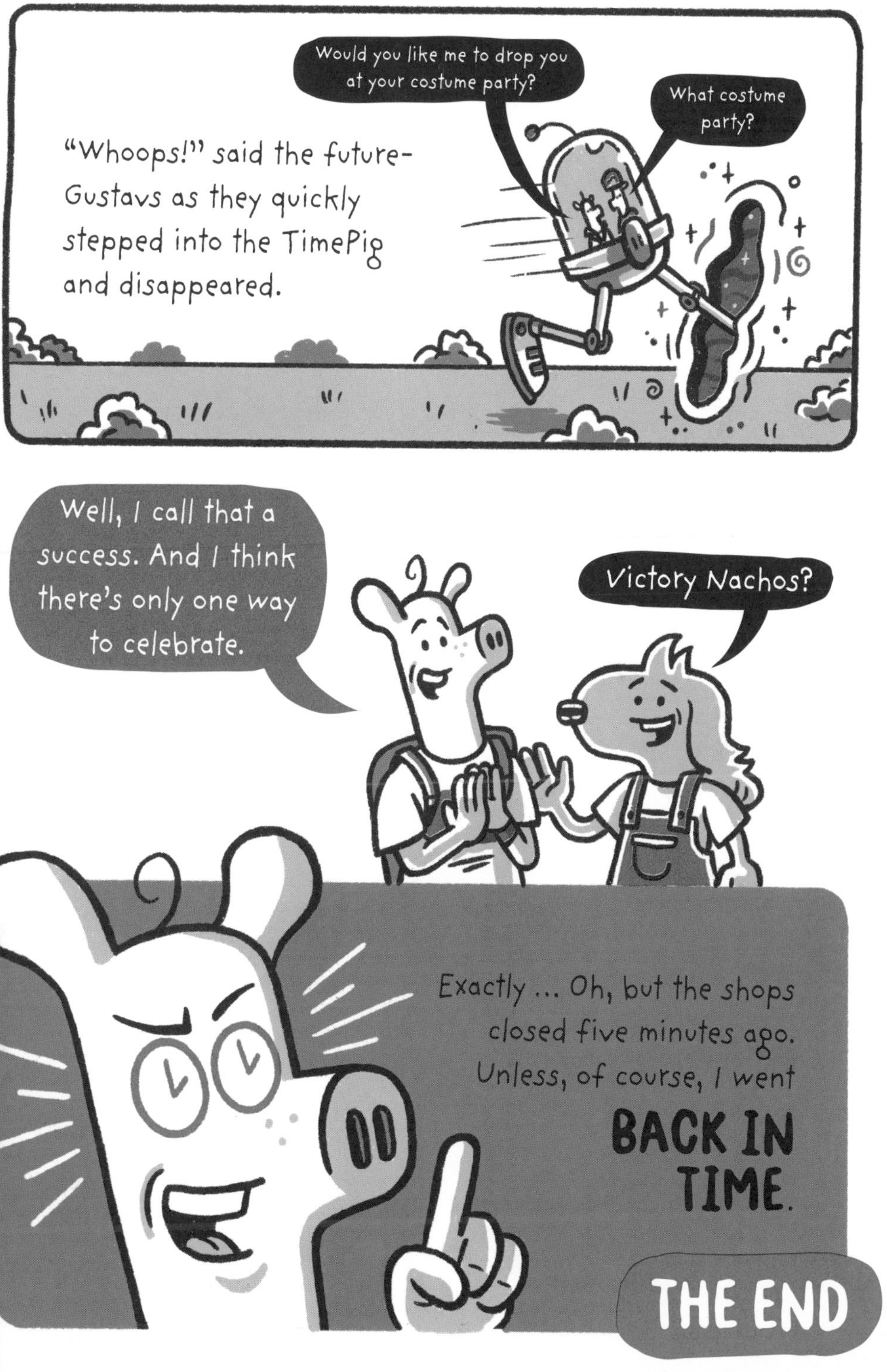
"Whoops!" said the future-Gustavs as they quickly stepped into the TimePig and disappeared.
Would you like me to drop you at your costume party?
What costume party?
Well, I call that a success. And I think there's only one way to celebrate.
Victory Nachos?
Exactly ... Oh, but the shops closed five minutes ago. Unless, of course, I went
BACK IN TIME.
THE END

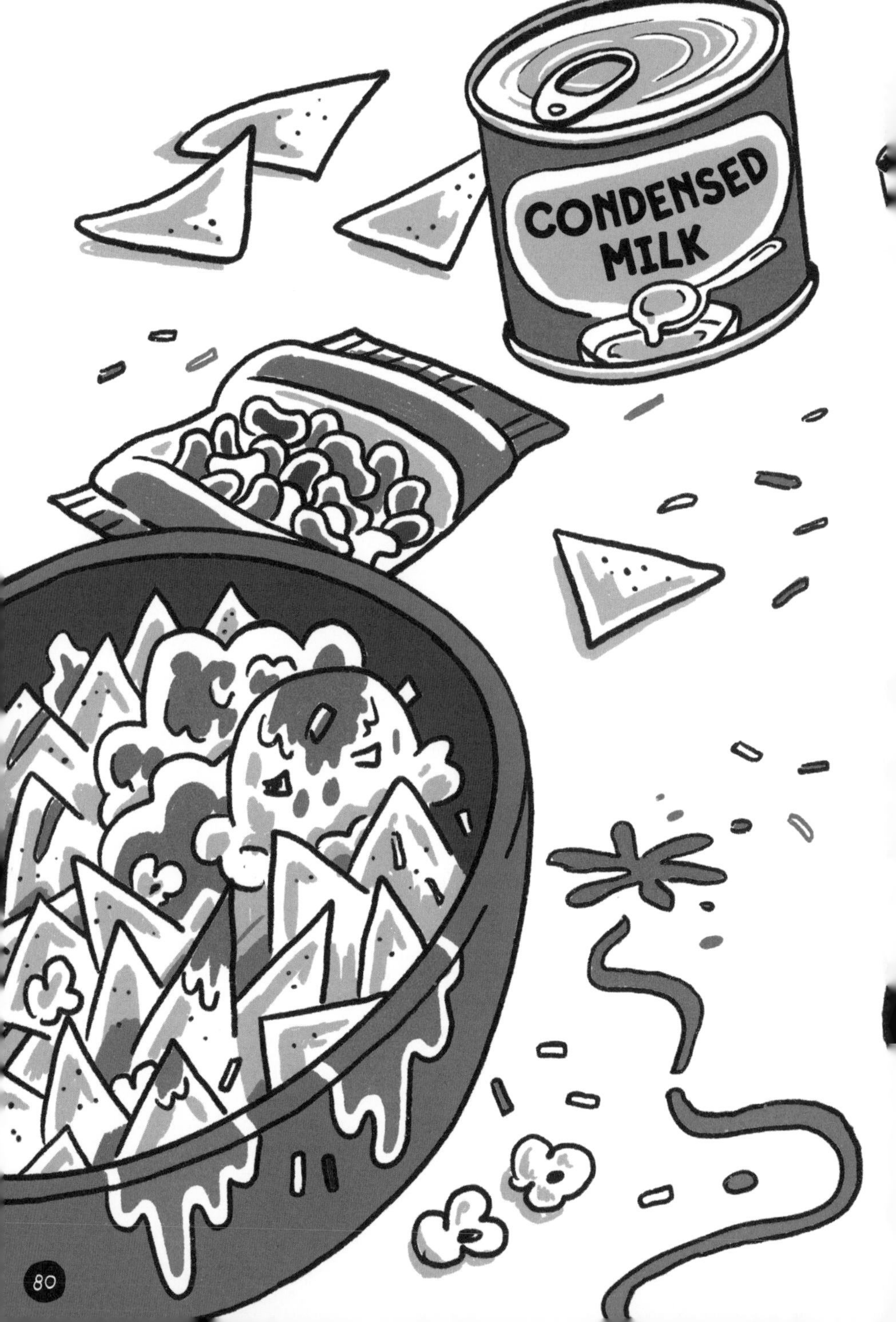
CONDENSED
MILK

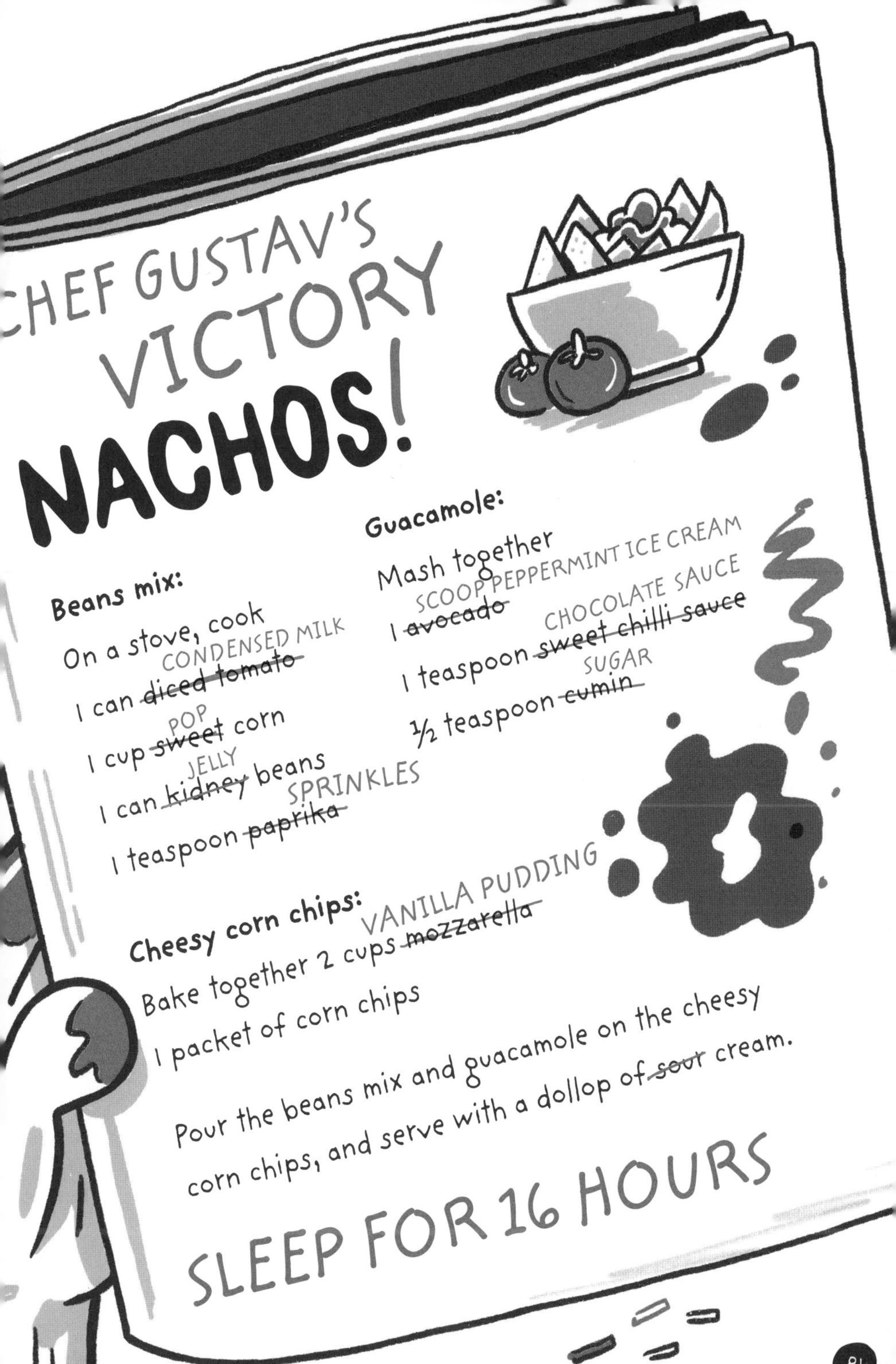
CHEF GUSTAV'S
VICTORY
NACHOS!
Beans mix:
On a stove, cook
1 can ~~diced tomato~~ CONDENSED MILK
1 cup ~~sweet~~ POP corn
1 can ~~kidney~~ JELLY beans
1 teaspoon ~~paprika~~ SPRINKLES
Guacamole:
Mash together
1 ~~avocado~~ SCOOP PEPPERMINT ICE CREAM
1 teaspoon ~~sweet chilli sauce~~ CHOCOLATE SAUCE
½ teaspoon ~~cumin~~ SUGAR
Cheesy corn chips:
Bake together 2 cups ~~mozzarella~~ VANILLA PUDDING
1 packet of corn chips
Pour the beans mix and guacamole on the cheesy corn chips, and serve with a dollop of ~~sour~~ cream.
SLEEP FOR 16 HOURS

# DETECTIVE GUSTAV
## AND THE
## GREAT PIG DAY MYSTERY

HAVE AN OINK-REDIBLE PIG DAY!

THE BIG SQUEEZE
—FROSTING DISPENSER—

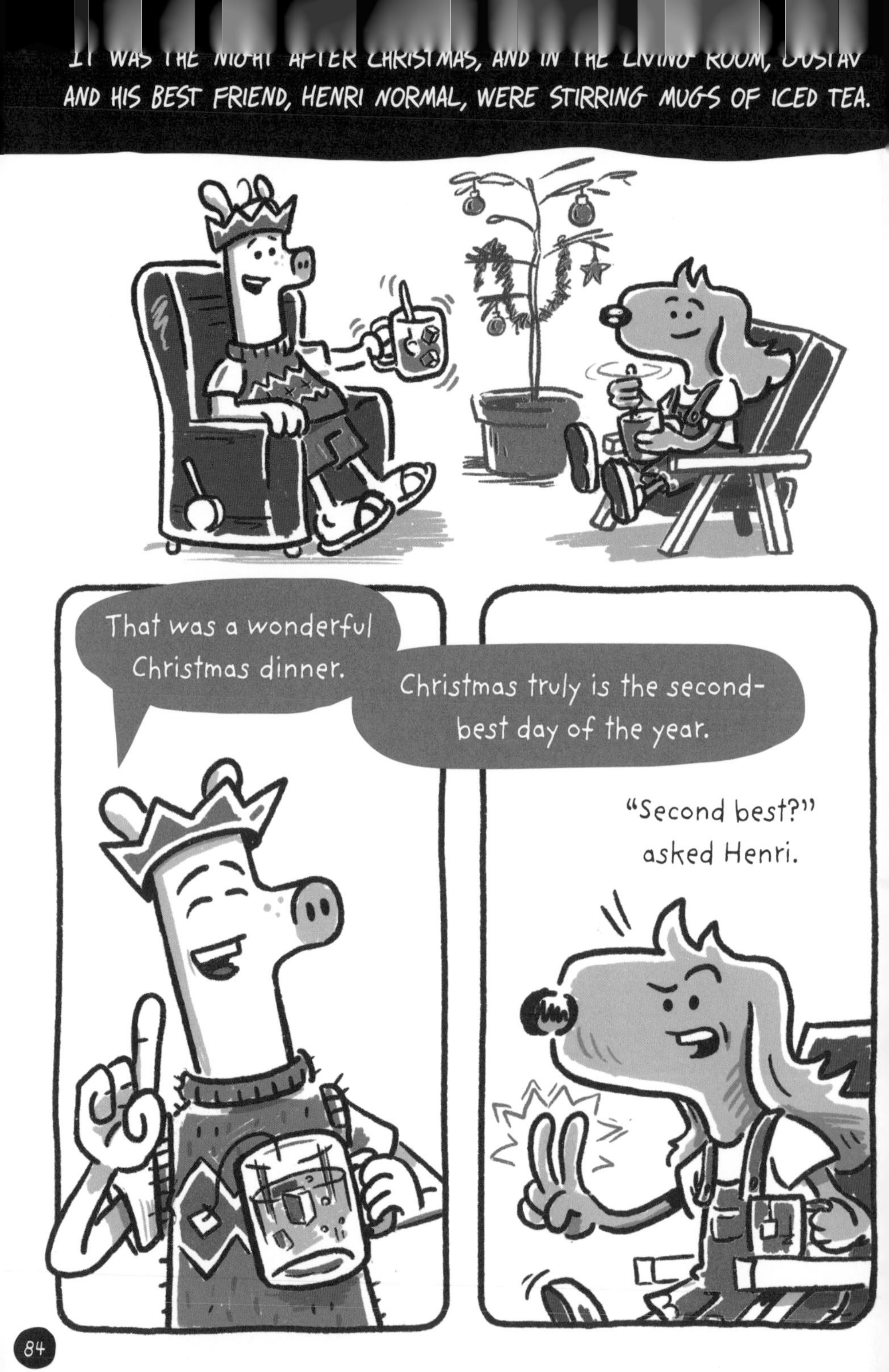
IT WAS THE NIGHT AFTER CHRISTMAS, AND IN THE LIVING ROOM, GUSTAV AND HIS BEST FRIEND, HENRI NORMAL, WERE STIRRING MUGS OF ICED TEA.
That was a wonderful Christmas dinner.
Christmas truly is the second-best day of the year.
"Second best?" asked Henri.

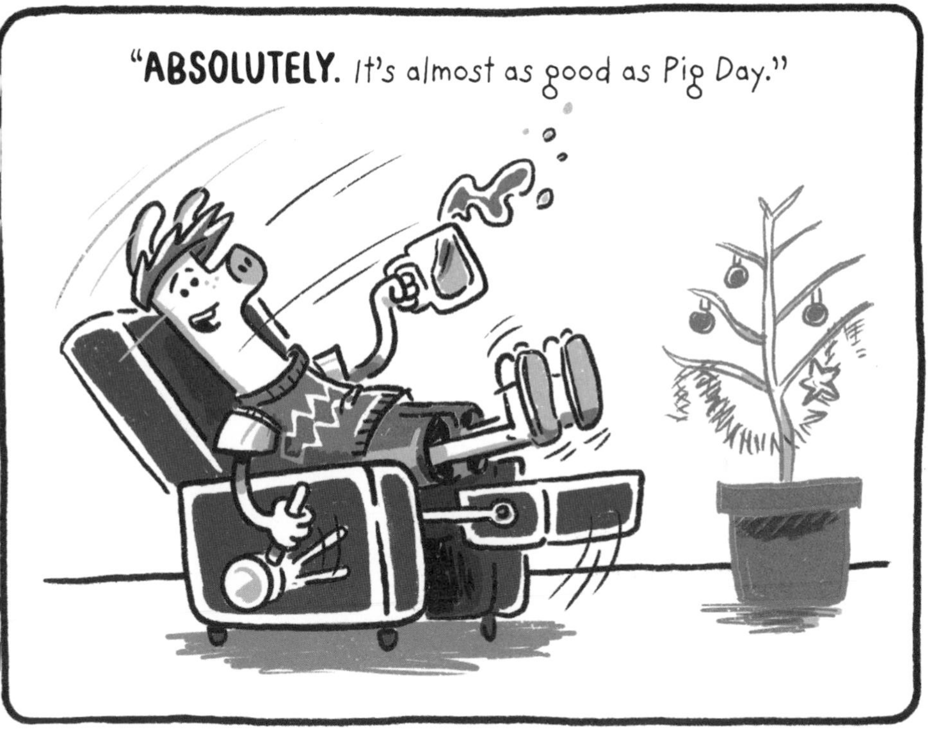
"ABSOLUTELY. It's almost as good as Pig Day."

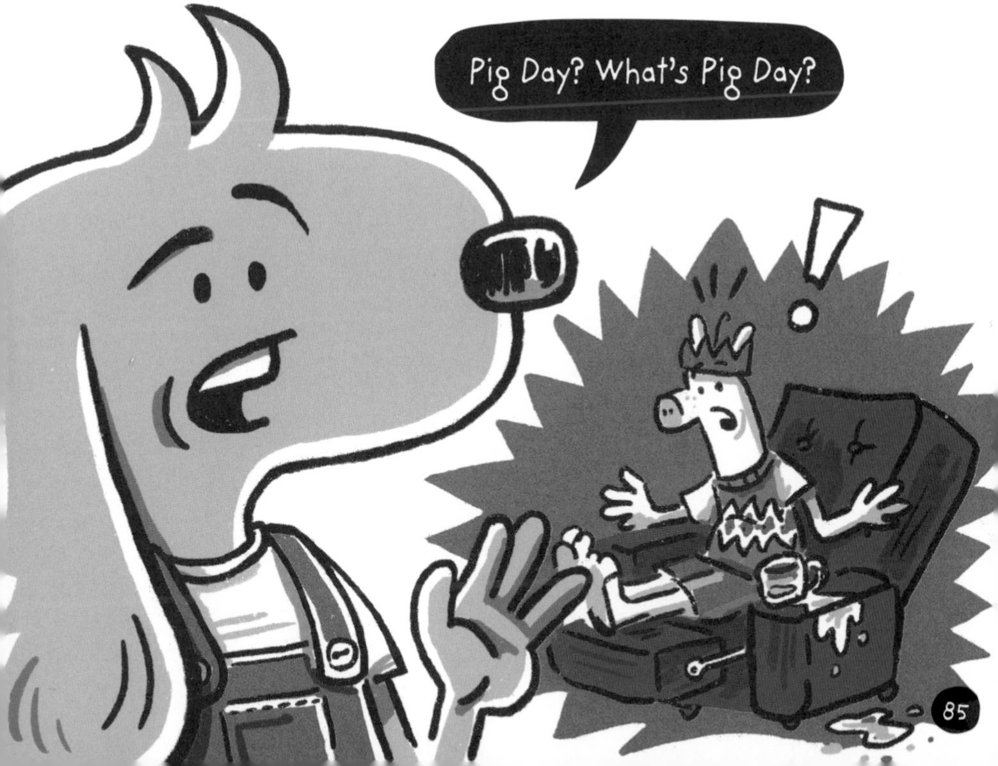
Pig Day? What's Pig Day?

"Only the most wondular, spectactulous, splendiffic day of the year!" beamed Gustav.

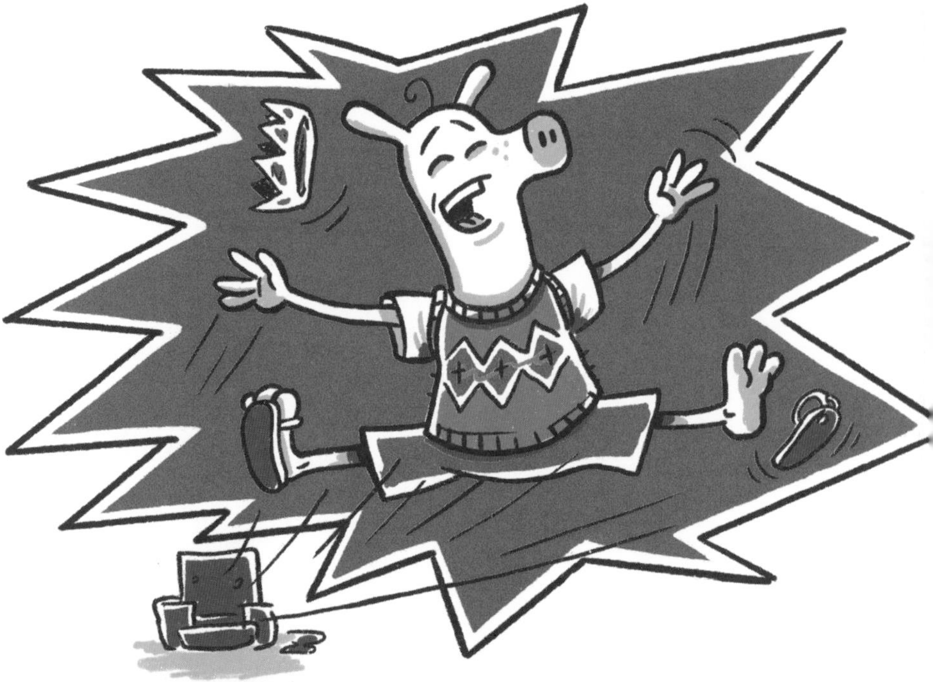

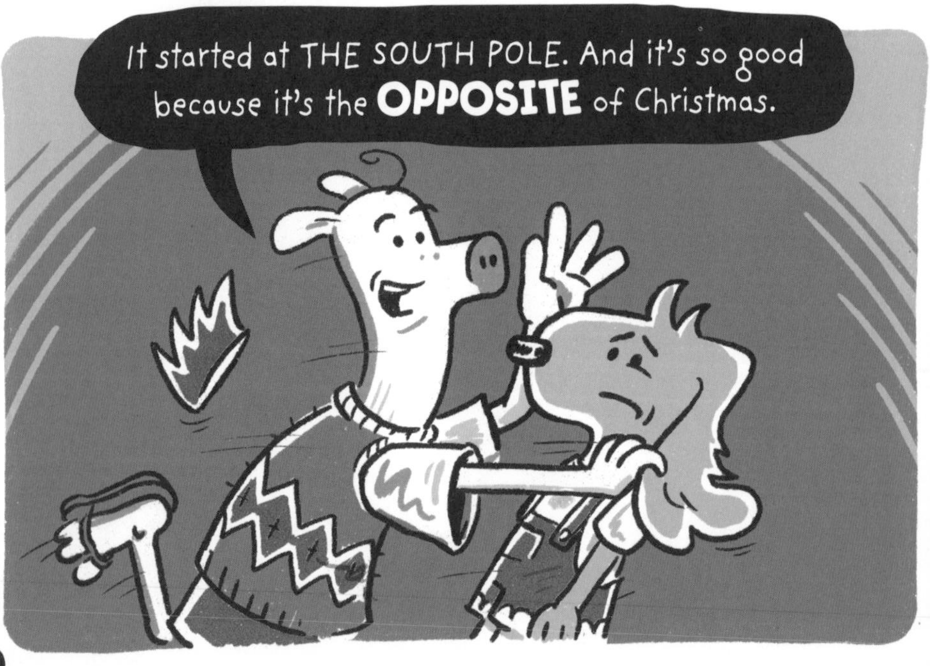
It started at THE SOUTH POLE. And it's so good because it's the **OPPOSITE** of Christmas.

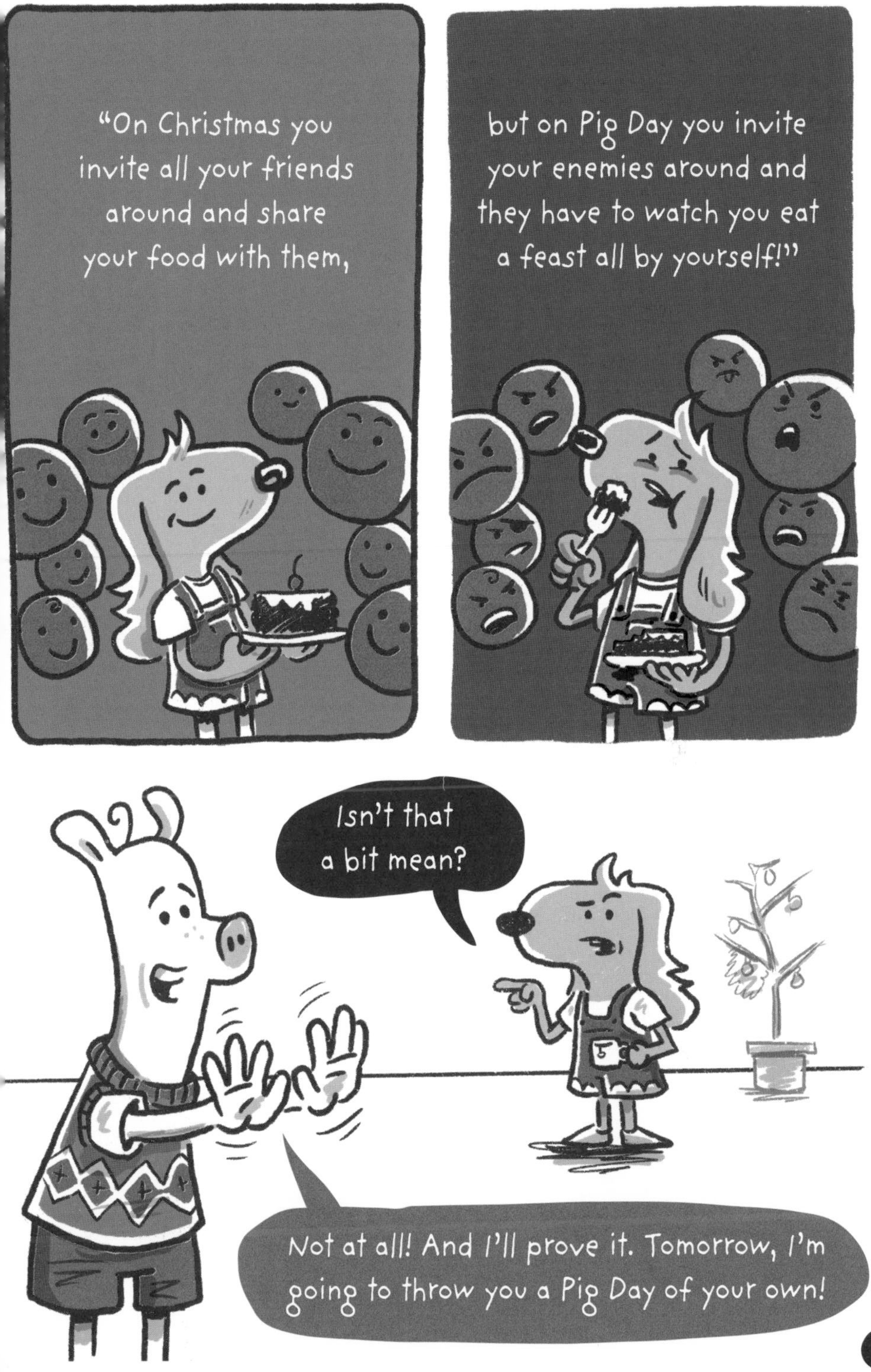
"On Christmas you invite all your friends around and share your food with them,
but on Pig Day you invite your enemies around and they have to watch you eat a feast all by yourself!"
Isn't that a bit mean?
Not at all! And I'll prove it. Tomorrow, I'm going to throw you a Pig Day of your own!

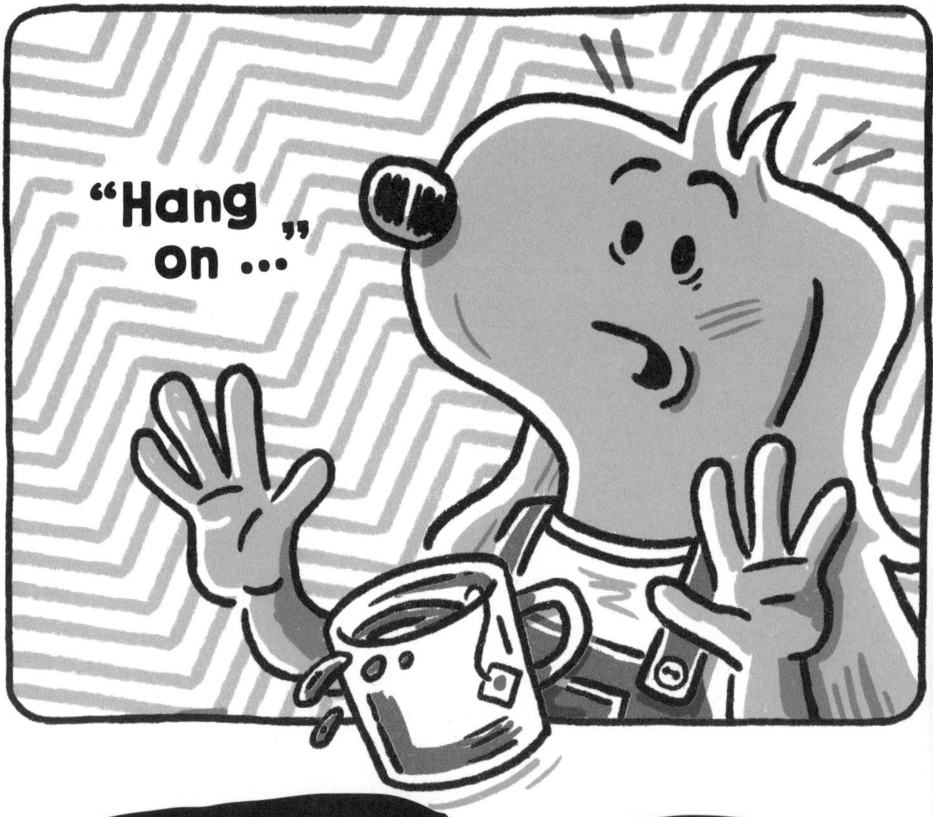
"Hang on ..."

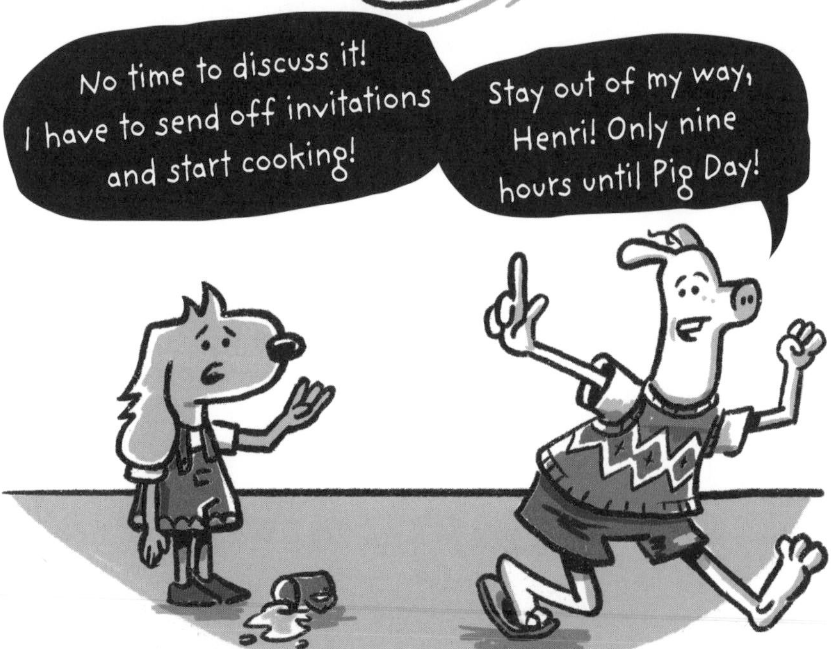
No time to discuss it! I have to send off invitations and start cooking!
Stay out of my way, Henri! Only nine hours until Pig Day!

So Henri went to bed, leaving Gustav baking late into the night.

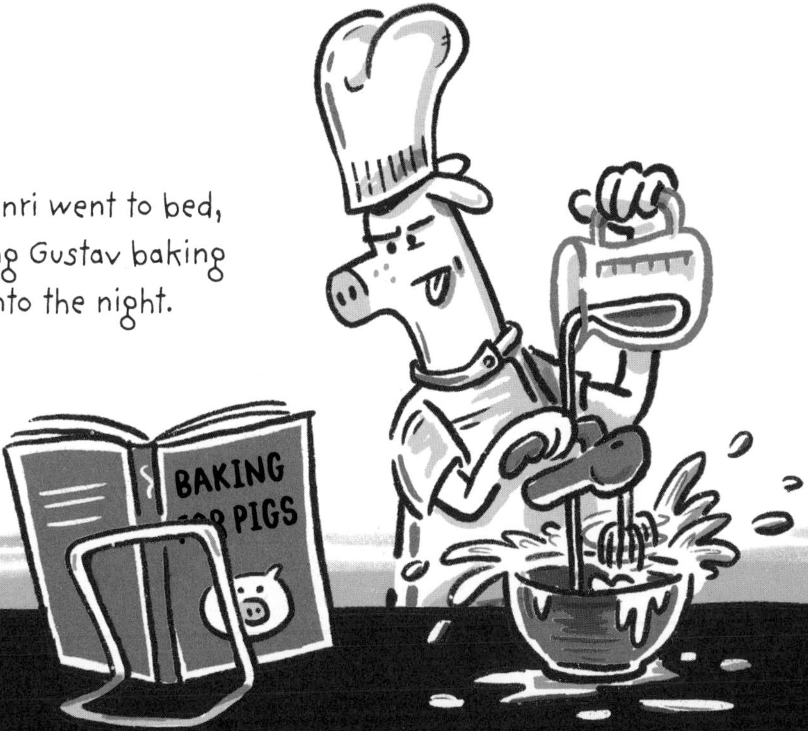
BAKING
PIGS

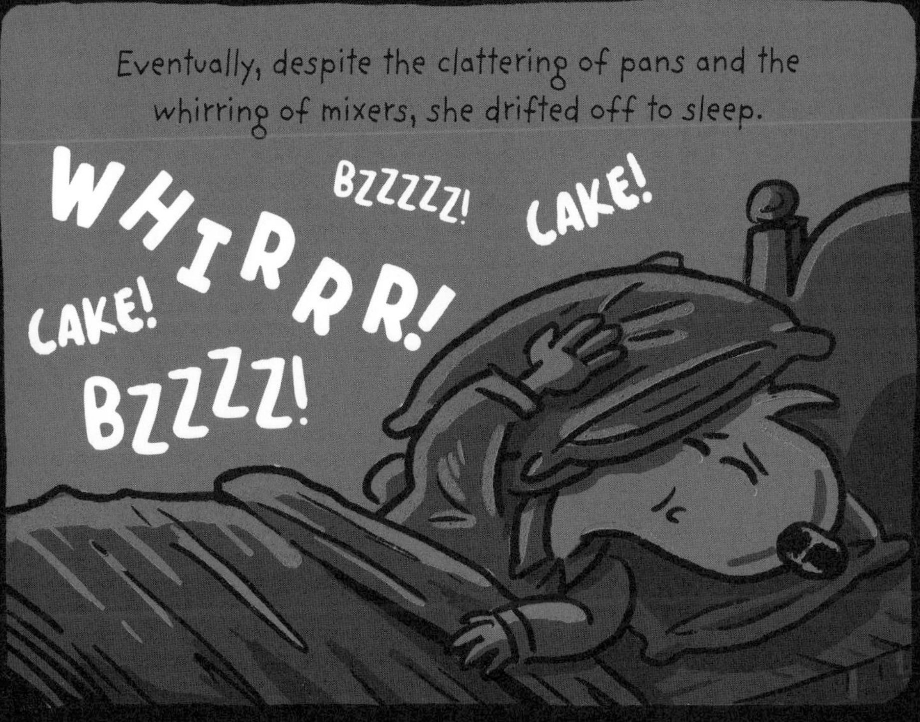
Eventually, despite the clattering of pans and the whirring of mixers, she drifted off to sleep.
WHIRRRR!
BZZZZZ!
CAKE!
CAKE!
BZZZZ!

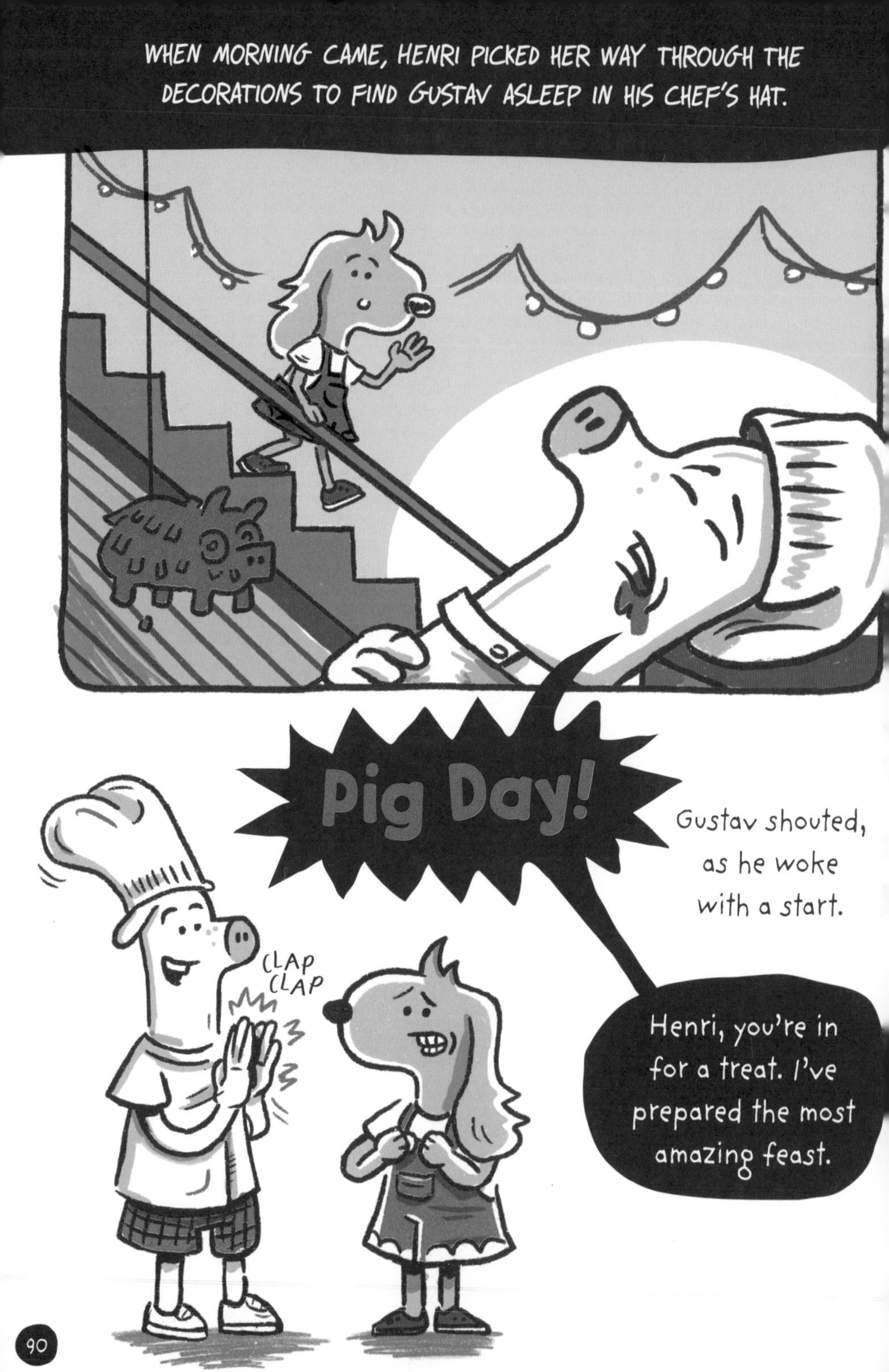
WHEN MORNING CAME, HENRI PICKED HER WAY THROUGH THE DECORATIONS TO FIND GUSTAV ASLEEP IN HIS CHEF'S HAT.
Pig Day!
Gustav shouted, as he woke with a start.
CLAP CLAP
Henri, you're in for a treat. I've prepared the most amazing feast.

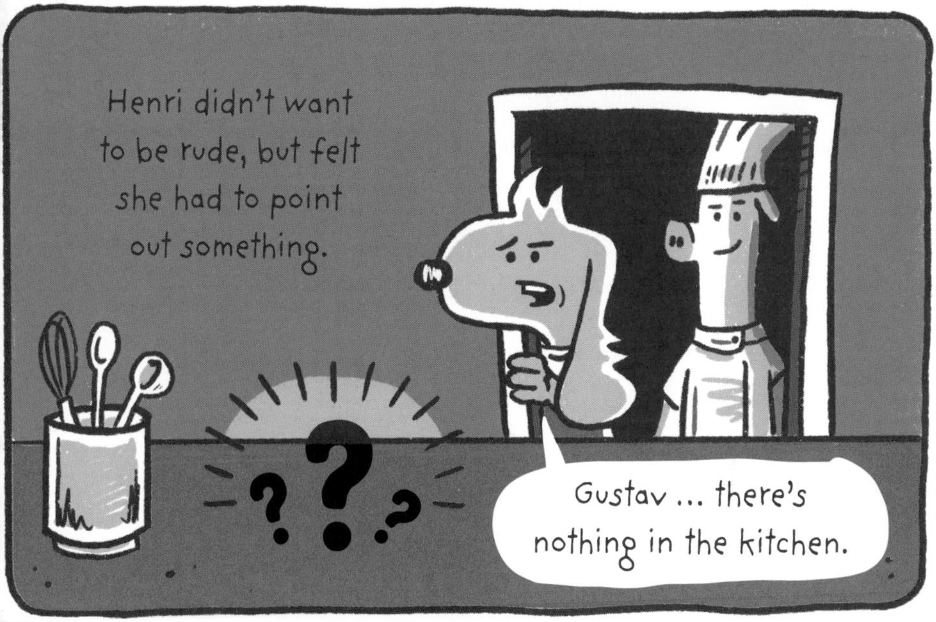
Henri didn't want to be rude, but felt she had to point out something.
Gustav ... there's nothing in the kitchen.

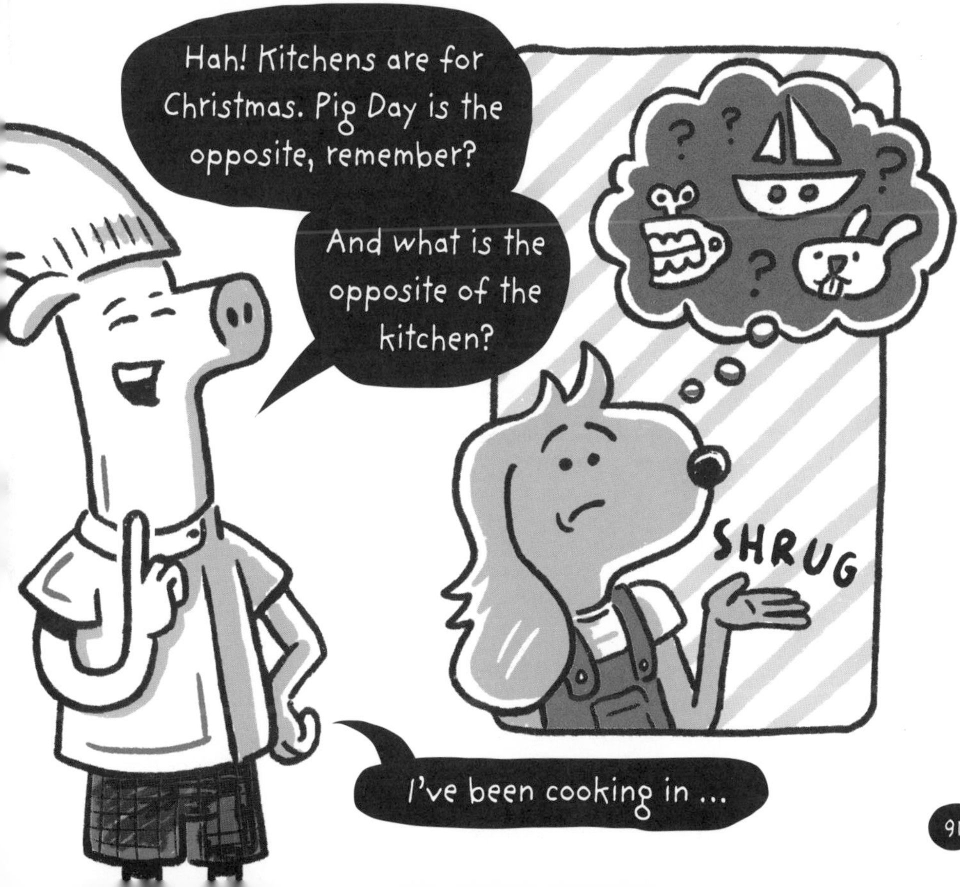
Hah! Kitchens are for Christmas. Pig Day is the opposite, remember?
And what is the opposite of the kitchen?
SHRUG
I've been cooking in ...

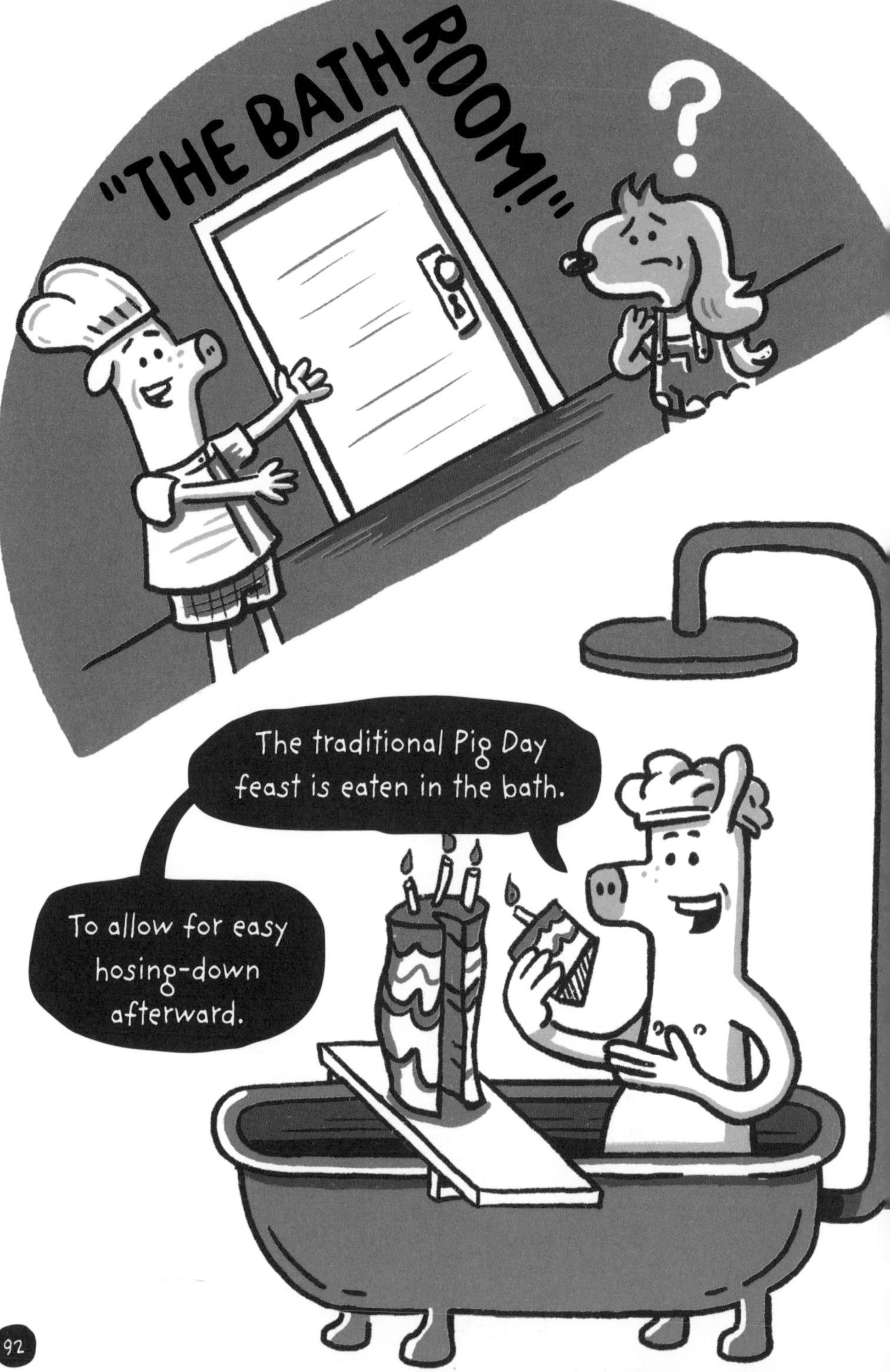
"THE BATHROOM!"
?
The traditional Pig Day feast is eaten in the bath.
To allow for easy hosing-down afterward.

"Now, the feast is a surprise, but I can allow you one peek through the keyhole before the guests arrive," said Gustav.

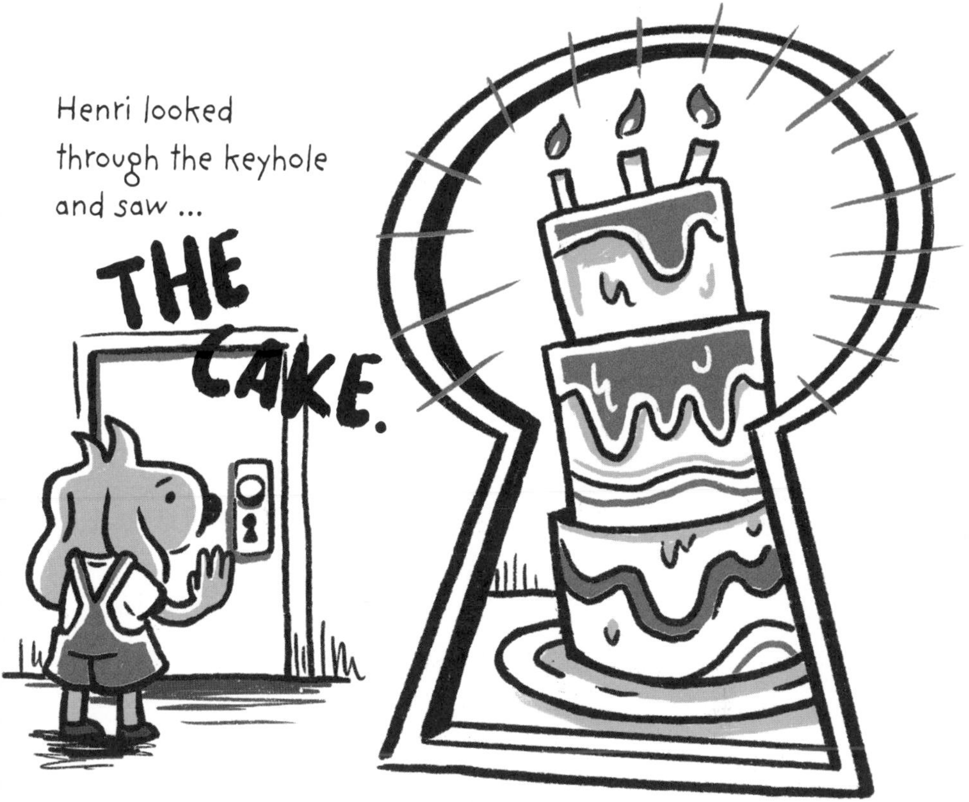
Henri looked through the keyhole and saw ...
THE CAKE.

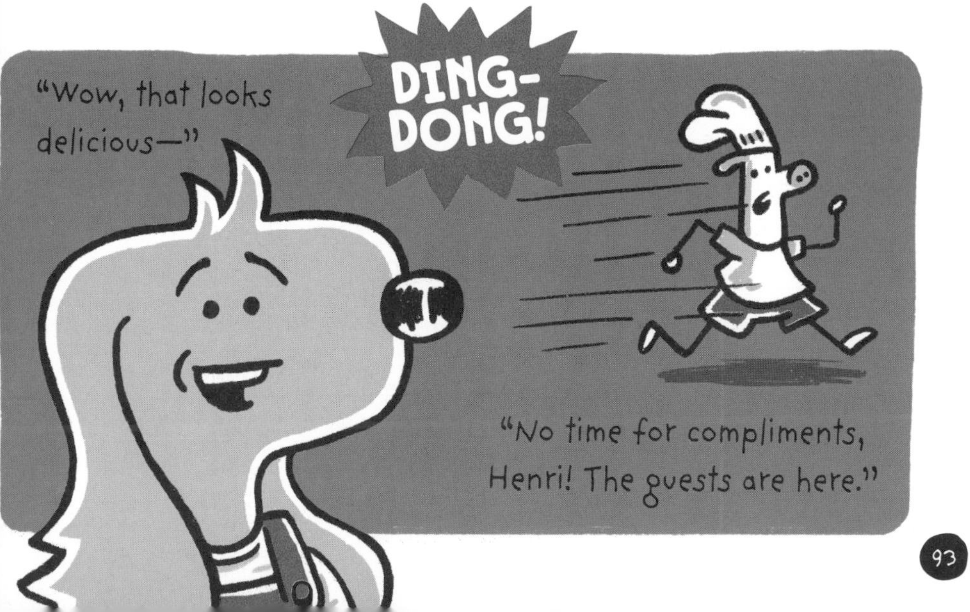
"Wow, that looks delicious—"
DING-DONG!
"No time for compliments, Henri! The guests are here."

The door opened and in sauntered:

# KING STEVE THE BEST, KING OF THE MOON.

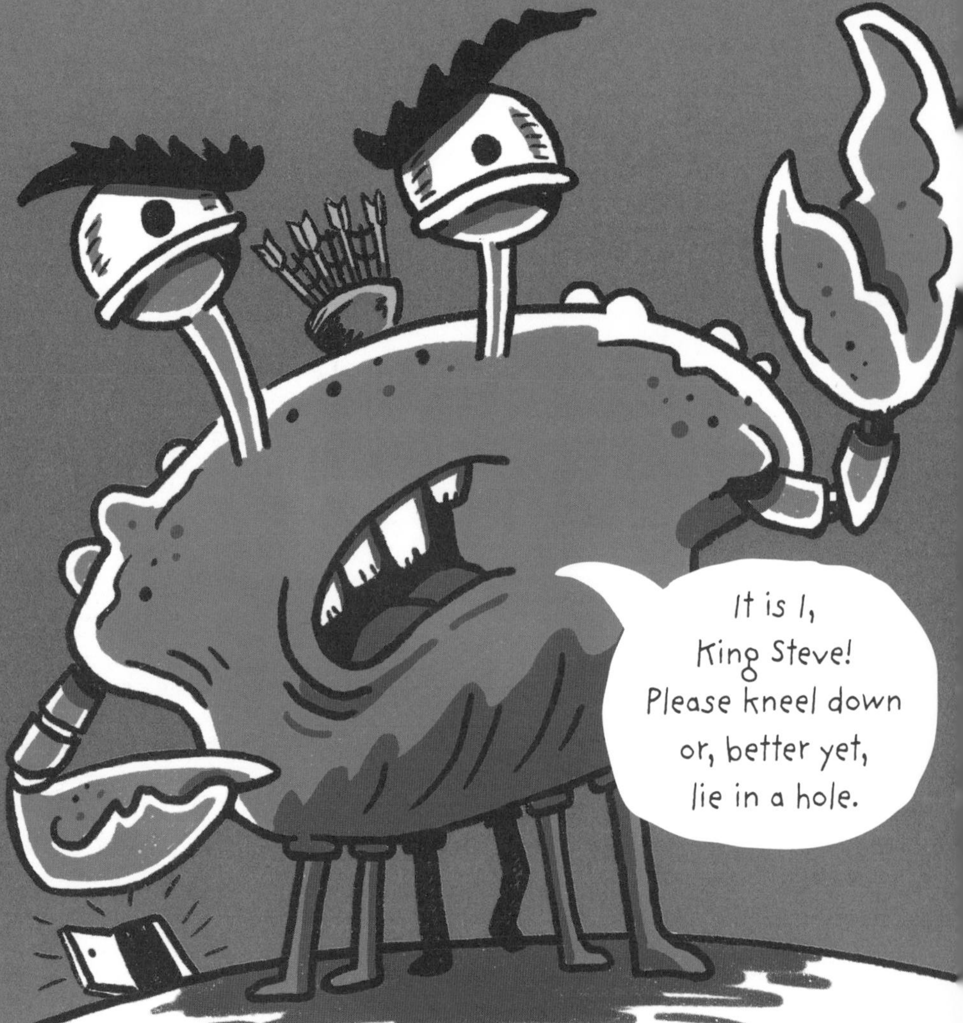
It is I, King Steve! Please kneel down or, better yet, lie in a hole.

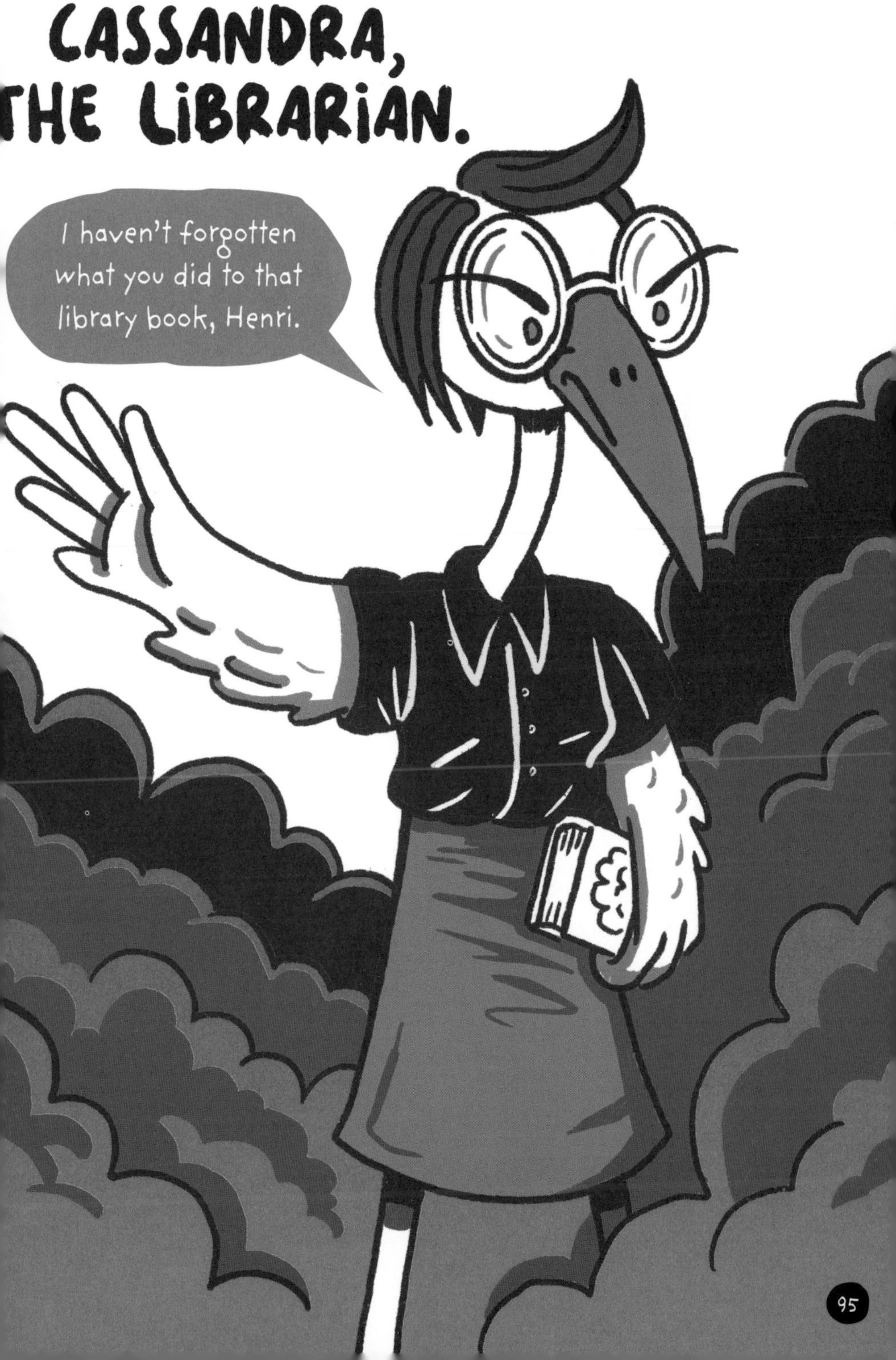
CASSANDRA,
THE LIBRARIAN.
I haven't forgotten what you did to that library book, Henri.

And Robert Swan.

I don't know either of you. I think I got this invitation by mistake.

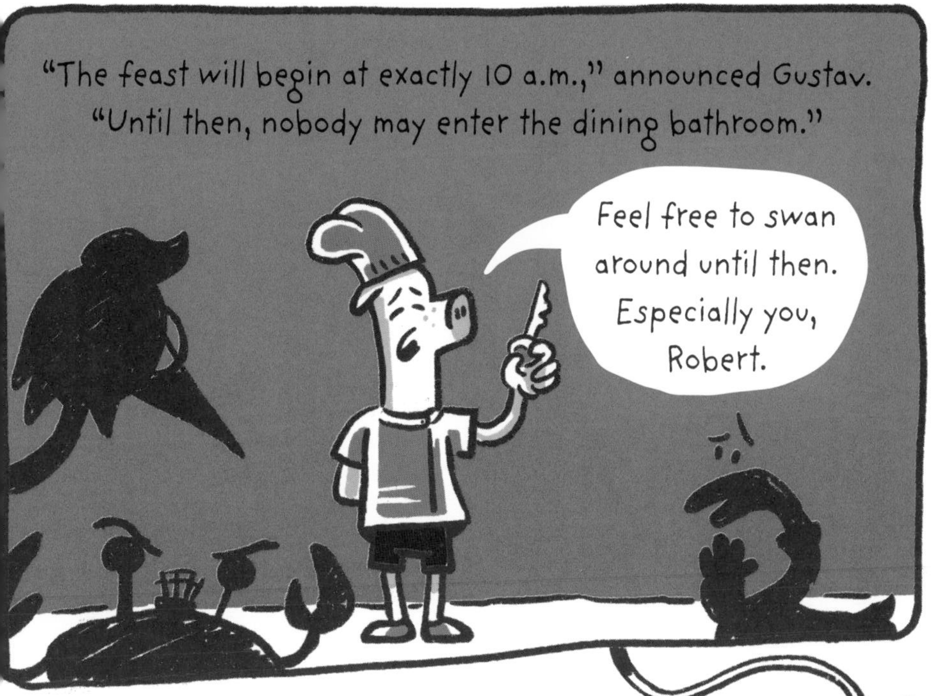
"The feast will begin at exactly 10 a.m.," announced Gustav. "Until then, nobody may enter the dining bathroom."
Feel free to swan around until then. Especially you, Robert.

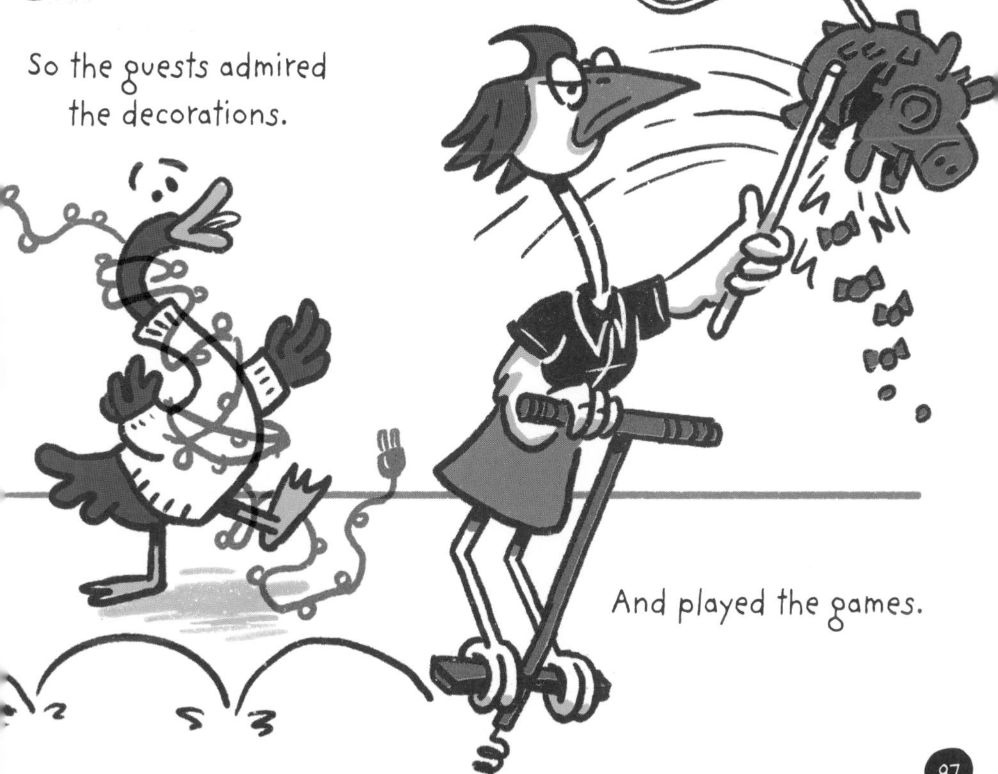
So the guests admired the decorations.
And played the games.

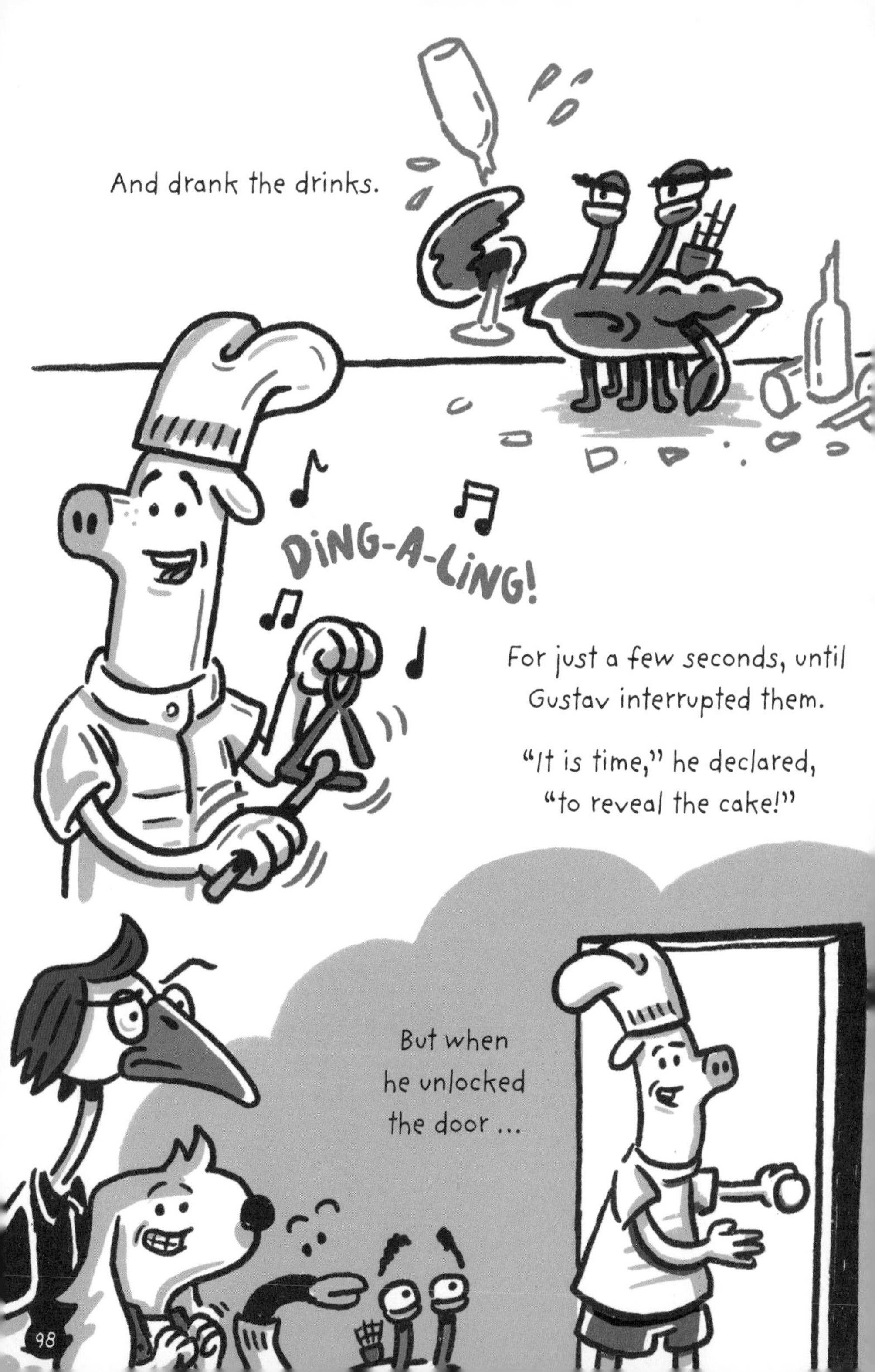
And drank the drinks.
DING-A-LING!
For just a few seconds, until Gustav interrupted them.
"It is time," he declared, "to reveal the cake!"
But when he unlocked the door ...

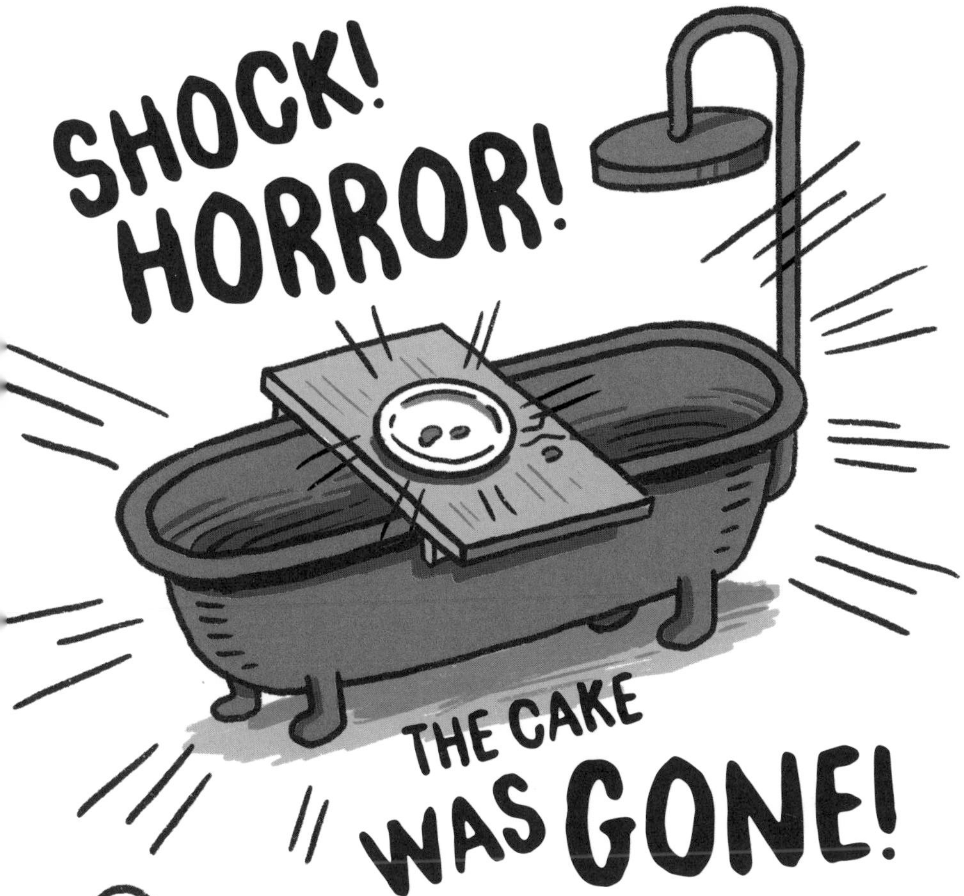
SHOCK! HORROR!
THE CAKE WAS GONE!

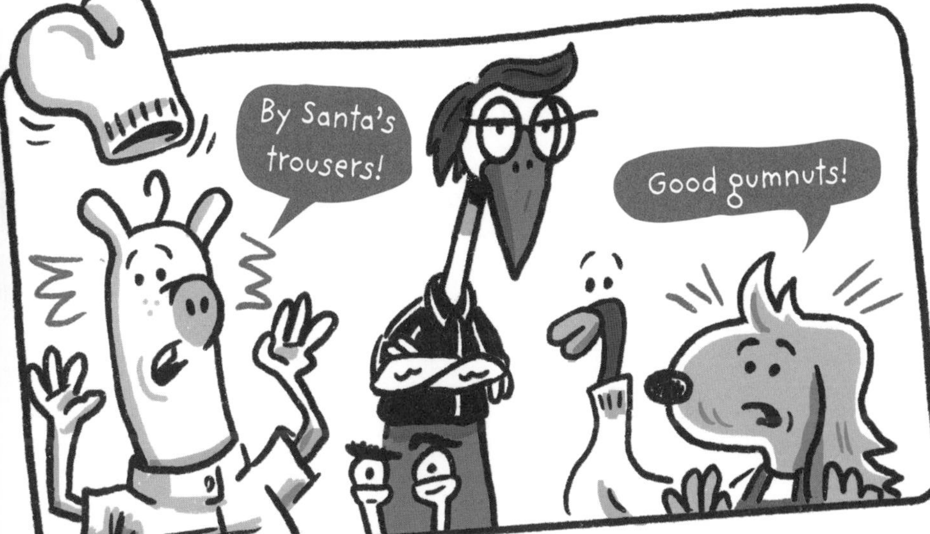
By Santa's trousers!
Good gumnuts!

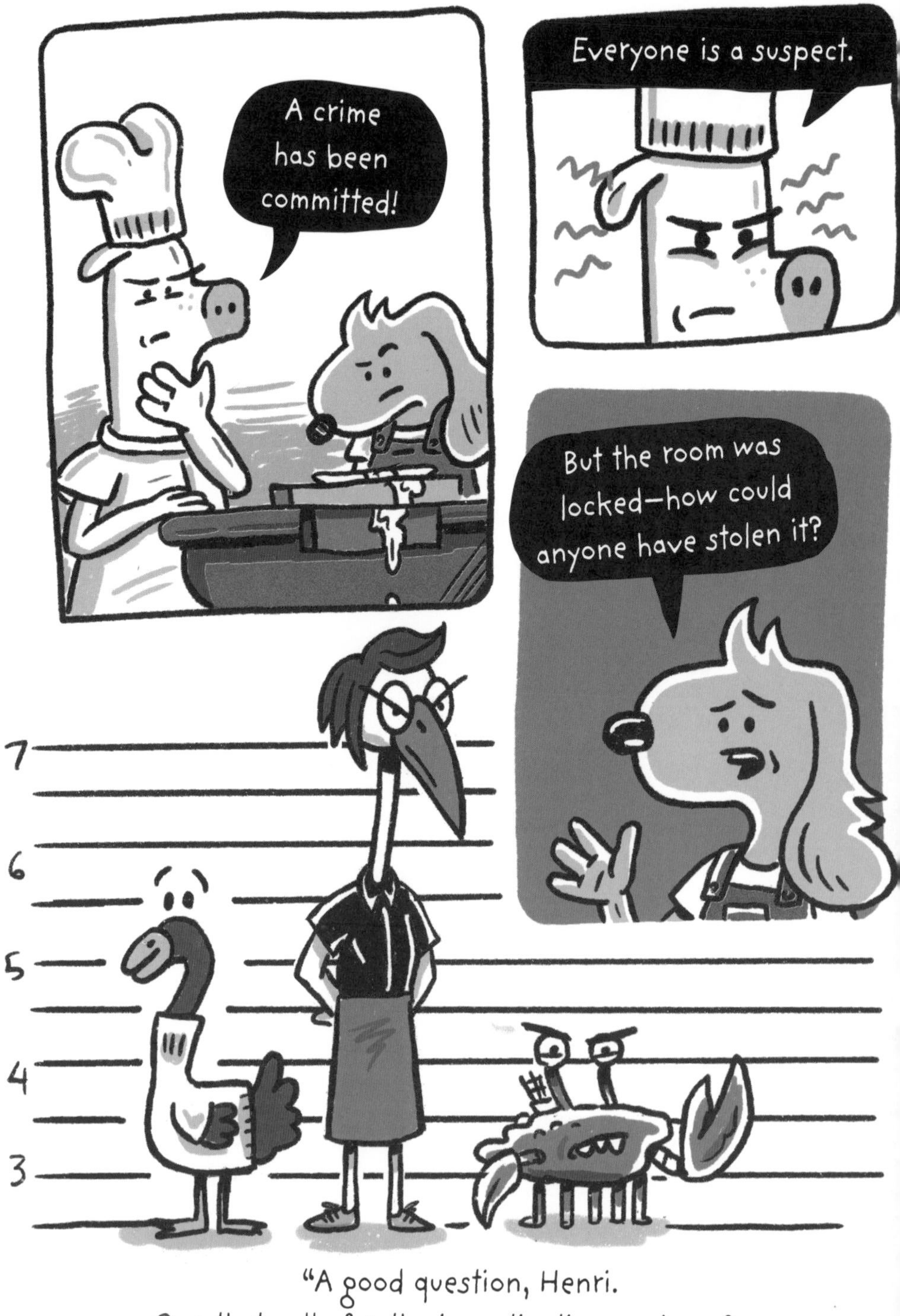
A crime has been committed!
Everyone is a suspect.
But the room was locked—how could anyone have stolen it?
7
6
5
4
3

"A good question, Henri.
One that calls for the investigative genius of ...

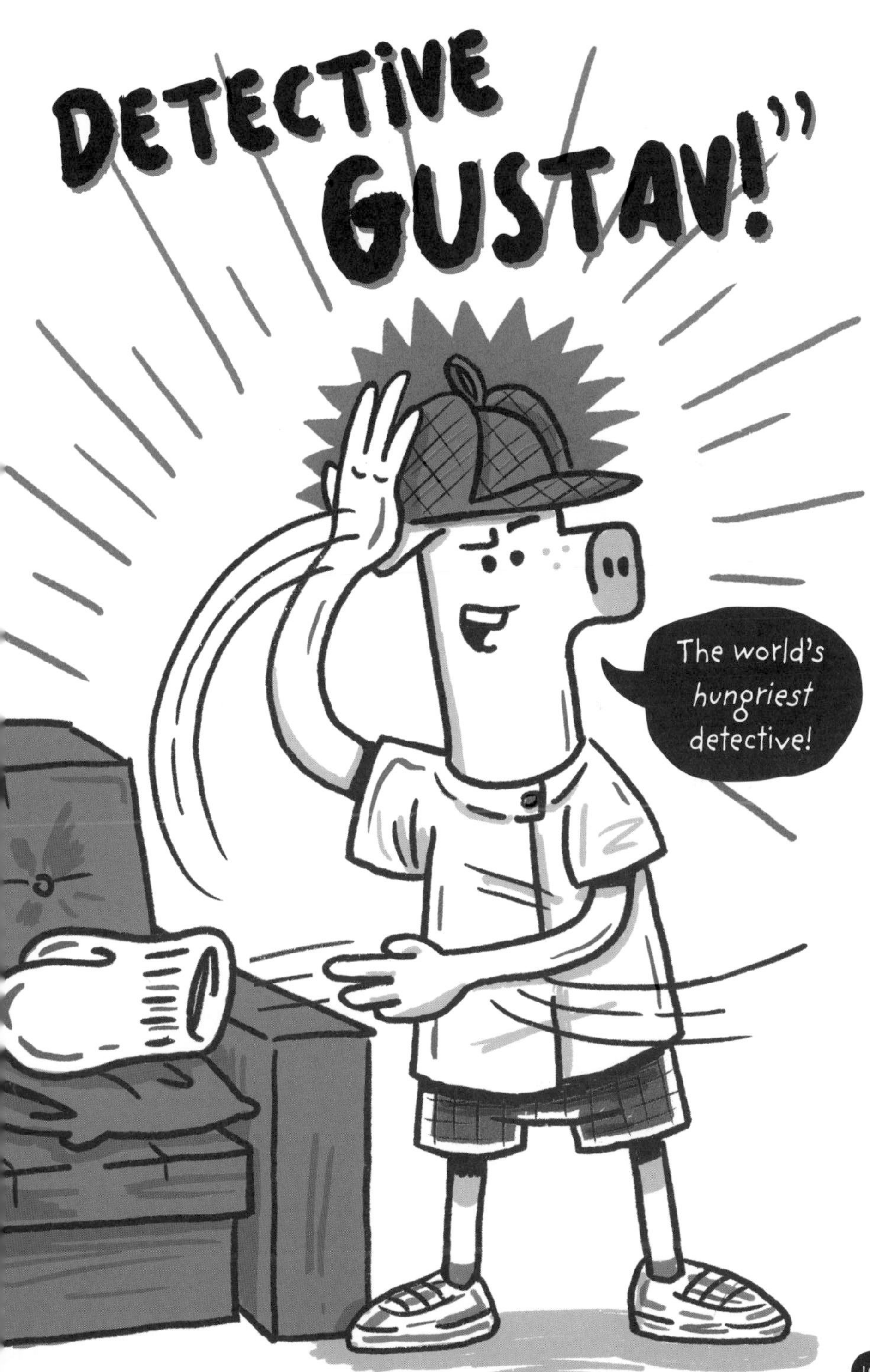
DETECTIVE GUSTAV!"
The world's hungriest detective!

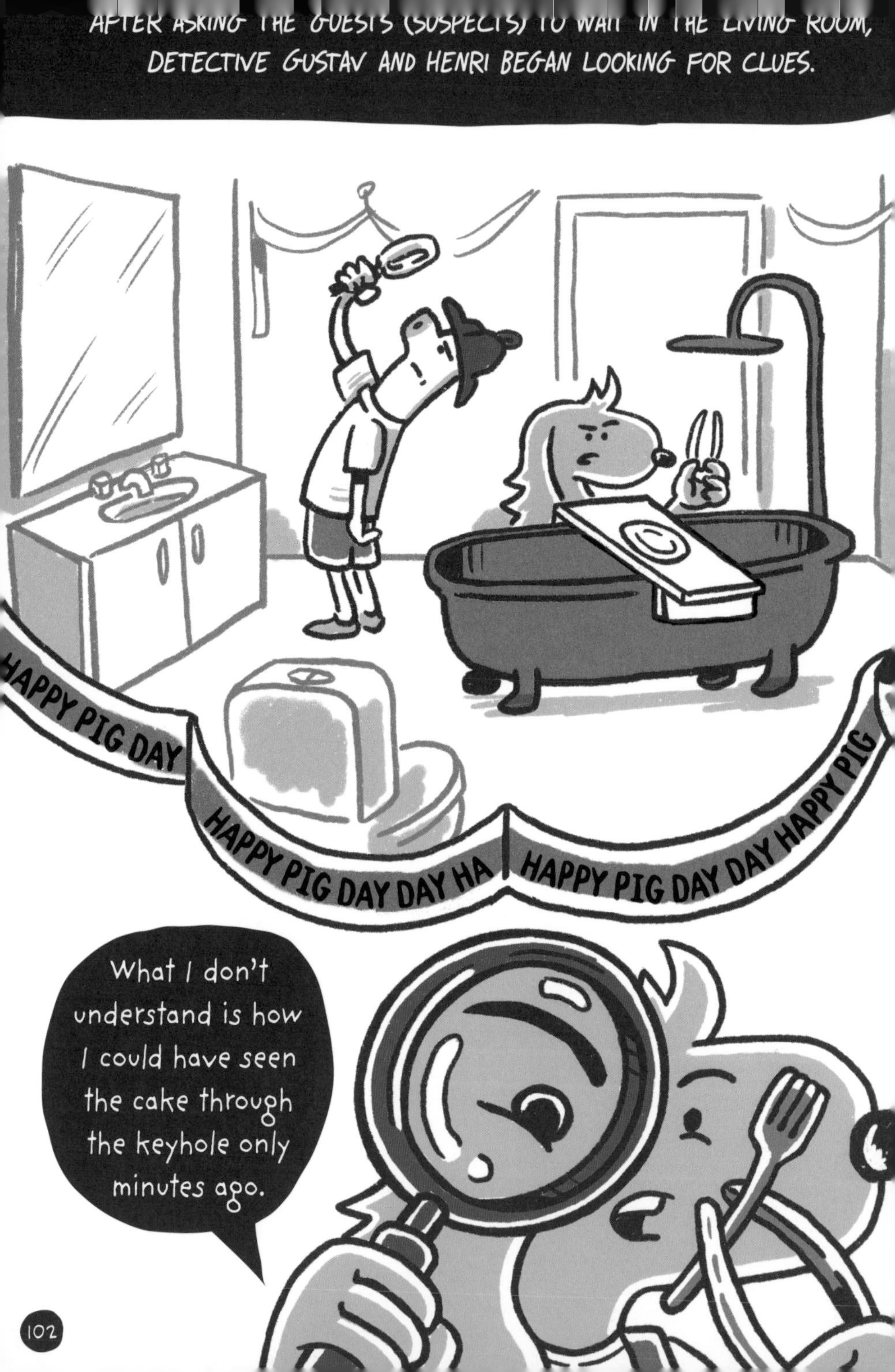
AFTER ASKING THE GUESTS (SUSPECTS) TO WAIT IN THE LIVING ROOM, DETECTIVE GUSTAV AND HENRI BEGAN LOOKING FOR CLUES.
HAPPY PIG DAY
HAPPY PIG DAY DAY HA
HAPPY PIG DAY DAY HAPPY PIG
What I don't understand is how I could have seen the cake through the keyhole only minutes ago.

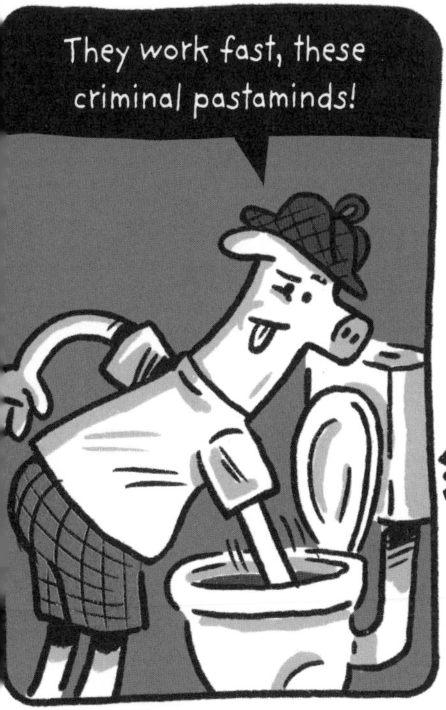
They work fast, these criminal pastaminds!

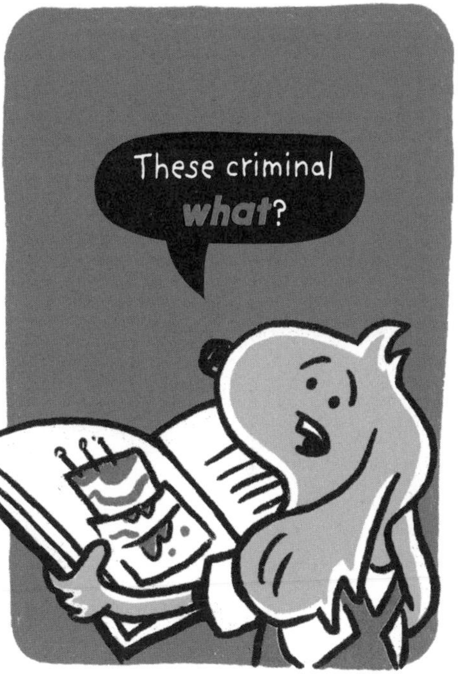
These criminal **what**?

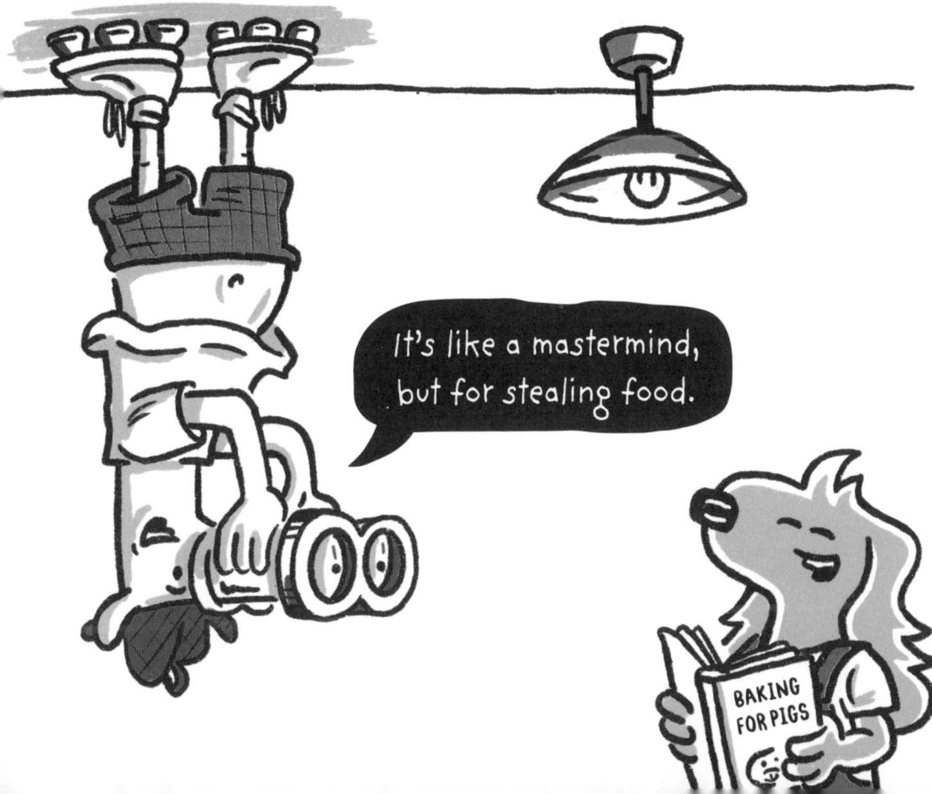
It's like a mastermind, but for stealing food.
BAKING FOR PIGS

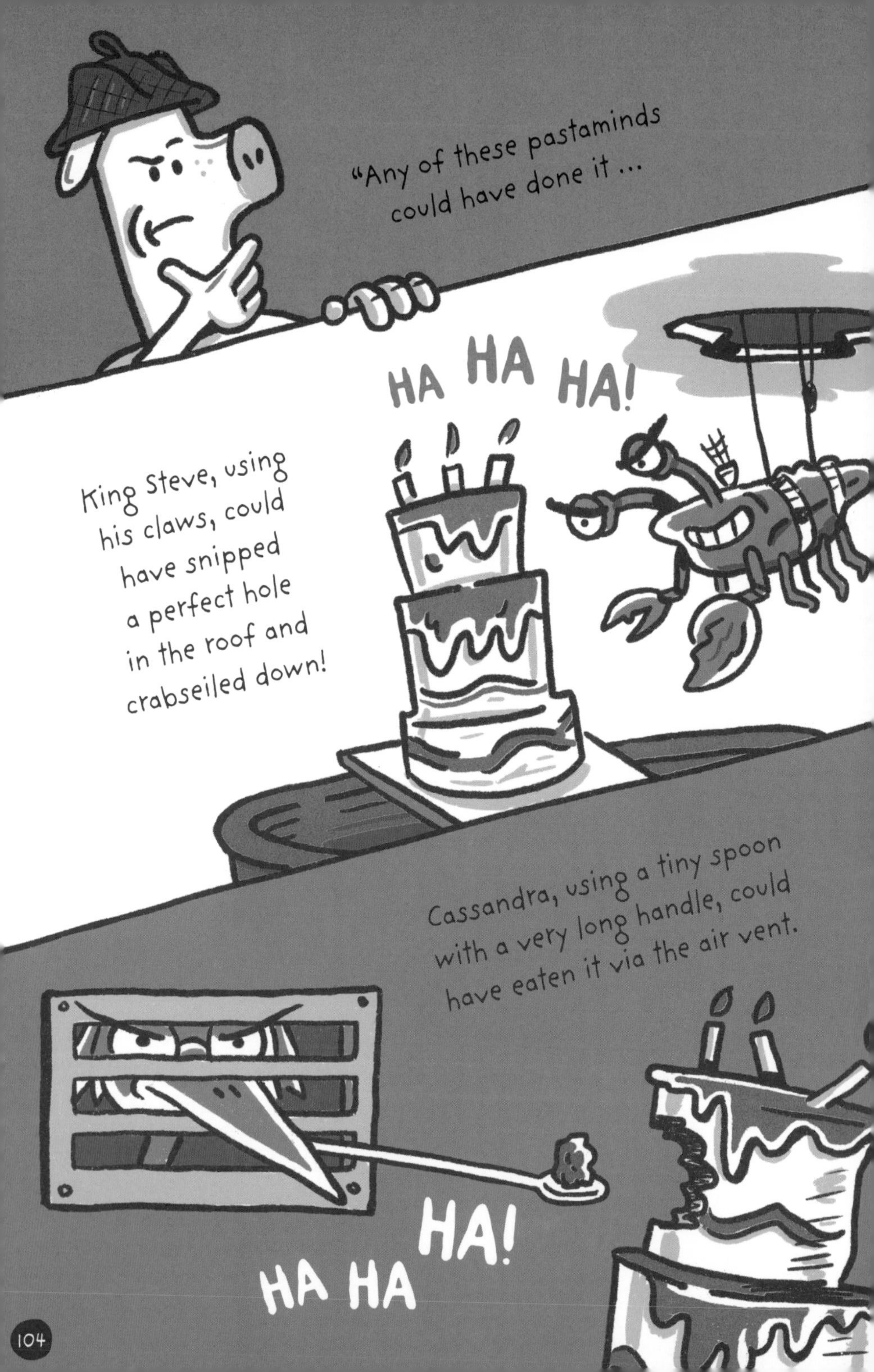
"Any of these pastaminds could have done it ...
HA HA HA!
King Steve, using his claws, could have snipped a perfect hole in the roof and crabseiled down!
Cassandra, using a tiny spoon with a very long handle, could have eaten it via the air vent.
HA HA HA!

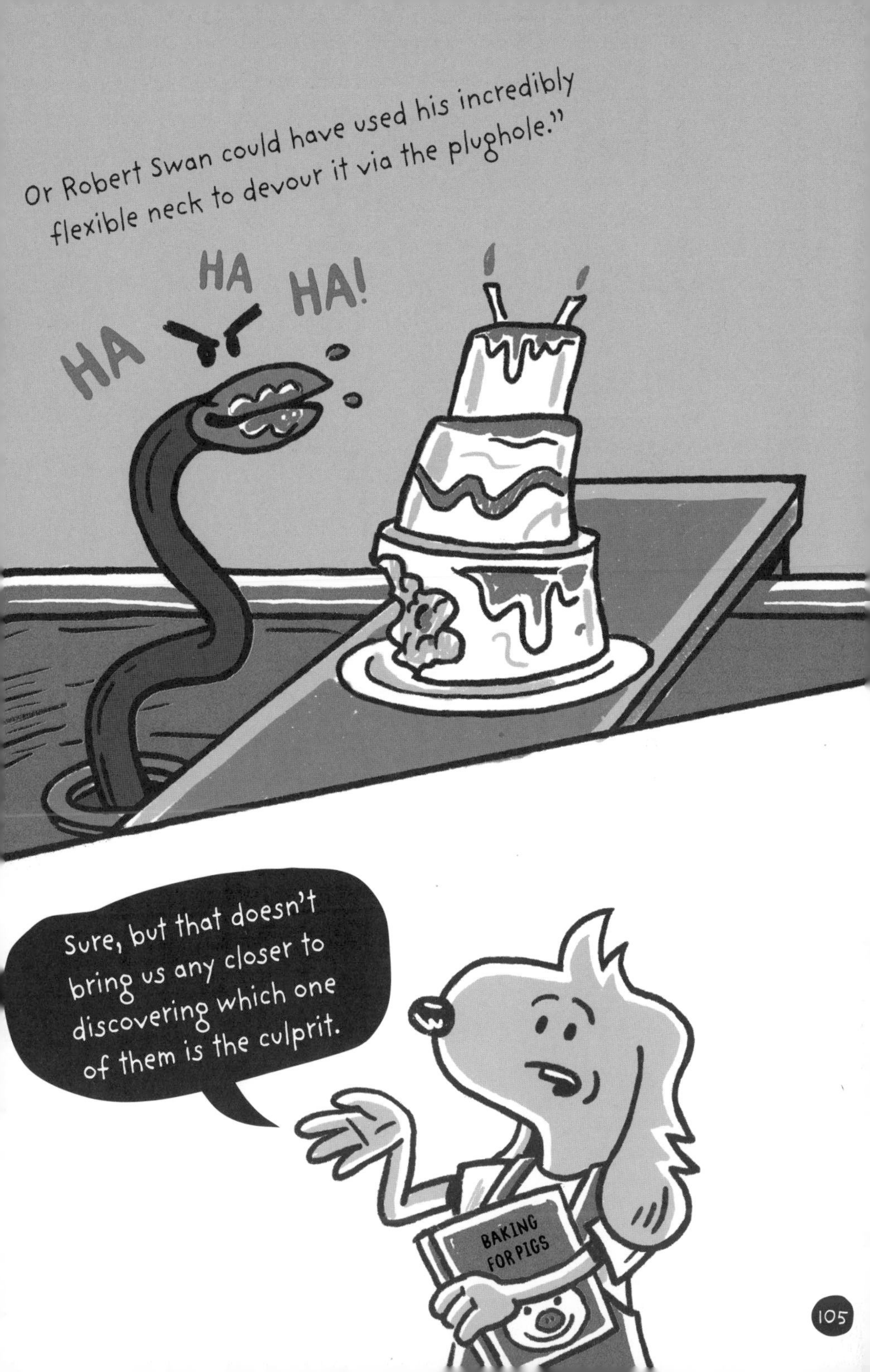
Or Robert Swan could have used his incredibly flexible neck to devour it via the plughole."
HA HA HA!
Sure, but that doesn't bring us any closer to discovering which one of them is the culprit.
BAKING FOR PIGS

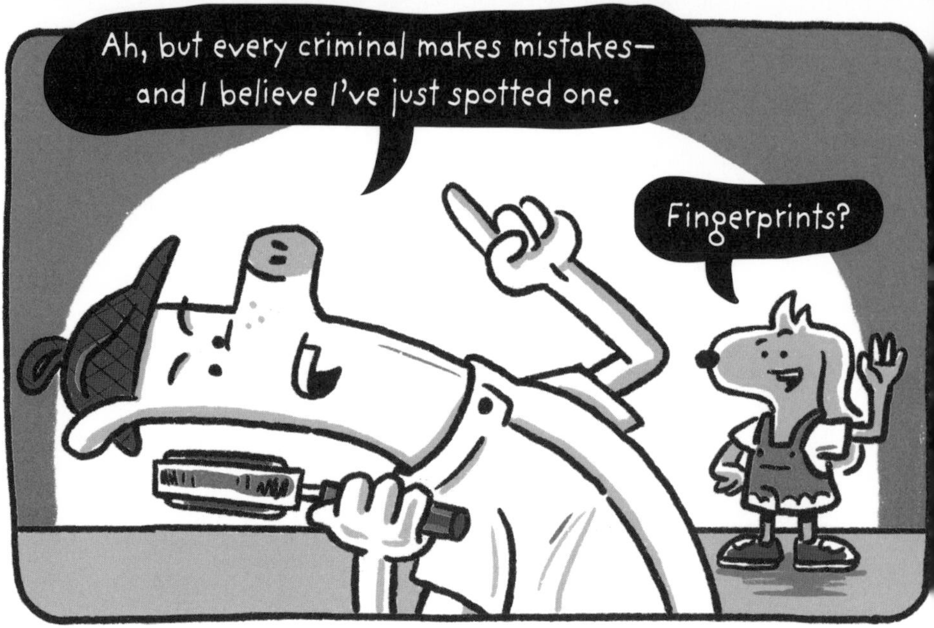
Ah, but every criminal makes mistakes—
and I believe I've just spotted one.
Fingerprints?

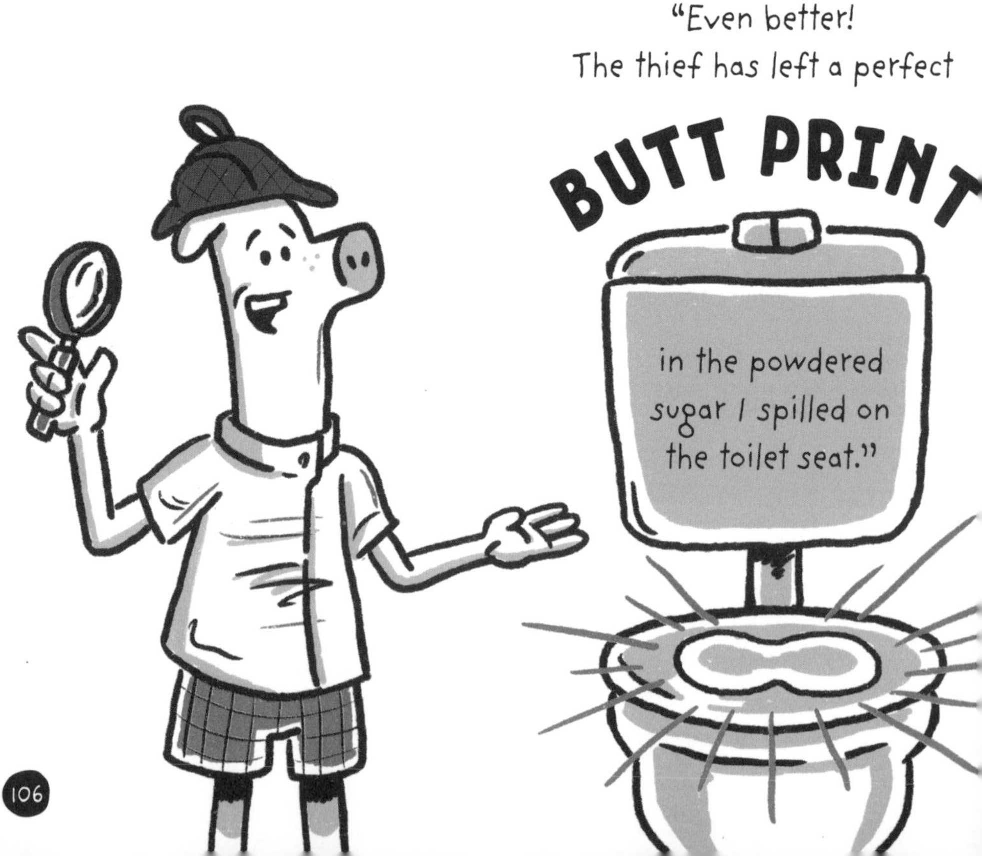
"Even better!
The thief has left a perfect
BUTT PRINT
in the powdered sugar I spilled on the toilet seat."

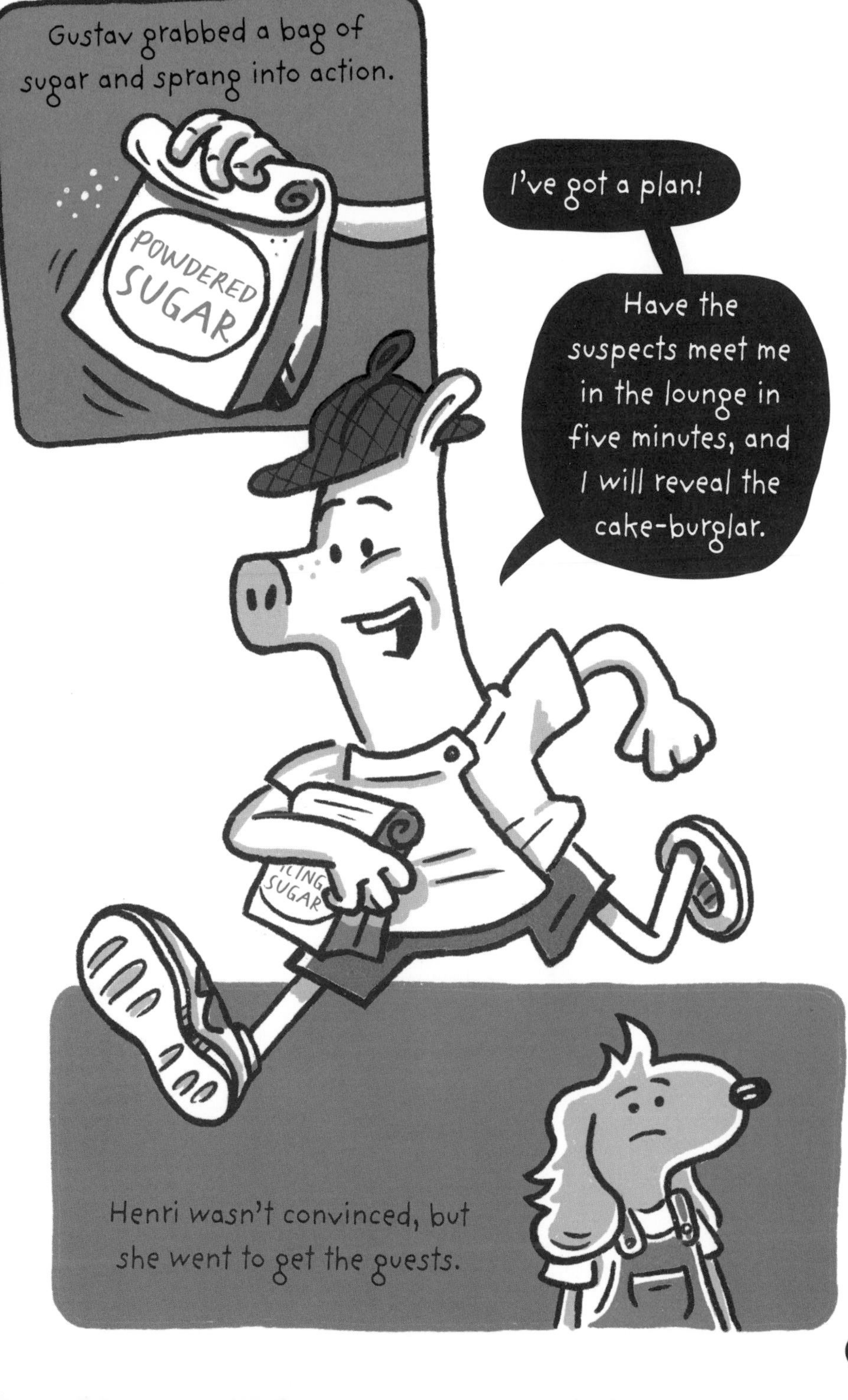
Gustav grabbed a bag of sugar and sprang into action.
POWDERED SUGAR
I've got a plan!
Have the suspects meet me in the lounge in five minutes, and I will reveal the cake-burglar.
Henri wasn't convinced, but she went to get the guests.

When everyone entered, Gustav was leaning on the mantlepiece.

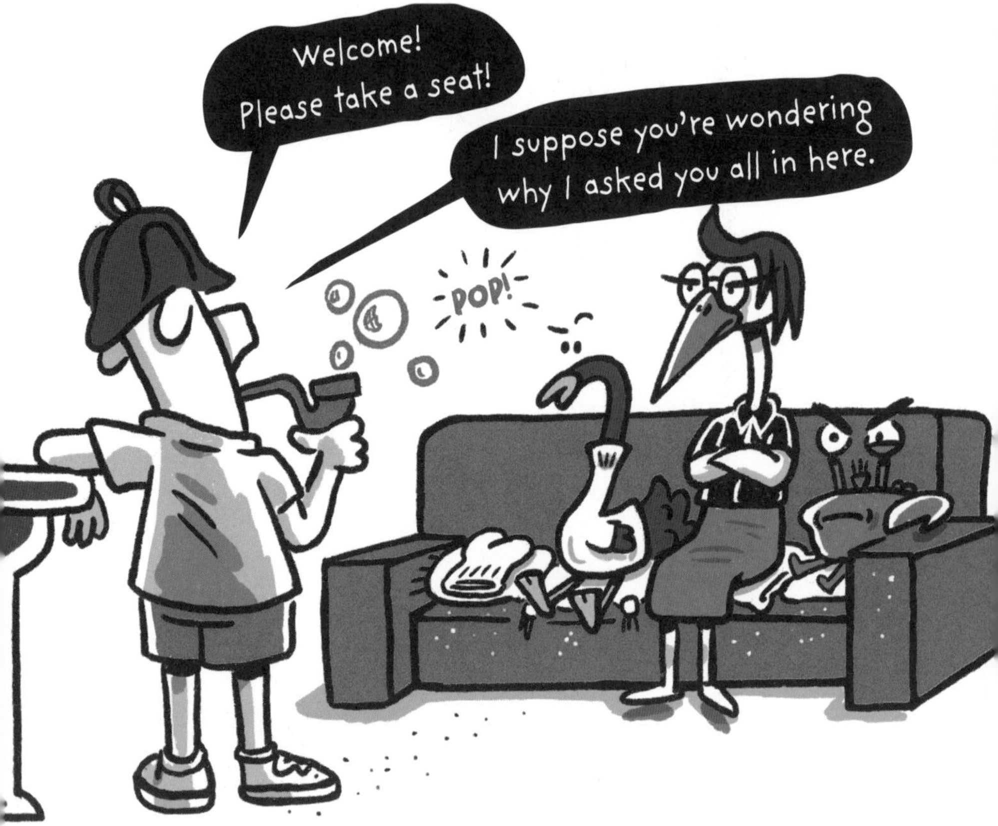
Welcome!
Please take a seat!
I suppose you're wondering why I asked you all in here.
POP!

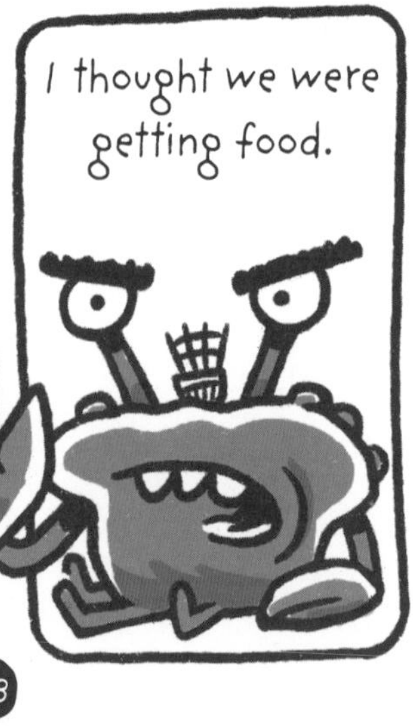
I thought we were getting food.

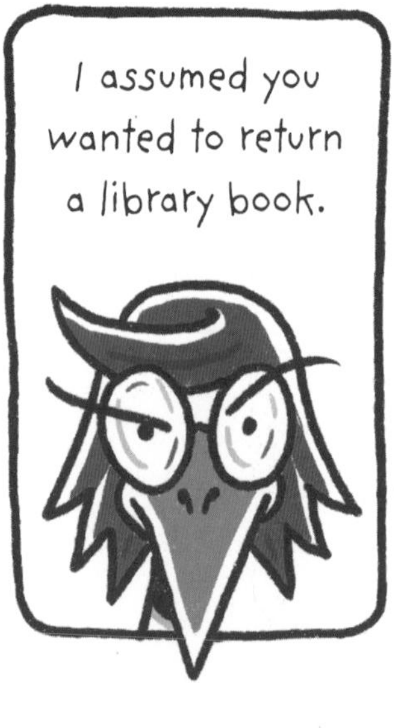
I assumed you wanted to return a library book.

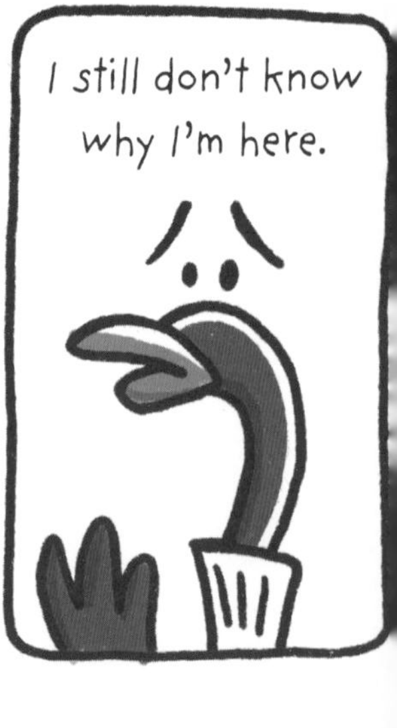
I still don't know why I'm here.

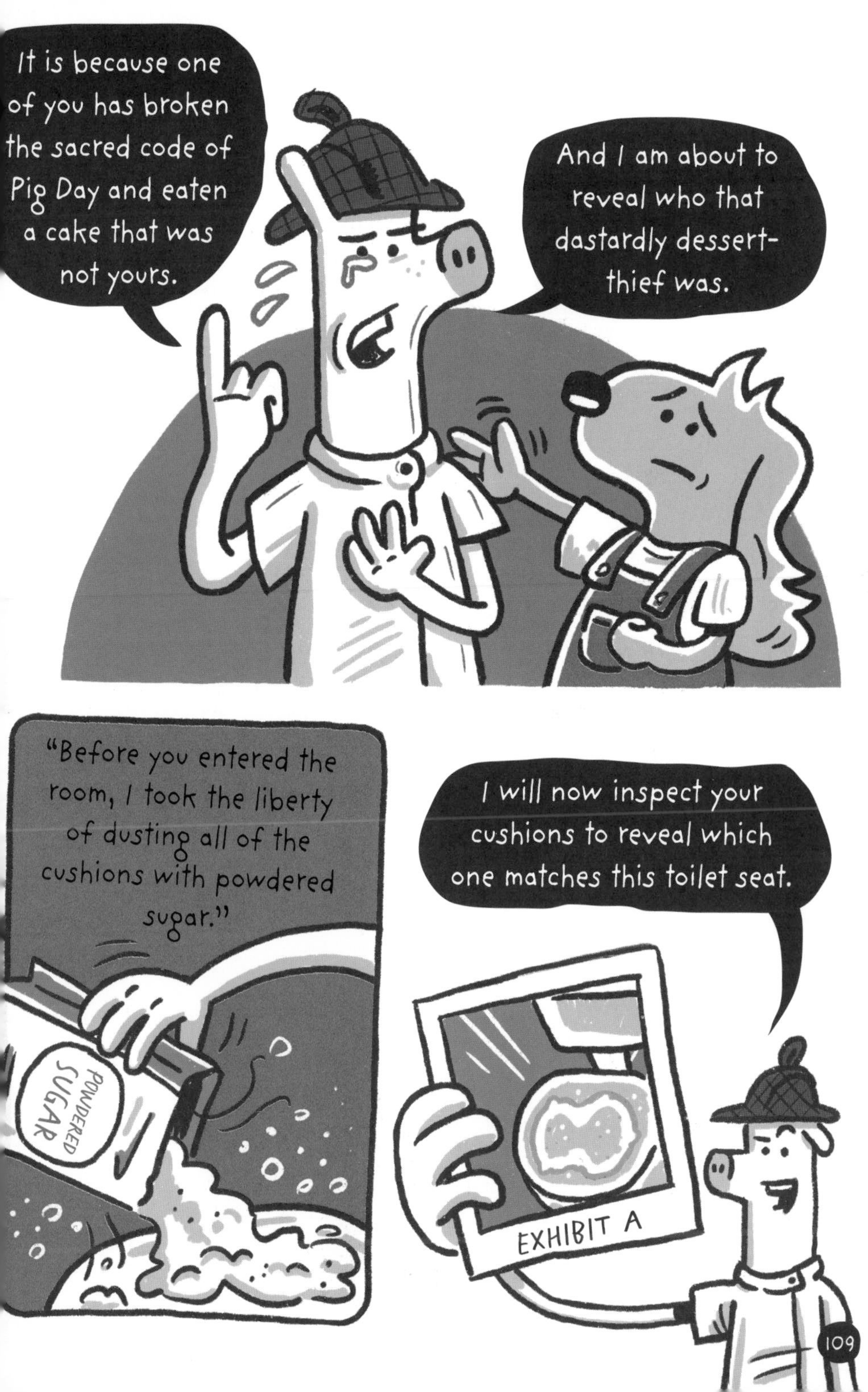
It is because one of you has broken the sacred code of Pig Day and eaten a cake that was not yours.
And I am about to reveal who that dastardly dessert-thief was.
"Before you entered the room, I took the liberty of dusting all of the cushions with powdered sugar."
POWDERED SUGAR
I will now inspect your cushions to reveal which one matches this toilet seat.
EXHIBIT A

Gustav revealed the cushions one by one.

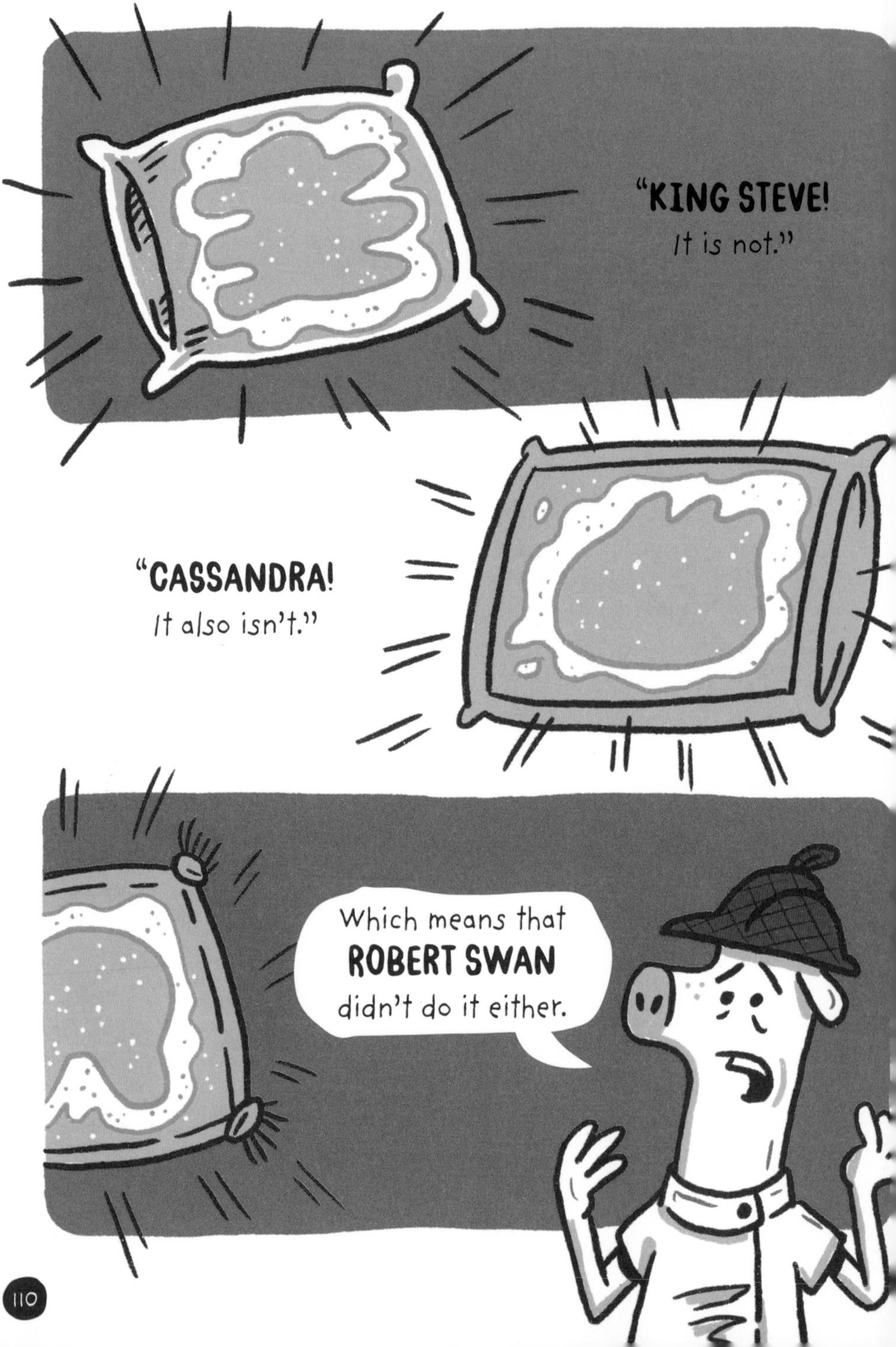
"KING STEVE!
It is not."
"CASSANDRA!
It also isn't."
Which means that ROBERT SWAN didn't do it either.

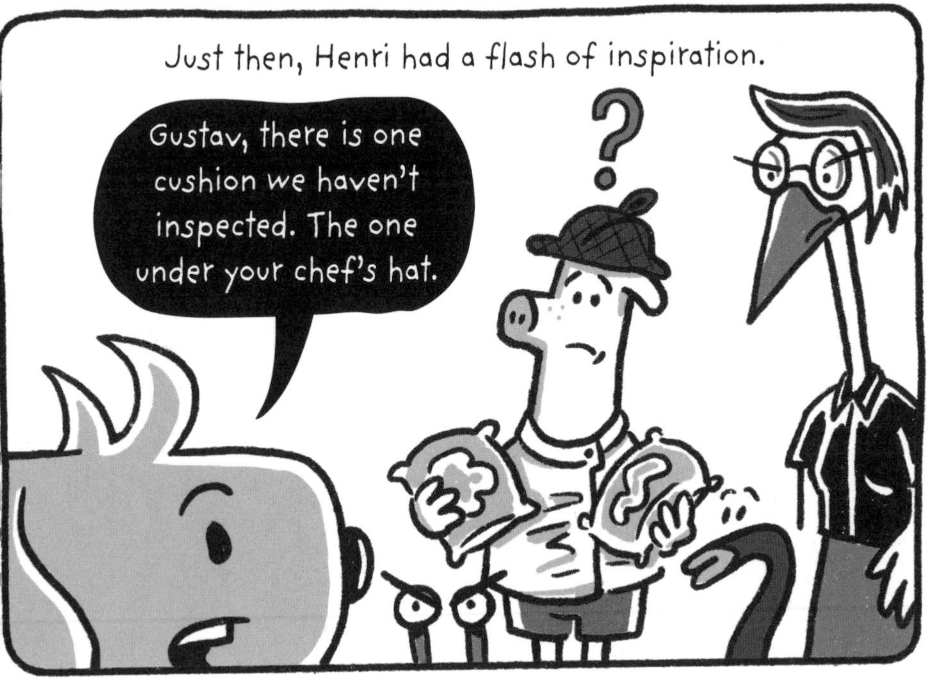
Just then, Henri had a flash of inspiration.
Gustav, there is one cushion we haven't inspected. The one under your chef's hat.

And when she lifted it up, the print was a ***perfect match***.

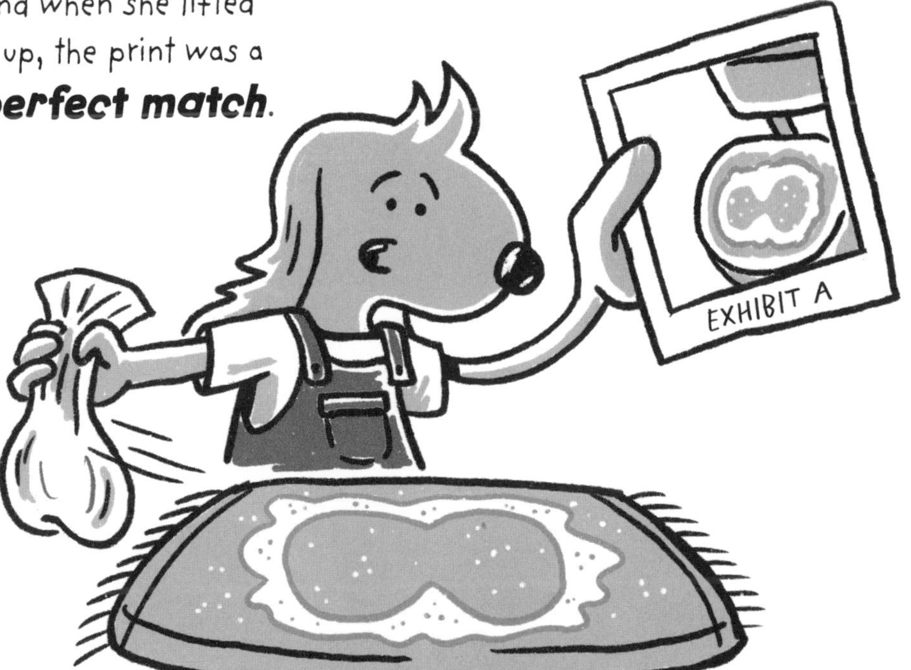
EXHIBIT A

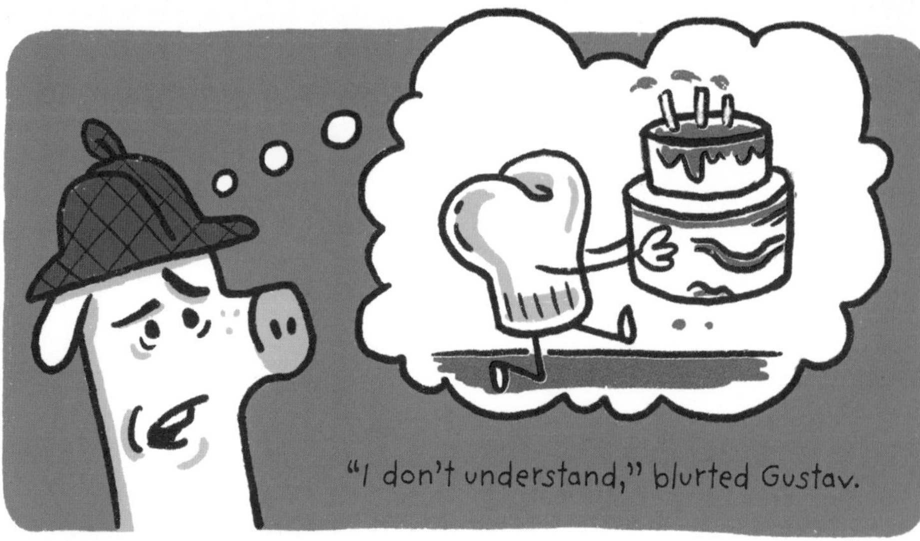
"I don't understand," blurted Gustav.

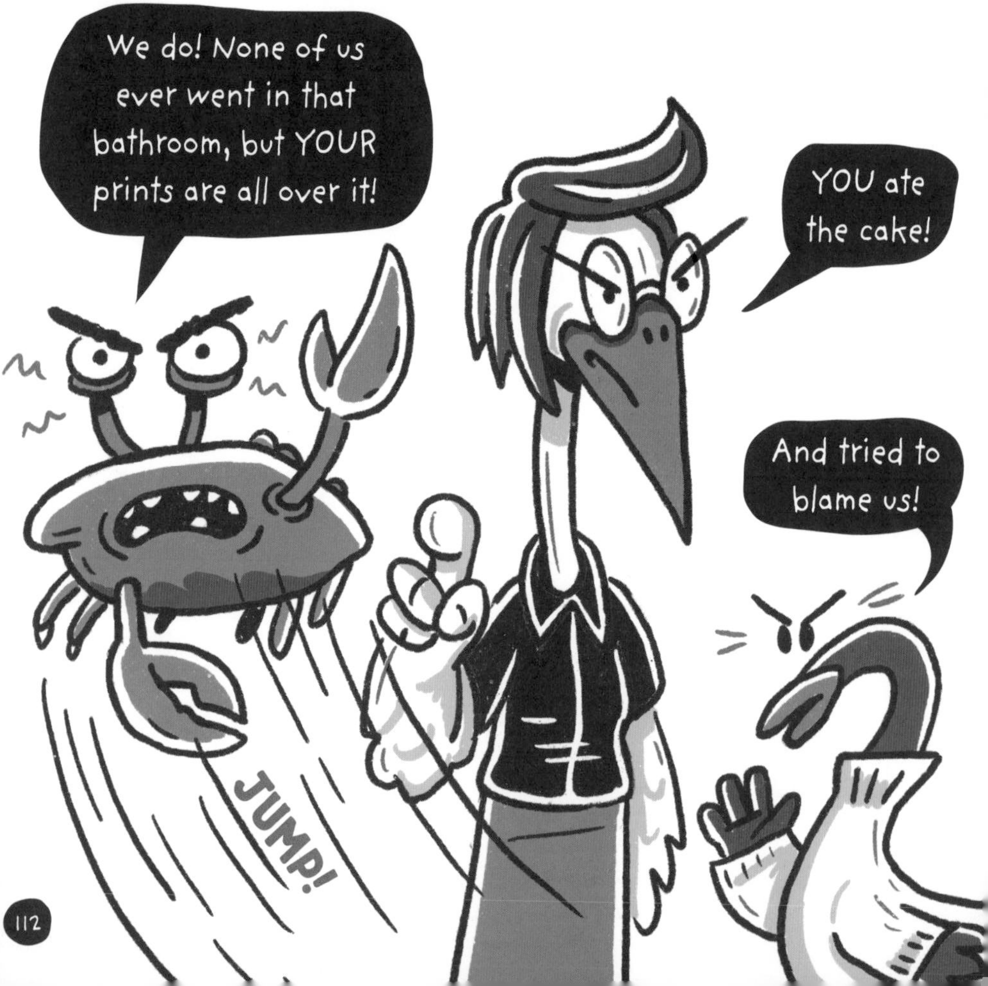
We do! None of us ever went in that bathroom, but YOUR prints are all over it!
YOU ate the cake!
And tried to blame us!
JUMP!

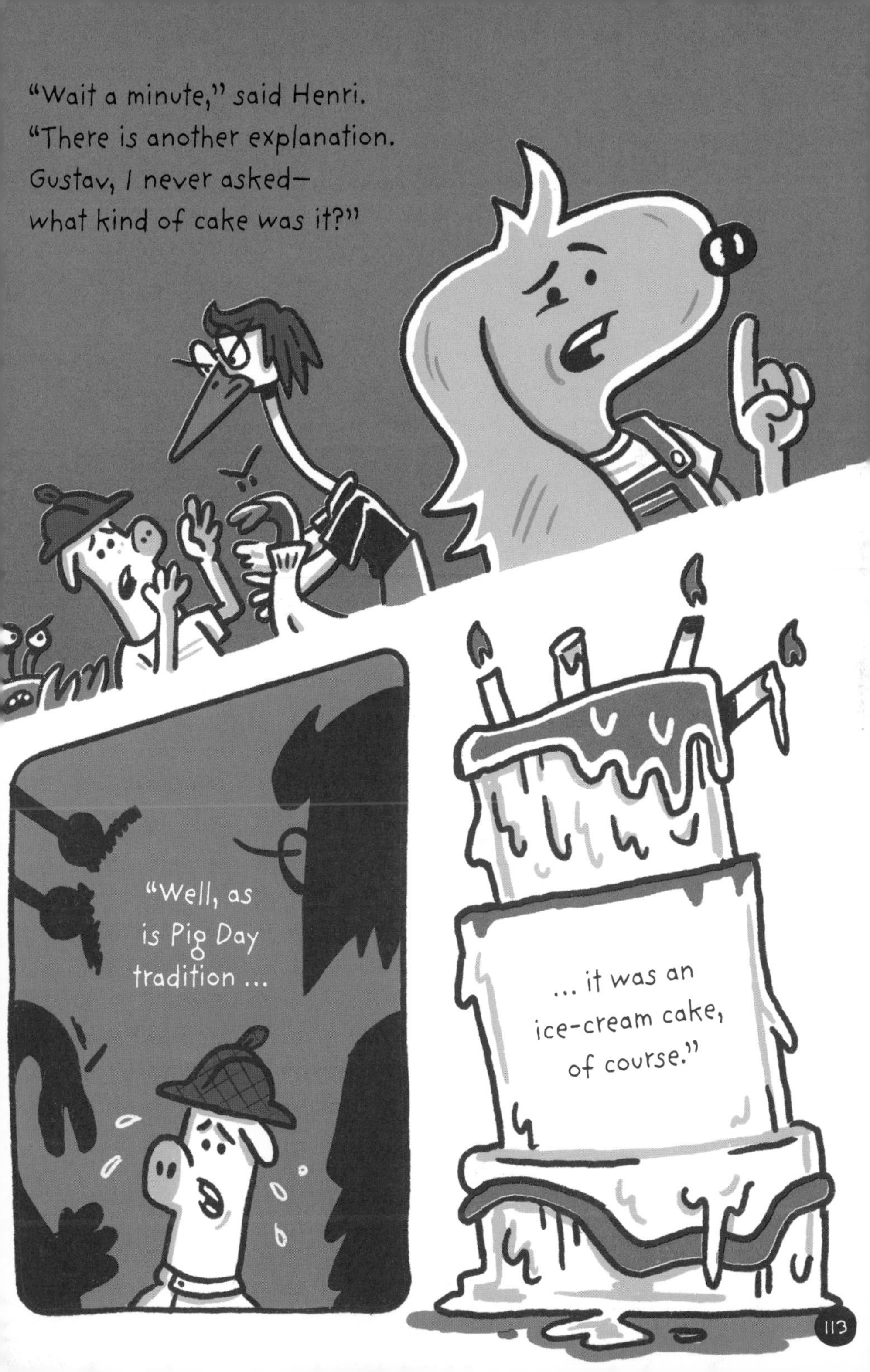
"Wait a minute," said Henri. "There is another explanation. Gustav, I never asked—what kind of cake was it?"
"Well, as is Pig Day tradition ...
... it was an ice-cream cake, of course."

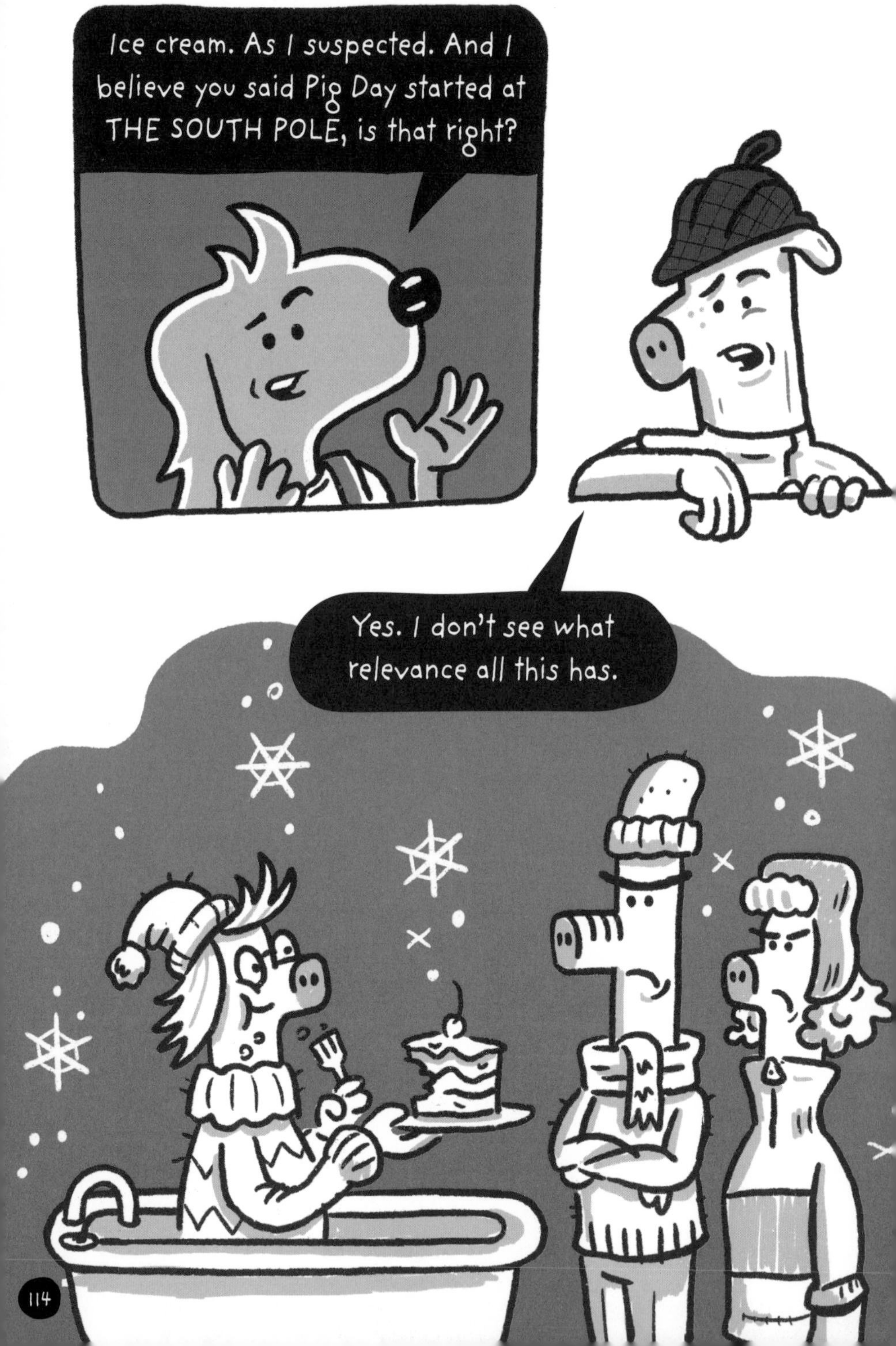
Ice cream. As I suspected. And I believe you said Pig Day started at THE SOUTH POLE, is that right?
Yes. I don't see what relevance all this has.

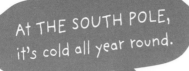

At THE SOUTH POLE, it's cold all year round.

But it's not icy here at all— it's the middle of summer.

And summer isn't cold. In fact, it is ... HOT.

I see ... and so the cake ...

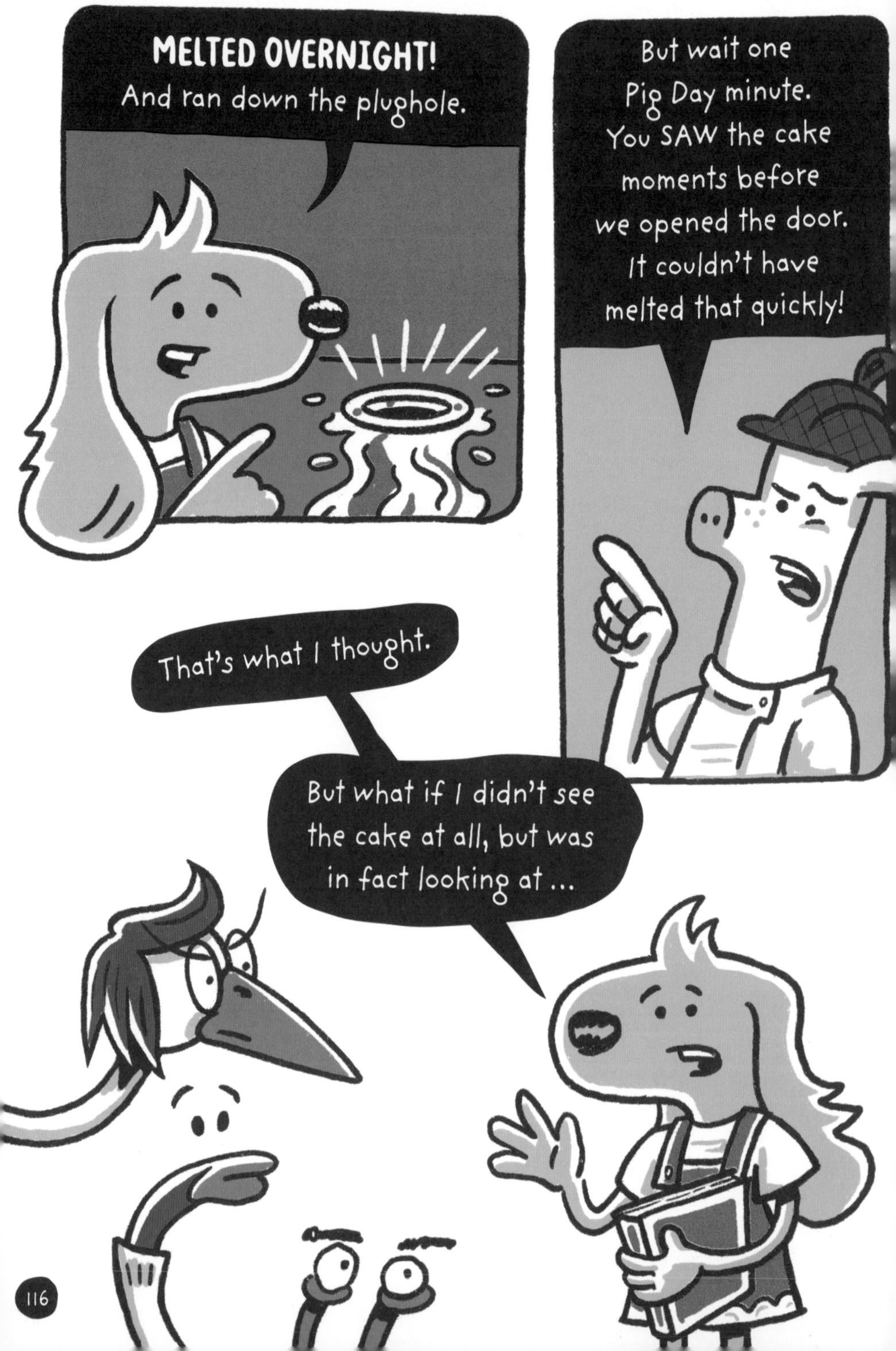

MELTED OVERNIGHT! And ran down the plughole.
But wait one Pig Day minute. You SAW the cake moments before we opened the door. It couldn't have melted that quickly!
That's what I thought.
But what if I didn't see the cake at all, but was in fact looking at ...

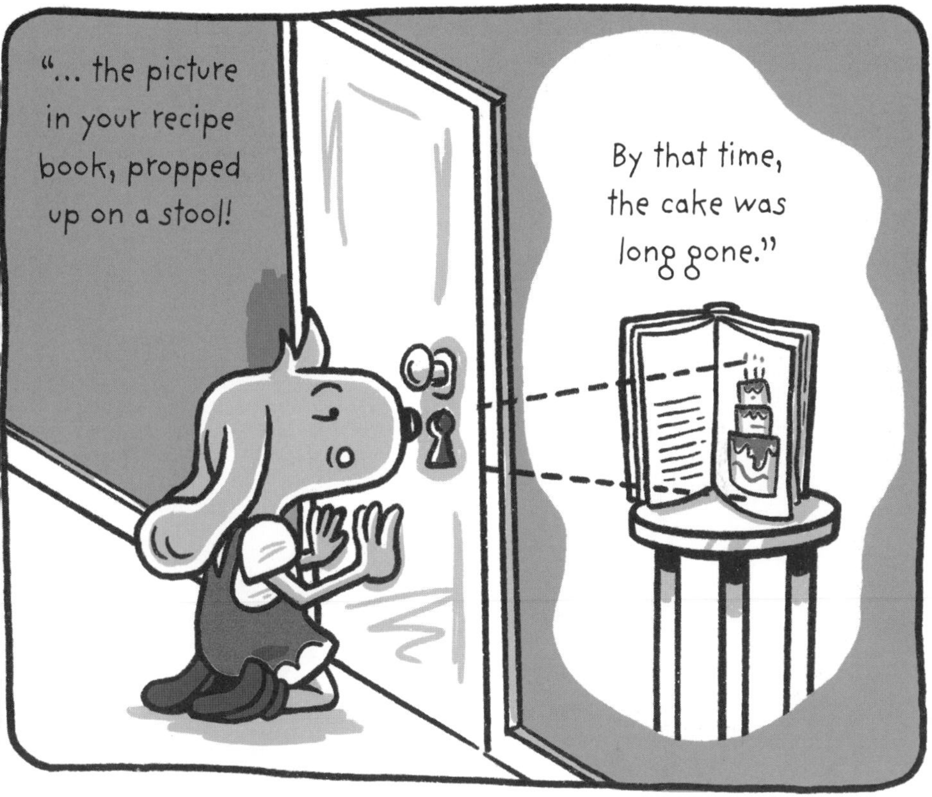
"... the picture in your recipe book, propped up on a stool!
By that time, the cake was long gone."

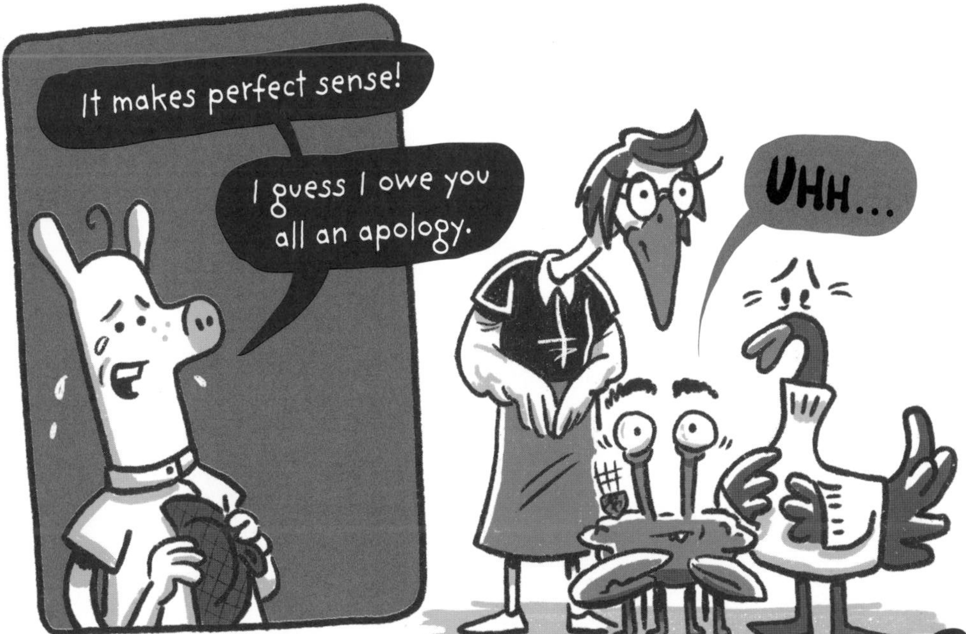
It makes perfect sense!
I guess I owe you all an apology.
UHH...

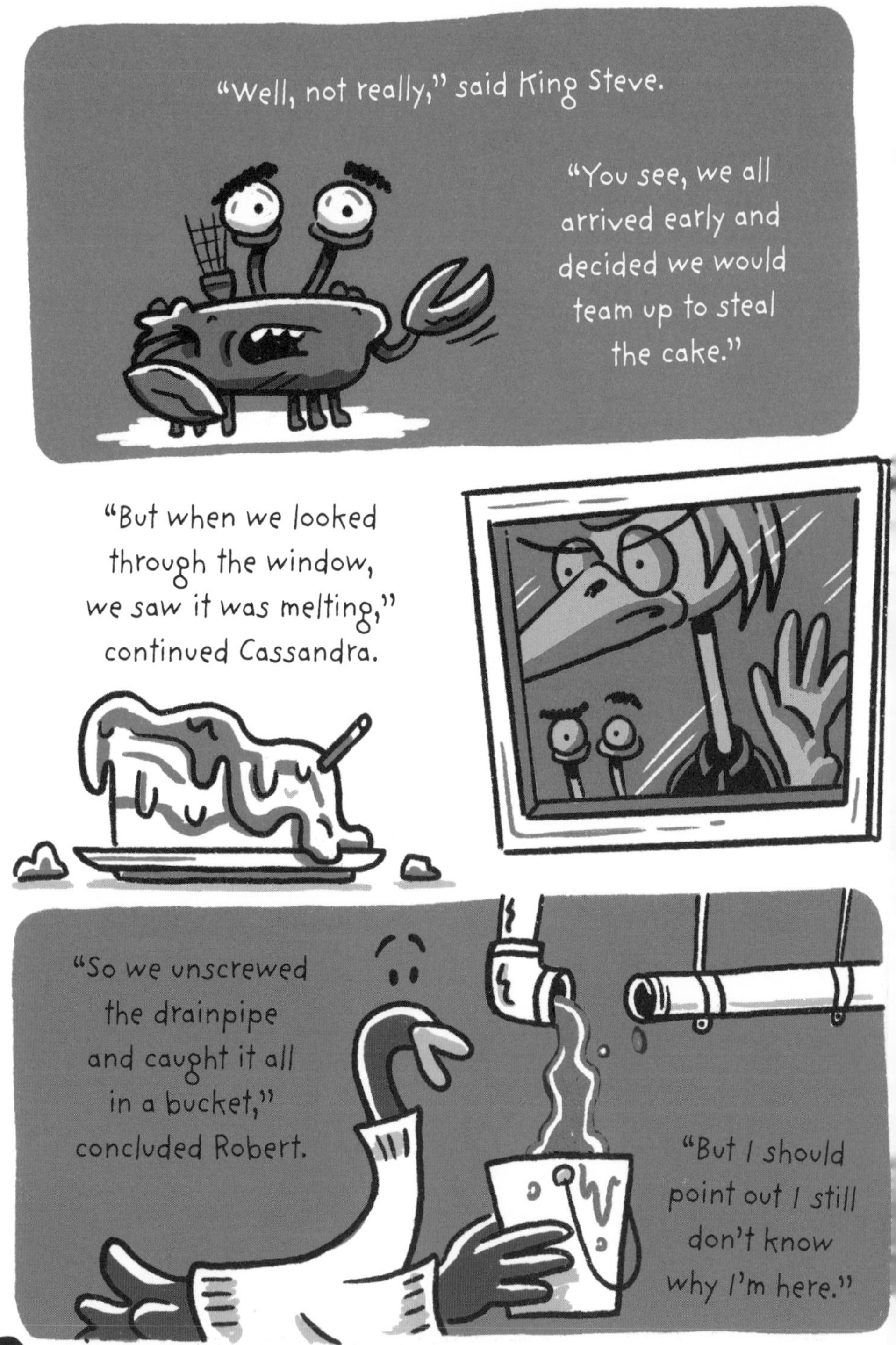
"Well, not really," said King Steve.
"You see, we all arrived early and decided we would team up to steal the cake."
"But when we looked through the window, we saw it was melting," continued Cassandra.
"So we unscrewed the drainpipe and caught it all in a bucket," concluded Robert.
"But I should point out I still don't know why I'm here."

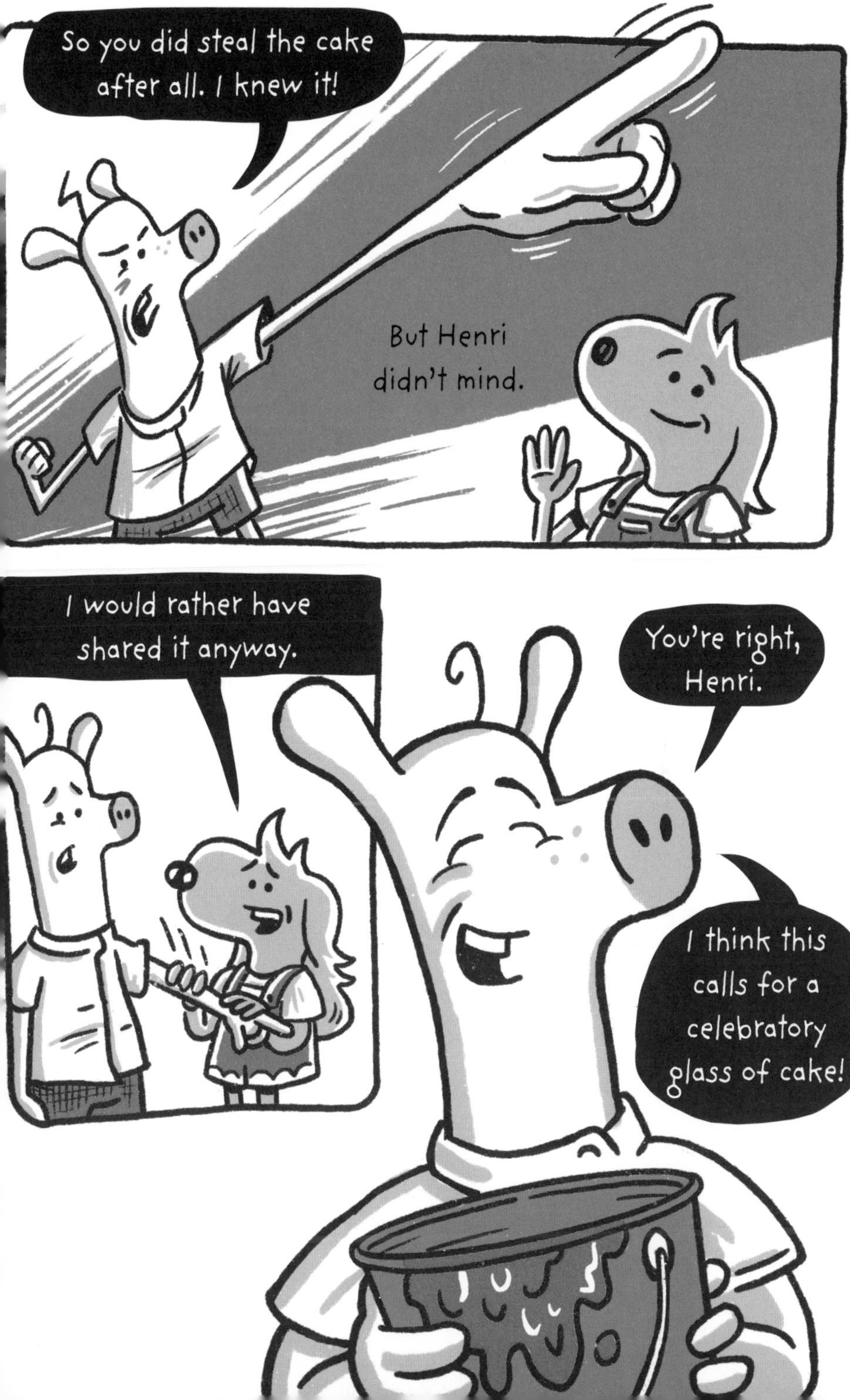
So you did steal the cake after all. I knew it!
But Henri didn't mind.
I would rather have shared it anyway.
You're right, Henri.
I think this calls for a celebratory glass of cake!

So they all drank melted ice-cream cake.
"Thanks for the best Pig Day ever, Gustav," said Henri.

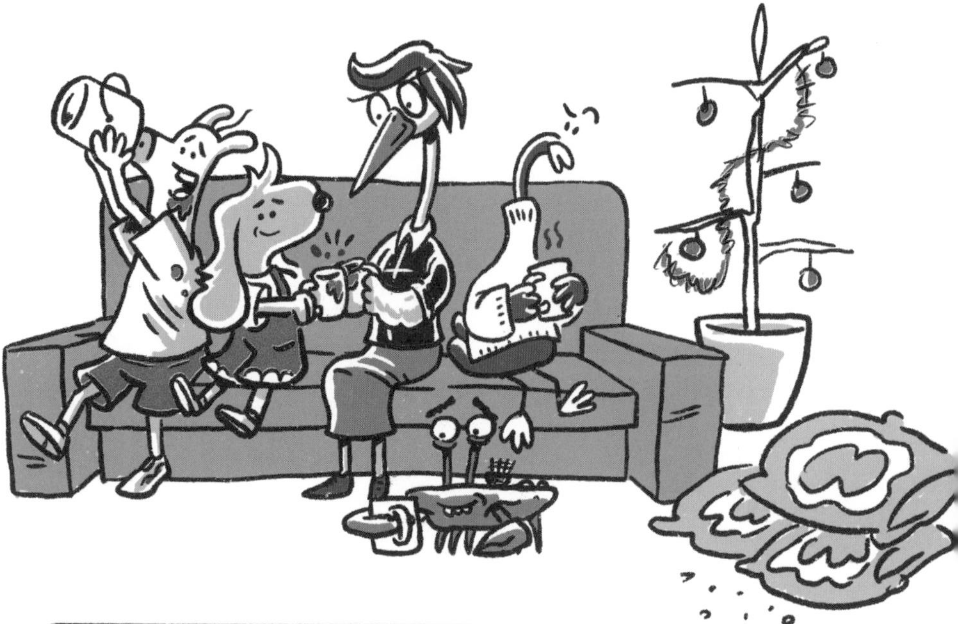

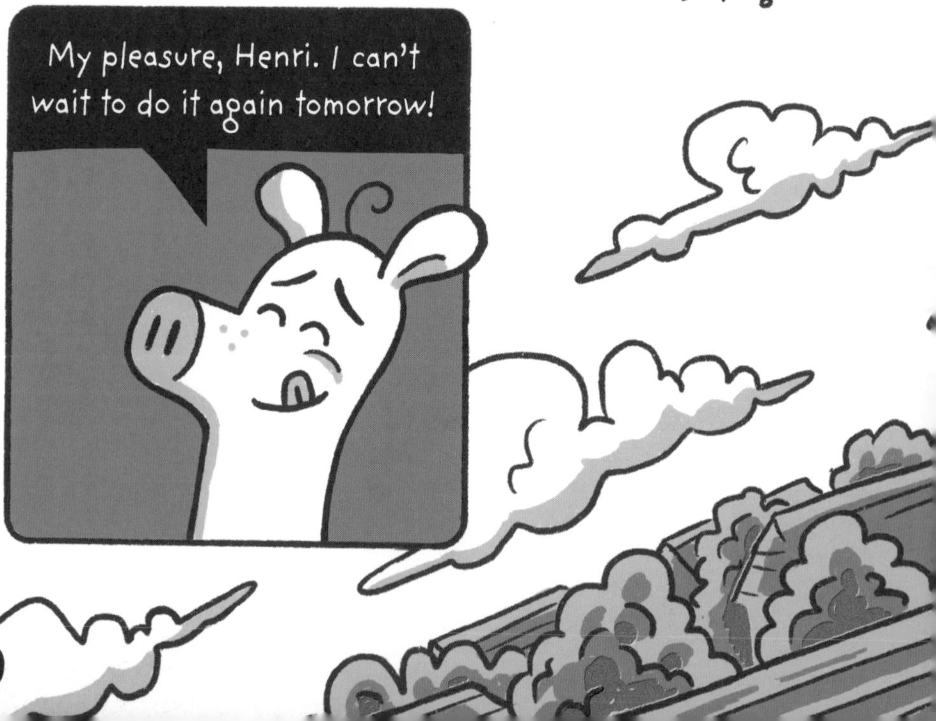
My pleasure, Henri. I can't wait to do it again tomorrow!

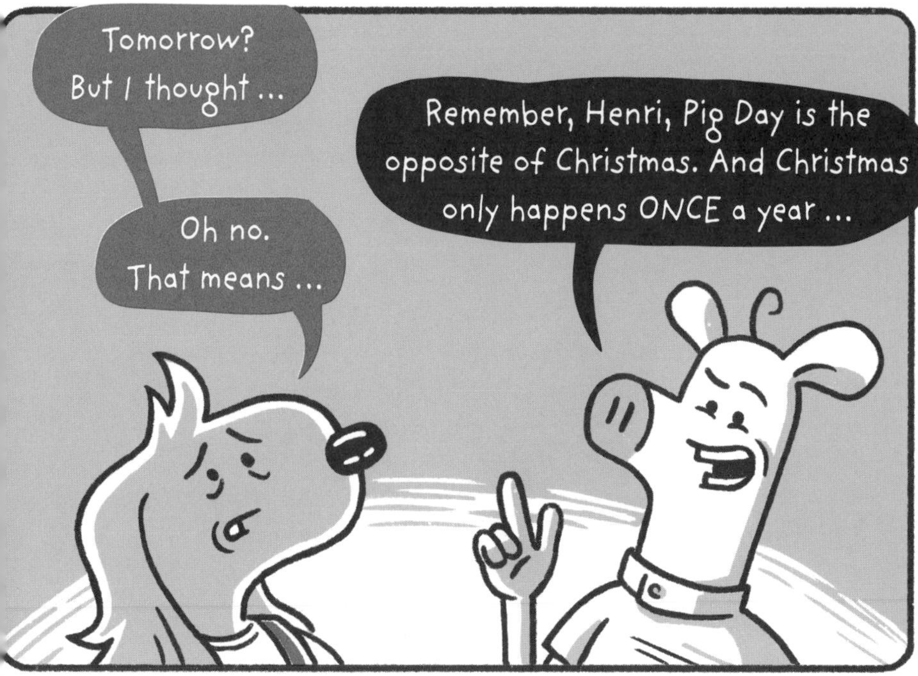
Tomorrow? But I thought ...
Oh no. That means ...
Remember, Henri, Pig Day is the opposite of Christmas. And Christmas only happens ONCE a year ...

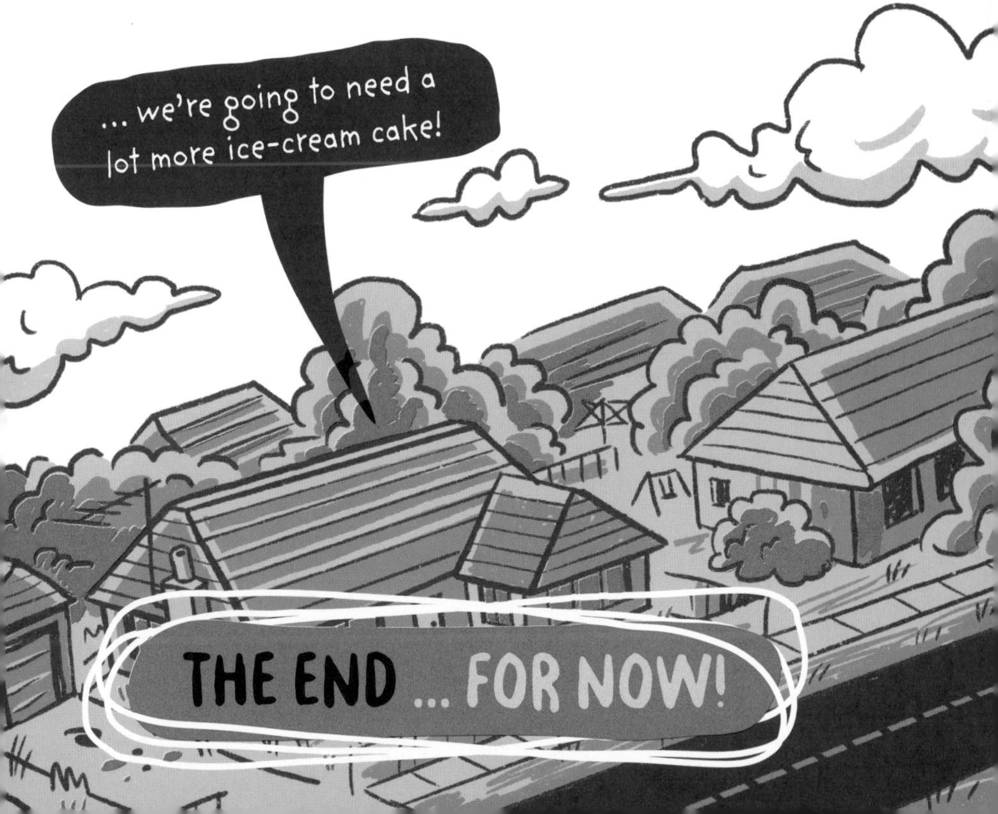
... we're going to need a lot more ice-cream cake!
THE END ... FOR NOW!

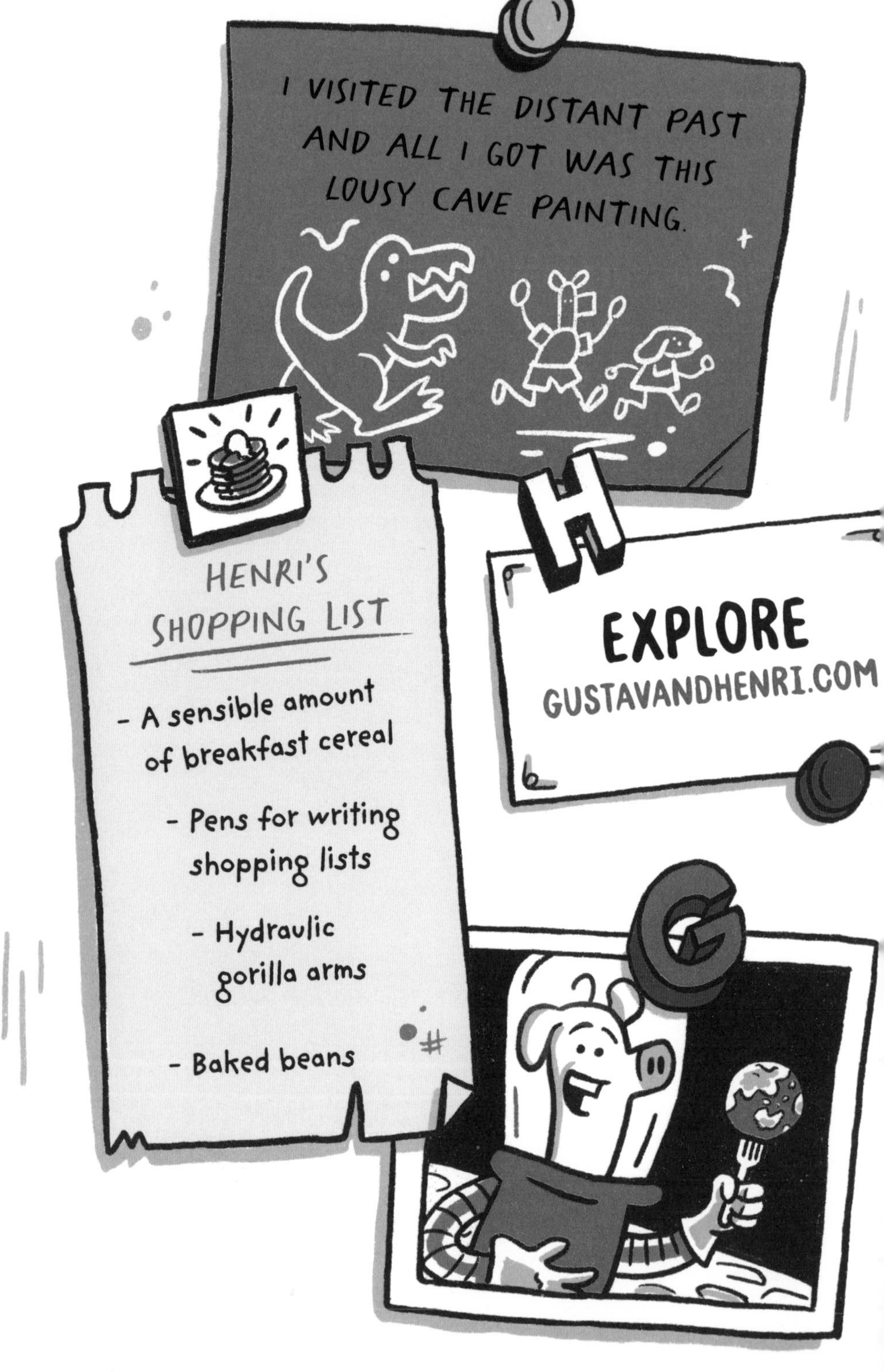

I VISITED THE DISTANT PAST AND ALL I GOT WAS THIS LOUSY CAVE PAINTING.
HENRI'S SHOPPING LIST
- A sensible amount of breakfast cereal
- Pens for writing shopping lists
- Hydraulic gorilla arms
- Baked beans
EXPLORE
GUSTAVANDHENRI.COM

# ANDY MATTHEWS
### (who drew the words)

Andy is a comedian who likes repairing bicycles. One day he hopes to learn to ride them. He created *Gustav & Henri* with

# PEADER THOMAS
### (who wrote the pictures)

Peader is an illustrator who likes doing silly voices* and designing impossible robots. He created *Gustav & Henri* with

*Hey! This is my normal voice!
—Peader

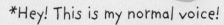

## FOR THE F.A.R CLUB.
## LET'S GO EXPLORING!
### -A.M.

## FOR AMY, WHO MAKES
## THE BEST PANCAKES.
### -P.T.

*Gustav & Henri Volume 1: Space Time Cake*
This edition published in 2022 by Red Comet Press LLC , Brooklyn, NY
First published in 2022 by Hardie Grant Children's Publishing, Australia

With special thanks to the spectaculous Carly Milroy
and the splendiffic Brian Colella for all their support.

Text copyright © 2022 Andy Matthews
Illustration copyright © 2022 Peader Thomas
Series design copyright © 2022
Hardie Grant Children's Publishing
Design by Pooja Desai
Library of Congress Control Number:
2022930004

ISBN (HB): 978-1-63655-036-7
ISBN (EBOOK): 978-1-63655-037-4
22 23 24 25 TLF 10 9 8 7 6 5 4 3 2 1

First Edition
Manufactured in China

Ahh, my favorite page of the book! The publishing information!

FSC
www.fsc.org
MIX
Paper from
responsible sources
FSC® C104723

RED COMET PRESS

RedCometPress.com